P9-DHS-746

DISCARDED

TIME
BOMB

OTHER BOOKS BY JONATHAN KELLERMAN

FICTION
Silent Partner (1989)
The Butcher's Theater (1988)
Over the Edge (1987)
Blood Test (1986)
When the Bough Breaks (1985)

NONFICTION
Helping the Fearful Child (1981)
Psychological Aspects of Childhood Cancer (1980)

JONATHAN KELLERMAN

TIME BOMB

BANTAM BOOKS
NEW YORK • TORONTO • LONDON • SYDNEY • AUCKLAND

A Bantam Large Print Edition

This is a work of fiction. Names, characters, places, and incidents are either the product of the author's imagination or are used fictitiously. Any resemblance to actual persons, living or dead, or locales is entirely coincidental.

TIME BOMB
A BANTAM BOOK

Bantam hardcover edition / October 1990
Bantam Large Print Edition / December 1990

ISBN 0-385-41578-8

Published simultaneously in the United States and Canada

Bantam Books are published by Bantam Books, a division of Bantam Doubleday Dell Publishing Group, Inc. Its trademark, consisting of the words "Bantam Books" and the portrayal of a rooster, is Registered in U.S. Patent and Trademark Office and in other countries. Marca Registrada. Bantam Books, 666 Fifth Avenue, New York, New York 10103.

PRINTED IN THE UNITED STATES OF AMERICA

BVG   0 9 8 7 6 5 4 3 2 1

This Large Print Book carries the Seal of Approval of N.A.V.H.

To my sister, Hindy Tolwin, with much love

Special thanks to Barbara Biggs and to all those writers who were there with counsel and/or kind words. To wit:

Paul Bishop, Lawrence Block, Dorothy Salisbury Davis, Michael Dorris, James Ellroy, Brian Garfield, Sue Grafton, Joe Gores, Andrew Greeley, Tony Hillerman, Stephen King, Dean Koontz, Elmore Leonard, the late Richard Levinson, William Link, Dick Lochte, Arthur Lyons, David Morrell, Gerald Petievich, Erich Segal, Joseph Wambaugh.

And, of course, Faye, whose strength, wisdom, and love could never be concocted in the wildest writer's fantasy.

Egad! What a talented bunch!

"And he gave it for his opinion, that whoever could make two ears of corn or two blades of grass to grow upon a spot of ground where only one grew before, would deserve better of mankind, and do more essential service to his country than the whole race of politicians put together."

—JONATHAN SWIFT

TIME
BOMB

1

Back to school.

It evokes memories of the tests we've passed, or the ones we've failed.

Monday. Milo's call punctuated a hard, gray November day that had finally erupted into rain.

He said, "Turn on your TV."

I glanced at my desk clock. Just after two-forty P.M.—talk show time. The cathode freak display. "What? Nuns who murder, or pets with ESP?"

"Just turn it on, Alex." His voice was hard.

"What channel?"

"Take your pick."

I flicked the remote. The sound came on before the picture. Sobs and whimpers. Then faces. Small faces, lots of them. Eyes wide with bafflement and terror. Fragile bodies blanketed and huddled together on the floor of a large room. Gleaming hardwood floors and chalk-white goal lines. A gym.

The camera moved in on a little black-haired girl in a puff-sleeved white dress as she accepted a plastic cup of something red. Her hands shook; the beverage sloshed; a false bloodstain spread on white cotton. The camera lingered, feasting on the image. The little girl burst into tears.

A chubby boy, five or six, cried. The boy next to him was older, maybe eight. Staring straight ahead and biting his lip, straining for macho.

More faces, a sea of faces.

I became aware of a mellow-voiced commentary—calculated sound bites alternating with strategic pauses. Sucked into the visuals, I let the words pass right through me.

Camera-shift to rain-slick asphalt, acres of it. Squat flesh-colored buildings spattered calomine-pink where the rain had penetrated the stucco. The voice-over droned on and the camera got manic— a flurry of visual slices, so brief they bordered on the subliminal: flak-jacketed, baseball-hatted SWAT cops crouched on rooftops, poised in doorways, and muttering into hand-held radios. Yellow crime-scene tape. Assault rifles; the glint of telescopic scopes; bullhorns. A cluster of grim men in dark suits conferring behind a barrier of squad cars. Police vans. Pulling away. Policemen packing and leaving. Then a sudden wide pan to something in a black zip-bag being carted away through the rain.

The owner of the mellow voice came on screen. Sandy-haired, *GQ* type in a Burberry trenchcoat and electric-blue crunch-knotted tie. The coat was soaked but his hair spray was holding up. He said, "Information is still trickling in, but as far as we can tell, only one suspect was involved and that individual has been killed. Here we see the body being taken away, but no identity has been released. . . ."

Zoom in on black bag, wet and glossy as sealskin. Stoic morgue techs who might have been taking out the garbage. The bag was hoisted up and into one of the vans. Slam of door. Close-up of the reporter squinting into the downpour, playing intrepid war correspondent.

". . . Recapping then, Nathan Hale Elementary School in the West Side community of Ocean Heights was the scene of a sniping that took place approximately forty minutes ago. No deaths or injuries are reported, except for that of the sniper, who is reported dead and remains unidentified. The exact circumstances of the death are still unknown. Previous rumors of a hostage situation have turned out to be false. However, the fact that State Assemblyman Samuel Massengil and City Councilman Gordon Latch were *at the school* at the time of the shooting has fueled reports that an assassination attempt may have been involved. Latch and Massengil have been on opposite sides of a controversy concerning the busing of inner-city children to underpopulated schools on the West Side and had planned a televised debate, though at present there is no indication if the shooting was related to—"

"Okay," said Milo. "You've got the picture."

As he spoke I spotted him standing behind the open door of one of the squad cars, one hand over his ear, the radio speaker pressed to his mouth. A background figure, too far away to make out his features. But his bulky figure and the plaid sport coat were giveaways.

"Alex?" he said, and I watched him scratch his head on screen. A weird juxtaposition— phone-a-vision. It faded as the camera swung back to the wet, empty schoolyard. A second of blank screen, station identification, a promise of resumption of "our regular programming" followed by a commercial for weight-loss surgery.

I switched off the TV.

"Alex? You still there?"

"Still here."

"All these kids—it's a real mess. We could use you. I'll give you directions. Use my name with the uniform at the command post. Ocean Heights isn't far from your neck of the woods. You should be able to make it in, what? fifteen, twenty minutes?"

"Something like that."

"Okay, then? All these kids—if anything's got your name on it, this one does."

"Okay."

I hung up and went to get my umbrella.

2

Ocean Heights adheres to the west end of Pacific Palisades, awkward as a pimple on a cover girl's chin.

Conceived by an aerospace corporation as a housing tract for the hordes of engineers and technicians imported to Southern California during the post-sputnik boom, the district was created by bulldozing lime groves, landfilling canyons, and performing radical surgery on a few mountaintops. What emerged was a slice of Disneyana: a "planned community" of flat, wide, magnolia-lined streets, perfect square sod lawns, single-story ranch houses on quarter-acre lots, and small-print deed covenants prohibiting "architectural and landscaping deviance."

The corporation is long gone, vanquished by poor management. Had it leased the houses instead of selling them, it might still be in business, because L.A. land-grab mania has pushed Ocean Heights prices into the high six-figure mark and the tract has emerged as an upper-middle-class refuge for those craving salt air seasoned with Norman Rockwell. Ocean Heights disapproves of the untrimmed, septic-tank-and-home-grown-dope ambience of neighboring Topanga, glares down like a dowager aunt upon the beach-blanket licentiousness of Malibu. But the view from the bluffs is often hazy. Fog, like complacency, seems to settle in and stay.

Milo's directions were precise, and even in the rain the drive went quickly—a spurt down Sunset, a turn onto a side street I'd never noticed before, three miles along a glassy canyon road that had a reputation for eating joyriders. A year of drought had ended with a week's worth of unseasonal autumn downpour, and the Santa Monica mountains had greened as quickly as home-grown radishes. The roadside was a tangle of creeper and vine, wildflower and weed—a boastful profusion. Nature making up for lost time.

The entrance to Ocean Heights was marked by the death of that boast: a newly surfaced avenue bisected by a median of grass and shaded by magnolias so precisely matched in contour and size they could have been cloned from the same germ cell. The street sign said ESPERANZA DRIVE. Beneath it was another sign: white, blue-bordered, discreet, proclaiming Ocean Heights a guarded community.

The rain took on power and spattered against

my windshield. A half mile later the police command post came into view: sawhorse barriers blocking the street, a domino spread of black-and-white squad cars, a battalion of yellow-slickered policemen projecting the guilty-till-proven-innocent demeanor of Iron Curtain border guards. Something else fed the checkpoint image: a group of about a dozen women, all Hispanic, all soaked and distraught, trying to cross the barriers, meeting stoic resistance from the cops. Other than that, the street was empty, shutters drawn on diamond-paned windows, color-coordinated panel doors dead-bolted, the sole movement the shudder of flowers and shrubs beneath the watery onslaught.

I parked and got out. The downpour hit me like a cold shower as I made my way toward the barricade.

I heard a woman cry out, *"Mi nino!"* Her words were echoed by the others. A chorus of protests rose and mingled with the hiss of the rain.

"Just a short while longer, ladies," said a baby-faced cop, struggling to appear unmoved.

One of the women called out something in Spanish. Her tone was abusive. The young cop flinched and looked over at the officer next to him—older, thickset, gray-mustached. Catatonic-still.

The young cop turned back to the women. "Just hold on now," he said, suddenly angry.

"Mi nino!"

Gray Mustache still hadn't moved but his eyes had settled on me as I approached. A third cop said, "Man coming up."

When I was within spitting distance, Gray Mustache gave a straight-arm salute, showing me the lines on his palm. Up close, his face was wet and puffy, laced with veins, and chafed the color of rare steak.

"No further, sir."

"I'm here to see Detective Sturgis."

The mention of Milo's name narrowed his eyes. He looked me up and down.

"Name."

"Alex Delaware."

He cocked his head at one of the other patrolmen, who came over and stood guard at the barrier. Then he went to one of the black-and-whites, got in, and talked into the radio. A few minutes later he came back, asked to see some ID, scrutinized my driver's license, and stared at me a while longer before saying "Go ahead."

I got back into the Seville and pulled forward. Two cops had cleared a car-sized space between the sawhorses. The Hispanic women surged toward it, automatically, like water down a drain, but were stopped by a shifting line of blue. Some of the women began to cry.

Gray Mustache was waving me through. I pulled up alongside of him, opened my window, and said, "Any reason they can't go see their children?"

"Go ahead, sir."

I drove on, braving a gantlet of accusing eyes.

Nathan Hale Elementary School was eight more blocks up Esperanza—a blacktop and flesh-stucco flashback to the images I'd just seen on the tube. Three empty school buses were parked at the curb, along with paramedics' vans and a few straggling press vehicles. The main building was sprawling and gray-roofed, skirted by a waist-high hedge of podocarpus. The front door was pumpkin-orange. Two cops guarded it from be-hind a cordon of yellow crime-scene tape. More palm-salutes, dirty looks, and radio checks before the chain-link gate to the school grounds was unlocked and I was directed around to the back.

As I made my way I noticed another tape cordon, wrapped around a small shedlike structure with wire-mesh windows, about seventy feet from the main building. Over the door was a sign: EQUIPMENT. Crime-scene techs kneeled and stooped, measuring, scraping, snapping pictures, getting drenched for their efforts. Beyond them the rain-blackened schoolyard stretched like scorched desert, vacant except for the distant galvanized geometry of a jungle gym. A single female re-porter in a red raincoat shared her umbrella with a tall young officer. What was passing between them seemed more flirtation than information transfer. They paused as I walked by—just long enough to decide I was neither newsworthy nor dangerous.

The back doors were tinted double-glass above three concrete steps. They swung open and Milo stepped out, wearing a quilted olive-drab car coat over the plaid sport jacket. All those layers— and the weight he'd put on substituting food for booze—made him look huge, bearish. He didn't notice me, was staring at the ground, running his hands over his lumpy face as if washing without water. His head was bare, his black hair dripping and limp. His expression said *wounded bear*.

I said, "Hello," and he looked up sharply, as if rudely awakened. Then his green eyes switched on like traffic lights and he came down the stairs. The car coat had large wooden barrel-shaped buttons dangling from loops. They bobbed as he moved. His tie was gray rayon, water-spotted black. It hung askew over his belly.

I offered him my umbrella. It didn't cover much of him. "Any problems getting through?"

"No," I said, "but a bunch of mothers are having a problem. You guys could use some sensitivity training. Consider that my initial con-sultation."

The anger in my voice surprised both of us. He frowned, his pale face deathly in the shade of

the umbrella, the pockmarks on his cheeks standing out like pinholes in paper.

He looked around, spotted the cop chatting
up the reporter, and waved. When the cop didn't
respond, he cursed and lumbered away, shoulders
hunched, like an offensive tackle moving in for the
crush.

A moment later the patrolman was sprinting
out of the yard, flushed and chastened.

Milo returned, panting. "Done. The mommies are on their way, police escort and all."

"The perquisites of power."

"Yeah. Just call me Generalissimo."

We began walking back toward the building.

"How many kids are involved?" I said.

"Couple of hundred, kindergarten through
sixth grade. We had them all in the gym, paramedics checking for shock or injuries—thank
God, nothing. The teachers took them back to
their classrooms, trying to do what they can until
you give them a plan."

"I thought the school system had people to
deal with crises."

"According to the principal, this particular
school has trouble getting help from the school
system. Naturally, I thought of you."

We reached the steps, where we were sheltered by an overhang. Milo stopped and placed a
heavy hand on my shoulder. "Thanks for coming
down, Alex. It's a goddam mess. I figured no one

would do a better job than you. I don't know what your schedule's like or if they'll be able to pay you, but if you can at least get them started on the right foot . . ." He cleared his throat and rubbed his face again.

I said, "Tell me what happened."

"Looks like the suspect got onto the school grounds before school opened, either by scaling or walking through—couple of the gates were left unlocked—proceeded into the storage shed, which had a dinky lock on it, and stayed there."

"No one uses the shed?"

He shook his head. "Empty. Used to be for athletic equipment. They keep all that stuff in the main building now. Suspect was settled in there until a little after noon, when the kids came pouring out for recess. Latch and Massengil and their people showed up by twelve-thirty and that's when the shooting started. Teachers began shoving the kids back in the building, but it was a real mob scene. Mass hysteria. Everyone falling over everyone else."

I glanced back at the storage shed. "TV said no one was hurt."

"Just the suspect. Permanently."

"SWAT?"

He shook his head. "It was over before SWAT got here. One of Latch's guys did the job. Fellow named Ahlward. While everyone else was diving for cover, he rushed the shed, kicked the door in and played Rambo."

"Bodyguard?"

"I'm not sure what he is, yet."

"But he was armed."

"Lots of people in politics are."

We climbed the steps. I took another look back at the shed. One of the mesh windows offered a clear view of the main building.

"It could have been a shooting gallery," I said. "Nearsighted sniper?"

He grunted and pushed the door open. The interior of the building was oven-warm, ripe with the mingled aromas of chalk dust and wet rubber.

"This way," he said, turning left and guiding me down a brightly lit hallway hung with children's artwork in fingerpaint and crayon, and health and safety posters featuring grinning anthropomorphic animals. The linoleum floor was clay-colored and mottled with muddy shoeprints. A couple of cops patrolled. They acknowledged Milo with stiff nods.

I said, "The newscast said Latch and Massengil were going to debate on camera."

"It wasn't set up that way. Apparently Massengil had a solo press conference in mind. Planned to make some speech about government tampering with family life, use the school as a backdrop, the whole busing thing."

"School know of his plans?"

"Nope. No one here had any idea he was coming down. But Latch's people found out about it and Latch decided to come down himself and confront him. Impromptu debate."

"Cameras ended up getting a better show," I said.

The doors off the corridor were painted that same pumpkin-orange. All were shut and as we passed, sounds filtered through the wood: muffled voices, the matter-of-fact sonata of a police radio, what could have been crying.

I said, "Think Latch or Massengil was the real target?"

"Don't know yet. The assassination angle brought the anti-terrorist boys zipping over from downtown. They're interviewing both of the staffs right now. As long as the political angle is a possibility, they're in charge—meaning I collect info and hand it over to them so they can classify it, then refuse to let me look at it on grounds that it's classified. Perquisites of power, hoo-ha." He gave a hollow laugh. "Top of that, the *FBI* just called from Westwood, wanting to know every-thing about everything, threatening to assign one of their guys as a *consultant*."

He hummed a few bars of "Send in the Clowns" and lengthened his stride.

"On the other hand," he said, "if it's your everyday, run-of-the-mill SoCal psycho killer gunning for innocent babies, none of the mucka-

mucks will give a shit, 'cause the psycho's dead—
no headline value—and yours truly will catch the
paperwork. Good old perquisites of power."

He stopped at a door marked PRINCIPAL,
turned the knob, and shoved. We entered a front
office—two straight-backed oak chairs and a secretary's desk, untended. To the right of the desk
was a door bearing a brown plastic slide-in sign
stamped LINDA OVERSTREET, ED.D. in white.
Milo knocked and pushed it open without waiting
for a reply.

The desk in the rear office was pushed to the
wall, creating an open space that accommodated a
sand-colored L-shaped sofa, tile-topped coffee
table, and two upholstered chairs. Plants in ceramic pots filled the corners. Next to the desk was
a waist-high shelving unit well stocked with
books, rag dolls, puzzles, and games. Framed
watercolors of irises and lilies hung on the walls.

A woman got up from the sofa and said,
"Detective Sturgis. Hello, again."

For some reason I'd expected someone
middle-aged. She was no older than thirty. Tall—
five eight or nine—leggy, high-waisted, and slim,
but with strong shoulders and full hips that flared
below a tight waist. Her face was long, lean, very
pretty, with a clear, fair complexion, rosy cheeks,
and fine features topped by a thick shag of
shoulder-length blond hair. Her mouth was wide,
the lips a trifle stingy. Her jawline was crisp and

angled sharply, as if aiming for a point, but ending in a squared-off cleft chin that granted her a bit of determination. She wore a charcoal cowl-neck sweater tucked into a knee-length denim skirt. No makeup other than a touch of eye shadow. Her only jewelry was a pair of square black costume earrings.

"As promised," Milo told her, "Dr. Alex Delaware. Alex, Dr. Overstreet, the boss around here."

She gave him a fleeting smile and turned to me. Because of her height and her heels, we were almost eye to eye. Hers were round and large, fringed with long, almost-white lashes. The irises were an unremarkable shade of brown but radiated an intensity that caught my attention and held it.

"Pleased to meet you, Dr. Delaware." She had a soft voice mellowed further by some kind of Southern twang. She held out her hand and I took it. Long-fingered and narrow, exerting no pressure. I wondered how someone with hands that submissive, that beauty-contestant voice, would handle a position of authority.

I said hello. She freed her hand and brushed her bangs.

"Thanks for coming down on such short notice," she said. "What a nightmare."

She shook her head again.

Milo said, "S'cuse me, doctors," and moved toward the door.

"See you later," I told him.

He saluted.

When he was gone, she said, "That man is kind and gentle," as if ready to argue the point.

I nodded. She said, "At first the kids were scared of him, scared to talk to him—his size. But he really handled them well. Like a good father."

That made me smile.

Her color deepened. "Anyway, let's get to work. Tell me everything I can do to help the kids."

She took a pad and pencil from her desk. I sat on the short section of the L-shaped sofa and she settled perpendicular to me, crossing her legs.

I said, "Are any of them showing signs of overt panic?"

"Such as?"

"Hysteria, breathing troubles, hyperventilation, uncontrollable weeping?"

"No. At first there were tears, but they appeared to have calmed down. At least the last time I looked they seemed settled—amazingly so. We've got them back in their classrooms and the teachers have been instructed to let me know if anything comes up. No calls for the last half hour, so I guess no news is good news."

"What about physical symptoms—vomiting, urinating, loss of bowel control?"

"We had a couple of wet pants in the lower grades. The teachers handled it discreetly."

I probed for symptoms of shock. She said, "No, the paramedics already went through that. Said they were okay. Remarkably okay, quote unquote—is that normal? For them to look that good?"

I said, "What do they understand about what's happened?"

She looked puzzled. "What do you mean?"

"Has anyone actually sat down and explained to them that there was a sniper?"

"The teachers are doing that now. But they have to know what happened. They heard the shots, saw the police swarm the campus." Her face tightened with anger.

I said, "What is it?"

She said, "That someone would do that to them. After all they've been through. But maybe that's why they're handling it okay. They're used to being hated."

"The busing thing?"

"The busing thing. And all the garbage that resulted from it. It was a match made in hell."

"Because of Massengil?"

More anger.

"He hasn't helped. But no doubt he speaks for his constituents. Ocean Heights considers itself the last bastion of Anglo-Saxon respectability. Till recently, the locals' idea of educational contro- versy was chocolate-chip or oatmeal cookies at the bake sale. Which is fine, but sometimes reality just has to rear its ugly head."

She drummed her fingers and said, "When you came in, did you notice how big the yard was?"

I hadn't, but I nodded.

She said, "It's a huge campus for such a small neighborhood, because thirty-five years ago, when the school was built, land was cheap, Ocean Heights was supposed to boom, and someone probably landed a juicy construction contract. But the boom never materialized and the school never came close to functioning at capacity. Until the budget crunches back in the seventies, no one paid much attention to that kind of thing. Who'd complain about small classes? But resources started to dry up, the Board began examining head count, efficient allocation of resources, all that good stuff. Most white schools were experiencing a dropping census but Hale was a real *ghost* town. The kids of the original homeowners were grown. Housing had gotten so expensive that few families with young children were able to move in. Those that could afford to live here could also afford to send their kids to private schools. The result was classroom capacity for nine hundred pupils and only eighty-six kids attending. Meanwhile, on the East Side, things were nuts—fifty, sixty per classroom, kids sitting on the floor. The logical thing seemed to be what the Board so quaintly terms 'modulated redistribution.' The B word. But totally voluntary, and one-way. Inner-city kids brought in, no locals bused out."

"How long's it been going on?"

"This is our second year. Hundred kids the first semester, hundred more the second. Even with that, the place was still a ghost town. But the locals felt crowded. Sixty of the eighty-six stragglers were transferred immediately to private schools. All the rest left mid semester. You would have thought we were importing the plague." She shook her head. "I can understand people wanting to be insulated, the whole idea of the neighborhood school. I know they must have felt invaded. But that doesn't excuse how ugly it got. Alleged *grown-ups* standing outside the gates waving signs and taunting the kids. Calling them greasers, wetbacks. *Vermin.*"

I said, "I saw it on TV. It was ugly."

She said, "During summer vacation we got vandalized—racist graffiti, broken windows. I tried to get the Board to send down some mental health people, someone to mediate with the community before the new school year started, but all I got were memos and countermemos. Hale's a stepchild that they're obligated to feed but don't want to acknowledge."

"How have the children reacted to all the hostility?"

"Very well, actually. They're so darned resilient, bless 'em. And we worked on it. Last year I met regularly with each class, talking to them about tolerance, respecting differences between people, the right to free speech, even if it's unpleasant. I had the teachers play games and do things to enhance self-esteem. We kept drumming into them how good they were. How brave. I'm no psychologist, but psych was my minor and I think I did at least a passable job."

I said, "Sounds like the right approach. Maybe that's why they're handling things well right now."

She waved off the compliment and her eyes moistened. "That's not to say everything was perfect—not by a long shot. They felt it—the hatred. Had to. A few families pulled their kids out of the busing program immediately, but most stuck it out, and after a while things seemed to be quieting down. I really thought this semester was going well. Hoped it had finally dawned on the good folks of Ocean Heights that a bunch of little kids weren't going to rape their daughters and rustle their cattle. Or maybe they just got bored— this place is *the* capital of Apathy. Only other issues that get them going are offshore oil drilling within a fifty-mile radius and anything that relates to landscaping. So I made sure our shrubs were well trimmed." Brief, bitter smile. "I was starting to think we could finally concentrate on *educating*. Then Massengil goes and dredges it all up—he's always had a special thing for us. Probably 'cause he's a local. Lives in Sacramento but keeps a house here for legal purposes. Obviously he views us as a personal burr in the butt."

She punched her palm. Her eyes were flashing. I altered my assessment about her ability to handle authority.

"The creep," she said. "If I'd known he was planning a dog-and-pony show today, I'd . . ."

She frowned, tapped her pencil on her wrist.

I said, "What?"

She hesitated, then gave another mirthless smile. "I was about to say I'd have met him at the gate with a loaded gun."

3

She looked down at her pad, realized she'd written nothing, and said, "Enough talk. What's your plan?"

"The first step will be to establish rapport with the kids. And the teachers. Your introducing me and explaining who I am will help that. Second, I'll focus on getting them to express their feelings about what happened—talking, playing, drawing."

"Individually or in groups?"

"Groups. Class by class. It's more efficient and more therapeutic—opening up will be easier if there's peer support. I'll also be looking for the high-risk kids—those who are especially high-strung, have had previous anxiety problems or experienced loss or an unusual amount of stress within the last year. Some of them may need one-on-one attention. The teachers can help by identifying them."

"No problem," she said. "I know most of them myself."

"The other important thing—maybe the toughest—will be to convince parents not to keep their children out of school for extended periods."

"What's extended?"

"More than a day or two. The sooner they get back, the easier it will be for them to adjust."

She sighed. "All right, we'll get on it. What do you need in the way of equipment?"

"Nothing much. Some toys—blocks, figurines. Paper and pencil, clay, scissors, glue."

"We've got all of that."

"Will I need a translator?"

"No. Most of the kids—about ninety percent—are Latino but all of them understand English. We've worked hard at that. The rest are Asian, including some pretty recent immigrants, but we don't have anyone on staff who speaks Cambodian or Vietnamese or Laotian or Tagalog or whatever, so they've come along pretty fast."

"Ye olde melting pot."

"Uh-uh, forbidden phrase," she said. "The memo god commands us to use *salad bowl*." She raised a finger and recited: "Every ingredient maintains its integrity, no matter how much you toss it around."

We left her office and stepped out into the hall. Only one cop remained, patrolling idly.

She said, "Okay. Now what about your fee."

I said, "We can talk about that later."

"No. I want things straight from the beginning—for your sake. The School Board has to approve private consultants. That takes time, going through channels. If I put in a voucher without prior approval, they can use that as an excuse not to pay you."

I said, "We can't wait for approval. The key is to get to the kids as soon as possible."

"I realize that, but I just want you to know what you're dealing with. Also, even if we go through channels, there're bound to be hassles getting you compensated. The Board will probably claim it has the resources to do the job itself; therefore there's no justification for bringing in anyone from the outside."

I nodded. "Same song and dance they pull with the parents of handicapped kids."

"You've got it."

"Don't worry about it."

"I worry about everything. It's my job," she said. Most of the softness in her eyes had melted away.

I said, "It's okay. Really."

"You realize we're talking potential freebie?"

"I realize. That's fine."

She looked at me. "Why are you doing this?"

"It's what I went to school to learn how to do."

There was distrust in her eyes. But she

shrugged and said, "Who am I to look a gift horse?"

We walked toward the first classroom. A door at the end of the corridor swung open. A tight cluster of nine or ten people poured out and barreled in our direction.

At the group's nucleus was a tall white-haired man in his sixties wearing a gray sharkskin suit that could have been purchased for Eisenhower's victory party. His face was stringy and hawkish above a long, wattled neck—beak nose, white toothbrush mustache, pursed mouth, eyes buried in an angry squint. He kept up a vigorous pace, leading with his head, pumping his elbows like a speed-walker. His minions were whispering at him, but he didn't seem to be listening. The group ignored us and blew by.

I said, "Looks like the esteemed assemblyman's run out of words."

She closed her eyes and exhaled. We continued walking.

I said, "What do you know about the sniper?"

"Just that he's dead."

"It's a start."

She turned sharply. "A start at *what*?"

"Dealing with the kids' fears. The fact that he's dead will help."

"You're going to get into gory details with them right away?"

"I'm going to be truthful with them. When they're ready for it."

She looked doubtful.

I said, "The key is for them to make some kind of sense out of a crazy situation. In order to do that they'll need as much accurate information as possible. Facts. About the bad guy—presented at their level, as soon as possible. The mind abhors a vacuum. Without facts, they'll fill their heads with fantasies of him that could be much worse than reality."

"Just how much reality do you think they need to absorb?"

"Nothing gory. Basics. The sniper's name, age, what he looks . . . looked like. It's crucial that they see him as human. *Destructible*. Gone forever. Even with facts, some of the youngest ones will be incapable of understanding the permanence of his death—they're not mature enough, developmentally. And some of the older ones may regress because of the trauma—temporarily 'forget' that dead people don't come back to life. So they're all vulnerable to fantasies of the bad guy returning. Of his coming back to get them again. Adult crime victims go through it—after the initial shock's worn off. It can lead to nightmares, phobias, all kinds of post-traumatic reactions. In children the risk is higher because kids don't draw a clear line between reality and fantasy. You can't eliminate the risk of problems, but by

dealing with misconceptions right away, you min-
imize it."

I stopped. She was staring at me, grimly, the
brown eyes unwavering.

"What I want," I said, "is for them to
understand that the bastard's truly *destroyed*. That
he's not some supernatural bogeyman that's going
to keep haunting them."

"Bastard" made her smile. "Okay. Just as
long as it doesn't end up scaring them more—"
She stopped herself. "Sorry. You obviously know
a heck of a lot more about this than I do. It's just
that they've been through so much for so long,
I've gotten protective."

"That's okay," I said. "Good to see someone
caring."

She ignored that. This one definitely didn't
like compliments.

"I don't know a thing about the *bastard*," she
said. "No one saw him. We just heard the shots.
Then there was a lot of panic—screaming and
shoving. We were trying to stuff the kids back into
the building, keeping their heads down. We ran as
fast and as far away as we could, trying to make
sure no one got trampled. No one even knew it
was over until that guy Ahlward came out of the
shed, waving his gun like a cowboy after the big
draw. When I first saw him, it freaked me out—I
thought *he* was the sniper. Then I recognized
him—I'd seen him in Latch's group. And he was

smiling, telling us it was all over. We were safe."

She shuddered. "Bye-bye, bogeyman."

The lone patrolman had tilted his head toward our conversation. He was young, handsome, coal-black, perma-pressed.

I walked up to him and said, "Officer, what can you tell me about the sniper?"

"I'm not free to give out any information, sir."

"I'm not a reporter," I said. "I'm a psychologist called in by Detective Sturgis to work with the children."

Unimpressed.

"It would be useful," I said, "for me to have as many facts as possible. So I can help the kids."

"I'm not free to discuss anything, sir."

"Where's Detective Sturgis?"

"I don't know, sir."

I returned to Linda Overstreet's side.

She'd heard the exchange. "Bureaucracy," she said. "I've come to believe it's a biological urge."

A door farther down the corridor opened, disgorging another group. This one revolved around a man in his early forties, mid-sized and chunky. He had a roundish, freckled face under an early-Beatles mop of gray-streaked dark hair which covered his brow. His clothes were formula junior-faculty: oatmeal-colored tweed sport coat, rumpled khaki pants, black-and-green plaid shirt,

red knit tie. He wore round tortoise-shell eyeglasses, the kind the British health service used to
give out for free. They rested atop a nose that
would have done a French bulldog proud. The rest
of his features were too small for his face—
pinched, almost effeminate. I thought of old pictures I'd seen of him. Long-haired and bearded.
The facial hair had made him look more seasoned,
twenty years ago.

The academic image was enhanced by the
people around him—young, bright-eyed, like students vying for the attention of a favorite profes-
sor. Each of them was final-exam solemn, but the
group managed to radiate a boisterousness that
was almost festive.

The round-faced man noticed us and stopped.

"Dr. Overstreet. How's everyone doing?"

"As good as can be expected, Councilman
Latch."

He came over to us. The staffers hung back.
With the exception of one bulky, blunt-faced,
red-haired man about Latch's age, none was older
than twenty-five. A clean-cut bunch, dressed for
success.

Latch said, "Is there anything I can do, Dr.
Overstreet? For the kids? Or your staff?"

"How about calling out the National Guard
for some protection?"

He flashed a brief, campaign-poster smile,

then turned serious. "Anything a little less . . . martial?"

"Actually," she said, "we could use some information."

"What kind of information?"

"About the sniper. Who he was, his motivation. Dr. Delaware here will be working with the children. He needs to know as much as possible in order to answer their questions."

He seemed to notice me for the first time, held out his hand and gripped mine hard. "Gordon Latch."

"Alex Delaware."

"Good to meet you, Alex. You're a psychologist? Psychiatrist?"

"Psychologist."

"From the School Board?"

Before I could answer, Linda said, "Dr. Delaware's a private practitioner recommended by the police. He's a specialist in childhood stress."

Latch's blue eyes focused behind his welfare specs. "Well, all power to you, and thanks for coming down on such short notice, Alex. It's been a horror—unbelievable. Thank God it turned out the way it did." He glanced back at his staffers, got nods from some of them. "What's your game plan—vis-à-vis the kids?"

I gave him a brief rehash of what I'd told Linda.

He took a moment to digest it. "Sounds right

on target," he said. "I was involved in your field once upon a time—majored in psych up at Berkeley. Crisis counseling, community mental health, primary and secondary prevention. We had a place in Oakland. Trying to integrate mental patients back into the community. Back in the good old days when humanism wasn't a dirty word."

"So I've heard." As had anyone who read the papers.

"Different times," he said, sighing. "Gentler and kinder. What happened today just underscores how far we've drifted. Damn, what a tragedy!"

Linda said, "What can you tell us about the sniper, Councilman Latch?"

"Not much, I'm afraid. We don't know much ourselves. The police have been awfully close-mouthed, as is their wont."

She said, "Mr. Ahlward would know something. If he feels up to it, perhaps he could educate us."

Latch looked over his shoulder again. "Bud? C'mere, please."

The red-haired man raised pinkish eyebrows and stepped forward. He wore a brown suit, white shirt, solid brown knit tie, had the kind of over-developed upper body that makes custom tailoring a necessity. This suit was off the rack and hung on him like a tarp. His hands dangled loosely at his sides, big, pale, fuzzed with copper. His hair was tightly curled and he wore it close to his head. He had a fleshy, jutting jaw and lazy amber eyes that remained fixed on his boss.

"Councilman?" Up close he smelled of cigarette smoke.

"Bud, these good people want to know about the sniper. What can you tell them?"

"Nothing yet," said Ahlward. He had a soft, boyish voice. "Sorry. Cops' orders." He zipped a finger across his mouth.

Latch said, "Nothing at all, Bud?"

"ATD was real clear on that, Councilman."

Latch turned back to us. "Anti-Terrorist Division. You might recall them from a couple of years ago. The lovely fellows who were spending taxpayers' money on surveilling innocent taxpayers? We've since gotten them to clean up their act, so I suppose we'll have to let them do their thing, for the moment. And they were adamant about keeping things under wraps until they're sure they've got the big picture. Bud's on his way downtown right now to give a formal statement. If we're all lucky, things'll clear up soon after that." To Ahlward: "Bud, soon as you get the green light vis-à-vis informational flow, make sure these good folks get anything they want. Immediately. Understood?"

"You bet," said Ahlward.

Latch nodded. Ahlward returned to the group.

"Thank God for Bud," said Latch, loud

enough for the group to hear. Someone patted
Ahlward on the back. The red-headed man
appeared unmoved. Standing with the others but
not one of them. A distant look had settled on his
face—Zen placid, as if he'd projected himself to
another place, another time. Not a hint that he'd
spent his lunch hour shooting someone to death.

"Okay, my friends," said Latch, taking a step
backward. "It's been a long day that shows no sign
of ending. Dr. Overstreet, if you need anything,
bypass the red tape and come straight to me. I
mean it. Let's get things on an even keel, once and
for all. Dr. Delaware, sounds like the kids are in
good hands, but you, too, feel free to get in touch
if there's anything I can do."

He reached into his jacket, removed some
business cards from a leather holder, and gave
them to us. A two-handed grasp of Linda's hand,
then mine, and he was gone.

Linda crumpled the card. Her face had tightened.

I said, "What's the matter?"

"Suddenly he's Mr. Helpful," she said, "but
last spring, when the kids were being put through
hell, I tried to get his help. Ocean Heights is part
of his district, even though I'm sure he didn't get
too many votes here. I thought because of his
reputation, all the civil rights stuff he used to be
into, he'd come down, talk to the kids, show them
someone with power was on their side. If for no

other reason than to use it for public relations. I must have called his office half a dozen times. Not even a return call."

"He came down today. To square off against Massengil."

"Some kind of ulterior motive, no doubt. They're all the same." She blushed. "Listen to me. You must think I'm a foursquare ballbuster."

"You might very well be," I said, "but I'd have to study you under more optimal circumstances in order to be able to come to a conclusion vis-à-vis that issue."

She opened her mouth, then broke into laughter. The cop down the hall pretended not to hear.

The classroom was large and bright and filled with an unaccustomed silence. Only the rain broke the quiet, sloshing against the windows in an insistent car-wash rhythm. Twenty pairs of eyes stared back at me.

I said, "I'm the kind of doctor who doesn't give shots. I don't look in kids' eyes or ears, either." Pause. "What I do is *talk* with kids and *play* with them. You guys like to play, don't you?"

A few blinks.

"What kinds of games do you like to play?"

Silence.

"How about ball? Any of you like to play ball?"

Nods.

"Handball?"

An Asian boy with a soup-bowl haircut said, "Baseball."

"Baseball," I said. "What position do you play?"

"Pitch. Soccer and football and basketball too."

"Jumpin' rope," said a girl.

"Pizza Party," said the Asian boy.

"That's a board game," explained the teacher. A stylish black woman in her forties, she'd relinquished her desk to me with eagerness, pulled a chair into a corner, and sat, hands folded, like a punished student. "We have that here in class. We have lots of board games, don't we, class?"

"I like to be mushrooms," said the Asian boy.

"Peppers," said another boy, small-boned, with long, wavy hair. "Hot peppers. *Muy caliente!*"

Giggles.

I said, "Okay. What other board games do you like to play?"

"Checkers."

"Chutes and Ladders!"

"Checkers!"

"I already *said* that!"

"Chinese checkers!"

"You Chinese!"

"No way. I'm *Viet*namese!"

"Memory!"

"I like to play too," I said. "Sometimes for fun and sometimes to help kids when they're scared or worried."

Return of silence. The teacher fidgeted.

"Something very scary happened today," I said. "Right here in school."

"Someone got killed," said a dimpled girl with coffee-colored skin.

"Anna, we don't *know* that," said the teacher.

"Yes," insisted the girl. "There was *shooting*. That means *killing*."

I said, "You've heard shooting before."

She nodded with vehemence. "*Uh*-huh. On my *street*. The gangbangers drive by and shoot into the houses. That means killing. *My* papa said so. One time we had a bullet hole in our garage. Like this." She measured a space between thumb and forefinger.

"My street too," said a crew-cut boy with an elfin face and bat ears. "A dude got killed. Dead. Boom boom boom. Inna face."

The teacher looked ill.

A few of the boys began to pantomime shooting, using their fingers for guns and half-rising out of their seats.

"Sounds scary," I said.

A boy laughed and shot at a girl. She said, "*Stop* it! You're *stupid*!"

The boy swore at her in Spanish.

"*Ramon!*" said the teacher. "Now you just settle down. Let's all of us settle down, class." Her glance at me said *Where'd you get your degree?*

I said, "It's fun to play shooting, because it makes us feel strong. In charge—the boss over our lives. But when it really happens, when someone's really shooting at us, it isn't too funny, is it?"

Headshakes. The boys who'd laughed hardest suddenly looked the most frightened.

I said, "What do you guys understand about what happened today?"

"Some dude was shootin' at us," said the Asian boy.

"Tranh," said the teacher. "We don't know that."

"Yeah, he was shootin' at us, Miz Williams!"

"Yes, Tranh. He *was* shooting," she said. "But we don't know who he was shooting *at*. He could have been shooting into the air." A look to me for confirmation.

"He was shooting at *us*," insisted Tranh.

I said, "Do any of you know what happened to him?"

"He got shot?" said the girl named Anna.

"That's right. He got shot and *he's* dead. So he can't hurt you. Can't do *anything* to you."

Silence as they appraised that.

The boy named Ramon said, "What about his friends, man?"

"What friends?"

"Like if he's a homeboy and the other home-boys are gonna come back and shoot us again?"

"No reason to think he's a homeboy," I said.

"But what if he's a stoner, man?" said Ramon. "Or a *cholo*."

"Who is he?" asked another girl, chubby, with black Shirley Temple ringlets and a quiver in her voice.

Twenty faces, waiting.

I said, "I don't know yet. No one does. But he's gone. Forever. You're safe from him."

"We should kill him *again*!" said Ramon.

"Yeah! *Kill* him! Shoot him with a twenty-two!"

"With a Uzi!"

"Push his face inna pizza so he don't breathe no more!"

"Push his face in *ca-ca*!"

The teacher started to say something. I stilled her with a glance. "How else could you hurt him?"

"Kill him!"

"Cut him up and feed him to Pancho—that's my dog!"

"Shoot him, boom, inna balls!"

"Ay, los cojones!"

Laughter.

"Boom!"

"Cut him up and grind him up and feed him to *my* dog!"

"You don't got no dog, Martha!"

"Do so! Got a real mean pit bull and he'll eat *you*!"

I said, "Shoot him, stab him, push his face down. Sounds like you guys are really mad."

"Yeah, man," said Ramon. "What you think, man? He try to kill us, we gonna kill him back!"

"We can't kill him," said the chubby girl.

"Why's that?" I said.

"Because he's big. We're just kids. We got no guns."

"That's dumb," said Tranh. "We can't kill him 'cause he's already dead!"

"Kill him *again*!" shouted someone.

"Find out where he lives," said Ramon, "and kill his fuckin' *house*!"

The teacher said, "Language!"

The chubby girl didn't look reassured. I said, "What's the matter?"

"Actually," she said, "we can't do nothing. We're kids. If people wanna be mean to us all the time, they can."

"Honey, no one wants to be mean to you," said the teacher.

The chubby girl looked at her.

"Everyone likes you, Cecelia," said the teacher. "Everyone likes all of you."

The chubby girl shook her head and began to cry.

By the time I finished, the rain had abated. I made a stop at Linda Overstreet's office, but it was locked and no one answered my knock. As I left the building I saw Milo in the yard, near the cordoned storage shed. He was talking to a slim, dark-haired man in a well-cut blue suit. He noticed me and waved me over.

"Alex, this is Lieutenant Frisk, Anti-Terrorist Division. Lieutenant, Dr. Alex Delaware, the clinical psychologist who'll be working with the kids."

Frisk checked me over and said, "How's it going, Doctor?" in a tone that let me know he didn't much care.

"Fine."

"Good to hear it." He flashed a barrel cuff and consulted his Rolex. He was young and tan, the dark hair permed in a neat cap, and wore a mustache that had taken a long time to trim. The blue suit was expensive, the shirt Turnbull & Asser or a knockoff. The tie that bisected it was heavy silk patterned with dancing blue parallelograms on a background of deep burgundy. His eyes matched the parallelograms; they never stopped moving.

He turned to Milo and said, "I'll let you know. Afternoon, Doctor." He walked away.

"Spiffy dresser," I said. "Looks like a TV cop."

"Young man on the way up," said Milo. "Masters in public administration from S.C., good connections, D-Three by the age of thirty, promoted to loot three years later."

"Is he taking over the case?"

"You just heard—he'll let me know."

We walked across the schoolyard.

"So," he said, "how'd it really go?"

"Not bad, really. I managed to meet briefly with all the classes. Most of the kids seem to be reacting normally."

"Meaning?"

"Meaning lots of anxiety, some anger. It's the anger I tried to harness—get them to feel more in control. I told the teachers to contact the parents and prepare them for possible appetite loss, sleep problems, psychosomatic stuff, clinginess, some school phobia. Some of the kids may need individual treatment, but a group approach should work for most of them. The important thing was getting to them quickly—you done good."

He said, "What'd you think of Ms. Principal?"

"Feisty lady."

"Texas lady," he said. "Cop's kid—daddy

was a Ranger, brought his work home. She knows this scene by heart."

"She didn't mention any of that to me."

"Why should she? With you she probably talked *feelings*."

I said, "*Her* main feeling right now is anger. Plenty of it simmering beneath the surface. It's been building since she got here—she's been dealing with lots of crap and getting very little support. She tell you about the vandalism?"

He frowned. "Yeah. First I'd heard of it. The School Board reported it directly to downtown—it never went any further."

"Bad P.R.?" I said.

"Perish the thought."

"Sounds like the school's been embroiled in politics since they brought the kids in. Think the sniping was political?"

"At this point, who knows?"

"Latch or Massengil have any theories? About being targets themselves?"

"I wouldn't know," he said. "Kenny Frisk and the ATD boys did all the interrogation. Hush-hush behind closed doors. Afterwards Kenny comes out and informs the rest of us peons that official policy is tight lips. All press releases to emanate from ATD. *Informational infractions* will be severely dealt with."

I searched his face for signs of anger. All I saw was a big, white mask.

A few steps later he said, "Though with politicos, good luck keeping their lips from flapping."

"So far Latch seems to be complying," I said. "I ran into him in the hall as he was leaving. Tried to get some information from him and received zip."

He turned his head and looked at me. "What kind of information?"

"Some sort of basic description of the sniper. Who he was. Anything tangible. The kids need to form an image of their enemy." I repeated the rationale I'd given Linda and Gordon Latch. "They're already asking questions, Milo. It would increase my effectiveness to be able to answer some of them."

He said, "Just basics, huh? Who he *was*."

I nodded. "Of course, any details you can tell me would be useful. Short of an 'informational infraction.' "

He didn't smile. "Details. Well, first thing I can tell you is that you're operating on a false premise."

"What's that?"

"It wasn't a *he*. It was a *she*."

4

The restaurant was dim and mock-English: collections of tankards and heraldic shields displayed on rough-textured dun walls, dartboards in "Ye Olde Pub Room," lots of distressed crossbeams, the tallowy, sweet smell of seared meat. A catacomb jumble of small dining rooms. A respectful maitre d' had seen to it that ours was empty.

Milo looked up from his T-bone, put down his knife, and took something out of his coat pocket that he slid across the table.

A piece of white paper, folded double. In the center was a photocopy of a driver's license.

The photo was dark and blurred. A young female face, oval, unsmiling. A little weak-chinned. Thin neck. White blouse. Dark straight hair, cropped short. Straight-edge bangs hovering above arched eyebrows.

I searched the features for something—some harbinger of violence. The eyes looked a little

dull. Sullen. Heavy-lidded, shallow as rain pud-
dles. But that could have been the poor quality of
the copy or weariness at waiting in line at the
DMV. Other than that, nothing. Average. A face
you'd never notice.

I read the ID data.

HOLLY LYNN BURDEN
1723 JUBILO DR
OCEAN HEIGHTS CA 90070

SEX: F HAIR: BRN EYES: BLUE
HT: 5-05 WT: 117 DOB: 12-12-68
RSTR: CORR LENS

"Local girl," I said.
"Very local. That address is five blocks from
the school."
"Jubilo Drive. Spanish for 'joy.' And I think
Esperanza means 'hope.' "
"A-plus, Sherlock. You caught the pattern.
The street next to Jubilo's Belleza Court.
'Beauty.' Some optimistic urban planner."
"Hispanophile urban planner," I said.
"Guess the locals don't share the spirit."
"Hey," he said, "street names are one thing;
letting them marry your sister's another."
I examined the picture again, reread the
information. "What do you know about her?"
"Just what you see in front of you. Frisk says

ATD will be checking out known associates—
going through their subversive files to see if her
name comes up. When he left us he was on his
way to her house."

"Nineteen years old," I said and gave him the
paper. He folded it back up and put it away.

"Now forget you saw it, Alex. *I'm* not even
supposed to have a copy."

"Why not?"

"Official ATD document."

"How'd you get it?"

He shrugged and began sawing his steak.
"After the print boys finished, Frisk designated
one of the offices as a 'data collection center.' Had
all the evidence hoarded in there, I just happened
to saunter in when he just happened to take a leak.
There just happened to be this Xerox machine that
kept whispering, 'Turn me on, big boy.' You
know how I've always been a sucker for the soft
touch."

"Why all the obsession with secrecy, Milo?
Once Frisk gave you her name, you could have
gotten the license yourself. Hell, I could get it
*my*self."

"That's the way ATD works—comes from
spending too much of their time hanging around
Washington. The Department sends them there—
and to FBI heaven at Quantico. Seminars. Hob-
nobbing with the cloak-and-dagger freaks. Makes
'em insufferable. But them's the rules—no sense

bucking without any payoff. Besides, it shouldn't take long for things to ease up. Only a matter of time before the whole case goes public."

"How long?"

"Unless something interesting turns up about the late Ms. Burden in somebody's files, Frisk plans on releasing her name to the press around noon tomorrow. Soon as that happens, you can tell your kids the bogeyman looks like their friendly neighborhood babysitter."

"How's he going to stall the press in the meantime?"

"The old fashioned way: lie. 'Sorry, ladies and gentlemen, no definitive ID pending autopsy.' Which is almost true—she did take a couple of bullets in the face. But you could still tell it was the same face as the one on the license."

I imagined the young, bland countenance swollen, perforated, bleeding; shook that picture out of my head and said, "Around noon should work out, anyway. I'm meeting with the kids at one."

"Great. But if, for some reason, Frisk hasn't gone public, neither do you, okay? I've got enough troubles without leaks getting traced back to me this early in the game."

"What kind of troubles?"

"The usual." His expression said: Change the subject.

We ate for a while. My mind kept drifting

back to the license photo. "A girl sniper," I said. "Hard to believe."

"Women's lib, Alex," he said with his mouth full. "They're trying to catch up to us in the asshole division."

"Then they've got a long ways to go," I said. "I remember County Jail—visiting Jamey Cadmus in the violent psych ward. One thing that impressed me was that they had twenty rooms for males, only two set aside for females, and those two were rarely *used* for females. What percentage of violent crime is committed by women?"

"Less than ten," he said. "But the stats get interesting when you look at the age pattern— violent offenders under eighteen. The rate for males is still much higher than it is for females, but the overall rate for males is dropping, while for females it's going up. The gap is closing. And even without the numbers, I'd know there's something happening, Alex. On the streets. I can sense it—rules of conduct breaking down. Maybe Manson's girls broke the ice, I don't know—Squeaky and the other one taking potshots at Ford, those assholettes in the SLA. Now the gangbangers have started using fems as triggermen . . . trigger*persons*. They figure the courts will go easier on psychopaths in dresses, and they're right. So far. Meanwhile, more and more Bonnies wanting to be Clydes."

He cut a large piece of T-bone free and

stuffed it in his mouth. "Hell," he said, still chewing, "nastiest thing I've seen this year was some stenographer over in Mar Vista doing in her boyfriend with a Chinese cleaver. Jilted-lover stir-fry. Call the Frugal Gourmet."

I looked at the sirloin on my fork and put it down.

"Bon appétit," he said.

"Thanks."

"Of course," he said, "the distaff does have a long way to go. We've got thousands of years of experience behind us. Tankfuls of testosterone. But they're working on it—the whole goddam culture's changing. Female wrestlers, girls pumping iron, shooting steroids, talking dirty. Hell, you ever see women flipping off truckers on the freeway till recently? They're feeling their oats, pal."

I made another go at my steak.

"Prime, huh?" he said, taking another mouthful.

"Prime."

"Private stock. Management knows me." He patted his gut. "Which is to love me. Big tips and it's cholesterol heaven."

He dipped a piece of meat in steak sauce. "Don't get me wrong, it's not like I have a thing against the fairer sex. Just telling it the way I see it."

"I know that."

"Yeah, well, sometimes people assume, you know?"

"I swore off assumptions for Lent."

He gulped another gargantuan piece of steak. The meat was bloody-rare and some juice dribbled down his chin. He dabbed at it. "Did I ever tell you I once had a girlfriend?"

"Never."

"Yup. High school days."

"I'm not surprised."

"No? What the hell *does* it take to surprise you?"

"How about an honest politician?"

His laugh was harsh. "Yeah, find one, put him in the cage next to the condor."

I said, "Why bother?"

He laughed some more.

"Any indication the Burden girl was aiming at Latch or Massengil?"

"Ye olde participatory democracy?"

"I'm serious, Milo. Being able to tell the kids they weren't the targets would make my job easier."

"Then, by all means, go ahead and tell 'em."

"No," I said. "If I say it, I want it to be true."

"Sorry, then," he said. "Nothing solid to give you. She didn't leave any political message at the scene, far as I know. No fringies have called yet expressing solidarity, and Frisk said he didn't recognize her name offhand from his subversive lists, though like I said, they'll be running her through the software. Maybe he'll turn up something at her house—some diary, or wacko manifesto. Meanwhile, all we've got is one dead girl and lots of question marks."

He thought for a moment. "If she *was* trying for one of them, my guess would be Massengil. Looks like no one except Latch's insiders knew their boy was going to be there."

"The press knew."

He shook his head. "Uh-uh. Only about Massengil. That much I confirmed from talking to the reporters. The invite came from Massengil's staff this morning. It was supposed to be a one-man show. Latch didn't announce he was coming. The idea was to surprise the enemy."

"How'd Latch find out Massengil was going to be there?"

"Once the press knew, it wouldn't be too hard for anyone to find out, would it?"

I said, "Anyone?"

"Anyone in the grapevine. Frisk does his job correctly, that's the first thing he'll check about her. Maybe she once worked for Massengil—or Latch. Or knew someone who did. No one on either staff recognized her name, but she could have been low-level—stuffing envelopes, whatever. Some meek little gofer they treated like shit, never took the time to notice. She swallows it for a while, then quits. No one notices she's gone.

Meanwhile, she's smoldering, making plans for vengeance. Fits the mass-killer profile. Then again, maybe the political thing was coincidental—Latch and Massengil had nothing to do with it. Maybe all she wanted to do was kill kids, and bigger game intruded."

"Local girl makes bad," I said. "Wonder if she attended Hale."

"Revenge for a bad report card?"

"Got anything that makes more sense?"

"As a matter of fact I don't," he said. "So far this is your quintessential senseless crime—as opposed to all the real sensible ones we get."

"Were the reporters there when the shooting started?"

He shook his head. "No. The press conference wasn't called until one. Massengil showed up half an hour before, walking around the yard, 'observing.' Latch dropped in on him a few minutes later."

I said, "If Latch's intention was to upstage Massengil, why not arrive when the media were in place? Make a dramatic entry."

"We wondered about that too. According to Frisk, Latch's explanation was that his object wasn't to confront Massengil but to *defuse* him. He was giving Massengil a chance to call the whole thing off before the cameras showed up."

"Saint Gordon."

"Yeah, and I'm Mother Teresa. My guess is

his real intention was to *spook* Massengil, work him up good. Massengil's got a reputation for having a short fuse—got into a punch-out with another politico couple of years ago, likes to yell back at hecklers, go head to head. Latch probably figured in half an hour he could get the guy *apoplectic* by the time the media showed. *Really* make a jerk out of him. Then the shooting started and took the edge off their little drama."

"One of the kids told me it sounded like war," I said.

"How would he know?"

"She. From Cambodia."

"Oh. Tell you one thing, old Holly was no pro-warrior. The rifle was a Remington Seven-hundred Classic. Bolt action, scoped. Nine pounds, stripped—one of the heavier ones they make, lots of kick. Not a girl's gun. You just don't pick up something like that, go boom, and hope to hit your target."

"Even with the scope?"

"Sighting and aiming wouldn't have been the problem, Alex. Holding *on* to the damned thing would be. According to the license she weighed under a hundred and twenty. And she hadn't gained anything since applying for it. I saw the body—skinny, no muscle on her. Unless she had plenty of practice, she might as well have brought a cannon to shoot mice. Women succeed in the shooting game, they get up nice and close, use a comfortable little handgun. Not that a handgun would have been of much use in a sniping situation."

"The license also said corrective lenses. Was she wearing her glasses?"

"Yup. Took a bullet in one of them, glass went right into the eye socket. Like shrapnel."

"How many shots did she get off before Ahlward stormed the shed?"

"Looks like three out of six rounds—though to listen to the teachers and kids, she had a machine gun; it was a regular blitz. But panic'll do that, magnify things. And some of what they heard was probably Ahlward shooting *her*—he put eight right in her."

"There's your pro," I said, remembering the redheaded man's calm. "Ex-cop?"

"Nope. Frisk said some kind of ex-military commando."

"Hard-ass type for a guy like Latch to employ."

"Not if Latch is a pragmatist. It's like that old bumper sticker that used to be on half the lockers at the academy: 'Mugged? Call a hippie.' Latch may spout the love-and-compassion line, but when it comes to saving his ass he ain't gonna hire Cesar Chavez."

"How'd Ahlward get into the shed?"

"Same back door Burden used. She left it

unlocked—I told you she was no pro. He ran around the back, waltzed right in, and pow."

I thought again of the face on the driver's license. Superimposed a mesh of blood and glass over the dull face.

"What is it?" said Milo.

"Nothing."

"My, my, my. You feel *bad* for her, don't you?"

"Not really."

"Not *really*?" He clucked his tongue. "Jesus, Alex, you turning mushy on me? I thought by now I'd raised your consciousness."

I said, "The whole thing's pathetic, Milo. A girl, holed up with a rifle she couldn't handle— God knows what's going through her head."

"So?"

"So I guess it just would have been nicer for the bad guy to be badder."

He put his fork down and stared at me. "Oh, she could have been plenty *bad*. No thanks to *her* she wasn't real *bad*. Just imagine a couple of lucky shots—couple of those cute little kids catching rifle slugs in—"

"Okay," I said, "I get the point."

"Good," he said, crumpling his napkin. "Get it and keep it. Situation like this, got to keep the old priorities straight. Now, how about some dessert?"

5

I got home by eight, picked up calls, did paperwork and chores, then spent half an hour with a new acquisition: a cross-country skiing machine. A genuine implement of torture that left me a sopping ball of sweat. In the shower I kept thinking about terrified children and evil babysitters. So much for aerobic cleansing.

At nine I watched the news on one of the local stations. The shooting at Nathan Hale was the lead story: file clips of weeping kids followed by the official LAPD statement delivered by Lieutenant Kenneth Frisk. The ATD man was articulate and at ease with the cameras as he sidestepped questions; his designer duds and mustache, prop-room photogenic. New-age cop. Lots of style, very little substance.

Armed with few facts and needing to stretch the broadcast, the newspeople flashed more file clips: a segment on Massengil's State House fistfight, a year before, with an assemblyman from the northern part of the state named DiMarco. The bout had taken place in the chambers of the legislature, the two of them going at it verbally— some esoteric issue having to do with gerrymandered districts. Massengil had come out of it without a scratch; DiMarco had suffered a bloody lip. The camera showed the loser pressing a crimson handkerchief to his mouth, then cut to footage taken today: DiMarco leaving his Sacramento office. Asked about Massengil's temper and how he thought it related to the sniping, he passed up a chance for retribution, said it wouldn't be prudent to comment at this time, got in his state-issued car and drove away. Discretion, or a loser's reticence.

Next came a retrospective on Gordon Latch—the speedy, compressed history that only a TV photomontage can accomplish, beginning with a twenty-year-old film: Latch, hirsute and bright-eyed, marching with Mario Savio at Berkeley, shouting slogans, getting busted at the People's Park. Cut to a hippie-style marriage in Golden Gate Park to the former Miranda Brundage. The bride, only child of a movie tycoon, former art history grad student at Berkeley, former Young Republican fashion plate programmed for Deliberate Understatement and the Junior League, had worn tie-dye.

Latch had radicalized her fast. She got arrested with him regularly, dropped out of school, lived in splendid Telegraph Avenue squalor. To the press, the irony was irresistible: In Hollywood circles, Fritz Brundage had long been regarded as a crypto-fascist—a prime mover behind the McCarthy-era blacklist and a passionate union-buster. The media covered his daughter's wedding as if it were hard news. Latch played to the cameras, enjoying his role as First Radical. Soon after the wedding he took Miranda to Hanoi, recorded messages for the Viet Cong exhorting GIs to desert their posts. The networks were there with open mikes. The Latches returned to the United States topping the Ten Most Hated List, fielding death threats and possible prosecution for sedition.

They went into seclusion at a ranch owned by the old man. Somewhere up north. People wondered why Fritz had given them sanctuary. The government decided not to prosecute. There were rumors of Fritz's calling in markers. Latch and Miranda stayed out of the public eye for five years, until Fritz died, then emerged, the heirs to a fortune. Freshly barbered and mature. Apologetic for Hanoi, self-proclaimed "democratic humanists," eager to work within the system.

A move to the West Side of L.A., a couple more years of good works—environmental activism, groceries for the homeless, charity camps for disadvantaged youths—and Latch was ready for the electoral process: a City Council seat vacated by the car-crash death of a well-loved incumbent with a well-hidden drinking problem and an ab-horrence for delegating authority. No designated successor, a sudden vacuum filled by Latch. And some generous monetary transfers from the former Brundage estate to the party's coffers.

The only protests against Latch's nomination came from veterans' groups. Latch met with them, ate crow, said he'd grown up, had a vision for the city that transcended partisan politics. He ran against token opposition. Regiments of college students went door-to-door in the district distrib-uting potholders and talking clean air. Latch won, made an acceptance speech that sounded down-right middle-of-the-road. Miranda seemed content to host political teas.

She photographed well, I noticed. Kneeling on the beach scraping tar off an oil-slicked peli-can.

End of montage. The anchorman offered a two-sentence review of the racial tensions at Hale. More shots of crying kids. Worried parents. A long view of the empty schoolyard.

The tail end of the story was an interview with a portly, white-bearded psychologist named Dobbs, billed as an expert on childhood stress who'd been enlisted by the School Board to work with the children. That held my attention.

Dobbs had on a three-piece suit that looked as if it had been woven from Shredded Wheat, and toyed with a heavy-looking watch chain as he spoke. His face carried a lot of loose flesh and he pursed his lips a lot, which made him look like a rubber Santa mask gone sour. He used home-grown jargon that made my head reel, talked a lot about crisis intervention and moral values—had plenty to say about how society had lost its moral fiber. I kept waiting for him to hold up a book jacket.

The phone interrupted his spiel.

"Dr. Delaware?"

"Speaking."

"This is Linda Overstreet. You gave me this number, so I figured it was all right to use it."

"Sure, Linda. What's up?"

"Have you by any chance been watching the news?"

"Got it on screen right now."

"So you saw him—Dobbs."

"In all his tweedy glory."

"He's lying, believe me. No one called him in on anything. I know because I spoke to the Board this afternoon and they hadn't gotten them-selves in gear yet."

"What's going on?"

"I don't know. What I do know is that Dobbs has got connections with the Board. So he proba-bly assumed they'd give him the okay, just went steamrolling ahead on his own."

"What kind of connections?"

"A couple of years back, after one of the earthquakes, he presented a very slick proposal to the Board: crisis intervention free of charge, at several schools—including the one where I was in training. What he actually ended up *doing* was having his assistants administer computerized tests to the kids and hand out brochures. Nothing hands-on. Couple of weeks later, some of the parents started getting phone calls informing them the tests had shown their kids to be suffering from severe emotional problems. Strongly *advising* them to bring the kids in for individual therapy. Those who resisted got follow-up calls, letters, not-so-subtle pressure. Funny thing is, all of the ones who were followed up lived in high-priced ZIP codes."

"The poor get poorer and the rich get therapy?"

"Yup. The Board got a few complaints about the hard sell, but overall they were pleased with Dobbs because he hadn't cost them a dime and they got testimonials from some of the parents of the kids who went for treatment, saying it had been helpful."

"Are his credentials on the level?"

"Far as I know."

"Hold on for a second. I'll check."

I went into the library, got an American Psychological Association directory, and came back on the line.

"What's his first name?"

"Lance."

I thumbed to the D's, found a bio on *Dobbs, Dr. Lance L.,* and skimmed it. Birthdate in 1943, Ph.D. 1980, in educational counseling from a land-grant college in the Midwest. Internship and postdoctoral training at a drug rehab center in Sacramento. State license in '82. Director of Cognitive-Spiritual Associates, Inc., since '83. Two addresses: West L.A. and Whittier.

"Looks bona fide," I said.

"Maybe, but with assistants doing all the work, what's the big deal if he himself is qualified? I see him as a self-promoter—the kind who loves to see himself on screen."

"This is L.A.," I said. "People demand *more* than their fifteen minutes of fame."

She laughed. "So you're not ticked off?"

"Why should I be?"

"You do the work; he takes the credit. Seems to me I spend half my time dealing with ego stuff, stepping on toes. Guess I'm sensitized to it."

"My toes feel fine."

"Okay," she said. "I just wanted to keep things straight. If Dobbs's people show up, I'll handle it."

"Thanks. And thanks for calling."

"Sure."

Silence.

I said, "How's everything going at school?"

"Good as can be expected." Her voice broke. "It's just starting to sink in, how close we all came . . . what a mess the whole thing is."

"How're *you* doing?"

"Oh, I'll survive. What I'm really concerned about is the kids. I talked to a few of the teachers and the feedback I got on your sessions was positive."

"I'm glad."

"How do they look to you—the kids?"

"Scared. But nothing abnormal. What's encouraging is that they seem able to express it. You and the teachers have obviously done a good job over the past two years."

"What are they scared of, specifically?"

"The youngest ones are concerned about separation from their parents, so you may see some school phobia and increased absenteeism from them. The older ones talked more about pain and suffering—trying to imagine what it felt like to be shot. Some discussion of death. Some anger's starting to come out, too, which is good. Anger and fear are incompatible in kids—one drives out the other. If they can harness their anger and focus it, it'll help them feel more in control in the long run."

"Anger heals, huh?" she said. "Maybe I should try it."

"Maybe," I said. "Though I have to be

honest: With adults the fear-anger thing isn't that clear-cut."

"Figures. Why should life be simple? Anything else I should know?"

"I've made a list of about twenty kids who seem extra-fragile. I'll keep an eye out for others. Any of the high-risk kids who still look shaky within the next few days will need individual attention and I'll want to meet with their parents."

"When do you want the parents?"

"How about Friday?"

"I'll get Carla on it first thing in the morning."

"Thanks. How're you doing with the parents—persuading them to send their kids back?"

"So far so good. I've been through this before, with the busing, so most of them trust me. But it's not easy telling them we've provided a safe place for learning for their kids. We'll keep trucking."

"Good luck."

"Thanks. I saw you leaving today with Detective Sturgis. Learn anything new on the sniper?"

Remembering Milo's warning, I hedged. "The police don't know much yet. Expect to be finding out more soon."

"Sounds like the old cop shuffle."

That reminded me of what Milo had told me

about her father. "Guess you'd know about that."

"What do you mean?"

"Detective Sturgis told me you were a cop's kid."

"Did he?" she said, suddenly chilly. "Yes, that's true. Well, have a good evening, and thanks again."

"See you tomorrow, Linda."

"Maybe not," she said. "I'll be running around all over the place. If you need anything, ask Carla. Good night."

"Good night."

I placed the phone in its cradle. The chill lingered. Milo hadn't said anything about her being touchy about her background. I wondered about it. But not for long. Too many other things on my mind.

Tuesday morning was crystalline—the kind of nose-tweaking, palate-tickling weather L.A. earns after a storm. I checked the morning paper for an update on the shooting, found nothing, and scanned the TV and the all-news radio stations. Just rehash. I returned calls, finished a couple of child-custody reports, working until just before noon, when I took a break for a pepper beef sandwich and a beer.

Remembering Milo's prediction, I turned the TV on again, flipped channels. Game shows. Soaps. Vocational training commercials. I was just about to switch it off when a press conference cut into one of the serials.

Lieutenant Frisk. More than ever, his tan, his teeth, and his perm made him resemble a soap opera cop, and the conference seemed like a continuation of the serial, just another scripted scene.

He straightened his tie, smiled, then proceeded to give Holly Lynn Burden her own ration of fame, enunciating her name, repeating it, spelling it, adding her birthdate, the fact that she lived in Ocean Heights, and was believed to have had psychiatric problems.

"All indications," he said, "are that Miss Burden was working alone, and no evidence of any political affiliation or conspiracy has been found, though we're still investigating at this time."

"What do you have," asked a reporter, "by way of a motive?"

"None, at this time."

"But you said she had psychiatric problems."

"That's true."

"What kinds of problems did she have?"

"We're still looking into that," said Frisk. "Sorry I can't be any more specific at this time."

"Lieutenant, was she gunning for the children, or was this an assassination attempt?"

"We're still collecting data on that as well.

That's all, at this time, folks. Get back to you soon as we have more."

Segue back to the soap: a cocktail party full of beautiful people, haute-coiffured and haute-cuisined, but riddled with angst.

I knotted my tie and put on my jacket. Time for school.

I arrived at Hale at 12:45—lunch hour but the yard was empty. A grizzled man in shabby clothes was walking up and down the sidewalk in front of the school. He carried a ten-foot cross and wore a sandwich sign proclaiming JESUS IS LORD on the front, NO HEAVEN WITHOUT REDEMPTION on the back. A middle-aged cop stood at the entrance to the gate, watching him. Blue uniform, but not LAPD. I got close enough to read the insignia on his sleeve. School police. I gave him my name, he checked it against a list on a clipboard, asked for ID verification, and unlocked the gate.

The man with the cross had shuffled halfway down the block. Now he turned and shouted, "Suffer the children!" in a hoarse voice. The school cop looked at him as if at a puddle of vomit, but made no move. The cross-man resumed his march.

I entered the yard. The storage shed was still wrapped with crime-scene tape. Despite the fine weather, a sense of desolation hung over the grounds—gloom coupled with tension, like the pause between thunderclaps. Maybe it was the emptiness, the lack of childish laughter. Or maybe just my imagination. I'd had the same feeling before . . . at deathbeds.

I pushed that aside and checked in with Linda Overstreet's secretary. Carla was young, tiny, and efficient. She had a punk hairdo and a smile that said life was a big joke.

I went to the first classroom. Yesterday there'd been two dozen students; today I counted nine. The teacher, a pale young woman just out of training, looked defeated. I gave her an encouraging smile, regretted not having the time to do more. As I took her place at the front of the classroom, she excused herself, sat in the back, and read a book.

The pattern of absenteeism repeated itself in every other class—at least half of the children had stayed home. Many of the ones I'd tagged as high-risk were among the missing. Therapist's dilemma: those who need help the most, run the farthest from it.

I concentrated on the help I could offer, went to work reestablishing rapport, giving the children time to ventilate, then introducing them to their bogeywoman: telling them Holly Burden's name, the few facts I knew about her. They were skeptical about the notion of a female sniper. Many of the youngest kids kept calling her "him."

I had them draw her, mold her out of clay,

build her out of blocks. Rip her up, smash her, bludgeon her, erase her. Kill her, again and again.

Blood and glass . . .

Through it all, I kept talking, kept reassuring.

It went on that way until, in one of the fourth grade classes, the mention of Holly Burden's name made the teacher go pale. A woman in her fifties named Esme Ferguson, she was a tall, square-faced bleached blonde, heavily made-up, conservatively tailored. She left the room and didn't return. Some time later I spotted her in the hall, caught up with her, and asked if she'd known Holly Burden.

She took a deep breath and said, "Yes, Doctor. She was from here."

"From Ocean Heights?"

"From *Hale*. She was a *student* here. I *taught* her. I used to teach sixth grade. She was in my sixth grade class. Years ago."

"What do you remember about her?"

Penciled eyebrows rose. "Nothing, really."

"Nothing at all?"

She bit her lip. "She was . . . odd. The entire family's odd."

"Odd in what way?"

"I really can't . . . This is too hard to talk about, Doctor. Too much happening all at once. Please excuse me. I have to get back to class."

She turned her back on me. I let her go,

returned to my work. To talk of the *odd* girl. Try to explain madness to children.

Madness, as it turned out, was something these children grasped easily. They loved the word *crazy,* seemed to revel in it, in graphic discussions of deranged people they'd known. Their view of mental illness was skewed toward blood and guts: wet-brained vagrants carving each other up in alleyways over a bottle of redeye; hebephrenic bag ladies walking in front of buses; drooling molesters; shrieking youths run amok on PCP and crack cocaine. Random bursts of psychotic poetry at the corner mini-market.

I sat back, listened to all of it, tried to cloak myself in the therapist's objectivity. After a couple of hours, the world they lived in began to overwhelm me.

In the past, when working with children who'd been traumatized, I'd always taken pains to put the traumatic event in context. Isolating disaster as a freak bit of cruelty. But looking into the knowing eyes of these kids, listening to their experiences, I heard myself faltering, had to force a note of confidence into my voice.

My last class of the day was a rowdy bunch of sixth graders whose teacher hadn't shown up. I let the frazzled substitute out on parole, and was about to begin when the door opened and a young Latina walked in. She had teased, frosted hair, wore a tight, knit scarlet dress, and had matching inch-long nails. Her smile was glossy and happy-face wide. In one hand she carried a huge brief-case; in the other, a red purse.

"Hi, kids," she announced. "I'm Dr. Mendez! How are *you* all doing today?"

The children looked at her, then at me. Her gaze followed theirs.

"Hi," she said to me. "I'm Dr. Mendez. I'm a *clinical psychologist*. And you must be Mr. . . ?"

I held out my hand. "*Dr.* Delaware. I'm a clinical psychologist too."

Her smile went stale.

"Um . . ." she said, still staring at my hand. The purse dropped from her hand.

The kids started laughing. She bent—awkwardly because of the tight dress—and retrieved it. They laughed harder.

I said, "Hold on a minute, guys," and asked her to come out into the hall. I closed the door. She put her hands on her hips and said, "Okay, what's going on?"

"Good question, Dr. Mendez."

"I'm here to do therapy with them—for the sniping."

"So am I. I've been doing it since yesterday."

"I don't understand," she said, flustered.

"The police called me in."

"To investigate?"

"To help."

"This makes no sense at all," she said.

I said, "Do you work with Dr. Dobbs?"

She pulled out an engraved business card and handed it to me. PATRICIA MENDEZ, M.A. COGNITIVE-SPIRITUAL ASSOCIATES, INC. Two addresses: on Olympic Boulevard in West L.A., and in Whittier. Four phone numbers. Tiny print at the bottom identified her as a Psychological Assistant to Lance L. Dobbs, Ph.D., and gave his license number.

I handed it back to her and said, "Have you checked with the principal? She should be able to clear things up."

"She wasn't in. But I'm here on authority of the School Board—they're *really* in charge, you know, not the police."

I said nothing.

Her briefcase was making her shoulder sag. She lowered it to the floor.

I said, "I think you should check in with the principal, anyway."

"Well"—She folded her arms across her breast—"I only know what I was told."

"Sorry you wasted time coming down here."

She frowned, thought. "Look, I'm just here to do my job. Couldn't you go to another class?"

"These kids have been through plenty. They need the comfort of routine. Predictability."

"I can provide that," she said.

"By walking in right in the middle of my session? Fitting *them* to *your* agenda?"

She tensed but smiled. "You seem to be coming from a hostile place. Possessiveness."

"And you seem to be coming from a deceptive place, Ms. Mendez. Billing yourself as a doctor with just a master's degree. Pretending to be a psychologist when you're an assistant."

She opened her mouth, closed it, and opened it again. "Tha . . . that's just a technicality. Next year I'll be a Ph.D."

"Then next year you'll be telling the truth."

"If you're implying there's something—"

"How many classrooms have you been to, so far?"

"Seven."

"Didn't anyone mention I'd been there?"

"They didn't . . . I—"

"You didn't really take the time to talk to them, did you? Just blew in, did your canned bit, and blew out." I looked down at the briefcase. "What's in there? Brochures?"

"You're a very hostile man," she said.

A wave of laughter rose from inside the classroom. Then a thump—overturned furniture.

I said, "Look, it's been fun but I have to go. Until you check in with the principal and clear this up, please stay away from the kids. For their sake."

"You can't order me—"

"And please think twice about misrepresenting yourself. The Board of Medical Examiners wouldn't be pleased."

"Is that a threat?"

"Just sound advice."

She tried to look tough and failed miserably. "It's my job," she said, almost pleading. "What am I supposed to do?"

"Check in with the principal."

"You keep saying that," she said.

"It keeps being a good idea," I said, turning the doorknob. The sound on the other side grew louder.

"Just a minute," she said. "Are you bilingual?"

"No."

"Then how in the world are you going to help them?"

"Their English is fine."

"That's not what I've been told."

"Then you've been misled. In more ways than one."

The sky was dimming as I left the yard. I saw Linda Overstreet just outside the gate, talking to the man with the cross. Trying to explain something to him. He stared at the sidewalk, then raised his head abruptly and seemed to swoon.

She backed away. He moved toward her, went nose to nose with her, wagging his finger.

She attempted to talk back; he talked over her, gestured more wildly. She finally gave up, turned her back on him and walked away. He opened a toothless black hole of a mouth and began shouting—something raw and incoherent.

She made it to the gate before noticing me, gave a what-can-I-do shrug, stopped and waited until I caught up with her. She was wearing a black linen dress, simply cut, suitable for mourning. But the contrast with her blond hair and fair skin lent a touch of unintended glamour.

"Getting religion?" I said.

She grimaced. "Crazy old jerk. He showed up early this morning, screaming about the whore of Babylon, suffer the children, all this other garbage. I tried to explain to him that the kids didn't need any more disruption, but it's like talking to cement—he has this tape in his head, keeps on playing it."

"What about the school cop?"

"See him anywhere?" she said, pointing to the unguarded gate. "Gone at three, won't stay a minute later. And not much good when he *is* here, standing around with his clipboard. Claiming he's not authorized to deal with Old Screamo as long as all he does is mouth off—right to free speech and all that. He's giving *me* a civics lesson."

The cross-bearer howled louder.

"What is it, the phase of the moon?" she said. "Brings them crawling out of the woodwork?

Speaking of crawlies, you've already made an enemy."

"Ms. Red Dress?"

She nodded. "She came bursting into my office on the verge of tears, claiming you'd *humiliated* her." She gave her arm a dramatic wave. "What really happened?"

I told her.

She said, "You really need this, don't you? Try to help us out and get embroiled in all this political garbage."

"I can take it in small doses," I said. "The question is, how do you stand it?"

She sighed. "Sometimes I wonder. Anyway, don't worry about her. I told her not to come back until I see the proper forms—gave her a stack to fill out. If there's a call from the Board, I'll deal with it the way they deal with nuisances—ignoring them, putting them on hold, memo blizzard. By the time they take a meeting and decide what to do, you'll probably be finished and out of here and the kids will be all right. How're they doing?"

"The ones that showed up are doing fine," I said.

Her face fell. "Yes, fifty-eight percent absent and my ears are still burning. I'd like to think I was persuasive, but let's face it, how can I in good conscience tell them everything will be okay?" She shook her head. I thought I saw her lip tremble but she covered it with a grimace.

"Wouldn't it be something if they finally won because of something like this?" she said. "Some stupid crazy? Anyway, don't let me keep you."

"On your way out or in?"

"Out. I'm right over there." She pointed across the street to a white Ford Escort.

I walked her to it. She unlocked the car and put her briefcase inside.

I said, "I'd think the principal would get a private parking slot."

"The principal usually does. But the entire grounds are still closed off, orders of the police. No parking, no foot traffic. We've had to keep the kids inside for lunch and recess—not that they're exactly begging to go back out."

"It's important they do go back out," I said, "to desensitize their fears of the yard. How long did the police say they needed it closed?"

"They didn't. No one's been here at all today, collecting evidence or anything, so I can't see the point— I mean, what could there be left to find out? Guess I'd better check it out. Meanwhile, you have a nice evening."

I opened the car door.

"A gentleman," she said, getting in. "How nice."

I searched her face for sarcasm, saw only weariness. The black dress had ridden up. Very long, white legs . . .

"Take care," I said, closing the door. "See you tomorrow."

"Listen," she said, "I'm heading out for some dinner—nothing fancy, but I wouldn't mind some company."

She blushed, looked away, jammed the key into the ignition and turned it. The Escort's engine came to life with a poorly tuned sputter, belched, and finally caught. When it had settled to an idle, I said, "I wouldn't mind some company either."

She blushed deeper. "Uh, just one thing—you're not married or anything, are you?"

"No," I said. "Neither married nor anything."

"That probably sounds weird to you, my asking."

Before I could answer, she said, "It's just that I like to keep things straight, give a wide berth to trouble."

"Okay," I said.

Her laugh was brittle. "Not that it's worked too well so far."

6

I followed her to a place of her choosing, on Broadway in Santa Monica. All-you-can-eat salad bar with enough produce to stock a county fair exhibit, seafood on a grill, lots of woodsmoke, lazy fly fans, Alphonse Mucha reproductions on paneled walls, sawdust on the floor. Nothing really good or really bad, budget prices.

We constructed our salads and took them to a back booth. Linda ate with enthusiasm, went back for a refill. When she finished the second bowl, she sat back, wiped her mouth, and looked sheepish.

"Good metabolism," she said.

"Do you exercise a lot?"

"Not a fig—Lord knows my hips could use it."

I thought her hips looked fine, but kept it to myself. "Count your blessings."

The entrees came and we ate without talking, comfortable with the silence, as if we were old friends, using the silence to decompress. After a few minutes she said, "What do you think of the sniper—being a girl and all."

"It took me by surprise. By the way, one of your teachers—Mrs. Ferguson—told me she knew her. Had taught her in sixth grade."

"Taught her at Hale?"

I nodded.

"Good old Esme. She didn't say a thing to me—par for the course. But if anyone would remember, it would be her. She's been around for years and she's a local. All the rest of us are recent transfers. Or carpetbaggers, as we've been called. What else did she have to say about her?"

"Just that she was odd. Her family was odd."

"Odd in what way?"

"She didn't get more specific. Didn't want to talk about it."

"The Ferg tends to get overwhelmed—a little Victorian," she said. "To her, *odd* could mean anything . . . using the wrong fork at dinner. But I'll have a talk with her, see what I can learn."

"What about transcripts?" I said. "Can you look them up?"

"There may be some old records, but I'm not sure. Before we started busing the East Side kids in, the place was cleaned up. Most of the files were moved downtown. I'll check tomorrow."

"How long have you been working at Hale?"

"Since last year—they brought me in with the

buses. First assignment out of postdoctoral probation. I think they sensed I was trouble, wanted to
get rid of me quickly and thought a few months at
Hale would do it."

I said, "It is a hell of a way to start."

She grinned. "Fooled 'em and stuck it out.
Too young and too dumb to know better."

"Same thing happened to me when I started
out," I said. "I was offered a very tough job right
out of fellowship—working with kids with cancer.
By the time I was twenty-seven I was directing a
program for two thousand patients, overseeing a
staff of a dozen. Trial by ordeal, but looking back,
I'm glad I did it."

"Cancer. How depressing."

"It was, at times. But also uplifting. Lots of
the kids went into remission. Some were cured—
more and more each year. We ended up doing a lot
of rehab—helping families cope, pain reduction,
sibling counseling—clinical research that could be
applied almost immediately. That was satisfying:
seeing your theories come to life. Being useful in
the *short* term. I really felt I was doing some good,
making an impact."

"Twenty-seven. God. How old were you
when you got your Ph.D.?"

"Twenty-four."

She gave a low whistle. "Whiz kid, huh?"

"Nah, just obsessive. I started college at
sixteen, kept pushing."

"Sounds like false modesty to me," she said. "Actually, I was sixteen when I started, too. But in my case it really was no big deal. Small school back in Texas—anyone with fluent English and half a brain skipped."

"Where in Texas?"

"San Antonio."

I said, "Nice town. I was there about ten years ago, consulting to the med school. Took a river ride, ate grits for the first time, picked up a pair of boots."

"Remember the Alamo," she said, gripping her coffee cup hard.

More chill. Time to veer onto a different road.

I said, "So here we are, couple of precocious kids. Enjoying the fruits of success."

"Oh, yeah," she said, still tense. "Ain't that a hoot."

"What made you decide to stop teaching and go back for your doctorate?"

"I could give you all these highfalutin explanations, but truth be told, I wasn't a very good teacher—not enough patience. I found it hard to deal with the ones who weren't bright. I mean, I could sympathize with them in the abstract. But I'd grind my teeth waiting for them to come up with the right answer." Shrug. "Not too compassionate, huh?"

"Compassionate enough to shift gears."

"What choice did I have?" she said. "It was either that or become a witch and go home hating myself each night. You, on the other hand, must have tons of patience."

"With kids, yes. Not always with the rest of the world."

"So how come you don't do therapy anymore? Detective Sturgis told me you're retired. I was expecting an old guy."

"I stopped a few years ago, haven't gotten back yet—long story."

"I'd like to hear it," she said.

I gave her an abridged version of the last five years: Casa de Los Niños, death and degradation. Getting overdosed on human misery, dropping out, living on real estate investments made during the California boom of the late seventies. Then redemption: missing the joys of altruism, but reluctant to commit to long-term therapy, making a compromise—limiting myself to time-limited consultations, forensic referrals from lawyers and judges.

"And cops," she said.

"Just one cop. Milo and I are old friends."

"I can understand that—you both have that . . . heat. Intensity. Wanting to do more than just coast by." She laughed, sheepish again. "How's that for sidewalk psychoanalysis, Doc?"

"I'll take my compliments any way I can get 'em."

She laughed, said, "Real estate investments, huh? Lucky you. I don't know what I'd do if I didn't have to work. I mean, sometimes I really despise my job. Maybe I'd opt for Club Med full time."

"Your present job can't be too easy on the old patience."

"True," she said, "but at least now I can close my door, get ticked off, scream my head off, throw something—Carla's tolerant. I just didn't want to be losing it in front of the kids—taking it *out* on them. Also, what you were talking about, the chance to *do* something, to be effective—on a large-scale basis—is appealing. I mean, if I can institute something systemic, something that really works, I'm affecting a couple of hundred kids at one time. But what I really hate is knowing what has to be done, knowing how to go about doing it, and having all these stupid roadblocks thrown in my way."

She shook her head, said, "I really hate bureaucrats. Then some days I sit back, look at all the crap on my desk, and realize I *am* one."

"Ever think of doing something else?"

"What, and go back to school? Nossir. I'm twenty-nine already. Comes a time you have to just settle down and bite the bit."

I wiped my brow. "Twenty-nine? Whew. Ready for the old porch rocker."

"Sometimes I feel I could use one," she said. "Look who's talking—you're not much older."

"Eight years older."

"Whoa, grandpa, tighten the truss and pass the Geritol."

The waitress came over and asked if we wanted dessert. Linda ordered strawberry short-cake. I chose chocolate ice cream. It tasted chalky and I pushed it aside.

"No good? Have some of this."

Then she blushed again. From the intensity of her color, she might have offered me a bare breast. I remembered how she'd warded off compliments, pegged her as afraid of intimacy, distrustful—nursing some kind of wound. My turn at sidewalk analysis. But then again, why shouldn't she be reticent? We barely knew each other.

I took some cake, less out of hunger than not wanting to reject her. She removed most of the whipped cream from her cake, ate a strawberry, and said, "You're easy to talk to. How come you're not married?"

"There's a certain woman who could answer that for you," I said.

She looked up. There was a crumb of cake on her lower lip. "Gee, I'm sorry."

"No reason to apologize."

"No, I really am sorry. I didn't mean to pry. . . . Well, yes, of course I did, didn't I?

That's exactly what I was doing. Prying. I just didn't realize I was prying into anything sore."

"It's okay," I said. "Just about healed. We all have our sore spots."

She didn't take the bait. "Divorce is so rotten," she said. "Common as brown sparrows, but rotten just the same."

"No divorce," I said. "We were never married, though we might as well have been."

"How long were you together?"

"A little over five years."

"I'm sorry."

"No reason for you to apologize for that either."

I realized my tone was sharp—irritation at doing all the revealing.

Tension filled the space between us like an air balloon. We busied ourselves with dessert, let it deflate gradually.

When we were through, she insisted on separate checks and paid with cash. "Well, Dr. Alex Delaware," she said, putting away her wallet, "it's been edifying, but I've got to get home and attack some paper. Will you be coming by tomorrow?"

"Same time, same station."

We stood. She took my hand in both of hers. That same soft, submissive touch, so at odds with the rest of her. Her eyes were soft coals, burning.

"I really want to thank you," she said.

"You're a very nice man, and I know I'm not always the easiest person in the world to be around."

"I'm not always Joe Mellow either."

Face to face. Tight silence. I wanted to kiss her, contented myself with walking her to her car and watching the movement of her hips and legs as she got into it. As she drove off, I realized we'd talked more about ourselves than the sniping.

But alone, back in the Seville, thoughts of the sniping kept intruding. I picked up an evening final at a 7-Eleven near Barrington, drove to Westwood and north through the village, and examined the front page as I waited out a red light at Hilgard and Sunset.

Two photos—one of the storage shed, titled SNIPER'S LAIR; the other a head shot of Holly Lynn Burden—shared center top. To the right a 64-point headline shouted SNIPER FIRE BREAKS OUT AT SCHOOL. LATCH AIDE ENDS IT. CHILDREN ON PLAYGROUND FLEE IN PANIC. FEMALE SNIPER SLAIN BY COUNCILMAN'S STAFFER.

The head shot looked as if it had been taken from a high school yearbook: white collar over dark sweater, single strand of pearls, starched pose. Same face I'd seen on the photocopied driver's license, but younger, some baby fat softening the edges. Longer hair, flipped at the shoulders. Dark-framed eyeglasses, that same sullen dullness behind them.

The light turned green. Someone honked. I put down the paper and joined the chrome-surge onto Sunset. Traffic was slow but insistent. When I got home I started reading, skimming the recap of the shooting, slowing down when I got to the bio of the shooter.

Holly Burden had lived all nineteen years of her life in the house on Jubilo Drive, sharing it with her father, Mahlon Burden, fifty-six, a "widower and self-employed technical consultant." The contents of the father's police interview hadn't been made public and he'd declined to talk to the press, as had a brother, Howard Burden, thirty, of Encino.

Through "School Board records" the paper had found out about Holly attending Hale but didn't quote Esme Ferguson or anyone else who remembered her.

The future sniper had gone on to attend a nearby public junior high, then Pacific Palisades High School, where she'd dropped out one semester short of a diploma.

Guidance counselors had trouble remembering her, but an adviser at the high school managed to locate grade transcripts showing her to have been a poor student with "no participation in extracurricular activities." The few instructors who remembered her at all described her as quiet, unobtrusive. One English teacher recalled she'd had "motivational problems, wasn't academically oriented or competitive," but hadn't participated in remedial programs. Not an alumna to brag about, but no one had picked up the slightest hint of serious mental disturbance or violence.

Neighbors "along the quiet, tree-lined street in this affluent West Side district" were a good deal more forthcoming. Speaking anonymously, they described the Burdens, *père et fille,* as "unfriendly, secretive"; "not involved in the community, they stuck to themselves." Mahlon Burden was characterized as "some kind of inventor—some people think he's eccentric"; Holly was termed "a weird girl who hung around the house all day, usually inside—she never got any sun, was white as a ghost." "No one really knew what she did with herself—she was a dropout, didn't go to school or do any kind of work." "There were rumors she was sick. Maybe it was mental."

The reporter used that *maybe* as a bridge to the next focus of the article: guesswork about the state of Holly Burden's psyche proffered by the usual pack of experts willing to pontificate without benefit of data. Prominent among the guessers was "Dr. Lance L. Dobbs, clinical psychologist and Director of Cognitive-Spiritual Associates of West Los Angeles, an authority on the psychological impact of childhood stress, hired by the School Board to treat the young victims at the school."

Dobbs termed the dead girl a "probable antisocial schizoidal personality or sociopath—it's the kind of aberrant character that's made, not born," and went on to lambaste society for "not meeting the spiritual growth needs of its young people." He described his treatment plan as a "comprehensive and systematic program of crisis intervention, including the use of bilingual therapists. We've already begun working with the victims and have made excellent progress. However, based on prior experience, we do predict severe reactions on the part of some youngsters. They will have to be treated more intensively."

Never-never land.

The article ended with a profile of the hero of the day.

Darryl "Bud" Ahlward, forty-two, listed as Councilman Gordon Latch's "chief administrative assistant." More than just a bodyguard, unless that was Latch's way of getting high-priced muscle on the city payroll. And muscle did seem to be what Ahlward was all about: former Marine drill instructor, commando, body-builder, martial arts expert. All of which fit the tight-lipped, macho posture I'd seen yesterday.

What *didn't* fit was that kind of crypto-soldier working for someone of Latch's political pedigree. Apparently, Latch had been asked about it before, explained it by citing a "mutual rapport between Bud and myself, especially vis-à-vis environmental issues."

I put the paper aside.

A pebble-toss of whos, whats, hows.

No whys.

I called my service for messages. Routine stuff except for a request to phone Assemblyman Samuel Massengil's office, accompanied by two numbers—one local, one with a 916 area code. Sacramento. Curious, I phoned the L.A. number, got a recorded message expressing Assemblyman Massengil's eagerness to be of service to his constituents, followed by a list of other offices and numbers where many "municipal and county services" could be obtained, thus avoiding contact with Assemblyman Massengil.

Finally, a beep. I left my name and number and went to bed with a head full of questions.

7

At eight-thirty the next morning I got a call from a woman with a laugh in her voice. She introduced herself as Beth Bramble, executive assistant to Assemblyman Samuel Massengil. "Thank you for returning our call, Doctor."

"Executive assistant," I said. "Bud Ahlward's counterpart?"

Pause. "Not quite, Dr. Delaware."

"You don't have a black belt?"

Another pause, briefer. "I've never known a psychiatrist with a sense of humor."

"I'm a psychologist."

"Ah. Maybe that explains it."

"What can I do for you, Ms. Bramble?"

"Assemblyman Massengil would like to meet with you."

"For what purpose?"

"I really don't know, Doctor. He's flying back up to Sacramento this afternoon for a vote, and would be pleased if you could join him this morning for coffee."

"I assume this is about the Hale School."

"That's safe to assume," she said. "What's a good time for you?"

"I'm not sure there is one. My work with the children is confidential."

"The Assemblyman is well aware of that."

"The last thing I want is to get involved in politics, Ms. Bramble."

"I assure you, Doctor, no one has any intention of corrupting you."

"But you have no idea what this is about."

"No, I'm sorry, I really don't—just delivering the message. Would nine-thirty be too early?"

The invitation intrigued me, but it smelled bad; my instinct was to stay away. Given Massengil's temper, it was a tricky situation. Reject him and he just might vent more of his spleen on the school. Then there was the matter of my curiosity. . . .

I said, "Nine-thirty's okay. Where?"

"Our district office is on San Vicente. In Brentwood."

She gave me the address and thanked me for my cooperation. After she hung up, I realized the laugh had left her voice early in the conversation and never returned.

A blue plastic sign stamped with the state seal was visible just above the address numerals,

half-obscured by the leaves of a scrawny hibiscus.
The building was anything but imposing, nothing
remotely governmental about it. Two stories of
white stucco moderne, trimmed with sand-colored
brick and sandwiched between a larger, glass-
fronted medical structure and a mini-mall whose
main attraction was a frozen yogurt parlor. Svelte
people in sweats streamed in and out of the parlor,
concerned more with body tone than better government.

Fronting the building was a tow-away zone. I
turned the corner, hooked into an alley, and parked
in a visitor's slot. Pushing open an iron gate, I
stepped into more fresh air—the basic garden
office setup: half a dozen suites on each floor, each
with its own entrance, arranged in a right angle
around a jungle of banana plants, clump bamboo,
and asparagus fern.

The district office occupied two suites on the
ground floor of the building, its neighbors an
insurance broker, a graphic artist, a travel agent,
and a publisher of technical manuals. The door to
the first suite instructed me to please use the door
to the second. Before I had a chance to comply, it
swung open and a woman stepped out into the
garden area.

She was in her mid- to late thirties, with
blue-black hair drawn back and tied in a tight bun,
a full face, icy gray-green eyes, a fleshy mouth,
and ten pounds of extra weight in all the right

places. She wore a tailored black suit that flaunted the weight, a white silk blouse, and black string tie fastened by a huge smoky topaz. The suit skirt ended at her knees. Her spiked heels were long and sharp enough to render grave bodily harm.

"Dr. Delaware? I'm Beth Bramble." Her smile was as bright and durable as a camera flash. "Won't you come in. The Assemblyman's free."

I resisted the urge to ask if the Assemblyman was also easy and followed her inside. She swayed when she walked—more flaunting—and led me into a reception area. Soft, spineless music flowed from an unseen speaker. The furnishings were vintage highway motel—wood-grain and Mylar, ostentatiously frugal. The walls were lime-sherbet grasscloth hung with a few blurry nautical prints and Rockwell reproductions. But most of the vertical space was covered by photos, scores of them, framed in black: Massengil entertaining foreign dignitaries, presenting trophies, holding aloft official proclamations crowded with calligraphy, gripping chromium-plated groundbreaking shovels, doing the banquet circuit surrounded by alcohol-glazed, tuxedoed, rubber-chicken eaters. And mixing with *the people*: wheelchair-trapped oldsters, sooty-faced firefighters, children in Halloween costumes, athletic team mascots dressed as hyperthyroid animals.

She said, "He's a beloved man. Twenty-eight years representing this district."

It sounded like a warning.

We made a sharp left turn, came to a door marked PRIVATE. She rapped once, opened it, stepped back, and ushered me in. When the door closed she was gone.

The office was small and beige, borderline-shabby. Massengil sat behind a plain, scuffed walnut desk. A gray suit jacket was draped over a gray metal file cabinet. He wore a short-sleeved white shirt and tie. The desk top was protected by a sheet of glass and bare except for two phones, a legal pad, and a bell jar of cellophane-wrapped hard candies. On the wall behind him were more photos and a diploma—a forty-year-old degree in engineering from a state college in the Central Valley.

Perpendicular to the desk was a hard brown sofa with wooden legs. A man sat on it, portly, white-bearded. Loose face, ruddy complexion. Santa Claus with indigestion. Just like on TV. Another vested suit, this one lead-heavy loden green, bunched up around the shoulders. Shiny gold watch chain and fob, which he toyed with. A fly-straining melon of belly protruded beneath the points of the vest. His shirt was yellow with a starched spread collar; his tie, a green paisley fastened in an enormous Windsor knot. He kept playing with the chain, avoiding my eyes.

Massengil stood. "Dr. Delaware, Sam Massengil. Appreciate your dropping by." His voice was thin as charity soup, louder than it had to be.

We shook hands. His was large, hard with callus, and he squeezed my fingers a bit too tightly for the camaraderie he was trying to fake. A man prone to excess, though that didn't apply to fashion. His shirt was wash-and-wear out of the sale bin, his tie a riot of powder-blue eagles soaring across a beige polyester sky. The short sleeves revealed arms too long even for his pro- tracted body, scrawny but knotted with muscle and coiled with white hairs. Arms lathed by manual labor. A face sun-spotted and wrinkled as dried fruit. One side of the white toothbrush mustache was longer than the other, as if he'd shaved with his eyes closed. He looked every day of his age, but hard and fit. Rail-splitting? I couldn't see him jogging with the yogurt crowd.

He sat back down, continued to look me over.

I said, "I didn't realize there were going to be three of us, Assemblyman."

"Yes, yes. This is a distinguished colleague of yours, Dr. Lance Dobbs. Dr. Dobbs, Dr. Delaware."

"I've seen Dr. Dobbs on television."

Dobbs gave a faint smile and nodded, made no effort to rise or shake hands.

I said, "What can I do for you, Assembly- man?"

Massengil and Dobbs exchanged glances. "Have a seat, won't you?"

I took a chair facing the desk. Dobbs shifted position, the better to study me, and the brown couch squeaked.

Massengil held up the bell jar. "Candy?"

"No thanks." No sign of the promised coffee.

"How 'bout you, Lance?"

Dobbs took the jar, palmed some candy, unwrapped a green one, and put it between his lips. He made wet noises, turning it between tongue and lips. Gazing past me, over at Massengil. Expectant. I thought of a soft, spoiled kid used to parental protection.

As if cued, Massengil cleared his throat and said, "We appreciate your coming down on such short notice, Doctor."

"All in the interests of good government, Assemblyman."

He frowned, exchanged another look with Dobbs. Dobbs ate another candy and made a lateral move with his eyes—some kind of signal. I began to wonder about their relationship. Who was the parent.

Massengil said, "Well, no sense shilly-shallying. Obviously, this is about the tragedy at the school. It's been some couple of days, hasn't it, Doctor?"

"Yes, it has, Assemblyman."

"Now we know you've been working with

those kids. Which is fine, as it stands, absolutely fine." A smile that looked as if it hurt. "Now, exactly how *did* you get involved?"

"The police asked me to get involved."

"The police." Another smile. Photo-opportunity caliber. I put a black frame around it. "I see, I see. Wasn't aware the police did that kind of thing."

"What kind of thing is that, Assemblyman?"

"Referring to *specialists*. Getting involved in social welfare issues. Are you on some kind of official police referral list?"

"No. One of the detectives is a friend of mine. I've worked with traumatized children be-fore. He thought—"

"One of the detectives," said Massengil. "I'm a great friend of the police, you know. Best friend they have in Sacramento, in fact. Crime bill needs pushing, I'm the first one the police chief comes to. County sheriff too."

He turned to Dobbs, was prompted again by a small nod. "So. A *detective* referred you. Which *detective* might that be?"

"Detective Sturgis. Milo Sturgis. He's the new D-Three—the new supervising detective at Westside Robbery-Homicide."

"Sturgis," he said, contemplative. "Ah, yes, the big, heavy fellow with the bad skin. They didn't let him in when they conducted the interro-gation." Throat clear. Another exchange of glances. Pause. "He's homa*sex*ual, I'm told, though you wouldn't know it to look at him."

He waited for an explanation. When I offered none, Dobbs made a small, satisfied sound, as if I'd behaved predictably.

"Well," said Massengil, "is he?"

"Is he what?"

"Homa*sex*ual."

"Assemblyman, I don't think Detective Sturgis' sex life is—"

"No need to shilly-shally. Sturgis' sex life is common knowledge in the Police Department. Quite a bit of resentment, too—colleague-wise—regarding his promotion. His being in the Department in the first place, what with all the diseases and related hazards."

My nails were digging into the arms of my chair. "Is there anything else, Assemblyman? I've got to be getting over to the school."

"Ah, the school. How's it going with those youngsters?"

"Fine."

"That's good." He leaned forward, put his hands on the desk, fingers blunt and splayed, yellow-nailed. "Let me ask you this point-blank. You one too?"

"One what?"

"Homa*sex*ual."

"Assemblyman, I don't—"

"The thing is, Doctor, everything's a real

mess, societally speaking. I think we can all agree
on that, right? My responsibility is to make sure
things don't get any messier than they've already
gotten. It's a crazy world we're living in—punks
shooting at elected public servants, big government forcing alternative life-styles down people's
throats, moving children around like truck produce. Pushing ivory tower theories not backed up
by real life experiences. Making no one happy at
either end—no the people or the youngsters. You,
being in your line of work, should know all about
that, though I've got to tell you it seems to me
more often than not that people *in* your line of
work forget all about reality, push for this'n that,
quick fix here, quick fix there. Causing more
erosion."

He picked up the bell jar, caressed it, said,
"*Erosion.* That's an important word—the soil's
got a lot to teach us. 'Cause when you boil it all
down, we're talking erosion of standards. *Boundaries.* Gradual but severely *deleterious,* just like it
is when the soil erodes. Everything boils down to
that. Preservation or erosion—what stays; what
goes. This is my district, son, my responsibility.
For close to thirty years it's *been* my responsibility. I fly up and down between here and Sacramento three times a week, using airplanes the way
other people use cars, because this world we live
in's a big one, this district is the part of that world
that's *my* responsibility, and I've got to cover it,

know what's going on in terms of every part of it. And when I see changes I don't like—*erosion*—I step in."

He paused for dramatic effect, a dime-store Cicero.

Dobbs said, "Sam—"

"Hold on a minute, Lance. I want the doctor here to know . . . where I'm coming from." Another big smile. "How's that for your contemporary lingo? Where I'm *coming* from. And where I'm coming from is a posture of professional responsibility for my district, wanting . . . needing to know if standards are being compromised, the boundaries loosened up any further. Wanting to know exactly who's in charge."

"In charge of what?"

"Systems. Systems of *influence*. *Educational* systems. *Psychiatric treatment* systems. Anything that influences impressionable young minds."

Dobbs smiled and said, "Dr. Delaware, given what the children have been through, we obviously need to make sure they're being given optimal treatment."

"We?"

"We," said Massengil. "My *team*."

"Dr. Dobbs is part of your team?"

Another flash of ocular Morse code.

"He's *on* the team," said Massengil, boasting but sounding oddly defensive. "Along with lots of other good people."

Dobbs said, "I've worked extensively with the Assemblyman's staff—management seminars."

"You bet," said Massengil, too quickly. "Top-notch stuff." He ticked off on his fingers. *"Foundations of Character. Pathways to Leadership. Spiritual Growth in Service of the Soul."*

Dobbs smiled, but seemed wary, a drama coach watching the performance of an unreliable ingenue.

Massengil said, "We've all of us benefited from Dr. Dobbs's input—the whole staff has. So you see, we're not opposed to your line of work per se, as far as it goes. But we just need to know who's doing it. Lance is someone we know and trust, because he understands the real world, the realities of the district. Real life and its spiritual underpinnings. That's why *he* was asked to treat those kids after the earthquake, why *he's* exceptionally qualified to treat these youngsters." Wide smile. "Now, all of a sudden you're involved, which is fine as far as it's gone—we appreciate your enthusiasm and we thank you kindly. But we don't know *who* you are, what your *background* is."

I gave him my academic credentials, using the long form.

He half-listened and stroked the bell jar. "Sounds fine, sir. But you still haven't answered the main, important question."

I said, "Am I gay? No, I'm not. But Detective Sturgis *is* my friend—do you think I'm in danger of catching it?"

The creases around his eyes tightened into paper cuts and his fingers curled on the desk top. Clawing the glass, whitening the horny nails. But he kept smiling, showed those brown teeth. "No telling *what* can be caught nowadays, right? Bottom line, we're all after the same thing, aren't we?"

"What's that?"

"Cleaning up the mess. Doing right by those youngsters. Seeing to it that they become good citizens. I'm sure you want that just as much as we do, now don't you, Doctor?"

"Right now," I said, "I'm less interested in teaching them civics than in helping them sleep through the night."

His smile faded.

Dobbs said, "All Assemblyman Massengil is saying is that values are crucial when working with these children—any children. Maintaining an order."

"What kind of order?"

"A system of values. Being overt and aboveboard with one's personal value system is a necessity in clinical work—one that's too often neglected. Children need that kind of security. The knowledge that their significant others *believe* in something. Surely you wouldn't disagree."

Massengil said, "Let's get down to brass tacks, Doc. We greatly appreciate everything you've done. I'm sure you've made a great start, psychology-wise. From now on, though, Lance's people are gonna take over. The way it was supposed to be in the first place."

I said, "I can't agree to that, Assemblyman. Breaking off and starting with someone new would only confuse the children further—weaken whatever sense of security they've rebuilt."

He gave his head a choppy wave. "Don't you worry about that. I'm sure Lance will be able to remedy that."

"Absolutely," said Dobbs. "If you're using a standard crisis-intervention mode, it should be no problem to transfer from one attachment figure to—"

I said, "Come on, Doctor. The last thing the children need is more unnecessary change."

Before he could answer I stood and looked down at Massengil. "Assemblyman, if you're really interested in their welfare, keep your politics out of their lives and let me do my job."

Massengil put his hands on the arms of his chair, sucked in his breath, and rounded his shoulders as if preparing to lift himself up. But he stayed in place, all the tension rising to his face, compressing and darkening it, like meat turned to pemmican in the sun.

"*Politics,* eh? Like that's some sort of dirty

word? Like it's somehow criminal to want to serve
God and country? I've got news for you, young
man. People don't want to hear that kind of
libertine guff anymore. They respect competence,
experience, know who their leaders are, where the
bedrock lies." He shook a finger at me. "If it's
politics you find so objectionable, let me tell you
something. Your *homasexual* friend got his *promotion* 'cause of politics. He called *you* in 'cause
of politics. And this whole mess started in the first
place 'cause of *politics*—*those kids* and the agita-
tors behind them are making a deliberate choice to
bring politics into their lives every morning they
get on that bus from Boyle Heights and head west!
So if you want to talk about politics, let's talk
about the whole damned picture!"

I said, "I'm not concerned with any of that.
All I care about is helping them deal with being
shot at."

"Wasn't *them. Me! I* was the target. Because
of what I stood for. Put in the cross-hairs by some
vicious radical punk trying to erode the boundaries!"

"Is that what you told ATD?"

He hesitated for a moment, looked at Dobbs,
then back at me. "What I know is my business.
Preservation and erosion. Fact is, it's about time
someone took charge of that school, set things
right. Place is nothing but an open sore on the face
of the district, social experimentation at the ex-

pense of stability. I try to talk straight about it and nearly get gunned down in cold blood. There's your being shot at!"

He was breathing hard and his fingers had left wet marks on the glass.

Dobbs said, "Sam. Assemblyman." He made a faint wiggling motion with one hand, then lowered it, like a magician de-levitating an assistant. Massengil settled back down and let out breath.

"All right, Doctor," said Dobbs. "Let's emphasize cooperation, not confrontation. Work together. I'd be happy to integrate you into my program."

All smiles.

I remembered what Linda had told me about his earthquake "program" and shook my head. "That would be pointless, Dr. Dobbs. I'm well into my treatment; the children are responding well. There's simply no reason to complicate things."

The smile lingered but turned condescending. "Are you sure that isn't ego talking, Doctor?"

"Not ego," I said. "Just good common sense."

"A contradiction in terms, if there ever was one, Dr. Delaware. If good sense was common, we'd both be out of business, wouldn't we? Same goes for good values."

"Values," I said. "Like truth in advertising?"

He pursed his lips. Before he could get them in gear, I turned to Massengil and said, "Yesterday, at the school, I met one of Dr. Dobbs's staff, handing out cassette tapes. Misrepresenting herself as a psychologist and claiming a doctorate she didn't have. Two violations of the state business code, Assemblyman. How's that for *erosion*?"

Massengil looked at Dobbs.

Dobbs laughed and said, "Picayune, Sam. A technicality. Patty Mendez is a good gal, but green. Not well-versed yet in all the red tape the bureaucrats throw at us. Dr. Delaware here was pretty rough on her. I've talked to her, set her straight."

Massengil stared at him for an instant, then swung his eyes back to me. "You heard that. Let's not go making a mountain out of a molehill."

"How about we get back on track?" said Dobbs gently.

"Right," said Massengil. "I want Lance involved. One way or the other. Plain and simple."

I looked at Dobbs. Self-satisfied. In control. Suddenly I understood. All the cross-glances, hand signals.

The bond between them went beyond management seminars.

What they had was deeper.

Something with a parent/child flavor to it.

It explained the odd defensiveness Massengil

had shown when I'd asked about Dobbs's being on his team.

We've all of us benefited, the whole staff.

All of us. Not just *me*.

Patient and therapist? The bedrock of the community baring his psyche to Santa Claus?

Why not?

Psychotherapy under the guise of management seminars would be a nifty cover, legitimizing Dobbs's presence in Massengil's office and sparing Massengil the trip to the doctor's office. Spiritual Growth in Service of the Soul . . . mind-probing disguised as "brainstorming." The bills could be laundered among the office invoices. . . .

Massengil's thin voice snapped me back to the present. Making another speech. More gobbledygook about values . . .

I said, "Gentlemen, if that's all, I'm on my way. And I expect to finish what I started without further interruption."

"You're making a big mistake," said Massengil. "A damned big one."

"No, *you* are," I said, loud enough to surprise all three of us. "The latest in a series of mistakes. Like using the school—exploiting *those youngsters*—to further your own agenda. Obsessing on trivial nonsense when there are so many important issues to deal with. And if you are right about being the target, you did a lot worse than that—you drew a killer to that yard, put those kids in mortal danger."

Massengil shot up and came around the desk. "You snotty fag bastard!" Froth had collected in the corners of his mouth. Flecks of it flew as he talked and one of them settled on his tie.

Dobbs looked pained. "Sam!" he said, struggling to his feet, trying to restrain the older man. But Massengil was strong for his age and fueled by rage. The two of them wrestled awkwardly for a moment. Then Dobbs said "Sam!" sharply, and Massengil stopped struggling.

He glowered at me from behind Dobbs's sloping loden shoulder. "Loudmouthed snot."

Dobbs turned and gave me a look-what-you've-done glare.

I said, "You have a very impolitic temper, Assemblyman."

Massengil said, "Don't worry, Lance. He's out. You're in. Got my word on it. Plain and simple."

I said, "Assemblyman, here's something plain and simple: The slightest attempt to interfere with my treatment and I'm going straight to the press. They don't have many facts on the shooting itself, and you can bet they'll be overjoyed to pick up a juicy side angle—political meddling."

Massengil surged forward. "Now, you just—" Dobbs held him back but gave me a threatening look himself.

I walked to the door. "So juicy they'll drool, Assemblyman. Doctors who aren't doctors, a 'crisis intervention' program that hasn't begun despite Dr. Dobbs's inspired little TV speeches. A non-program that your office has already paid for. Sounds like poor fiscal policy at best, multiple fraud at worst. Someone's going to want to know why—why the connection between you and Dr. Dobbs is so strong that you're willing to stretch this far. At the very least there'll be an ethics investigation. You know how those things get when they pick up momentum. So let's see if those hungry newshounds think it's picayune."

The color drained from Massengil's face. Dobbs's face froze. He picked up his watch fob and began rubbing it hard.

I turned my back on them and left.

Beth Bramble was outside the office, smoking a long, pink, silver-tipped cigarette.

"Everything go okay?" she said, smiling. Squeezing the laugh back in.

"Peachy keen." My jaws ached from tension and my voice was hoarse.

She stopped smiling, looked back at the office door.

"Don't worry. He's all right," I said. "Still beloved."

8

Good show of cool, but as I walked to the Seville the anger hit me. I found a pay phone near the yogurt place and put in a call to Milo. He was out and I left a message to phone. I went inside, bought a cup of coffee, drank it, and took a refill while standing at the counter. Lots of ambient conversation about pulse rates. Mine was racing.

I got out of there and drove to the school, traveling slowly, trying to settle down, arriving a little before eleven, still keyed up and not ready to face the kids.

I parked, did a little deep breathing, and got out of the car. Both the school cop and the crossbearer were gone. As I walked toward the gate a car came tooling slowly down the street. Silver-gray compact. Honda Accord in need of a wash, the body dimpled and scarred, the finish not much shinier than primer. But a single display of Kalifornia-kustom flair caught my eye: gleaming blackened windows that wrapped around the car like electrician's tape, making the lackluster paint-work appear even more tarnished. Windows that would have seemed more in place on a stretch limo.

The little gray car stopped to let me cross, lingered, and continued cruising for a block before turning left. I walked onto the school grounds.

Linda was in her office, behind a pile of paperwork. When she saw me she swiveled, stood, and smiled. She was wearing a blue oxford button-down shirt and khaki skirt, brown boots with sensible low heels. The bit of leg that showed was smooth and white. Her hair was swept back and fastened at the temples with tortoise-shell barettes, revealing small, close-set ears adorned with tiny gold studs.

"Hi. You're early," she said, pushing aside some papers.

"Got thrown off my schedule."

Deep breathing or not, there was still ire in my voice.

She said, "What is it?"

I told her about the confrontation with Mas-sengil and Dobbs, leaving out the part about Milo's sexuality.

"The bastards," she said and sat back down. "Trying to profit from tragedy."

I took a chair opposite her.

"That's what you get for being a nice guy," she said.

"I wasn't such a nice guy half an hour ago. When Massengil started leaning on me, things got hot. Hope I didn't make things worse for you."

"Don't worry about it." She sounded weary.

"How much damage can he do?"

"Nothing in the immediate, other than make more noise—which is unlikely after the shooting." She thought for a moment. "I guess he *could* try to screw the school budget when it comes up next year in Sacramento. But it would be hard for him to target Hale specifically. So don't worry about it. Just keep doing your thing."

"He's a strange one," I said. "Really rough around the edges, not at all well-spoken."

"What'd you expect? A statesman?"

"Some sophistication—polish. He's been at it for twenty-eight years. On top of the crudeness, he's got a nasty temper. Surprising he's lasted this long."

"He probably knows who to punch out and who to kiss up to—that's the whole game, isn't it? And over twenty-eight years he's fixed plenty of potholes. Besides, being rough around the edges probably works well here—the whole cowboy thing."

"He's got to have something going," I said. "Hasn't had any opposition for the last two elections. I know, 'cause I'm a constituent. I keep leaving the space blank."

"I'm a constituent too. I write in Alfred E. Newman."

I smiled.

She said, "Might we be neighbors, sir?"

"I live up in Beverly Glen."

"Beverly Glen and where?"

"North of Sunset, up toward Mulholland."

"Mmm, real pretty up there," she said. "Way out of my league. All I've got is a little hutch near Westwood and Pico." Mischievous smile. "Guess neither of us loyal constituents has much chance of getting *our* potholes fixed."

"Better learn to mix your own asphalt," I said. "Or cozy up to Dr. Dobbs."

"Speaking of which," she said and took something off her desk and handed it to me.

It was a cassette tape, white plastic with black lettering that had smeared. The title was KEEPING A CLEAR MIND, AGES 5–10. *Copyright 1985, Lance Dobbs, Ph.D. Cognitive-Spiritual Associates, Inc.*

"This is what Little Miss Phony Doc was handing out before you aced her," she said. "I confiscated all of them, took one home, and listened to it last night. Far as I can tell, what it comes down to is brainwashing. Literally. Dobbs goes on about how bad thoughts make children sad and angry. Then he tells them to imagine their mommies taking their brains out and scrubbing them hard with soap and water until they're all clean, all the bad thoughts are gone, and what's left are good, clean, sparkly thoughts. Sounds hokey to me. Is there any way something like that could be beneficial?"

"Doubtful," I said. "Techniques like that have been used with chronically ill people—positive thinking, guided imagery, trying to get them to focus away from their discomfort. But generally those patients are screened and counseled first—encouraged to express their feelings before they try to clean their heads. That's what our kids need right now. To unload."

"So you're saying this could hurt them—jam them up?"

"If they took it too seriously. It could also cause guilt problems if they started to view their fear and anger as 'bad.' To kids, *bad* means they've misbehaved."

"Damn quacks," she said, glaring at the cassette.

"Was there anything on the tape that would hold a child's interest?"

"Not that I heard," she said. "Just some ditsy music in the background and Dobbs droning on like some kind of oily guru. Real low budget."

"Then there's probably not much risk. The kids wouldn't sit through it long enough to be damaged."

"Hope so."

"Low budget," I said. "Just like Massengil's

interior decorating. I can see why that kind of thing would appeal to him—a quick fix, no mucking around with anything psychologically threatening. And outwardly cost-effective—two hundred kids treated at one time. Dobbs could probably rig up some computerized test showing the kids were doing great; then the two of them throw a press conference and end up heroes."

I put the tape in my pocket. "I'll take it home and give it a listen."

She said, "What really burns me is the grief we go through trying to get mental health funds out of the legislature. They're always demanding outcome studies, proof of efficacy, pages of statistics. Then a creep like Dobbs gets his mouth on the government tit with this kind of nonsense."

"That's because the creep has a special in."

"What?"

"I can't be certain but I'd be willing to bet he's Massengil's therapist."

She lowered her chin and raised her eyebrows. "Old Blowhard in analysis? C'mon. You just said he wouldn't go for anything psychologically threatening."

"He wouldn't. Dobbs probably couches it in nonthreatening—non*therapeutic* terminology. Muscle-relaxation training, management efficiency. Or even something quasi-religious—one of the seminars had something to do with the soul."

"Down on the old knees and emote?"

"Whatever it is, I'm pretty sure there's something going on between them." I told her what I'd seen of the interchange between Dobbs and Massengil, the cues and covert looks. "When I hinted at exposing the nature of their relationship, Massengil almost lost his cookies."

"Oh, boy," she said. "There's a charming image for you." She touched a finger to her lips. "Wonder what kink he's having straightened."

"Maybe it's temper control, or relief of some kind of stress-related symptom like hypertension. Dobbs seemed accustomed to calming him down and Massengil obeyed him. As if they'd practiced together."

"A minor league Eagleton," she said, shaking her head. "Wouldn't play too well with the good folks of Ocean Heights, would it?"

"Hence the seminar cover," I said. "And extra payoffs to Dobbs for being discreet—like referrals after the earthquake. And the tapes. How much you want to bet Massengil's office paid for them? For a minor investment Massengil's buying the chance to come out of this whole thing smelling fragrant. He and Dobbs had no way of knowing I'd get there first—after Dobbs had already started talking to the press. The scandal potential is there. At the very least Massengil would look like a damn fool."

She shook her head. "Same old story. You'd

think I'd get used to it. I hope all of this hasn't soured you too much."

I realized that talking about it had leeched the anger out of my system. "Don't worry. I've seen worse. Anyway, I'm here to work. How many kids showed up?"

"A few more than yesterday, but not nearly enough. A lot of the parents couldn't be reached by phone during working hours. Carla and I will try again tonight."

I noticed how tired she looked and said, "Nice to see you haven't been soured."

She examined a cuticle. "One does what one can."

I said, "I see the school guard is gone."

"Must mean we're safe, huh?"

"You don't feel safe?"

"Actually, I do. I truly believe Massengil brought things to a head. The worst is over."

The look on her face didn't jibe with her words. I said, "What is it, then?"

She opened a drawer, pulled out a manila envelope, and handed it to me.

Inside were three sheets of paper, one blue-ruled and torn from a spiral notebook, the others cheap white stationery, unmarked. The message on one of the white sheets had been typewritten on an old manual; the other was handwritten in very dark penciled block letters. The blue-ruled sheet was covered with bird-scratch red-ballpoint cursive.

Different hands, the same message:

SPICK LOVER!!! FUCK YOU MONGREL RACEMIXER BICHES!!!

YOUR DAY OF RECKON IS SOON. REPENT OR BURN WITH ALL NIGGER TYPES IN DAMN NIGGER HELL . . .

ILLEAGALS GO BACK TO BEANERLAND. NO MORE STEALING JOBS FROM AMERICAN WORKING PEOPLE . . . WHITE PEOPLES LIBERATION FRONT.

She said, "I used to get this kind of swill regularly, but it had stopped. Guess it brings back memories of how rough things were in the beginning."

"Have you told the police?"

She nodded. "I called that detective from the terrorist squad—Frisk. He had me read all of it to him over the phone, said he'd send someone over to pick up the letters. But he didn't sound too hurried—kind of bored, actually. Didn't care that I'd gotten my fingerprints all over it or that Carla had thrown out the envelopes. I asked him about putting the guard back on duty, just for a while. The guy was no great shakes but better than nothing, right? Frisk said the guard had been supplied by the school district and it was out of his bailiwick, but that it really didn't seem to be anything to worry about—the perpetrator had acted alone. I asked him what about copycats, and he said that was highly unlikely."

"Did you tell him about the crossbearer?"

"Old Elijah? That's how I think of him— crazy prophet, down from the hills. I mentioned it, but Frisk said there was nothing he could do unless the turkey actually broke a law or unless I went to court and got a restraining order. Incidentally, he showed up again this morning—Elijah. Shouting through the fence about hell and perdition. I went out to him and told him he'd done good work here—everyone had heard the word. Then I asked if I could read his Bible with him. He jumped on that, turned to something from Jeremiah, death and destruction of the Holy Temple. You should have seen the two of us, reciting out on the sidewalk. After we finished I told him he should check out Hollywood Boulevard—lots of needy spirits aching for salvation over there. He called me a woman of valor, blessed me, and marched away singing."

When I stopped laughing, I said, "Crisis intervention. You've got the knack, Doctor."

"Right. All the time I was stroking the moron's ego, what I really wanted to do was give him a good kick in the pants."

"Any word from Frisk on when the kids will be allowed back in the yard?"

"They're allowed as of this morning. When he said there was nothing to worry about security-wise, I asked him about releasing the yard. He said, 'Oh, yeah, sure, go ahead.' He'd clearly forgotten about it—no big deal to him that we've had to keep two hundred kids cooped up. We are not talking paragon of sensitivity."

I said, "Did he have anything more to say about the shooting?"

"Not a blessed thing. And I asked."

"Did you tell him about Ferguson knowing the Burden girl?"

She nodded. "He said to have her phone him—that same bored tone. Doing me a great big favor. Old Esme called in sick, so I phoned her at home and delivered the message. While I had her on the line I asked her what she remembered about the girl. Didn't turn out to be much: Holly was a loner, not very bright, tended to space out in class, had trouble learning. But she did have one nugget of gossip—the girl had a black boyfriend. Old Esme lowered her voice when she delivered that. As if I cared. As if it really mattered, now. She also said the father's got a reputation for being a little strange. Works out of his house, some kind of inventor—no one's really sure how he supports himself. Incidentally, I did paw through our old records and found nothing on her. Apparently all the records that old were brought downtown. I called downtown and they informed me a manual search was being made of her transcripts; anything to do with her was classified information, orders of the police."

"A boyfriend," I said.

"You think that's significant?"

"Not that he was black. But if the relationship was relatively recent, he might be able to tell us something about Holly's state of mind. Did Ferguson say anything else about him besides that he was black?"

"Just that. Capital B. When I didn't comment on it, Esme started making flu noises and I hung up."

"Somehow I sense she's not your favorite person."

"I'm sure it's mutual. She's a grind, biding her time until pension. I wouldn't count on getting any insight from her on the Burden girl or anything else."

I said, "Speaking of insight, has Ahlward or anyone else from Latch's office called yet?"

"About what?"

"Vis-à-vis informational flow," I said in a puffed-up voice. "We good folks were supposed to get anything we wanted as soon as the police gave the old green light, right?"

"Promises, promises."

"Not that it matters, at this point. In fact it's better he's stayed away. The kids don't need any more political involvement."

"Neither do the adults," she said.

The noon bell rang outside in the hallway, loud enough to vibrate the office walls. I got up. "Time to heal young minds."

She walked me to the door. "In terms of reaching the parents, I don't know if Friday gives us enough time. How about Monday?"

"Monday would be fine," I said.

"Okay. We'll keep calling. I want you to know I really appreciate all you're doing."

She looked beaten.

I felt like putting my arms around her. Instead I smiled and said, "Onward. *Non illegitimati carborundum.*"

"Ah, on top of everything else, the man's a Latin scholar. Sorry, Prof. I took Spanish."

I said, "Inscription on ancient Roman tomb: Don't let the bastards wear you down."

She threw back her head and laughed. I kept the sound in my head as I went to class.

9

The children greeted me with eagerness, talking freely. I had the younger ones build replicas of the storage shed with blocks, manipulate figurines representing Holly Burden, Ahlward, the teachers, themselves. Acting out the shooting, over and over, until boredom set in and visible anxiety diminished. The older students wanted to know what had caused Holly Burden to go bad, caused her to hate them. I assured them she hadn't targeted them, had been deranged, out of control. Regretted having little with which to back that up.

A sixth-grader said, "What made her crazy?"

"No one knows."

"I thought that was your job, knowing what makes people crazy."

I said, "*Trying* to know. There's still a lot we don't understand about craziness."

"I got an aunt who's crazy," said a girl.

"She got it from you," said the boy next to her.

And they were off. . . .

I walked out of the last classroom sapped but feeling a sense of accomplishment, wanted to share that feeling with Linda and brighten up her day. But her office was locked and I left the school.

As I got in the Seville I noticed a car turn a corner and approach. Slowly. Silver-gray Honda. Dirty. Black windows.

It pulled up alongside me, stopped.

I power-locked the Seville. The Honda remained in place, engine idling, then suddenly drove off.

I snapped my head around and made out four digits and three letters of a license number. Held the information in my head until I could retrieve pen and paper from my briefcase and write it down. Then I sat there trying to figure it out.

Some kind of intimidation?

Or just a curious local, checking out the carpetbaggers?

I thought of the racist filth Linda had shown me and wondered if there could be a connection.

I looked over at the school grounds, graying in the autumn twilight. A handful of students remained in the yard, waiting to be picked up, playing under the watchful eyes of a teacher's aide. The school buses were gone, transporting kids from suburbia back to the mean streets—but which streets were meaner?

I watched the children frolic. Enjoying their newly paroled schoolyard.

Hide and seek.

Kickball. Hopscotch.

Losing themselves in the game of the moment.

So trusting it hurt.

I looked up and down the street before pulling out. Drove home too fast and kept checking my rearview mirror.

The first thing I did when I got in the house was pick up the phone and dial West L.A. Robbery-Homicide.

This time, the new D-Three was in.

"Hey, Alex. Got your message, tried to call. Kind of crazy right now—"

"Strange things are happening, Milo. Let's talk."

"Sure. Later," he said, in a voice that let me know he wasn't alone. "Let me handle a few things and I'll get back to you on that."

He rang the bell shortly before seven and, operating on reflex, went straight into the kitchen. I stayed on the leather sofa, watching the roundup of the news.

Nothing new on the shooting: just close-ups of Holly Burden's yearbook picture, a School Board official reporting that a "detailed and extensive manual search of several years of school records" had confirmed her attendance and graduation from Nathan Hale Elementary School but revealed no new insights. Then more psychiatric speculation, including one theory that she'd returned to Hale to take revenge for some imagined slight. When asked to fill in the details, the psychiatrist demurred, saying he was speaking theoretically—in terms of "classical psychodynamic wisdom." Dobbs came on again, in a segment that looked prerecorded. Caressing his watch fob, still talking about his treatment program at Hale, blasting "society." I wondered how long he'd keep up the charade.

Milo returned with a comice pear in his mouth, one of a dozen sent me each year as a gift by a grateful patient now living in Oregon.

He chomped. "Nice to see you're buying good healthy food again."

"All for you," I said. "Nutrition for a growing boy."

He patted his belly and sat down, scowling.

The camera drew back from Dobbs's rubber face. The psychologist was stroking his beard, had put on a sad, sanctimonious expression—part mourner, part huckster.

Milo snorted and began humming "Jingle Bells."

I said, "Yeah, the resemblance *is* striking, but this guy's no saint."

"Better be careful. He knows if you're naughty or nice."

Dobbs's pronouncements on spirituality dissolved into a commercial.

Milo stretched his feet out and said, "Okay, you promised me strange. Time to deliver."

I started with my encounter with Massengil and Dobbs.

He said, "I don't know that I'd classify any of that as *strange,* Alex. Seems like good old politics as usual: the asshole feels the school is his turf, wants his boy in on anything that goes on there. You have to think like these guys do—power's their dope. You've *infringed.* Of course he's gonna get offended."

"So what should I do about it?"

"Not a goddam thing. What can he do to you?"

"Not much," I said, "but he might be able to do something to *you.* He talked about how your promotion had caused resentment."

"I'm quaking," Milo said, and wiggled his hand. "But he's right in one regard. The troops are *not* happy with my ascension up the administrative ladder. One thing to tolerate a faggot; whole other ball of wax to take *orders* from one. Make things worse, the other D-Threes are getting antsy with my 'approach to the job.' Most of them are your basic desk jockeys, marking off time. My wanting to work the streets makes them look like the comatose slugs they are. The only other guy who stays active is the Homicide D-Three out in West Valley. But he's a born-again, doesn't like deviates, so there's no bonding potential there. Still, no sense pissing and moaning, right? Don't do the crime if you can't hack the slime. Besides, getting rid of me would be more trouble than it's worth—Department's like one of those dinosaurs with the pea-sized brains. Impossible to budge, real easy to get around if you watch your step. So don't worry about me, do your job, and forget it."

"That's exactly what Linda said."

He grinned. "*Linda*? We're on first-name basis, hoo-hoo."

"Down, Rover."

"*Linda*. All that fluffy blond hair, the southern accent. But *feisty*—gives her an appealing edge. Not a bad choice at all, pal. Time for you to be getting back into the social swing, anyway."

"No one's made any *choice*."

"Uh-huh." He made rude sounds. "*Leenda. Muy leenda*."

"How's Rick?"

"Fine. Don't change the subject."

I said, "That's exactly what I'm going to do."

I told him about the silver Honda. He looked unimpressed.

"What did it do other than stop for a few minutes?"

"Nothing. But the timing was weird. It was there when I arrived, driving by when I left."

"Maybe someone thinks you're cute, Alex. Or could be it's just one of the locals, playing paranoid posse, checking out the neighborhood for strangers, thinking *you're* the weirdo."

"Could be."

"If it would make you feel better," he said, "give me the license number."

I did and he copied it down.

"Service with a smile," he said. "Anything else I can do for you?"

I said, "Massengil seemed sure he was the target. You hear anything backing that up?"

"Nothing—not that Frisk has opened his files to me. Maybe the old coot knows something, but what's more likely is that he's got an inflated sense of self-worth, thinks he's actually worth shooting. Or maybe *he's* the paranoid one and that's what Santa's treating him for."

He ate more pear, said, "Some milk would go well with this," and went to get some. He returned, drinking out of the carton.

"Something else you should know about," I said, and told him about the hate mail.

"Your basic bedbugs," he said. "Too bad she has to go through it."

"She said Frisk didn't take it too seriously."

"To tell the truth, Alex, there's not much you can do with that kind of garbage. Now if it turns out the Burden girl was affiliated with some racist group, that'll be different."

"Would Frisk tell you if she was?"

"Not until after he put on his Giorgio suit, smiled into the camera, and told the greater metropolitan area first. But chances are, if she was highly political he'd know already. ATD's got everything computerized, would have moved on her known associates and I would have heard it through the old interoffice rumor transport system."

"Is there anything new you can tell me about *her,* Milo? The kids are asking."

"I've learned a few things by way of my source at the coroner's but I doubt it's the kind of info that'll help you. She was wearing black— jeans, sweater, shoes, everything down to the undies."

"Sounds like a commando getup."

"Or ninja nutcase. Or her taste in couture ran to basic black and a string of bullets. Or maybe she just didn't want to be seen in the dark—who the hell knows? What else—yeah, she was clean, drug-wise and booze-wise, an intact virgin, in excellent physical health prior to being perforated.

Stomach contents showed she'd eaten around six the previous evening. There was a paper cup with urine in it in the shed. The chemical composition of the pee implied she'd been camped out there some time during the night, sipping and waiting. Sound like something you want to tell the kids?"

I shook my head. "I learned something too. She had a black boyfriend."

He put down the milk carton. "Oh, yeah? Where'd you hear that?"

"One of the teachers at Hale lives in the neighborhood, taught her years ago. She told Linda about the boyfriend and Linda told me. Linda told Frisk but he wasn't any more interested than he'd been in the hate mail."

He ran his hand over his face. "Boyfriend, huh? Active or ex?"

"That's what I wanted to know. If he was recent, he might know something, right? But the teacher never said."

"Not that active, anyway," he said. "The intact virgin part. Got a name?"

"No. Just what I told you."

"Well," he said, "interracial dating's no crime. Officially."

I thought back to the hate mail. *Racemixer biches.* "Even casual interracial dating would be considered a *felony* in Ocean Heights, Milo. Meaning she might have gotten a lot of social punishment for it—nasty comments, ostracization, or worse. And it also implies she was anything but a racist—wouldn't have been likely to be shooting at those kids."

"Unless she and the boyfriend had a nasty breakup and she started resenting all minorities."

"Maybe," I said. "Here's a more likely scenario: What if coming face to face with local racism radicalized her and turned her against someone she viewed as racist. A racist authority figure."

"Massengil?"

"Maybe she and Massengil even had some kind of confrontation before the shooting. Something he'd never admit to. You should have seen how he reacted when I accused him of drawing a killer to the school, Milo. It definitely struck a nerve. With his temper, even a minor confrontation with her could have gotten ugly. Combine that with her history of psychological problems. . . . By the way, where did Frisk come up with that?"

He shook his head in disgust. I resolved to stop evoking feelings of impotence.

"Anyway," I said, "mix those elements and you've got something potentially explosive. It would explain why Massengil was so sure he was the intended target."

Milo thought about it, said, "Guess it's feasible, but good luck proving it."

I said, "Don't you think it's worth talking to the boyfriend? Checking out known associates?"

"Sure. But it's possible Frisk has already done it."

"He didn't mention it to Linda."

"He wouldn't. Guy would swear off orgasms if it gave him the upper hand."

"He who dies with the most secrets wins?"

"You got it."

"Must be a blast working with him."

"Oh, yeah. Like a cattle prod to the prostate. Anyway, what's this teacher's name?"

"Esme Ferguson. She teaches fourth grade. She called in sick this morning. You can get her home number from Linda."

He copied down the name. "She have anything else to say about the late Ms. Burden?"

"Lousy student, used to space out in class, not too social. Fits with what the neighbors told the papers about her hanging around the house all day."

"How," he said, "does she meet a black guy if she spends all her time just hanging around the house? In that neighborhood."

"Good question."

He closed his pad, put it back in his pocket. "Only *good* question, my friend, is one that can be answered."

"Profound."

"Yeah. Someone profound said it— Heidegger, Krishnamurti. Or maybe it was Harpo Marx. Squeak squeak."

He finished the pear with two ferocious bites and emptied the milk carton.

"Sounds more like Zeppo," I said. "Care for some dessert?"

10

After he left I listened to the white cassette. The contents were nothing that would have intrigued a grade-schooler: synthesized harp music that sounded as if it had been recorded underwater and Dobbs talking in the syrupy-sweet, patronizing tone people who don't really like kids put on when they talk to them.

The gist of the message was Play Ostrich—clean your brain, blot out reality in order to make it go away. Pop psych in all its superficial glory; Freud would have turned over in his grave. B. F. Skinner wouldn't have pushed the reward button.

I turned off the tape recorder, ejected the cassette, and lobbed a two-pointer into the nearest wastebasket, wondering how much Dobbs charged per tape. How many copies he'd peddled to the state, via Massengil's expense account.

The phone rang. I took it in the kitchen.

"Hi, Alex, it's me."

A voice that had once soothed me, then cut me. First time I'd heard it in months.

"Hello, Robin."

She said, "I'm working late, waiting for some lacquer to dry. Just wanted to see how you're doing."

"I'm doing fine. How about yourself?"

Let's hear it for sparkling repartee.

She said, "I'm fine too."

"Burning the midnight oil?"

"The Irish Spinners just got into town for a concert at McCabes. The airline damaged a bunch of their instruments and I'm doing the repairs."

"Ouch," I said, imagining my old Martin guitar in splinters. "Emergency surgery."

"I *feel* like a surgeon. The poor guys were devastated and they've been hanging around the shop, looking over my shoulder. I finally shooed them away. So now they stay outside in the parking lot, pacing and wringing their hands like relatives waiting for a prognosis."

"How is the prognosis?"

"Nothing a little hot glue and artful splicing shouldn't be able to fix. How about you? What've you been up to?"

"Repair work also." I told her about the sniping, my sessions with the children.

"Oh, that. Alex, those poor little kids. How are they doing?"

"Surprisingly well."

"Not surprising. They're in the best of hands. But wasn't there another psychologist, talking about it on TV?"

"He's limited himself to talk. Which is all for the best."

"He didn't impress me either. Too glib. Lucky for the kids they got you."

"Actually," I said, "the main reason they're coping relatively well is they've grown up with violence, seen lots of hatred."

"How sad . . . Well, I think it's great you're getting involved with them—using your talents."

Silence.

"Alex, I still think about you a lot."

"I think about you too." As little as possible.

"I . . . I was wondering—do you think it's reached a point where we could get together sometime, to talk? As friends?"

"I don't know."

"I realize I'm coming at you out of left field with this. It's just that I was thinking about how rare friendship is—between men and women. Part of what we had *was* friendship. *Best* friendship. Why do we have to lose that? Why can't that part of it be preserved?"

"Makes sense. Intellectually."

"But not emotionally?"

"I don't know."

More silence.

"Alex, I won't keep you. Just take care of yourself, okay?"

"You too," I said. Then: "Stay in touch."

"You mean that?"

"Sure," I said, not knowing what I meant.

She wished the kids at Hale well, and hung up.

I stayed up and watched bad movies until sleep overtook me, sometime after midnight.

The Santa Ana winds arrived in the darkness. I awoke on the sofa and heard them shrieking through the glen, sucking the moisture out of the night. My eyes felt gritty, and my clothes were twisted around me. Not bothering to remove them, I made it to the bedroom, crawled under the covers, and collapsed.

Sunrise brought a glorious Thursday morning, skies scoured and buffed a perfect Delft blue, trees and shrubs varnished a luminous Christmas green. But the view through the French doors had the jarring, cold perfection of a computer-fabricated Old Master. I felt sluggish, drugged by dream residue. Confusing hyperactive images had embedded themselves in my subconscious like fishhooks. Too much pain to tug them loose; time to play ostrich.

I dragged myself into the shower. As I was toweling off, Milo called.

"Ran the plates on the Honda. The car is an

'83, registered to a New Frontiers Technology, Limited. Post office box in Westwood. Ring any bells?"

"New Frontiers," I said. "No. Sounds like some kind of high-tech outfit—which would make sense if the driver was one of the locals."

"Whatever. Meanwhile, thought you might want to know I've got an appointment this Saturday with Mrs. Esme Ferguson. Her *residence,* at two. Tea and sympathy, pinkies extended."

"I thought Frisk was doing all the interviewing."

"He has first dibs but he never called her. He's just about ready to close the case. Apparently, nothing political's come up on Burden in anyone's files—no criminal record, not even a parking ticket. No funny phone calls that can be traced from her home to anywhere else, no job at Massengil's or Latch's. So they're considering it a nut job and are ready to file it as a solve. Isn't it nice when things go smoothly?"

Back at Hale by ten. Several dozen children were out on the yard for morning recess, running, climbing, hiding, seeking. The asphalt sparkled like granite under an unencumbered sun.

I finished my group sessions by noon, reserving the rest of the day for individual evaluations of the children I'd tagged as high-risk. After a couple more hours of evaluation, I decided five of them would be okay; the rest could use one-on-one treatment.

After spending another couple of hours doing play therapy, supportive counseling, and relaxation training, I checked in Linda's office. Carla was going through a pile of forms. Her punk-do was wrapped in a blue bandana and she looked around twelve years old.

"Dr. Overstreet's downtown," she said. "At a meeting."

"Poor Dr. Overstreet."

Her smile seemed less carefree than usual.

"Any of Dr. Dobbs's people been by?" I said.

"No, but someone else has." She put her finger in her mouth and made a gag-me gesture.

"Who?"

She told me.

"Where?"

"Probably one of the classrooms—your guess is as good as mine."

I didn't have to guess. I heard the music as I walked down the hall. Awkward attempts at blues riffs tooted on a harmonica with warped reeds.

I pushed open the classroom door and found a dozen or so fifth-graders looking quieter than I'd ever seen them.

Gordon Latch was sitting on the desk, legs folded yogi-style, jacket off, tie loosened, sleeves rolled to his wrists. A chromatic mouth organ was in one hand; the other caressed his gray-brown mop of hair. Behind him stood Bud Ahlward, wearing a charcoal-colored sack suit, back to the chalkboard, arms across his bulky chest, expressionless.

He was the first to notice me. Then Latch turned, smiled, and said, "Dr. Delaware! Come on in and join the party."

The teacher was sitting at the back of the room, pretending to grade papers. One of the younger ones, just out of training, quiet, with a tendency to be underassertive. She looked up at me and shrugged. The room had gone silent. The kids were staring at me.

Latch said, "Hey, guys," put the harmonica to his lips, and blew a few bars of "Oh, Susanna." Ahlward tapped one wing-tipped foot, concentrating. As if keeping rhythm required great effort. Latch closed his eyes and blew harder. Then he stopped, gave the kids a wide smile. A few of them squirmed.

I walked toward the desk.

Latch lowered the harmonica and said, "Bud and I thought it would be useful to drop by. Give these guys a chance to ask questions." Half-wink, lowered voice: "Vis-à-vis our prior discussion."

"I see."

"Brought L.D. too," he said, hefting the harmonica. Turning back to the kids, he gave a cheerleader flourish with the harmonica hand. "What's L.D. stand for, guys?"

Rustling from the seats. Childish mumbles.

"Right," said Latch. "Little Dylan." Toot, inhale, toot. "Old L.D. here, had him since Berkeley—that's a college up north, near San Francisco, guys. Any of you know where San Francisco is?"

Nothing.

Latch said, "They had a giant earthquake there a long time ago. Big fire too. They've got a great big Chinatown there and the Golden Gate Bridge. Any of you hear of the Golden Gate Bridge?"

No volunteers.

"Anyway, old L.D. here is my little trusted musical buddy. He helped me get through some long days—days with lots of homework. You know about homework, don't you?"

A few nods.

Ahlward lifted one foot and inspected the bottom of his shoe.

Latch said, "So. Anything *you* guys want to hear?"

Silence.

Ahlward uncrossed his arms and let them dangle.

Latch said, "Nothing at all?"

A boy in the back said, "Bon Jovi. 'Living on a Prayer.' "

Latch clicked his tongue a couple of times, tried a few notes on the harmonica, and moved it away from his lips, shaking his head. "Sorry, amigo, that's not in my repertoire."

I said, "Councilman, could I talk to you for a moment? Privately."

"Privately, huh?" Mugging for the kids, he lowered his voice to a stage whisper: "Sounds pretty mysterious, huh?"

A few children responded with shaky smiles; most remained stolid. Up at the chalkboard, Ahlward had crossed his arms again and was alternating his gaze between the view out the window and a spot on the rear wall, over the heads of the children. Bored and watchful at the same time.

I cleared my throat.

Latch checked his wristwatch and slipped the harmonica into his shirt pocket. "Sure, Dr. Delaware, let's talk." Full wink. "Hang in there, guys."

He got off the desk, flipped his jacket over one shoulder, and came my way. I held the door open for him and we stepped out into the hall. Ahlward followed us, silently, but remained in the doorway of the classroom. Latch gave him a short nod and the redheaded man closed the door, resumed the folded-arms, Secret Service stance, and looked up and down the corridor, a reflexive watchdog.

Latch pressed his back flush against the wall

and bent one leg. The harmonica sagged in his pocket. The lenses of his welfare glasses were crystal-clear, the eyes behind them restless. "Good group of kids," he said.

"Yes, they are."

"They seem to be handling things pretty well."

"That's true too."

"Though it seems to me," he said, "that they're a bit understimulated—not to know where San Francisco is, the Golden Gate Bridge. The system's failing them, has a long way to go before it does right by them."

I said nothing.

He said, "So. What's on your mind, Alex?"

I said, "With all due respect to your intentions, Councilman, it would be best to let me know the next time you're planning to drop in."

He seemed puzzled. "Why's that important to you?"

"Not me. Them. To keep things predictable."

"How so?"

"They need consistency. Need to feel a stronger sense of control over their environment, not have any more surprises thrown at them."

He lifted his glasses with one hand and rubbed the bridge of his nose with the other. I noticed that the skin behind the freckles was ruddy, tinged with bronze; since the sniping he'd taken some sun.

When the spectacles were back in place he said, "Maybe we got our signals crossed, Alex, but I thought this was exactly what you wanted. Exactly what you said you wanted that first time we met. Accurate information—firsthand information. Bypassing the red tape. Bud and I have been cleared by the cops in terms of informational flow, so I figured why not?"

"What I had in mind was something a little more organized," I said.

He smiled. "Going through channels?"

"That's not always a bad idea."

"No, of course not. The thing is, Alex, this wasn't really planned. Believe it or not, we public servants do get spontaneous once in a while."

Grinning. He waited until I smiled back, then said, "What happened was, Bud and I were literally in the neighborhood. Driving down Sunset on our way from a meeting in the Palisades—keeping the developers in check. Give those boys a free rein and the whole coastline will be a strip mall inside of a month. It was a hellacious couple of hours, but we came out of it better than when we went in and I was feeling pretty good about my job—that's not always the case. So when Bud mentioned that we were coming up on Ocean Heights, I said to myself, why *not*? It had been on my mind to get back here soon as the police cleared us but I'd been too caught up with backlog—dealing with the investigation set me back a couple of days. Things really piled up. But I felt badly about not keeping my word. So I told him to turn off, use the time we did have profitably."

"I understand, Councilman—"

"Gordon."

"I appreciate what you wanted to do, Gordon, but with all these kids have been through, it's best to coordinate things."

"Coordinate, huh?" His blue eyes stopped moving and got hard. "Why do I feel all of a sudden as if I'm back in school myself? Being called into the principal's office?"

"That's not what I intend—"

"Coordinate," he said, looking away from me and giving a short, hard laugh that percussed in his chest and died before it got to his throat. "Go through channels. That's exactly the kind of thing we tell taxpayers when they come up to the mike in Council chambers and ask us for something we don't intend to give them."

I said, "What exactly is your plan, Gordon?"

He turned back to me. "My plan? I just told you there was none."

"Your intention, then, in terms of the kids."

"My *intention*," he said, "was to break the ice with a little help from L.D., then field their questions. Give them a chance to throw stuff at me—anything they want. Give them a chance to find out the system can work *for* them, once in a while. Give them the opportunity to learn from Bud what it feels like to be a hero. My intention was to listen to *their* feelings and share *mine*— what it felt like to be under fire. The fact that we're all in this together—we'd better pull together or the planet's in trouble. I was just about to get into that when you came in."

Sidestepping the reproach, I said, "Were you planning to do that in every class?"

"Sure. Why not?"

"To do it thoroughly might take quite a bit of time. Several days. The media are bound to find out you're here. Once they do, we run the risk of more commotion."

"The media can be handled," he said quickly. "My only goal is to protect the little guys."

"From what?"

"Not what, Alex. *Whom*. The users. People who'd think nothing of exploiting them for personal gain."

He emphasized the last three words and paused, shot a knowing look over at Ahlward, who remained stoic.

"The sad thing is," he said, "with what they've experienced here—what they've seen of the political process—they run a heavy risk of growing up cynical. *Uninvolved*. Which doesn't bode well for us as a society, does it? We're talking stagnation, Alex. To the extent that that kind of thing takes over on a large scale, we're really in trouble. So I guess what I want is for them to see that there can be another side to politics. That there's no need to stagnate or give up."

From erosion to stagnation. My second dose of political rhetoric in as many days.

I said, "Another side as opposed to the one represented by Assemblyman Massengil?"

He smiled. "I won't kid you. My opinions on Assemblyman Massengil are public record. The man's a dinosaur, part of an era that should be long-forgotten. And the fact that he's involved has made me take a special look at this situation. This city's changing—the entire state is. The *world* is. There's a new age of transworld intimacy that won't be stopped. We're inexorably linked to Latin America, to the Pacific Rim. Cowboy days are gone, but Sam Massengil hasn't the vision to conceive of that." Pause. "Has he been causing any more problems for you?"

"No."

"You're sure? Don't be shy about letting me know, Alex. I'll ensure you're not caught in the middle."

"I appreciate that, Gordon."

His flipped his jacket forward and slipped it on. Patted his hair. "So," he said, smiling, "this must be fulfilling work."

"It is."

"I notice there's this other psychologist doing

a lot of speechifying to the media. Fellow with a beard."

"Lance Dobbs. So far he's limited his involvement to talk."

"You mean he hasn't actually been here?" Indignation, mock or otherwise.

"No, he hasn't, Gordon. One of his assistants came by but I convinced Dr. Dobbs that too many cooks would spoil the broth and she hasn't been back since."

"I see," he said. "That's certainly true—too many cooks. True in lots of other regards."

I didn't respond.

He said, "So. You feel you have it worked out. With Dr. Dobbs."

"So far so good."

"Excellent. Good for you." He paused, touched his harmonica pocket. "Well, good luck and more power to you."

The old two-handed grip and a nod at Ahlward. The redheaded man moved away from the door and smoothed his lapels. From inside the classroom came shouts and laughter, the young teacher's voice, tight with frustration, trying to be heard over the tumult.

Latch turned his back on me. The two of them began walking away.

I said, "Planning on coming back, Gordon?"

He stopped, and lowered his eyebrows, as if pondering a question of cosmic proportions.

"You've given me food for thought, Alex. I really heard you. About doing it right. Coordinating. So let me bounce it around, check my calendar, and get back to you."

I waited until the corridor was empty, then followed at a discreet distance, made it to the door, and watched them crossing the yard, ignoring the children playing there. They then left the grounds, got into a black Chrysler New Yorker, Ahlward driving, and rode away. No other vehicles pulled out behind them. No retinue of young scrubs, no sign of the media. So perhaps the in-the-neighborhood story was genuine. But I had trouble buying it. Latch's eager response to my question about Massengil, his questions about Dobbs, convinced me his agenda had been other than altruistic.

And the timing was too cute, coming so soon after my summons to Massengil's office. Not that yesterday's visit had been public knowledge. But Latch had already displayed access to Massengil's itinerary—the day of the sniping. Ready to do battle on camera.

Now the two of them were would-be heroes. A couple of sharks, vying for a tooth-hold in the underbelly of tragedy. I wondered how long it would go on.

Politics as usual, I supposed. It reminded me of why I'd dropped out of academic medicine.

I left the school and tried to put all thoughts of politics out of my mind long enough to get some dinner down. Driving quasi-randomly, I ended up on Santa Monica Boulevard and stopped at the first place I spotted that offered easy parking, a coffee shop near Twenty-fourth Street. Someone had begun holiday decorations—plastic poinsettia on each table; windows frosted and painted with mistletoe; spavined, bucktoothed reindeer; and a few baby-blue menorahs. The good cheer hadn't spread to the food and I left most of my roast beef sandwich on the plate, paid, and left.

It was dark. I got into the Seville and pulled out of the lot. Traffic was too heavy for a left turn, so I headed west. Another car's headlights filled my rearview mirror. I didn't think much of it until a few blocks later, when I turned right again and the lights stayed with me.

I drove to Sunset.

Still the headlights. I could tell, because the left one flickered.

Narrowly spaced beams. Small car. Compact car. Too dark to determine the color or make.

I joined the eastbound flow on the boulevard. Each time I looked into the mirror, the headlights stared back at me like a pair of yellow, pupilless eyes.

I caught a red light at Bundy. The headlights edged up closer. A filling station was at the nearest corner, the pre-embargo type—expansive lot, full-serve pumps, pay phone.

I rolled forward. The headlights followed suit. When the amber light flashed for the north-south traffic, I rolled for two seconds, then made a sharp turn up the driveway, kept going until I reached the pay phone.

The car with the flickering headlight started up and drove across the intersection. I followed it, taking in as many details as I could. Brown Toyota. Two people in front. Female passenger, I thought. I couldn't see the driver. The passenger's head turned, facing the driver. Talking to each other. Not even a glance in my direction.

I scolded myself for being paranoid, got back on Sunset, and drove home. The operator at my service gave me an earful of messages—one from Milo, the rest all business. I put in return calls, reaching one late-working attorney, a bunch of answering machines, and the desk sergeant at Robbery-Homicide, who told me Detective Sturgis was out, and no, he had no idea what the call had been about. I took the mail in, changed into shorts, running shoes, and a T-shirt, and went for a night jog. The Santa Anas had returned, gentler; I ran with the wind, felt airborne.

I came back an hour later and sat by the fishpond, unable to make out the koi as anything more than bubbles on the black surface of the water. But hearing them, hearing the song of the waterfall, my mind started to clear.

I stayed there a while longer, then went back up to the house, ready for the present tense. I thought of phoning Linda, tried to convince myself my motives were purely professional, then realized I didn't have her home number. Neither did Information. I viewed it as an omen, settled in for another night alone.

Nine o'clock. Evening news on the local station; I was becoming a tragedy junkie. I cracked a Grolsch, settled back, and clicked the remote.

The broadcast began with a regurgitation of the usual international mess, followed by a machine-gun spatter of local crime stories: an armored-van robbery at a savings and loan in Van Nuys, one guard killed, the other in critical condition. A Pacoima crack-smoker who'd gone berserk and stabbed his eight-year-old son to death with a butcher knife. A five-year-old girl snatched out of her front yard up in Santa Cruz.

Tough competition; nothing on the Hale sniping.

I sat through ten minutes of the feathery stuff that passes for human interest journalism in L.A. Tonight's main feature was a millionaire Newport Beach urologist who'd won the lottery and vowed his life-style wouldn't change. Next came shots of the new Rose Queen opening a shopping mall in Altadena.

Happy talk between the anchors.

Weather and sports.

The doorbell rang. Probably Milo, here to tell me, in person, what he'd called about.

I opened the door, directing my eyes upward toward Milo's six-foot-three level. But the eyes that stared back were a good nine inches lower. Bloodshot gray-blue eyes behind eyeglasses in clear plastic frames. Bloodshot but so bright and focused, they seemed to pierce the glass, dominating a smallish, triangular face. Pasty complexion rendered sallow by the bug-light over the door. Mouth tightly set. Small, thin nose with narrow nostrils flanking an incongruous bulb-tip. Wispy brown-gray hair blowing in the night wind. A nondescript face above a tan windbreaker zipped to the neck.

My gaze fell to his hands. Pale and long-fingered, wringing each other.

"Dr. Delaware. I presume." Nasal voice. Not a trace of levity. The hackneyed line rehearsed . . . No, more contrived than that. *Programmed.*

I looked over his shoulder. Down in the carport was a silver-gray Honda with blackened windows.

I was suddenly certain he'd been standing out there for a while. My neck hairs prickled and I put one hand on the door and took a step backward.

"Who are you and what do you want?"

"My name is Burden," he said, making it sound like an apology. "My daughter's . . . There's been some . . . trouble with her. She . . . I'm sure you know."

"Yes, I do, Mr. Burden."

He extended both hands in front of him, knitted together, as if containing something precious or lethal. "What I . . . I'd like to talk to you, Dr. Delaware, if you could spare the time."

I stepped back and let him in.

He looked around, still wringing his hands, eyes bouncing around the living room, like a billiard trick shot.

"You have a very nice home," he said. Then he started to weep.

11

I let him in and sat him down on the leather sofa. He sobbed tearlessly for a while, making dry, choking noises, hid his face in his hands, then looked up and said, "Doctor . . ."

Then nothing.

I waited.

His glasses had slid down his nose. He righted them. "I . . . May I please use your . . . facilities?"

I pointed him down the hallway to the bathroom, went into the kitchen, made strong coffee, and brought it back, along with cups and a bottle of Irish whisky. I heard the toilet flush. A few minutes later he came back, sat down, folded his hands in his lap and stared at the floor, as if memorizing the pattern on my Bukhara.

I put a cup of coffee into his hands and offered the whisky bottle. He shook his head. I spiked my own drink, took a long, hot swallow, and sat back.

He said, "This is . . . Thank you for allowing me into your home." His voice was nasal, oboelike.

"I'm sorry for your loss, Mr. Burden."

He shielded his face with one hand and moved it from side to side, as if trying to shake off a bad dream. The hand holding the cup trembled badly and coffee sloshed over the sides and onto the rug. He uncovered his face, put the cup down, rattling it against the glass top, snatched a napkin, and scrambled to mop up.

I touched his elbow and said, "Don't worry about it."

He backed away from the contact but allowed me to take the sodden napkin from his hand.

"I'm sorry . . . It . . . I don't mean to intrude."

I took the napkin into the kitchen in order to give him more time to compose himself. He got up and paced the room. I could hear his footsteps from the kitchen. Rapid, arrhythmic.

When I returned, his hands were back in his lap, his eyes back on the rug.

A minute passed slowly, then another. I drank coffee. He just sat there. When he made no attempt to speak, I said, "What can I do for you, Mr. Burden?"

He answered before the last word was out of my mouth. "*Analyze* her. Learn the truth and tell them they're wrong."

"Tell who?"

"*Them*. The police, the press, all of them. They're delusional. Saying she shot at *children,* was some kind of homicidal *monster*."

"Mr. Burden—"

He shook his head violently. "*Listen* to me! *Believe* me! There was no earthly way she would . . . *could* do anything like that. No way she would use a *gun*—she hated my . . . She was pacifistic. Idealistic. And never *children*! She *loved* children!"

I imagined the final scene in the storage shed. Her lair. Black clothing, a rifle, a cup of urine.

He shook his head, said, "Impossible."

"Why come to me, Mr. Burden?"

"For *analysis,*" he said, with just a trace of impatience. "*Psycho*-analysis. That's your specialty, isn't it? Childhood motivation, thought processes of the developing organism. And despite her age, Holly was a child. Psychologically. Believe me, I should know. That would put her within your professional purview, wouldn't it? Am I correct?"

When I didn't respond right away, he said, "Please, Doctor. You're a scholar, an in-depth man—this should be right up your alley. I know I've chosen right."

He began reciting the titles of studies I'd published in scientific journals. Ten-year-old articles. In perfect chronological order. When he was finished, he said, "I do my research, Doctor. I'm thorough. When things count, it's the only way."

The sorrow gone from his face, replaced by a haughty smile—an A student expecting praise.

"How'd you find me, Mr. Burden?"

"After I spoke to the police it became clear to me they weren't after the truth, had preconceived notions. Just plain lazy, concerned with wrapping things up. So I began observing the school, hoping to learn something—anything. Because nothing they told me made sense. I recorded the license plates of anyone going in and out of the school grounds and checked them against my files. Yours cross-checked with several of my lists."

"Your lists?"

The oboe played a couple of long notes close to laughter. "Don't be alarmed—it's nothing ominous. Lists are my business. I should have mentioned that in the beginning. Mailing lists. Direct mail advertising. Applied *demography*. Data that can be called up with regard to occupation, ZIP code, marital status—any number of variables. You were on the mental health specialist list. Subclass 1B: Ph.D. clinical psychologists. Yet you weren't the psychologist who's been talking to the media, claiming he's been treating the children. It made me curious. I investigated you further. What I learned gave me hope."

"My journal articles gave you hope?"

"Your articles were good—scientifically

sound. Relatively hard methodology for a very soft science. That showed me you're a thorough thinker—not some civil servant just coasting. But what really heartened me were the data I obtained from the lay press—newspaper articles. The Casa de Los Niños case. The Cadmus scandal. You're obviously a man who seeks the truth singlemindedly, doesn't run from challenges. I'm a good judge of character. I know you're the man for me."

More A-student hubris. And something else: a hunter's smile.

Where had the grief gone? A spooky little man.

I said, "Speaking of the truth, how about showing some identification. Just to be thorough."

"Certainly. It always pays to be thorough." He produced a cheap wallet and from it plucked a driver's license, Social Security card, and several credit cards. The photo on the license had a furtive, sullen look that reminded me of a dead girl. I glanced at the credit cards, all gold, all in the name of Mahlon M. Burden. Returned to the license photo and stared at it some more.

"I know what you're thinking," he said, "but for the most part, she resembled her mother."

I gave him back his ID.

"She had her mother's innate goodness, as well," he said. "Compassion for all living things.

This whole thing is a travesty—you've got to help me."

"Mr. Burden, what is it exactly you think I can do for you?"

"Conduct a psycho-biography. The life and times of Holly Lynn Burden." Mention of her name made his gaze waver for an instant; then it hardened with intent. "Apply the same tools of scholarship you apply to your research and become the resident expert on my little girl—on what made her tick. Delve as deep as you like. Be unsparing with your questions. Do whatever it takes to get to the root of this mess. Learn the truth, Dr. Delaware."

I took my time answering. His eyes never left me.

"Sounds like you're talking about two separate things, Mr. Burden. Reconstructing your daughter's life—what's known as a psychological autopsy. And *vindicating* her. One may not lead to the other."

I waited for the explosion. What I got was more of the hunter's smile.

"Oh, it will, Dr. Delaware. It will. A father knows."

A father knows. A mother knows. How many times had I heard that before.

"There's something you should know," I said. "You're obviously not happy with the way the police are handling things, but it was the police who called me in."

"Unless you'd lie to make them happy, that doesn't bother me."

"Something else. I can't promise you confidentiality. On the contrary. My first allegiance is to the children at Hale. My main goal is helping them cope with what happened, and I can't let anything distract me from that. If I found out something negative about Holly and disclosing it would serve a therapeutic purpose, I'd disclose. Unpleasant things could become public knowledge."

"I'm not frightened of the truth, Dr. Delaware. Solid data never scare me."

Boasting. I thought of him surveilling me, from behind blackened windows. Using his "files" to invade my privacy. Using tears to gain entry into my *lovely home*.

Assuming the patient role so that I'd play therapist?

No matter what his motivation, I'd been manipulated. I took another sip of spiked coffee and experienced a wave of lightheadedness. Alcohol or the strangeness of the moment?

I put the cup down, sat back, crossed my legs, and studied him. Tried to regain objectivity, pull out of the sorrow-sympathy circuit that he'd instigated on my doorstep.

"I absolutely accept your contingencies," he said. "Will you help me?"

He leaned forward on the sofa. Dry-eyed.

One part of me—the invaded householder—wanted him out of there. But I found myself considering his proposition. Because what he was offering me was exactly what I'd been telling everyone I wanted. A chance to understand the bogeywoman. The opportunity to mine some bit of information that might speed up the healing of the kids at Hale.

Delve as deep as you like. Be unsparing with your questions.

Given the recency of his tragedy, his inability at this point to confront what had really happened in the storage shed—that pledge meant little. He might start out by answering my questions and end up seeing me as the enemy. But somewhere in between, I might very well learn something.

At what price?

I said, "Give me some time to think about it."

That didn't please him; he tugged at the zipper-pull of his windbreaker, opened and closed the jacket, and kept staring at me, as if waiting for me to change my mind.

Finally he said, "That's all I can ask, Doctor."

He stood. Out came the cheap wallet. He handed me a white business card.

NEW FRONTIERS TECHNOLOGY, LTD.
MAHLON M. BURDEN, PRES.

A phone number with a Pacific Palisades exchange had been penciled beneath his name.

He said, "That's a private line—very few people have it. Call me, twenty-four hours a day. Chances are I'll be out of the office most of tomorrow—downtown, at Parker Center. Trying to get the police to release the . . . her body. But I'll be picking up messages."

His chin quivered and his face started to sag. Trying not to look at him, I saw him out the door.

I was still thinking about him when Milo called.

"Got a fix on your Honda," he said. "New Frontiers Tech is Burden's father's company."

"I know." I told him about the visit.

"He dropped in on you, just like that?"

"Just like that."

"Traced *you* by running *your* plates?"

"That's what he said."

"You get any sense he was dangerous?"

"Not really. Just odd."

"Odd in what way?"

"Calculating. Manipulative. But maybe I'm being too hard on him. The guy's been through hell. Lord knows I'm not seeing him at his best."

"Sounds to me like he piqued your professional curiosity."

"Somewhat."

"Somewhat. That mean you're gonna take him up on his proposition?"

"I'm thinking about it. Any problem if I do?"

"Doesn't bother me, personally, Alex, but are you sure you want to get in any deeper?"

"If I can learn something that would help the kids, I do. I made it clear to him that my first allegiance was to *them*. No confidentiality. He accepted it."

"He accepts it for now. But look at the guy's state of mind. Heavy denial: he's still claiming she's innocent. What happens when reality hits him? What happens after you go in and do your thing and come out concluding his little girl was a wacko with blood on the brain? How do you think he'll accept that?"

"I raised that possibility with him."

"And?"

"He said he was willing to take his chances."

"Right. He also tell you it was his rifle she took to that shed? Apparently the guy's a gun collector and she lifted one of his collectibles. What do you think that does to his ability to think straight about this?"

She hated my . . .

"When did you learn this?"

"Extremely recently." Pause. "Sources at the ballistics lab."

He cursed. I couldn't tell how much of his

resentment came from having to get facts on the investigation secondhand, how much from the possibility I might work with Mahlon Burden.

"So," I said, "you're saying I should turn him down?"

"*Me* telling *you* what to do? Perish the thought. I just want you to think carefully about it."

"That's exactly what I'm doing, Milo."

"While you had him there, did you ask him about the boyfriend?"

"I didn't ask him about anything. Didn't want to engage him until I was sure which way I was going to take it."

"Sounds like you're already engaged, pal. Only question is, when's the wedding?"

"What's bugging you, Milo?"

"Nothing. Oh, hell, I don't know. Maybe it's the idea of you working for the other side."

"Not for. *With*."

"Same difference."

"What puts him on the other side, anyway?"

"Good guys and bad guys. Know of a more meaningful distinction?"

"*He* didn't pull the trigger, Milo. All he did was sire her."

"She was nutso. Where did it come from?"

"What, guilt by procreation?"

A long, uncomfortable silence.

"Yeah, yeah, I know," he said. "Where's my

milk of human compassion for him—he's a victim too. It's just that I called you in to help the kids. Trying to do something positive in the middle of all this crap. I guess I don't want to see you used—to whitewash what she did."

"That would be impossible. What she did is *indelible,* Milo."

"Yeah. Okay, sorry. Don't mean to ride you. It's just been a terrific day. Just got back from another crime scene. Toddler murder."

"Oh, shit."

"Pure shit. Two-year-old victim. Mom's boyfriend gets loaded on ice and dust and God knows what else, uses the baby for punching practice. Neighbors heard the kid wailing all day, called Protective Services two weeks ago. Social workers came down last week, evaluated, wrote it up as 'high risk,' recommended removal from the home. But they hadn't gotten around to *processing* it yet."

"Jesus."

"Processing," he said. "Don't you just love that? Like sausage. Shit into the grinder, out the other end, tagged and wrapped. Can't wait to see what tomorrow brings. What new load of garbage will need to be *processed.*"

12

I mulled over Burden's offer without coming to any conclusion, woke up Friday morning still thinking about it. I put it aside and drove to the school to work with the ones I was sure were the good guys.

I could tell I was making progress: The children seemed bored, and a good part of each session was spent in free play. Most of the afternoon was spent working individually with the high-risk youngsters. A few were still experiencing sleep problems but even they seemed more settled.

Doing remarkably well.

But what would the long-term effects be?

By four I was sitting in an empty classroom thinking about that. Realizing how poorly my training had prepared me for the work I was doing, how few insights standard psychology had to offer about the effects upon children of traumatic violence. Perhaps my experiences could be useful to others—other victims and healers, certain to materialize soon in a world grown increasingly psychopathic. I decided to keep detailed clinical records, was still writing at five when a custodian lugging a mop and bucket stuck his head into the room and asked how long I was planning to be there. I collected my stuff and left, passing Linda's office. Carla's work space was dark, but the light was on in the inner office.

I knocked.

"Come in."

She was at her desk reading, slightly stooped, looking intense.

I said, "Cramming?"

She put her book down, swiveled around, and motioned toward the L-shaped couch. She had on an off-white knit dress, thin gold chain, white stockings with a subtle wave pattern running through them vertically, and medium-heeled white pumps.

"I was wondering if you'd drop by," she said. "Heard we had visitors yesterday."

"Oh, yeah," I said. "A veritable bath in the milk of human kindness."

"Lord. And it just keeps on coming."

She turned back toward the desk and took something out of a drawer. White cassette. "Three more boxes of these showed up this morning via registered mail. Carla didn't know what it was. She signed for the whole shebang."

"Just tapes, no people?"

"Just tapes. But Dobbs's office did call to confirm the delivery. Carla was out delivering memos to the classrooms and I took the call."

"Butt-covering," I said. "The mail registration is proof for any state auditors that he fulfilled his contract and is entitled to every penny Massengil paid him."

"That's what I figured. I asked to speak to him directly and they put him on. The yahoo was all sweetness and light. Wanting to know how the poor little things were doing. *Things*. He probably *sees* them as things. Assuring me he was on twenty-four-hour call in case of emergencies. I'll sleep so much better knowing that."

"And no doubt the phone call will be logged as professional consultation and billed for."

"He made sure to let me know you and he had *conferred*," she said. "That the two of you were *of one mind with regard to clinical issues*. He approves of your methods, Doctor—doesn't that make *your* day?"

"Sounds like he wants to compromise," I said. "We don't expose his little scam, let him make a few bucks on the tapes, and he backs off."

"How does that sit with you?"

I thought about it. "I can live with it if it means he stays out of the picture."

"So can I," she said. "What does that make us?"

"Realists."

"Ugh." She waved her hand. "I refuse to waste any more time on sleaze. How do the kids look to you?"

"Very good, actually." I gave her a progress report.

She nodded. "I've been hearing the same kind of thing from the parents we've spoken to on the phone. Definitely less anxiety. It's helped me to convince quite a few of them to send their kids back, so you've done a real good deed."

"I'm glad."

"At first, mind you, they were skeptical. Confused by what the kids were doing—drawing pictures of the sniper, tearing her up, getting mad. There's always that impulse to protect, try to hush things up. But results talk loudly. I've lined up at least a couple of dozen mothers for your Monday meeting."

"There's something else you should know about," I said. "Another visit." I told her about Mahlon Burden.

"How weird—out of the blue like that."

"It was, but he's pretty stressed. He's convinced Holly's innocent, wants me to conduct a psychological autopsy, show the world what made her tick. Somehow that's going to lead to proving her innocence."

Without hesitation she said, "I think you should do it. It's a great opportunity."

"Opportunity for what?"

"Learning. Understanding what went wrong—what *did* make her tick."

"I can't be sure I'll come up with anything significant, Linda."

"Whatever you come up with, it'll be more than we've got now, right? And the more I've been thinking about it—now that the shock's worn off—the weirder the whole thing is. A *girl*, Alex. What in the world could lead her to do something like that? Who was she shooting at? The media have basically dropped it. The police haven't told us a thing. If her father's willing to talk to you, why not take him up on it? Maybe you can learn something about her—some warning sign—that can help prevent something like this happening again."

I said, "His willingness to have me exhume her psychologically is being influenced by heavy denial, Linda. Once his defenses break down, he's likely to change his mind. If I start coming up with stuff he doesn't approve of, he'll probably end the whole thing."

"So? In the meantime, you learn what you can."

I didn't reply.

She said, "What's the problem?"

"My first allegiance is to the kids. I don't want to be perceived as being aligned with the bad guys."

"I wouldn't worry about that. You've earned your stripes around here."

"Milo—Detective Sturgis—has reservations about it."

"Sure he does. Typical cop-think—bunker mentality."

Before I could answer, she said, "Well, no matter what anyone thinks, in the end it's got to be your decision. So do what you feel is best."

She looked away, put the tape down, and began straightening the papers on her desk.

The chill . . .

I said, "I'm leaning toward telling him yes. I plan to let him know over the weekend."

"Ah, the weekend," she said, still straightening. "Can't believe this week's actually ending."

"Got a busy one lined up?"

"Just the usual scut. Chores, TCB time."

I said, "How about forgetting about business for a while?"

She arched her eyebrows but didn't look at me.

"Let me be more explicit," I said. "An early dinner—let's say in half an hour. Somewhere quiet, with a well-stocked bar. All shoptalk forbidden. Bring a little elegance into our otherwise humdrum lives."

She looked down at her dress, touched one knee. "I'm not exactly dressed for elegance."

"Sure you are. Hand me the phone and I'll make a reservation right now."

The eyebrows arched higher. She gave a small laugh and turned to me. "A take-charge guy?"

"When something's worth taking charge of." It came out sounding like a line. I said, "Hey, babe, what's your sign?"

She laughed harder and gave me the phone.

It took her a while to organize her things, write memos and reminders. I used the time to go into Carla's office and call in for messages. Two people who'd started college at sixteen, unable to let go of the compliant-kid role.

Finally, we left the building. She still looked tense, but she slipped her arm through mine.

The custodian was eager to lock up the school grounds and begin his weekend, so she drove the Escort onto the street and parked just outside the gate. We took the Seville and headed west. The restaurant I'd chosen was on a busy stretch of Ocean Avenue across from the bluffs that look down on the birth of Pacific Coast Highway. French but friendly, a clean white decor and canvas-topped front porch with a waist-high brick wall that allowed alfresco dining while segregating the sidewalk throng. We got there by six-fifteen. Several homeless people were competing with the parking valets for turf. I gave away a few dollars and got dirty looks from the valets.

We were seated at the bar for another twenty minutes before being escorted to a spot under the canvas. By eight-thirty, the Big-Deal-Pending folks would be tooling up in rented Mercedes and designer Jeeps that would have intimidated Patton, but at this hour we were opening the place.

Across the street, a grove of coco palms crowned the bluffs. Through the crosshatched trunks of the big trees, the sky was trapezoids of blood-red streaked with aqua, diluting to hammered copper near the horizon. As we sipped our drinks, it deepened to indigo. I watched the play of light and shadow on Linda's face. She'd pinned her hair up. A few fine golden strands had come loose near the nape of her neck. They caught the last hints of daylight and glowed like electric filament.

I said. "Isn't this better than TCBing?"

She nodded, rested her chin in her hand, and looked out at the sunset. Long graceful neck. Grace Kelly profile.

The waiter came, lit the table candle, and recited the daily specials. The kitchen must have overstocked on rabbit, because he kept pushing some kind of hare stew provençale.

She smiled up at him, said, "Sorry, but I just couldn't eat Bugs," and chose grilled white sea bass. I ordered steak in peppercorn sauce and a bottle of Beaujolais nouveau.

We drank and didn't say much. It took a long time to get served. When the food came she ate with the same gusto she'd shown the first time.

First time. Our second dinner. Despite that, despite all those chats in her office, I knew little about her.

I caught her eye and smiled. She smiled back but seemed preoccupied.

"What is it?" I said.

"Nothing."

"Not back at work, I hope."

"No, no, not at all. This is lovely."

"But there's still something on your mind?"

She ran a finger up the stem of her wineglass. "I guess I'm trying to figure out if this is a date."

"Do you want it to be?"

She shook her finger at me. "Now you sound like a *shrink*."

"Okay," I said, sitting up straight and clearing my throat. "Back to take-charge guy. It's a *date*, babe. Now be a good girl and eat your fish."

She saluted and put her hand down on the table. Long, graceful fingers that I covered with mine.

She took a deep breath. Even in the dim light I could see her color deepen. "I'm really pretty full. How about we skip dessert?"

Time had raced; it was nearly nine by the

time we got back in the car. She closed her eyes, put her head back, and stretched her legs. Then more silence.

I said, "How about a drive?" and when she nodded, headed north on Ocean and turned onto the ramp that leads down to Pacific Coast Highway. I slipped Pat Metheny into the tape deck and drove in the slow lane all the way to western Malibu, just past the Ventura County line. Mountains on one side, ocean on the other—past Decker Canyon, very little evidence of human disruption. I got to Point Mugu before beginning to feel drowsy. I looked over at Linda. The light from the dashboard was barely strong enough for me to make out her features. But I could see that her eyes were closed and she had a satisfied-child smile on her face.

The car clock said it was ten-fifteen. The highway sign said we were nearly at Oxnard. I thought of the last time I'd driven this way. To Santa Barbara, with Robin. I turned the car around, ejected Metheny, fed Sonny Rollins into the deck, and headed back to L.A. listening to the magic sax turn "Just Once" into something transcendental.

When I stopped at the light at Sunset Beach, Linda stirred and blinked.

I said, "Good morning."

She sat up. "Good Lord! Did I fall asleep on you?"

"Like the proverbial baby."

"How rude. I'm *sorry*."

"Nothing to be sorry for. Your serenity rubbed off on me."

"What time is it?"

"Ten after eleven."

"Unbelievable—I just lost two hours." She sat straighter and smoothed her hair. "I can't believe I just conked out like this."

I patted her wrist. "No sweat. I'll just expect total vivaciousness next time."

She gave a noncommittal laugh and said, "I guess you'd better take me back to get my car."

The light turned green. I got onto Sunset, reached the manicured magnolias of Ocean Heights just before midnight.

A cold, thick fog had settled in. Esperanza Drive was silent and blanketed by a crushing darkness. Not a soul on the street; the diamond windows of the ranch houses were black as obsidian, the low-voltage glow of landscaping spotlights dulled to amber smudges. Only a few illuminated doorbell buttons managed to pierce the vapor, orange discs that followed us, a battalion of tiny cyclops eyes.

My windshield clouded and I turned on the wipers. They scraped out a lazy four-four and I felt my eyelids droop.

Linda said, "Never been here at this hour. It's eerie—so . . . vacant."

I said, "L.A., but more so," and drove slowly toward the school. As we neared the spot where she'd left her car, I saw something. Two more eyes. Red irises. Taillights. Another car, parked in the middle of the street.

The fog had grown thicker; I couldn't see ten feet in front of me. I put the wipers on high, but the windshield kept beading with moisture and fogging up on the backbeat of the four-four. I reduced speed, rolled closer, saw movement through the haze—a manic blur of movement, trapped by my headlights. Then harsh music: dull percussion followed by a solo of breaking glass.

"Hey," said Linda, "what the—that's my car!"

More thumping and shattering. The crunch and scrape of metal against metal.

I gunned the engine and sped forward. Movement. Clearer, but not clear. Human movement. The pad of footsteps over the swoop-swoop of the wipers. Then another engine revving. I opened my window and screamed, "What the hell's going on!"

Tires squealed and the taillights diminished to pinpoints before disappearing into the mist.

I jammed the Seville into park and sat there, breathing hard. I could hear Linda's respiration racing ahead of mine. She looked terrified but made a move to get out. I held her wrist and said, "Wait."

"Oh, Jesus Lord."

I turned off the wipers. We endured an evil minute, then another. When I was convinced we were alone, I got out of the car.

Cold silent street. The fog had an ozone smell.

Beads of glass littered the street, vitreous against the damp pavement, like melting hail.

I looked up and down Esperanza. Down the row of ranch houses, still dark.

The silence stretched and became absurd. Not a hint of movement, not a single window yellowing, or the merest creak of curiosity.

Despite the racket, Ocean Heights slept soundly. Or pretended to.

Linda got out of the Seville. We examined her Escort. The windshield of the little car had been punched out. So had the windows on the driver's side. The hood had been caved in and was riddled with fissures that were raw metal around the edges. Bubbles of safety glass dusted the surface and pooled in the low spots.

"Oh no," she said, gripping my arm and pointing.

Another type of assault: the once-white roof was a cyclone scrawl of red and black spray paint.

Abstract art: a coiling, dripping portrait of hate.

Abstract except for one clear bit of representation.

Covering the driver's door, sprayed and resprayed for emphasis, its diagonal cruelty unmistakable even in the fog, was a black swastika.

13

Her hands were shaking too hard to get the key in the lock, so I opened the door to the school. She managed to find the corridor light and flip it on, and we went to her office, where I phoned Milo. He answered, sounding groggy. When I told him what had happened, he said, "Wait right there."

He arrived half an hour later. Thirty silent minutes with my arm around Linda's shoulders, feeling the rigidity of her body, then watching her pull away, pace, shuffle papers, fuss with her hair. When Milo walked in she composed herself, thanked him for coming, but seemed cold.

Something about cops . . .

If Milo noticed it, he didn't let on. He questioned her with a gentleness I'd seen him use with child witnesses, then put away his note pad and said, "Sorry you had to go through this."

"So what else is new," she said.

He stood. "I'll use your phone and get the

print boys down here, but that will take some time. So why don't the two of you go on home. I've got all the info I need."

She said, "No prints. Not another media circus."

Milo looked at me, then back at her. "Dr. Overstreet, we're in hear-no-evil territory—if anyone across the street saw what happened, they won't let on. And even if we manage to find an honest person, chances are they saw nothing worthwhile 'cause of the fog. So pulling prints from the car is really our only chance of getting anywhere."

"They were using crowbars or something like crowbars. What's the chance of pulling any prints from the car?" she said.

"Slim," he admitted. "Unless they slipped and touched the car. But *without* prints, we've got nothing—might as well forget the whole thing."

"That's what I want, Detective Sturgis. To *forget* it."

Milo scratched his nose. "You're saying you don't want to file charges?"

I said, "Linda—"

She said, "That's exactly what I'm saying. The children have been through enough. All of us have. The last thing we need is another fright, more attention."

I said, "Linda, if there's some danger, don't

you think the children and their parents should be aware of it?"

"There's no danger—this is just more of the same garbage we've had since the beginning. The sniping put us back in the spotlight and another cockroach crawled out. And there'll be others—phoning, mailing. Until they find someone else to pick on. So what would be the point of advertising this? No one would be caught and more kids would be scared into dropping out. That's precisely what *they* want."

Gutsy speech, but by the end of it she was talking in gulps, almost hyperventilating, and digging her nails into the arm of the couch so hard I heard fabric scrape.

I looked at Milo.

He said, "Did you keep any of the hate mail?"

"Why?"

"In the unlikely event we ever find the piece of shit who trashed your car, maybe we can match a print to one of the pieces of mail and add a federal charge to his grief. You'd be surprised how nasty those postal inspectors can get."

She said, "I told you I don't want to go public."

Milo sighed. "I understand that, and I promise you there'll be no official investigation. And that's why I said 'in the unlikely event'—'near impossible' would be more accurate. But let's say the perp returns—emboldened by getting away with it. And let's say someone catches him in the act. You're not saying you'd want us to let him go, are you?"

She stared at him, threw open a desk drawer, and yanked out a stack of envelopes bound with string.

"Here," she said, thrusting it at him. "My entire collection. I was going to donate it to the Smithsonian, but it's all yours. Happy reading."

"Who else touched the contents besides you and your secretary?"

"Just us. And Dr. Delaware."

Milo smiled. "I suppose we can rule him out."

She didn't respond.

"Got something to put it in?" he said.

"Always happy to oblige, Detective." She opened another drawer, found an interoffice mail envelope, and dropped the stack into it. Milo took it.

I said, "What about some kind of protection, Milo? Increased patrol."

Both of them turned to me, then exchanged knowing glances. Cop and cop's kid. I felt like a new immigrant who didn't know the language.

He said, "I can have a patrol car drive by once each shift, Alex, but it's unlikely to make a difference."

She told him, "Sorry for bringing you down

here. If I'd thought it out rationally, I wouldn't have bothered you."

"No bother," he said. "If you change your mind or need to file a report for insurance, let me know. I can push some paper for you, maybe speed things up. Meantime, let's get your car towed."

"If it still drives, I'll take it home myself."

I said, "You've got to be kidding."

"Why not?" she said. "The damage is probably all to the body. If it rolls, home it goes. I'll call my insurance company tomorrow and have it towed from there. The district will pay for a rental—one advantage of being a civil servant."

"Linda, without a windshield you'll freeze."

"Fresh air. I'll survive."

She searched in her purse and pulled out her keys.

I looked at Milo. His shrug said, *Nolo contendere*.

The three of us left the office, Linda walking several paces ahead, no one talking.

Outside, the street was still silent and seemed more dank, a sump for the haze. The Escort looked like a piece of junk sculpture. Linda got in through the passenger door. When she closed it, it made an unhealthy, rattling sound, and a few pieces of glass fell onto the street and tinkled like wind chimes.

Milo and I stood by as she jammed the key

into the ignition. The little car sputtered and belched and for a moment I thought there'd been mechanical damage. Then I remembered that it had sounded that way the first time I'd heard it.

She kept trying. Milo said, "Gutsy lady."

I said, "You think this is the right way to handle it?"

"She's the victim. It's her choice, Alex."

"That's not what I asked."

He ran his hand over his face. "Matter of fact, she's probably right. She knows the way things work, knows we'll never catch the assholes. All she'd buy would be more cameras and print space."

The Escort started, then stalled and died.

I said, "Okay. Sorry for calling you out for nothing."

"Forget it. I was restless anyway."

I recalled his grogginess over the phone but said nothing. He took out his keychain and began swinging it like a lasso. Looked at the swastika, then out at the row of darkened homes.

"Lovely times we're living in, Alex. National Brotherhood Week."

That reminded me of something. "How'd your meeting with Ferguson go?"

"Nothing dramatic. Call me tomorrow and I'll run it by you. Meanwhile, go and do your civic duty."

"What's that?"

"Make sure Dr. Blondie gets home in one piece."

He patted me on the shoulder and shambled to his car. Just as he drove away, the Escort's engine caught and stuck. Linda fed it gas. I walked up to the shattered window.

"I'll follow you home, Linda."

"Thanks, but I'm okay, it's really not necessary." Her face was streaked with tears but she was forcing a tough look—almost comically grave. The hand on the steering wheel was taut and ghost-white. I touched it. She pumped the gas pedal several more times. The Escort made a noise like an old man clearing his throat.

I said, "You might have radiator damage, something that's not obvious. The last thing we need is for you to get stranded somewhere."

She looked up at me. Lots of fine pale hair had come loose. Her mascara had run, creating sad-clown streaks.

I touched her cheek. "Come on—what are friends for?"

She looked at me again, started to say something, closed her eyes, and nodded.

I followed her east on Sunset, then south, past the darkened movie marquees of a deserted, littered Westwood Village, all the way beyond Pico and the post-moderne excess of the Westside Pavilion. Not far from Overland Avenue, where

I'd lived in a dingy flat during indigent student days.

The Escort clanged along—no taillights, one headlight—molting bits of glass and flecks of paint. The swastika made me think of a battered Nazi staff car. But despite its pathetic appearance, the wreck moved fast enough and I had to concentrate in order to stay with her as she made a series of abrupt turns down side streets. She came to a halt at an apartment complex at the end of a cul-de-sac.

The building was monolith-graceless, four stories of peach-colored texture-coat, with aqua-green tubular iron railing and just enough land-scaping to satisfy the zoning laws. There was a low roar in the distance: Through the branches of a malnourished pepper tree, the San Diego Free-way was a frantic light show.

A steep drive led down to a subterranean parking garage blocked by an aqua-green gate. She put a card in a slot and the gate slid open. Leaving the card in place, she drove through. I pressed the card to keep the gate open, retrieved it, and followed her. The garage was half empty and I found a spot next to her.

"Home sweet home," she said, getting out. Her hair was mussed, her cheeks rosy. She touched them. "Ah, the bracing vapors. There's something to be said for open-air motoring."

"I'll walk you in."

She said, "If you insist," but didn't sound annoyed.

We walked across the garage, took stairs up to the lobby, which was oppressively small, furnished with a single upholstered bench and a fire extinguisher, and papered in green foil patterned with silver bamboo.

"I'm on the third floor," she said and punched the elevator button. The lift was closet-sized. As the doors slid shut, we found ourselves standing close together. Flanks touching. Smelling each other's breath. Her perfume. My after-shave. All of it overlaid with the bitter, hormonal essence of stress.

She looked at the floor. "Some date, huh?"

"Just don't say I never took you anywhere interesting."

She laughed, then broke into loud, spasmodic sobs and tucked herself into a corner of the elevator. I put my arm around her and drew her to me. She put her head on my shoulder, hiding her face. I kissed the top of her head. She cried some more. I held her tighter. She looked up, mouth slightly parted. I wiped her face. Her cheeks felt frozen.

The elevator stopped and the doors opened.

"At the far end," she mumbled.

We made our way down a green-foiled hallway that smelled of mildew, both of her arms around my waist.

Inside, the place was sweet with her perfume. The living room was small and boxy, with oyster walls, potted plants, teak and polished-cotton furniture, apartment-grade gold carpeting ruled with vacuum tracks. Everything neatly ordered and lemon-oiled. I sat her down on a couch patterned with a fleecy blue-and-pink stripe, put her feet up on a matching ottoman, and removed her shoes. She covered her eyes with one arm and reclined.

The kitchen was tiny and opened to a six-by-six dining area that barely accommodated a stout-legged butcher-block table. A Mr. Coffee machine, a stack of filters, and a can of Colombian dark-roast sat on the counter next to an unmarked blackboard labeled THINGS TO DO. I brewed a couple of cups' worth and filled two L.A. ZOO mugs—zebra and koala—that I grabbed from an assortment hanging on an accordion rack next to the phone.

When I got back to the living room, she was sitting up, watching me, looking dazed, her hair still windblown.

I gave her the coffee, made sure she had a firm grip on the cup before taking a seat across from her.

She lowered her lips to the rim, breathed in coffee steam, and drank.

I said, "Anything else I can get you?"

She looked up. "Come closer. Please."

I sat next to her. We drank, drained our mugs.

"More?" I said.

She placed her mug on the coffee table, said, "Oh, Lord, what's next?" and rested her head on my shoulder again.

I put my arm around her. She sighed. I nuzzled her hair, smoothed it. She turned her head so that her mouth brushed against mine—the merest contact—then turned back the other way and pressed her lips to mine, first tentatively, then harder. I felt them yield. Her tongue was hot and mocha-rich, exploring my teeth, sidling against my tongue, pressing against it, teasing it.

Without breaking the kiss, I put my own cup down. Fastened, we hugged each other, squeezing hard.

She shuddered and stroked the back of my neck. I massaged her shoulders, allowed my hands to dip lower, run over the knobs of her spine, the lean contours of her body. She kissed me harder, made throaty urgent sounds. I touched padded hips. A knee. She guided me higher. I felt the inside of her thigh, smooth and cool and firm through nylon. She lifted herself, tugged down at her panty hose, denuding one long, white leg. I touched her. Bare flesh. Softer, cooler. Then a wave of heat. She flushed, shuddered harder. Her hands left my neck and scrambled at my fly. More fumbling, eyes closed. Then she located me.

Her eyes opened wide. She said, "Oh, God," caught her breath, and lowered herself.

She attended to me as if praying. When the feelings grew too intense, I pried her away, kissed her mouth, took her in my arms, stood, and carried her into the bedroom.

Blue-black darkness, just a hint of moonlight filtering through apartment-grade windowshades. A narrow brass bed covered in something that felt like satin.

We lay down, embraced, connected still partially clothed, and did a horizontal slow-dance, kissing all the while, moving together as if we'd been partners for a long time.

She came very quickly, unexpectedly, crying out, tugging my hair so hard the roots ached. I'd been holding back, gritting my teeth. I let go and felt my toes curl.

She breathed hard for a long time, clutching me. Then she said, "Oh, God, I can't believe I'm doing this."

I lifted myself up on my elbows. She pulled me down hard, fastened her arms around my back, and gripped me so tight I could barely breathe.

We began kissing again, softer. Got lost in it. Then she pulled away, gasping. "Phew. Okay. I need . . . to breathe."

I rolled off, caught my own breath. I was drenched with sweat, my clothing twisted and binding.

She sat up. My eyes became accustomed to the darkness, and I saw that hers were still closed. She reached behind her back and unzipped her dress, slipping her arms out of the sleeves and letting the fabric collapse around her. I made out the curves of her shoulders. White. Small-boned but strong. Delicious bumps atop each one. I kissed them. She gave a small cry, shook the hair out of her face, and leaned back on the flats of her hands. I unhooked her bra, freed her breasts, small but heavy. Hefted them, kissed them. She had tiny nipples, smooth and hard as pond pebbles.

We stripped and got under the covers.

She had a hungry mouth. A line of down that bisected her belly from umbilicus to mons. And those hips, jutting, nearly perpendicular to a small, tight waist. I gripped them and kneaded, felt fluid movement beneath the dermal sheath, heat and vitality. Her hands were warm again. She pulled me on top of her. Big, padded, welcoming hips, cradling me in a soft liquid core.

Again, she finished first, waited me out with a dreamy, content look on her face, then dropped off to sleep when I was through, holding me tight.

As she sank deeper and deeper into slumber, she maintained her hold around my waist, nestling her head in the crook of my neck, snoring lightly in my ear.

So different from Robin, who'd always signed off with a friendly, firm kiss, then rolled away, yawning, needing to stretch out. Needing space . . .

Robin, of the auburn curls and almond eyes. Firm body, strong worker's hands, musky, athletic pleasures . . .

This one. This stranger . . . soft, long-stemmed and white as a calla lily, almost limp in repose.

But this one needed me, held me fiercely as she dreamed.

One hand in my hair. The other clamped around my middle.

Holding on for dear life.

A soft prison.

I lay there, not moving, shifting my eyes around the room.

White furniture, prints on the walls. A couple of stuffed animals atop a dresser. Perfume bottles on a mirrored tray. Paperback books. A digital clock that said 1:45 A.M.

A car with a souped-up engine roared by three stories below. Linda jerked and her breathing stopped, then quickened, but she stayed fast asleep.

I became aware of other sounds. A toilet flush somewhere in the building. Another car. Then a low hum, deep and constant as a Gregorian chant. Freeway dirge. A lonely sound. Years ago, I'd taught myself to perceive it as a lullaby. . . .

She nuzzled in closer. One of my hands was

between her legs, beautifully trapped. The other had come to rest upon the stem of her neck. I felt a pulse, slow and strong.

I used one finger to tent the covers, peeked at our bodies plastered together, nearly the same length, but hers so much lighter, softer, hairless.

Salt-and-pepper still life on a narrow apartment bed.

I kissed her cheek. She gripped me tighter, dug her nails into my rib cage, and threw one leg over mine.

I wondered what I'd gotten myself into.

14

I awoke the next morning alone, smelling shampoo. The bathroom radiated moist heat as I passed it. She was sitting at the butcher-block table, wearing a black kimono printed with cherry blossoms. Her hair was wet and combed straight back. The water had darkened it to butterscotch. Her face was pale and scrubbed. Coral shells rode her ears. An untouched cup of orange juice sat in front of her. Without any makeup at all, she could have passed for a college student.

I said, "Good morning, Teach."

"Hi." Her smile was cautious. She drew the robe tighter. The few square inches of chest I could see were white dusted with a flush. I went behind her and kissed the back of her neck. Her skin smelled of lotion. She pressed her head back against my belly and rolled it back and forth. I touched her cheek, sat down.

She said, "What can I get you?"

"Just juice. I'll get it myself."

"Here, take mine." She handed me the glass. I drank.

She said, "So."

"So."

I looked toward the kitchen. "I notice your blackboard is blank. Any plans for today?"

She shook her head, looked preoccupied.

"Something the matter?"

Another shake of her head.

"What is it, Linda?"

"Nothing. Everything's fine." Wide smile.

"Okay." I drank juice.

She got up and began straightening a living room that didn't need it. Her hair hung down her back, flapping in a wet sheet against black silk. Her feet were bare, narrow, with curving toes, the nails polished pink, though her fingernails were unpainted.

Secret vanity. A woman who valued privacy.

I went to her and slipped my arms around her. She didn't resist but neither did she yield.

I said, "I know. So much so fast."

She gave a short, angry laugh. "For a long, long time I've pretended I had no needs. Now you come along and all of a sudden I'm a bundle of needs. It feels too much like weakness."

"I know exactly what you mean. It's been a long time for me too."

She turned around sharply, searched my face, prospecting for lies. "*Has* it?"

"Yes."

She stared some more, then grabbed my face with both of her hands and kissed me so hard I felt myself spinning.

When we broke, she said, "Oh, Lord, the danger signs are all flashing." But she took my right hand and pressed it to her left breast, over the heartbeat.

Afterward, she ran a bath for me, kneeled on the mat and scrubbed my back with a loofah. Too subservient for my taste but she insisted. After a minute or so I said, "Why don't you get in?"

"Nope." She touched her still-wet hair. "I'm already waterlogged."

She kept scrubbing. I closed my eyes. She began humming, something in a major key. I realized her voice was something special—sweet, with a controlled resonance. Trained pipes. I listened more intently. She hummed louder.

When she paused, I said, "You've got a really great voice."

"Oh, yeah, a regular diva."

I opened my eyes. She looked cross.

"Ever sing professionally?"

"Oh, sure—the Met, Carnegie Hall, sold out the Superdome. But the pull of the classroom was too darned strong. Hand me the shampoo."

The strain in her voice let me know I'd touched another nerve. How many danger zones along the pathway to knowing her? Tired of backing away, I said, "How long ago was it?"

"Ancient history."

"Couldn't be too ancient."

"College days. That's ancient enough."

"I played music in college too."

"That right?"

"Played guitar at nights, to put myself through."

"Guitar." Her mouth turned down. "How nice."

The chill.

I said, "Another danger zone, Linda?"

"What . . . what are you talking about?"

"When I get near certain topics—cops, now music—the No Trespassing signs start flashing."

"Don't be silly." She pointed toward the shampoo bottle. "Do you want me to do your hair or not?"

I gave her the bottle. She lathered. When she was through she handed me a towel and left the bathroom.

I toweled off, dressed, and went into the bedroom. She was sitting at her vanity, putting on eye shadow. Looking miserable.

I said, "Sorry. Forget it."

She began combing her hair. "The cop's name was Armando Bonilla. Mondo. San Antonio PD, rookie in a squad car. I was just twenty when I met him, a junior at U.T. He was twenty-two, an orphan. Old Mexican family, but he barely spoke Spanish. One of those Latin cowboy types you see in Texas. He wore his hair longer than the Department liked, spent his nights playing in a band. Guitar." She shook her head. "Good old guitar. Must be in my karma, huh?"

Her laugh was bitter.

"Six-string guitar and pedal steel. Flying fingers, self-taught—he was a natural. The other three guys in the band were cops too. More Latin cowboys. They'd known each other since sixth grade, joined the Department to have something stable, but the band was their first love. Magnum Four. Fantasies of recording contracts but none of them was ambitious or aggressive enough to pursue it and they never got out of the bar circuit. It's how I met them . . . met him. Amateur night at a place near the Alamo; they were the house band. Daddy was a Sunday fiddler, used to push music on me all the time. Push me to sing. Traditional country, western swing—the stuff *he* liked. I knew every Bob Wills song note for note by the time I was eight.

"That night he dragged me there, then made me get up and sing. Patsy Cline. 'I Fall to Pieces.' I was so nervous, my voice cracked. I sounded horrible. But the competition was thin and I came in first—gift certificate for a pair of boots and an invitation to join the band. They were into country rock—Eagles, Rodney Crowell, old Buddy Holly stuff. Mondo did a mean 'La Bamba,' putting on this humongous gag sombrero and this thick Spanish accent, even though he didn't know what all the words meant.

"They renamed the band Magnum Four and Lady Derringer. I started to get into performing. You would have thought Daddy'd be overjoyed— music plus a bunch of cops. But he didn't like the fact that they were Mexican—though he never would come out and admit it. In San Antonio the big myth is that brown and white live together in harmony, but that ain't the way it goes down when tongues loosen at the dinner table. So instead of just coming out and saying it, he griped about the kind of garbage we were playing, how late I was coming home from gigs, stinking of booze and smoke. Mondo tried to relate to him on a cop level—Daddy'd worked in the same Department, made sergeant before getting accepted into the Rangers. But that didn't make any difference. He cold-shouldered Mondo. Told me the guys were no-account punks masquerading as peace officers, nothing like the upstanding buckaroos of *his* day. The thing that made him maddest was that he'd gotten me into it in the first place. The more he bugged me, the more resolute I got. Closer to Mondo, who was really sweet and naïve beneath all the macho posturing. Finally, Daddy and I had a big fight—he slapped me across the face and I packed up and moved out of the house and into an apartment with Mondo and two of the band guys. Dad stopped speaking to me, total divorce. A month later—just after Christmas—Mondo and I got engaged."

She stopped, bit her lip, got up, and walked back and forth in front of the bed.

"About a month after the engagement, he got pulled out of uniform and put on some kind of undercover assignment that he couldn't talk about. I assumed it was Dope or Vice, or maybe some Internal Affairs thing, but whatever it was, it changed our lives. He'd work nights, sleep days, be gone for a week at a time. The band fell apart. Without him it was nothing. I used the extra time to study, but the other guys got depressed, started drinking more—bad vibes. Mondo started drinking too. And smoking dope, which was something he'd never done before. He grew his hair even longer, stopped shaving, wore ratty clothes, didn't shower regularly—as if the criminal thing were rubbing off on him. When I ragged him about it, he said it was part of the job—he was just playing a role. But I could tell he was really getting into it, and I wondered if things would ever go back to the way they'd been.

"Here I was, all of twenty, lonely, scared about what I'd gotten myself into, unable—and unwilling—to go back to Daddy. So I swallowed my pride, put up with whatever Mondo wanted— which really wasn't much. He was hardly ever around. Then, early in February, he traipsed in, the middle of the night, dirty and smelly, woke me up and announced he was moving out. Something really big, a new assignment—he'd be gone for at least a month, maybe longer. I started crying, tried to get him to tell me what was going on, but he said it was the job, I didn't need to know—for my sake I shouldn't know. Then he kissed my cheek— a passionless kiss, as if we were brother and sister—and left. It was the last time I saw him. Two days later he got caught in a dope burn and was gunned down, along with another rookie. The other guy survived but was a vegetable. Mondo was the lucky one—dead before he hit the floor. It was a big screw-up—dealers and junkies, and cops dressed as dealers and junkies, waging war at this dope factory out in the barrio. Four bad guys were killed too. The papers called it a slaughter-house, made a big deal about how poorly prepared the two of them had been for the assignment. Lambs to the slaughter."

She hugged herself, sat down on a corner of the bed, out of reach.

"After that, I fell apart, crying for days, not eating or sleeping. And there came good old Dad to the rescue, carrying me—literally—back home. Sitting me in the parlor, playing his old seventy-eights and fiddling for his little girl, just like old times. But I couldn't deal with that, and I got really hostile to him, snappish, fresh-mouthed. In

the old days he never would have tolerated it—
he'd have taken a switch to me, even at my age.
But he just sat there and took it, docile. *That*
scared me. But mostly I was angry. Enraged at
life. Insulted by God. And then the question marks
started bugging me. Why *had* Mondo been thrown
into something he wasn't equipped to handle?

"The funeral made it worse—all those gun
salutes and rah-rah speeches about valor. I rode to
the grave site in the same car as Mondo's commander and demanded to know what had happened. The bastard was an old friend of Dad's,
still considered me a child, and he patronized me.
But when I showed up at his office the next day
and got pushy, he lost patience—just like a father
would—and told me since Mondo and I had never
been legally married, just *cohabitating,* I had no
rights to any information or anything else,
shouldn't start thinking I could put in a claim on
Mondo's pension.

"I went home sobbing. Daddy listened, got
all indignant and protective, and told me he'd take
care of that S.O.B. Next day, the commander
came calling, Whitman's Sampler tucked under
his arm for me, bottle of Wild Turkey for Daddy.
All apologetic, calling me Miss Linda and Pretty
One—Daddy's pet name for me when I was little.
Sitting in the parlor and going on about how the
strain of the tragedy was getting to all of us, what
a great guy Mondo had been. Daddy nodding as if

he and Mondo had been best friends. Then the commander handed me an envelope. Inside were ten one-hundred-dollar bills—money the other cops had collected for me. Letting me know without saying it that even if I didn't legally have rights, he was granting them to me. I told him I didn't want money, just the truth. Then he and Daddy looked at each other and started talking in low, soothing tones about the dangers of the job, how Mondo'd been a true hero. The commander saying Mondo'd been picked for undercover because he was top-notch, had great recommendations. If only there were some way to turn back the clock. Daddy joining in, telling me about all the close calls *he'd* had, how scared and brave Mama had been when she was alive. How I had to be brave, go on and live my life.

"After a while it started to work. I softened up, thanked the commander for coming. Began to let my feelings out—to grieve. Started to finally be able to lay it to rest. Concentrate on what I was going to do with the rest of my life. Everything seemed to be going as well as could be expected until, about a month later, I got a call from Rudy—one of the other guys in the band—asking me to meet him at a restaurant out in the suburbs near Hill Country. He sounded uptight, wouldn't tell me what it was about, just that it was important. When I got there he looked terrible—drained, pale. He'd lost a lot of weight. He said he

was quitting the Department, moving the hell out
of state—to New Mexico or Arizona. I asked him
why. He said it was too dangerous sticking
around, that after what had been done to Mondo,
he'd never trust anyone in the fucking Department. I said what the heck are you talking about.
He looked around—he was really jumpy, as if he
was scared of being watched. Then he said, 'I
know this will blow you away, Linda, but you
were his lady. You've got a right to know.' Then
he told me he'd found out Mondo hadn't been
pulled off patrol because of his excellent performance. The opposite was true: He had a bad
record—demerits for subordination, the long hair,
borderline probation, low competence ratings.
He'd been given dangerous assignments as a favor
to someone."

She stopped, touched her gut. "Lord, even
after all these years it gets to me."

"Your dad."

Dull nod. "He and his old buddy, the commander. They set him up, put him in a situation
they knew he couldn't handle. Like throwing a
new recruit into the jungle—sooner or later, you
know what's going to happen. Lamb to the slaughter. Damned close to premeditated murder, said
Rudy, but nothing anyone could ever prove. Just
knowing it put *him* in jeopardy, which was why he
was getting the hell out of town.

"He left the coffee shop, looking over his

shoulder all the while. I drove away at about ninety per—feeling out of my body, numb, like a player in my own nightmare. When I got home Daddy was sitting in the parlor. Fiddling. Grinning. After one look at my face, he put his bow down—he knew. I started screaming at him, hitting him. He reacted very calmly. He said, 'Pretty One, what's done is done. No sense fretting.' I just looked at him, as if seeing him for the first time. Feeling nauseated, wanting to throw up, but determined he wouldn't see me weak. I snatched the fiddle out of his hands—an old Czechoslovakian one that he really loved. He'd been buying and trading them for years until he'd found a keeper. He tried to grab it but I was too fast for him. I held it by the peg head and smashed it against the mantelpiece. Kept smashing until it was splinters. Then I ran from that house and never returned. Haven't spoken to him since, though a couple of years ago we started exchanging Christmas cards again. He's remarried—one of those men who needs a woman around. Some bimbo from Houston, half his age. She'll get *his* pension, and the house I grew up in, and she'll be the one tending his old bones."

She closed her eyes and rubbed her temples. "Cops and guitars."

I said, "A long time ago."

She shook her head. "Nine *years*. *God*. Haven't had much of a taste for music for a long time—don't even own a phonograph—and here I am *humming* to you and playing geisha and I barely know you."

Before I could answer, she said, "Haven't had anything to do with *cops,* either, till this mess."

But I remembered that she'd mentioned being a Ranger's daughter to Milo. Pushing the door open a crack.

"Maybe the time's ripe for change, Linda."

A tear made its way down her cheek. I moved closer to be able to hold her.

15

After a while she got up and said, "There're some things I have to take care of. Boring stuff— shopping, cleaning. Been putting it off for too long."

"What are you planning to do for transportation?"

"I'll manage." Restless. Embarrassed by it.

I said, "I've got some things to take care of too. The glories of the single life."

"Oh, yeah."

We left the bedroom and walked to the front door, not touching. I opened the door and stepped out into the green corridor. Weekend-silent. The mildew smell seemed stronger. Newspapers lay in front of several doors. The headline was something about Afghanistan.

She said, "Thanks. You've been wonderful."

I held her chin and kissed her cheek. She gave me her mouth and tongue and gripped me for a moment, then pulled away and said, "Out, before I yank you back in."

"Is that a threat or a promise?"

She smiled, but so briefly it made me wonder if I'd imagined it. "You understand, I just need to . . ."

"Breathe?"

She nodded.

"Nothing like breathing to liven things up," I said. "Would asking you out for tomorrow night lower the oxygen level?"

She laughed and her damp hair shook stiffly. "No."

"Then how about tomorrow? Eight P.M. Take in a couple of art galleries, then dinner."

"That would be great."

We squeezed hands and I left, feeling a curious mixture of melancholy and relief. No doubt she viewed me as Mr. Sensitive. But I was happy to have some breathing space of my own.

When I got home, I called Milo.

He said, "How's she doing?"

"Coping."

"Called you an hour ago. No one home. Must have been an extended consultation."

"Gosh, you must be a detective or something."

"Hey, I'm happy for you. The two of you are cute together—a regular Ken and Barbie."

"Thanks for your blessing, Dad. What'd you learn at Ferguson's?"

"Good old Esme? That was fun. She reminded me of the kind of teachers *I* used to have—more into what lines had to be skipped than what you actually wrote in the composition. Her house had this permanent Lysol smell—made me feel as if I was polluting it just by being there. Porcelain poodles on the hearth, little groupings of miniature doggies in glass cases. But nothing animate. She had me leave my shoes at the door—thank God I'd worn the socks without the holes. But for all the spick and span, she has a nasty little mind. Textbook bigot to boot. First she tested the waters with a few sly comments about the city changing, all those Mexicans and Asians invading, and when I didn't argue, really got into how the coloreds and the other *outsiders* have ruined things. Listening to her, the school used to be a regular junior Harvard, chock full of genius white kids. *Refined* families. *Fabulous* school spirit, *fabulous* extracurricular activities. All her star pupils going on to bigger and better things. She showed me a collection of Dear Teacher postcards. The most recent one was ten years old."

"What did she have to say about the latest illustrious alumna?"

"Holly was a very *dull* student—*wholly* unmemorable. A strange girl—the whole family was

strange. Clannish, unfriendly, no pride of ownership in their house. The fact that no one really
knows what Burden Senior does for a living bugs
her. She kept asking *me* about it, didn't believe me
when I told her I had no idea what New Frontiers
Tech was all about. This is a lady who mainlines
conformity, Alex. Sounds like the Burdens broke
too many rules."

"Behavioral niggers," I said.

He paused. "You always did know how to
turn a phrase."

"In what way was Holly strange?"

"Didn't go to school, didn't work, rarely left
the house except to take walks at night—skulking,
Ferguson called it. Said she saw her a few times
when she was out trimming her flowers. Holly
was skulking along, staring at the sidewalk."

"Old Esme trims her flowers at night?"

"Twice a day. That tell you something about
her?"

"Did Holly always skulk alone?"

"Far as she knows."

"What about the boyfriend?"

"Sounds as if she was overstating, calling
him a boyfriend. Just a *colored boy* she saw Holly
talking to a few times. In old Esme's world view,
that implies fornication, but since we know Holly
was a virgin, the two of them might actually have
just talked. Or anything in between. Esme said the
boy had worked at the local grocery last year but

she hadn't seen him in a while. Bag boy and deliveries. She always felt nervous about letting him into her home—guess why. She didn't know much about him, just that he was Very Big And Black. But people tend to exaggerate what they're afraid of, so I wouldn't put heavy money on 'big.' "

I said, "Perceptual vigilance. Learned about it in social psych."

"*I* learned it interviewing eyewitnesses. Anyway, I couldn't even get a full name out of her. She *thought* his first name was Isaac or Jacob but wasn't sure. Something Jewish-sounding. She found it amusing that a *colored boy* would have a *Jewish* name. That launched her into another what's-this-world-coming-to speech. I kept waiting for her to segue to faggots, but she just droned on about stupid stuff until I found myself staring at the poodles."

"Sounds like a lonely lady."

"Three times divorced; men are beasts. She probably *talks* to the goddam poodles. I finally got out of there and stopped by the grocers—place called Dinwiddie's—to see if I could learn anything more about the boy, but the store was closed."

"Planning on going back?"

"Eventually."

"How about today?"

"Sure, why not? Not that it's likely to lead to

anything earth-shattering. But Rick's out doing good works at the Free Clinic. If I stick around I'll end up doing laundry."

Or drinking too much.

I said, "An hour, lunch on me?"

"Hour it is. But forget lunch. While we're at the market I can palm an apple, just like Pat O'Brien walking the beat. Always wanted to do that. Be a real cop."

Despite his pessimism, Milo arrived dressed for work: gray suit, white shirt, red tie, note pad in pocket. He directed me to a street named Abundancia Drive, which ran through the center of Ocean Heights and ended at a small town square, built around a treeless circular patch of lawn. A hand-lettered sign—the kind you see in the small parks of Mayfair in London—designated the patch as Ocean Heights Plaza. The grass was bare except for a white Lutyens-style garden bench chain-bolted to the ground next to a NO DOGS, NO BICYCLES warning.

Ringing the patch were business establishments. The most prominent was a one-story red brick bank done in retro-Colonial, complete with pillars, pediments, and limestone planters brimming with geraniums. The rest of the shops were also red brick. Red brick and gingerbread cute enough for a theme park.

I found a parking spot in front of a dry

cleaner's. Gold-leaf Gothic lettering was *de rigueur* for the storefronts. Welcome to the home of mixed metaphors. Ficus trees pruned low and trimmed to look like mushrooms grew from circular metal grilles embedded in the sidewalk, spaced so the plantings fronted every other store.

The shops were a classic village mix. Haberdasheries for both sexes, each with a soft spot for Ralph Lauren. Ye Olde Gift Emporium and Card Shoppe. Alvin's Apothecary complete with a stone mortar and pestle over Dutch doors. A medical building that could have passed for Santa's Workshop. Arno's Old World Jeweler/Watchmaker. Janeway's European Bakery. Steuben's Imported Sausage and Charcuterie. The Ocean Café.

Dinwiddie's Fine Grocers and Purveyors was a double-width enterprise with forest-green wainscoting and a cream-colored oval sign over the entry that read EST. 1961.

California antiquity.

The picture window was framed with green molding and dominated by a straw cornucopia, out of which tumbled a contrived flow of gleaming, oversized produce. More fruit was displayed in wooden crates slathered with old-fashioned painted labels. Each apple, pear, orange, and grapefruit had been polished to a high gloss and was individually cradled in damson-blue crepe.

"Looks like you picked the right place to palm," I said.

Inside, the place was bustling and spotless, cooled by wooden fly fans, serenaded by Muzak. GOURMET FOODS at the front. A liquor section big enough to intoxicate the entire neighborhood. Foodstuffs stacked to the rafters, everything neatly ordered, the wide aisles marked by overhead wooden signs painted that same dark green.

A pair of green-aproned women worked steadily at antique brass cash registers hooked up to computerized scanners. Three or four shoppers waited in each line. No one talked. Milo walked up to one of the registers and said, "Hi. Where's the owner?"

The cashier was young, chubby, and fair. Without looking up, she said, "In the back."

We made our way past PASTA and BREAD-STUFFS. Next to the DAIRY case was a green wooden panel door with a brass lock dangling from an open hasp. Milo pushed it open and we stepped into a short, dark hall, cold as a refriger-ator, rank with an old lettuce smell, and filled with generator noise. At the end was another door marked EMPLOYEES ONLY.

Milo knocked and opened it, revealing a small windowless office paneled in imitation knotty pine and furnished with an old mahogany desk and three red Naugahyde chairs. The desk was crowded with papers. A brass balance scale served as a paperweight for an inch-thick stack. An assortment of commercial calendars hung on the walls, along with a couple of faded hunting prints and a framed photo of a pleasant-looking, slightly overweight brunette woman kneeling next to two white-haired, ruddy boys of preschool age. A pine-ridged expanse of lake was in the background. The boys struggled to hold on to a fishing rod from which a healthy-looking trout dangled.

The obvious genetic source of the children's pigmentation sat behind the desk. Early thirties, pink-skinned, with thin, near-albino hair cut short and parted on the right. He had broad, beefy shoulders, a nub of a broken nose above a bushy mustache the color and consistency of old hay. His eyes were large, colored a curious tan-gray, and had a basset droop. He wore a blue broadcloth button-down shirt and red-and-blue rep tie under a green apron. The shirtsleeves were rolled up to the elbows. His forearms were pale, hairless, Popeye-thick.

He put down a hand calculator, looked up from a pile of invoices, and gave a weary smile. "Weights and Measures? We passed just last week, gentlemen."

Milo showed him his police ID. The blond man's smile faded and he blinked several times, as if forcing himself awake.

"Oh." He stood and extended his hand. "Ted Dinwiddie. What can I do for you?"

Milo said, "We're here to talk about the sniping at Hale Elementary, Mr. Dinwiddie."

"Oh, that. Horrible." His wince seemed involuntary and sincere. He blinked a couple more times. "Thank God no one was hurt."

"No one except Holly Burden."

"Oh, yes. Sure. Of course." He winced again, sat down, and pushed aside his paperwork.

"Poor Holly," he said. "It's hard to believe she'd go and do something like that."

"How well did you know her?"

"As well as anyone, I guess. Which means not much at all. She used to come in here, with her dad. I'm talking years ago, when she was just a little girl. Just after her mom died. Back when *my* dad was alive." He paused and touched the balance scale. "I used to bag and check after school and on Saturdays. Holly used to stand behind her dad's legs and peek out, then draw back. Really shy. She always was kind of a nervous kid. Quiet, as if she was in her own little world. I'd try to talk to her—she never answered back. Once in a while she'd take a free candy, if her dad would let her. Most of the time she ignored me when I offered. Still, there was nothing . . ."

He looked up at us. "Sorry. Please, sit down. Can I get you some coffee? We've got a new European roast brewing out in front in the sample pot."

"No thanks," said Milo.

We sat in the red chairs.

Milo said, "Any more recent impressions of her?"

"Not really," said Dinwiddie. "I didn't see much of her. They were usually delivery customers. The couple of times I did see her wandering around the streets, she looked kind of . . . detached."

"Detached from what?"

"Her surroundings. The external world. Not paying attention to what was going on. The kind of thing you see in creative people. I've got a sister who's a writer—very successful screenwriter. She's getting into producing. Emily was always like that, fantasizing, off in her own world. We used to kid her, call her Space Cadet. Holly was spacey but in her case I don't think it was creativity."

"Why's that?"

The grocer shifted in his chair. "I don't want to speak ill of the dead, but basically, Holly wasn't very bright. Some of the kids used to call her retarded—which she probably wasn't. Just dull, a little below average. But in her family that had to be especially tough—the rest of the Burdens were all pretty intellectual. Her dad's downright brilliant—used to work for the government as some kind of high-level scientist or mathematician. The mom did, too, I think. And Howard—her brother—he was a scholastic ace."

"Sounds like you knew the family pretty well."

"No, not really. Mostly I'd just deliver the groceries or go over there for tutoring. From Howard. He was a math whiz, totally brilliant with numbers. We were in the same class but he could have taught it. Lots of kids went to him for help. Everything came easy for him, but he really had a thing for math." He gave a wistful look. "He actually stuck with what he loved, became some sort of statistician. Has a great position with an insurance firm out in the Valley."

Milo said, "When you say you and he were in the same class, was that at Nathan Hale?"

Dinwiddie nodded. "All the kids went to Hale back in those days. Things were different." He fussed with the knot of his tie. "Not necessarily better, mind you. Just different."

I said, "How so?"

He fidgeted some more and lowered his voice. "Listen, I work here, live here, lived here all my life—it's a great neighborhood in many ways, great place to raise kids. But the people here pretend nothing will ever change. That nothing *should* ever change. And that's not too realistic, is it?" Pause. "Standing behind the register, or making a delivery, or coaching Little League, kind of gives you the chance to observe—you hear all sorts of things—ugly things from people you thought were decent, people your kids play with and your wife has coffee with."

"Racial comments?" Milo said.

Dinwiddie gave a pained look. "That's not to say it's any worse here than anywhere else— racism's fairly endemic in our society, isn't it? But when it's your own neighborhood . . . you'd just like it to be better."

Fairly endemic in our society.

It sounded like a phrase out of a textbook.

Milo said, "Do you think any of that—the local racial attitudes—are related to the sniping?"

"No, I don't," Dinwiddie said quickly. "Maybe if it had been someone else, you could make the connection. But I can't see Holly being racist. I mean, to be racist you'd have to be political, at least to some degree, wouldn't you? And she wasn't. Least as far as I knew. Like I said, she wasn't too in touch with her surroundings."

"What kind of political attitudes did her family have?"

"No idea if they had any," he said quickly. His hand flew to his tie again, and he blinked several times in succession. I wondered if something about the discussion was putting him on edge.

"Really, gentlemen, I just can't see any political connection," he said. "I truly believe whatever Holly did came from inside her—her own problem. Something intrapsychic."

"Mental problems?" said Milo.

"She'd *have* to be crazy to do something like that, wouldn't you say?"

I said, "Besides being 'spacey,' did she ever show signs of other mental problems?"

"That I couldn't tell you," said Dinwiddie. "Like I said, I haven't seen her in a long time. I was just talking theoretically."

Milo said, "When you saw her walking around the neighborhood, was this at night or during the day?"

"Day. I'm only talking a couple of times. I'd be on my way to make a delivery and she'd be making her way down the street, kind of a loose shuffle, staring down at the sidewalk. That's what I meant by spacey."

"Anything else you can tell us about the family that might relate to the shooting?"

Dinwiddie thought. "Not really, Detective. They were never real social. Marched to their own drummer, but basically they were decent people. You can tell a person's character when you check their groceries. When he was alive, my dad had a system for classifying folks—Grumblers, Skinflints, Nitpickers, Tomato Squeezers." A sheepish smile spread under the mustache. "Kind of an us-them thing. Happens in every profession, right? Don't let on to my customers or I'd be out of business."

Milo smiled and ran his finger across his lips.

Dinwiddie said, "It's funny. When I was younger I used to hear my dad come home and grouse, and think he was being intolerant, just didn't understand people. I majored in sociology in college, had all sorts of theories and explanations for why he'd become so misanthropic, how what he really needed was more intrinsic satisfaction in his work. Now here I am, doing the same job he did, and I find myself using the same labels."

I said, "Which of your dad's labels would you apply to the Burdens?"

"None, really. They were easy to deal with, never complained, always paid their bills right away with cash. Mr. Burden always had a generous tip ready, though he wasn't much for conversation. He always seemed busy with something, doing his own thing."

"Another spacey one?" said Milo.

"Not like Holly. With him, you always felt he *was* lost in thought. Thinking about something important. With Holly, it just seemed—I don't know—stuporous. As if she were withdrawing from reality. But if this is making her sound like some dangerous psychotic, that's not what I mean at all. She'd be the last person I'd expect to do anything violent. On the contrary, she was timid, a real mouse."

Milo said, "When did her mother die?"

Dinwiddie touched his mustache, then tapped

a fingertip absently to his tongue. "Let's see. I think Holly was four or five, so that would make it about fifteen years ago."

"What'd she die of?"

"Some sort of stomach condition, I think. Tumors or ulcers or something—I'm not sure. Only reason I remember it being the stomach is she used to buy a lot of antacids, really stocked up on them. Whatever it was, it wasn't supposed to be fatal, but she went in for surgery and didn't come out. Howard was pretty freaked out—all of us were. It was the first time anyone in the class had lost a parent. We were in high school—sophomores. Howard had never been much of a joiner, but after his mom died he really pulled away, dropped out of Chess Club and Debate Club, gained a whole lot of weight. He kept on getting good grades—that was like breathing for him—but he cut himself off from everything else."

I said, "How did Holly react?"

"I can't say I remember anything specific. But she was just a little kid, so I'd expect she was devastated."

"So you can't say if her spaciness was due to her mother's death?"

"No—" He stopped, smiled. "Hey, this sounds more like psychoanalysis than police work. I didn't know you guys did this kind of thing."

Milo hooked a thumb at me. "This gentleman's a noted psychologist. Dr. Alex Delaware.
He's working with the kids at Hale. We're trying
to get a picture of what happened."

"Psychologist, huh?" Dinwiddie said. "I saw
a psychologist being interviewed about the kids on
TV. Heavyset fellow, big white beard."

"Change of plans," said Milo. "Dr. Delaware's the one."

Dinwiddie looked at me. "How are they? The
kids."

"Doing as well as can be expected."

"That's real good to hear. I send my own kids
to private school." Guilty look. Shake of the head.
"Never thought I'd be doing that."

"Why's that?"

Another tug at his tie knot. "Truth be told,"
he said, "I used to be pretty much of a radical."
Embarrassed grin. "For Ocean Heights, anyway.
Which means I voted Democrat and tried to
convince my dad to boycott table grapes in order
to help the farm workers. That was back when the
last thing I wanted to do was run a grocery. My
actual goal was to do what you do, Doctor.
Therapy. Or social work. Something along those
lines. I wanted to work with people. Dad thought
that was soft work—the ultimate put-down. Said
eventually I'd come back to the real world. I set
out to prove him wrong, did volunteer work—with
crippled kids, Job Corps Inductees, adoption

agencies. Became a Big Brother for a kid out in East L.A. Then Dad dropped dead of a heart attack, left no insurance, just this place, and Mom was in no position to run it, so I stepped in. One semester short of my B.A. It was supposed to be temporary. I never got out."

His brow creased and his eyes drooped lower. I remembered his comment about Howard Burden, the wistful look: *He actually stuck with what he loved. . . .*

"Anyway," he said, "that's about all I can tell you about the Burdens. What happened over at Hale was a real tragedy. Lord only knows Mr. Burden didn't need any more. But hopefully time will heal." He looked to me for confirmation.

I said, "Hopefully."

"Maybe," he said, "people will even learn something from all of this. I don't know."

He picked up his calculator, tapped the buttons.

"One more thing, Mr. Dinwiddie," said Milo. "There's a young man who works or used to work for you, making deliveries. Isaac or Jacob?"

Dinwiddie's thick shoulders tightened and his breath caught. He let it out a moment later, slowly, deliberately. "Isaac. Ike Novato. What about him?"

"Novato," said Milo. "He's a Hispanic? We were told he was black."

"Black. A light-complected black. What's that . . . what's he got to do with any of this?"

"We were told he was friendly with Holly Burden."

"Friendly?" The shoulders hunched higher and shrugged.

Milo said, "He still work for you?"

The grocer glared at us. "Hardly."

"Know where we can find him?"

"It would be difficult to find him anywhere, Detective. He's dead, cremated. I scattered the ashes myself. Off the pier at Malibu."

Dinwiddie's gaze was angry, unyielding. Finally he looked away, down at his desk, picked up an order blank, gave it an uncomprehending look and put it aside.

"Funny you shouldn't know," he said. "That *I* should be telling *you*. Though I guess not, considering the size of this city, all the homicides you get. Well, he was one of them, gentlemen. Last September. Shot to death, supposedly in a drug burn, somewhere down in South Central."

"Supposedly?" said Milo. "You have doubts?"

Dinwiddie hesitated before answering. "I guess anything's possible, but I seriously doubt it."

"Why's that?"

"He was a straight arrow—just wasn't the dope type. I know cops think all civilians are naïve, but I did enough volunteer work with juvenile offenders to be a pretty good judge. I tried to tell that to the police but they never bothered to come down here and talk to me about him face to face. I only found out about the murder because when he hadn't showed up for work for two days running, I called his landlady and she told me what had happened, said the police had been by, told her it was a dope thing. I got the name of the detective on the case from her. I called him, told him I was Ike's employer, volunteered to come down to the station and give information. His attitude wasn't exactly enthusiastic. A couple of weeks later he called me back, asked me if I wanted to come down and identify the body. 'A formality'—his words—so that he could clear it. It was obvious that to him this was just a routine ghetto shooting—another case number. What really surprised me when I got there was that the detective himself was black. He hadn't sounded black over the phone. Smith. *Maurice* Smith. Southeast Division. Know him?"

Milo nodded.

"Classical self-hatred," said the grocer. "Turning all that rage against the self. All oppressed groups are at risk for it. Minorities in official capacities are really vulnerable. But in Smith's case it may be getting in the way of his doing his job."

"Why'd he need you to identify the body?"

"Ike had no family anyone could locate."

"What about the landlady?"

Dinwiddie shrugged again and stroked his mustache. "She's pretty old. Maybe she couldn't handle the stress. Why don't you ask Smith?"

"What else can you tell us about Novato?"

"Top-notch kid. Bright, charming, learned fast, not a lick of trouble. Always willing to do above and beyond the call of duty, and believe me, nowadays that's rare."

"How'd you hire him?"

"He answered an ad I put up on the bulletin board at the Santa Monica College job center. He was taking courses there, part time. Needed to work to support himself. The all-American work ethic, exactly the kind of thing Dad used to extol." The gray eyes narrowed. "Course, Dad never would have hired Ike."

I said, "Did you run into any problems having him work here? Given the attitudes you described."

"Not really. People will accept blacks in relatively menial positions."

Milo said, "Do you still have his job application on file?"

"No."

"Remember his address?"

"Venice. One of the numbered streets, Fourth Avenue or Fifth, I think. The landlady's name was Gruenberg."

Milo wrote it down. "What about a picture?"

Dinwiddie hesitated, opened a drawer, took out a color snapshot, and handed it to Milo. I craned and got a look at it. Group photo. Dinwiddie, the two cashiers out front, and a tall, lanky, mocha-colored young man, posed in front of the market, waving. Everyone wearing green aprons.

Ike Novato had light-brown kinky hair cut short, full lips, almond eyes, and a Roman nose. The stooped posture of one who'd reached full height early. Big, awkward-looking hands, shy smile.

"This was taken last Fourth of July," said Dinwiddie. "We always throw a big party for the local kids. Safe and Sane Celebration. Free candy and soda instead of fireworks. One of the parents brought a camera and took it."

Milo said, "Can I borrow this?"

Dinwiddie said, "Guess so. Are you saying there's some connection between Ike and what happened at the school?"

"That's what we're trying to find out," Milo said.

"I can't see that," Dinwiddie said.

I said, "Were there any problems with his doing deliveries? Having him come into people's houses?"

Dinwiddie's right hand curled into a fist. Mounds of muscle and sinew appeared along the massive forearm. "In the beginning there were a few comments. I ignored them and eventually they stopped. Even a stone *racist* could see what a decent kid he was." He tightened his other hand. "Chalk up one puny point for truth and justice, huh? But at the time I thought I was doing something important—making a stand. Then he goes down to Watts and gets shot. I'm sorry, but it still makes me angry. The whole thing was depressing."

"Any other reason for him to be down in Watts?" said Milo.

"That was Detective Smith's point. The street where he was shot was a notorious crack alley— why else would he be there except to make a deal? But I still have my doubts. Ike told me more than once how much he hated drugs, how drugs had destroyed his people. Maybe he was down there to *catch* a pusher."

"His people," said Milo. "Thought he had no family."

"I'm speaking generically, Detective. The black nation. And your Smith's the one who told me there was no family. He said they ran Ike's fingerprints through all the police files—missing kids, whatever—and nothing turned up. Said Ike had applied for his Social Security card only a few months before working for me. They had no record of any previous address. He told me it would be a Potter's Field situation if no one came forth and claimed the body." Wince. "So I took him home."

"What did the boy tell you about his background?"

"Not much. We didn't have extended discussions—it was a work situation. I got the impression he'd had a good education because he was pretty articulate. But we never went into detail. The name of the game around here is hustle, hustle, hustle."

"You never asked him for references?"

"He came from the college—they screen them there. And his landlady said he was reliable."

"Have you talked to the landlady since his death?"

"Just once. Over the phone. I asked her if she knew anything about his family. She didn't either. So I took care of everything. Did what I could. I figured cremation would be . . . I don't know, cleaner. Ecologically. That's what I want for myself."

He raised his hands and let them settle on the desk. "And that's about all I can tell you, gentlemen."

Milo said, "What was the relationship between him and Holly?"

"Relationship?" Dinwiddie grimaced. "Nothing romantic, if that's what you're getting at. He was on a completely different level than she was. Intellectually. There'd be nothing in common between the two of them."

"We've been told he was her boyfriend."

"Then you've been misinformed," Dinwiddie said, clipping his words. "Ocean Heights is flap-jaw capital of the world—too many small-minded people with too much leisure time. Take anything you hear around here with a container of salt. Iodized or otherwise."

Milo said, "We've been *informed* that Ike and Holly used to talk."

Dinwiddie's hand rose to his tie and loosened it. "What Ike did tell me," he said, "is that when he went to deliver to her house, occasionally they'd strike up a conversation. He said she was lonely. He felt sorry for her and took the time to make her feel good about herself—he was that kind of kid. She started preparing things for him—milk and cookies. Tried to keep him there. Which was really unusual for Holly—she never wanted to talk to anyone. I told Ike how unusual that was and I warned him."

"About what?" said Milo.

"The sexual thing, her developing a crush on him. You know the fantasies people have about blacks—all the hypersexual nonsense. Put black and white together and everyone assumes it's something dirty. Add to that the fact that Holly wasn't psychologically normal and the risk of trouble was *definitely* something to worry about.

To Ike's mind he was just being friendly—the way you'd be to a needy child. But I could see her reading more into his friendliness than he'd intended. Coming on to him, getting rejected, and screaming rape. So I advised him to be careful. For all of our sakes."

"Did he listen to you?"

Dinwiddie shook his head. "He thought I was worrying over nothing, assured me there was no danger of anything happening—Holly never got seductive. That all she wanted was a friend. What could I say to that? That he should reject her? Because she was white? What would that have said to him?"

Neither of us answered. Dinwiddie kept talking, in a low, deliberate tone, as if unaware of our presence. "One time I was driving home, doing a delivery that took me past the Burden house, and saw the two of them out in front. Ike was holding a bunch of books and Holly was looking up at him as if he were some kind of big brother. She and Howard had never been close. Ike looked more brotherly with her than Howard ever had. I remember thinking how strange it looked—a white kid and a black kid actually communicating. In Ocean Heights. It could have been a poster for tolerance. Then I thought how *stupid* it was that something as simple as that *would* be strange."

He punched a button on his calculator, studied the number that came up as if it were a puzzle.

"They were just a couple of kids," he said. "Trying to get through life. And now they're both gone. And I've got a special on asparagus."

16

He walked us out through the market. Business had slowed and the chubby cashier stood idle. I lifted a large yellow apple from its crepe bed and handed it to her along with a dollar bill. Before she could open her register, Dinwiddie said, "Forget it, Karen," and removed the bill from between her fingers. Handing it back to me, he said, "On the house, Dr. Delaware. And here's one for you, Detective."

"Can't take gifts," said Milo. "Thanks anyway."

"Then here's two for Dr. Delaware." Smiling but intense. I thanked him and took the fruit. He held the door open for us and stood on the sidewalk, next to a ficus mushroom, gazing after us as we drove away.

I cruised down Abundancia and came to a stop sign. There was a small golden sticker on each apple. Milo removed his, read it, and said, "Fiji. Hoo-hah, watch out, Gauguin."

I said, "That was Tahiti."

He said, "Don't nitpick," bit, chewed, swallowed. "A bit presumptuous, but fine nose and texture. These Ocean Heights folks sure know how to live."

I said, "Let's hear it for the good life," lifted my own apple like a toast glass, and took a bite. Crisp and sweet, but I kept expecting a worm to wiggle out.

I drove through the empty, picture-perfect streets. At the next stop sign Milo said, "So. What'd you think of El Grocero?"

"Frustrated. Likes to think of himself as a fish out of water but feels guilty about keeping his gills wet."

"Know the feeling," said Milo, and I regretted the flippancy of my remark.

He knew what I was thinking, laughed, and cuffed my arm. "Don't worry, pal. It's a privileged position, being on the outside looking in."

I turned onto Esperanza, and the conformist magnolias came into view. "Apparently the boyfriend wasn't a boyfriend."

"Maybe, maybe not. If this Novato kid did have a romance thing going with Holly, he wouldn't have told the boss."

"True," I said. "So all we really know about him is that he and Holly talked a few times. And that he's dead. Which in terms of—pardon the expression—understanding Holly could be relevant. If Ike meant a lot to her, his death could have tipped her over the edge."

"Trauma leads to rifle games?"

"Sure. The loss could have been especially traumatic for someone with her history—the early death of her mother. She closed herself off from the world. Withdrew. I've worked with patients who lost a parent at a young age and didn't get help. When you don't grieve, the sorrow just sits there and festers. You stop trusting, learn to hate the world. Holly was a loner. If Ike was the first person who really tried to relate to her, he could have become a substitute parent—Dinwiddie said she was looking up at him as if he were a big brother. Let's say he got her trusting again, brought her out of her shell. Then *he* dies. Violently. It triggers all the garbage she'd been sitting on for fifteen years. She explodes. Make sense so far?"

"As much sense as anything," he said. "You know better than I do."

I drove past another block of green lawns. A few people were out, walking dogs, washing cars. I thought of Linda's car, remembered the fog and dread that had settled over Ocean Heights last night. The broken glass, the hooked cross.

What other demons hid themselves, crouching and sniggering behind the diamond-paned windows?

Milo stared out his window and munched.

Cop-surveilling, force of habit. Pictures kept floating through my mind. Ugly possibilities.

When he turned away for a moment, I said, "What if Holly and Ike did more than just chat? What if they got into philosophical raps—the rotten state of the world, injustice, poverty, racism. Given Holly's sheltered life, the experiences of someone like Ike would have been a real eye-opener for her—could have really changed her. That's what happened in the sixties when white kids from suburbia went to college and encountered minority students for the first time. Instant radicalization. Someone else might have channeled it constructively—volunteer work, altruism. But Holly was vulnerable because of all that loneliness and anger and distrust. It's the classic lone assassin profile, Milo. She could have seen herself as Ike's avenger. Vanquishing Massengil—a *symbol* of racism—could have seemed noble."

"Vanquishing," Milo said. "Sounds pretty medieval. Maybe she just wanted to shoot kids."

"What would be her motive for that?" I said. "We've no indication she resented their presence."

"Look, Alex, you're talking about a probable nutcase. Who knows what she would have had *reason* to do? Who knows what kind of crazy things actually ran through her head? When you get down to it, how much do you really know about her, anyway?"

"Not much at all," I said, feeling suddenly like one of the pontificating TV experts.

I exited Ocean Heights, headed back on the winding canyon road toward Sunset. Milo said, "Don't sulk," and went back to looking out the window.

At the boulevard, I said, "Still entertaining questions, or is the cop-shop closed for the day?"

"Questions about what?"

"Novato's murder. The way Dinwiddie talked about him. Any of that intrigue you?"

He turned and faced me. "What about it is supposed to intrigue me?"

"It just seemed as if Dinwiddie developed a lot of . . . passion when he discussed Ike. Really tensed up, got emotional. He got really defensive when denying that Holly and Ike had been lovers. Could have been jealousy. Maybe there was something more than a working relationship between him and Ike."

Milo closed his eyes and gave a short, weary laugh.

"It happens," he said, with a wicked smile. Then he ran his hand over his face. "Yeah, I was thinking that myself—the guy did get awfully righteous. But if there was something sexual, don't you think he would be careful not to let on to us? I mean, how many Fiji apples do you think he'd sell if the good folks of Ocean Heights suspected him of *that*?"

"True," I said. "So maybe his emotionality was a result of exactly what he said it was—liberal guilt. Still, the picture he painted of Novato was kind of odd, don't you think? Black kid with a Latin name, comes from somewhere 'back east' but doesn't tell anyone where. Settles in Venice, enrolls in college in Santa Monica, gets a job in Whitebread Heaven, performs excellently in that job, inspires *some* kind of passion in his employer, makes friends with the girl no one talks to, then gets blown away in Watts. Not too long after, that girl goes for *her* gun and gets blown away herself."

Milo was silent.

I said, "Of course, I'm just a rank amateur civilian. Theorizing. The pros . . . that guy from Southeast—Smith—didn't think it was weird at all."

Milo said, "What'd I say about sulking?" But he looked bothered.

I said, "Do you really know Smith?"

"Casually."

"And?"

"Not the worst investigator in the world."

"But not the best."

Milo moved his bulk around, trying to get comfortable, frowning when he couldn't. "Maury Smith is average," he said. "Like most people in most jobs. Putting in time and dreaming about Winnebago Heaven. In all fairness to him, a place like Southeast Division'll do that to you even if you start out determined to be Super Cop. More bodies in one hot week than we see in six months. No matter what anyone says, those kinds of numbers will change your attitude about the sanctity of life—the same way war does."

"NAACP's been saying that for a long time."

"Nah, it's not racism. Okay, maybe some of it is. But what it really boils down to is *context*: One DB out of a hundred thou just ain't the same as one out of a hundred—I don't care how pure your heart is. And a DB in Crack Alley just ain't gonna merit the same care as one in Stone Canyon."

"Meaning Smith's investigation might have been cursory."

"Meaning a black kid gets gunned down in a bad black neighborhood with a Baggie of rock clutched in his hot little hands doesn't exactly shout high intrigue."

"We don't know Novato was carrying."

"Yeah. Well, I guess I can make a few calls and find that out."

He folded his arms over his chest.

I said, "Ready for lunch?"

"Nah, the goddam apple filled me. Complex carbohydrates. Who needs more?"

I kept my mouth shut.

A minute later he said: "Tell you what I'd really like. A tall, frosty, liver-eating Johnny Black or reasonable facsimile. In lieu of that, I'll make those phone calls and do the goddam laundry. What do you guys call that—repression?"

"Sublimation."

"Sublimation. Yeah. Drop me back at your place. Gotta go home and sublimate."

I didn't like the edge in his voice, but his expression warned off debate.

Besides, I had a call of my own to make.

17

Mahlon Burden's answering machine message was ten seconds of chamber music followed by a clipped "Leave your message," and three short beeps.

I said, "This is Alex Dela—"

Click. "Hello, Doctor. What have you decided?"

"I'm willing to explore the possibilities, Mr. Burden."

"When?"

"I've got time today."

"Doctor, I've got nothing but time. Name the place and the time."

"An hour. Your house."

"Perfect." Strange word considering his circumstances.

He gave me an address I already knew and followed it up with precisely detailed directions.

"An hour," he said. "Looking forward to it."

*   *   *

No pride of ownership. I'd expected something flagrantly deviant—slovenly—at 1723 Jubilo. But at first glance the house was like all the others on the block. Single-story ranch, the walls sided with aluminum designed to resemble wood, painted the green-gray of a stormy sea. The window casements and front door were the same gray—ah, the first bit of deviance, a monochrome statement when viewed alongside the neighboring houses with their carefully contrasting color schemes.

I parked, began noticing other misdemeanors. The small lawn, mowed and neatly edged but a half-shade paler than the sprinkler-fed emerald of all the others on the block. A few thin spots in the grass that threatened to raise the offense to felony level.

No flower beds. Just a girdle of creeping juniper separating grass from house. No trees, either—none of the dwarf citrus, avocados, or birch triplets that graced the lawns of the other homes.

The gestalt: austere, but hardly quirky. Ocean Heights was easily offended.

The front door had been left slightly ajar. I rang the bell anyway, waited, then walked into an entry hall carpeted with a disc of mock-Persian. Before me was a compact, square living room, white-walled, flat-ceilinged, and rimmed with an obtrusively ornate band of egg-and-dart crown molding. The carpeting was green wool, spotless but thin as the lawn, and looked to be about thirty years old. The furniture was of similar vintage, the wood stained oxblood, the chairs and sofas quilted and upholstered in a chrysanthemum print that shouted *spring,* pleat-skirted and sheathed in condom-snug clear plastic. Everything matched, every piece arranged with showroom precision. An *ensemble.* I was certain all of it had been bought at the same time.

I cleared my throat. No one responded. I waited and gave myself over to fantasy. A young couple Sunday shopping in some suburban department store—Sears or a counterpart. The smell of popcorn, the ding of elevator bells. One child in tow—a boy. The parents anxious, budget-conscious, but intent on acquisition. Furniture, appliances, soft rolls of carpeting. Cookware, dishes, all the brand-new, optimistic words it took to fill a proper 50's populuxe home: Pyrex, stainless, vinyl, Formica, rayon, nylon. Sheaves of receipts. Warranties. More promises. A shopping spree worthy of a game-show winner . . .

All those dreams reduced to an ensemble, static as a museum exhibit.

I said, "Hello?"

A white-painted brick mantel framed a fireplace that was too clean ever to have been used. No screen, andirons, or tools. The top of the mantel was as bare as the walls. White walls, blank as giant sheets of virgin notepaper.

The *tabula rasa* approach to domestic life . . .

Across the living room was a dining room two thirds its size. Crenelated molding. More green carpet, more notepaper walls. Pecan-finish china cabinet, matching buffet. A couple of souvenir plates on one of the cabinet shelves. Grand Coulee Dam. Disneyland. The rest of the shelves empty. An oval table surrounded by eight straight-backed, plastic-sheathed chairs and topped with a brown pad filled most of the floor space. A pass-through with sliding wooden doors was cut into the wall behind the head of the table, offering a view of a yellow kitchen.

I went over and peeked in. Thirty-year-old refrigerator and stove glazed with yellow porcelain. No magnets or reminders on the fridge. No cooking smells.

There was a doorway leading to the rear of the house. A note was tacked onto the threshold.

DR. D.: IN THE BACK. M.B.

Beyond the note, an unlit hallway lined with closed doors. White space deepening to gray. I stepped closer, made out the sound of music. A string quartet. Haydn.

I walked toward it, followed the right turn of the hallway, and came to a final door. The music was loud and clear enough to be live.

I turned the knob, stepped into a large, peak-ceilinged room, the planks and cross-beams painted white. Dark hardwood floor. Three walls of blond birch paneling; the fourth, a bank of sliding glass doors that looked out to a small backyard that was mostly cement driveway. A silver-gray Honda sat in front of a corrugated aluminum garage door.

The glass gave the room an indoor-outdoor look. What realtors used to call a lanai, back in the days when they were peddling tropical dreams. What had become, in this age of transience and marital fracture, the family room.

The Burden family room was big and cold and devoid of furniture. Devoid of nearly everything, except for six-figures' worth of stereo equipment arranged in a bank against one of the birch walls. Black-matte cases, black-glass instrument panels. Dials and digital readouts bleeping green and yellow and scarlet and gas-flame blue. Oscilloscopic sine waves. Fluctuating columns of liquid laser. Pinpoints of bouncing light.

Amps and preamps, tuners, graphic equalizers, bass-boosters, treble-clarifiers, filters, a reel-to-reel tape player, a pair of cassette decks, a pair of turntables, a compact disc player, a laser-disc player. All of it connected via a tangle of cable to a Stonehenge arrangement of black, fabric-faced speaker columns. Eight obelisks, spread throughout the room, big enough to project a heavy metal band into the bleachers of a baseball stadium.

A string quartet flowed out at medium volume.

Three quarters of a quartet. Both violin parts and the viola.

Mahlon Burden sat on a backless stool in the center of the room cradling a cello. Playing by ear, eyes closed, swaying in tempo, thin lips pursed as if for a kiss. He had on a white shirt, dark trousers, black socks, white canvas tennis shoes. His shirt sleeves were bunched carelessly at the elbows. Gray stubble flecked his chin, and his hair looked unkempt.

Seemingly unaware of my presence, he played on, fingers assuming positions along the ebony board, bearing down, quivering with vibrato. Floating the bow across the strings in a horsehair caress. Controlling his volume so perfectly that the cello meshed seamlessly with the recorded sounds regurgitated by the speakers.

Man and machine. Man as machine.

To my ears he was good, symphony quality or close to it. But I was put off by the sterile staginess of the whole thing.

I was here to exhume, not to be serenaded. But I heard him out, kept waiting for him to make a mistake—some flaw in tempo or sour tone that would justify an intrusion.

He kept playing perfectly. I endured an entire

movement. When the piece was finished he kept his eyes closed but flexed his bow arm and took a deep breath.

Before I could say anything, the next movement began, opening with an arpeggiated solo by the first violin. Burden smiled as if meeting an old friend, readied his bow.

I said, "Mr. Burden."

He opened his eyes.

I said, "Very pretty."

He gave me a blank look and his face twitched. The second violin joined in. Then the viola. He glanced back at the columnar speakers, as if making eye contact with their fabric faces could somehow forestall the inevitable—forestall what he'd initiated.

The moment for the cello's entry arrived. The music flowed, exquisite but incomplete. Unsettling. Like a beautiful woman without a conscience.

Burden gave one last look of regret, then stood, put his cello in its case, then the bow. Out of a trouser pocket came a small black remote-control module.

A single button push.

Fade to black.

The silence emptied the room of more than music. I noticed for the first time that the birch paneling was really some kind of photoprinted plyboard. The scuffmarks on the hardwood stood out harsh as keloid scars. The sliding glass door hadn't been cleaned in a while. Through the cloudy panes, the concrete and grass view was depressing.

Family room without a family.

He said, "I play every day without fail. Concentrate on the technically challenging pieces."

"You play very well."

Nod. "At one time I had ambitions of doing it for a living. But it's not a very good living unless one is extremely lucky. I never counted on luck."

Uttered with more pride than bitterness. He walked over to the stereo bank.

"I believe in doing things systematically, Dr. Delaware. That's my main talent, actually. I'm not much in terms of innovation, but I do know how to put things together. To create systems. And to use them optimally."

He fondled the equipment, then began delivering a lecture on each of the components. Waiting out delay tactics was one of *my* talents. I just stood there and listened.

". . . so you might be asking yourself, why two cassette players? This one"—he pointed—"is conventional magnetic tape, but *this* one is DAT. Digital audio tracking. State of the art. The inventors hope to compete with CDs, though I'm not yet convinced. Still, the sound quality is impressive. I had a prototype a full year before it hit the market. It interfaces quite well with the rest of the system. Sometimes that's a problem: Components will meet individual specifications but not blend well with other members of the system. Like an instrument that's been tuned to itself with no regard for the rest of the orchestra. Acceptable only in a very limited context. The key is to approach life with a conductor's perspective. The whole greater than its parts."

He moved his hand as if wielding a baton.

I gave him a dose of therapist's silence.

He stroked a black glass face and said, "I suppose you'll want to know about our origins— Holly's origins."

"That would be a good start."

"Come with me."

We walked down the hallway. He opened the first door on the left and we entered a white-walled room with a single window covered with gray drapes. The drapes were drawn. Light came from a spindly chrome halogen lamp in one corner. The carpeting was an extension of the green I'd seen in the living room.

From the size and placement I guessed it had once been the master bedroom. He'd converted it into an office: one wall of sliding mirrored closet doors and, against the other three, white Formica cabinet modules arranged in a U, shelves on top, cabinets on the bottom, black Formica work space sandwiched in between. The shelves were filled with boxes of floppy disks, computer manuals, software manuals, hard-disk replacement units, stationery, office supplies, and books—mostly reference works. One entire wall was given over to phone directories—hundreds of them. Conventional, business only, something called the *Cole Reverse*, compendia of ZIP codes, and a hand-lettered volume entitled ZIPS: *SUBANALYS*.

The walls behind the desk tops were lined with power strips—a continuous stripe of electrical outlets, each connected to something by stout black cable: three PC work-stations, each with a brushed-steel and black vinyl secretary chair, battery backup, laser printer, and phone modem. An additional ten multiline phones, five connected to more modems and fax machines, the others to automatic answering machines; a trio of automatic dialers; a huge batch-copying Xerox machine sunk into one of the cabinets, only the top half of its bulky chassis visible; a smaller, desktop copier, an automatic check-writer, an electronic postage meter. Other apparatus I couldn't identify.

The room buzzed and hummed and flashed, phones ringing twice before answering machines kicked in. Fax machines excreting sheets of paper at odd intervals, each sheet falling neatly into a collecting bin. The computer monitors displayed amber rows of letters and numbers bunched in groups of four and five—an incomprehensible series of alpha-numeric codes that moved across the screen in tiny increments, like cars in a traffic jam.

A herky-jerky electromagnetic kinesis that worked hard at simulating life.

Burden looked proud—paternally proud. His clothes blended with the room. Black-and-white camouflage.

This was where he went to disappear.

"My nerve center," he said. "The hub of my enterprises."

"Mailing lists?"

He nodded. "As well as marketing consultations to other corporations—demographic targeting. Give me a ZIP code and I'll tell you worlds about a person. Give me a street address and I'll go a good deal further—predict trends. It's what led me to this."

Another conductor's flourish as he slid open a drawer, removed a booklet, and handed it to me.

Heavy stock. Glossy. A title in bright-yellow computer-type lettering: *New Frontiers Technology, Ltd.* over a jet-black banner.

Below the title, an ostentatiously muscular dark-haired man, naked from the waist up and wearing yellow Spandex pants, straddled a meter-laden exercise machine. Cords ran from the equipment to a yellow belt around his waist and to a matching sweatband. His deltoids, pecs, and biceps were hypertrophied meat-carvings. Veins popped as if worms had burrowed under his skin;

every bead of perspiration stood out in vitreous bas-relief. His smile said pain was the ultimate high. Behind him, a similarly hewn blond woman in a yellow body suit and a belt/headband hookup created a marathon blur on a cross-country skiing machine—not unlike the one I had at home. The cords and headgear made them resemble candidates for electrocution.

I turned a page. Mail-order catalogue. One of those yuppy-stroking affairs that seemed to arrive in the mail every day. I thought I remembered throwing this one out.

You were on the mental health specialist list.

I had bought my ski machine from a catalogue. But not this one . . .

Burden was staring at me, prouder than ever. Waiting. I knew what I was expected to do. Why not? All part of the job.

I examined the catalogue.

The inside cover was a two-paragraph letter above a color photo of a handsome, broad-shouldered man in his mid-thirties. He had wavy hair, luxuriant walrus mustaches, and a clipped beard—the Schweppes man in his prime. He wore a pink button-down shirt with a perfect collar roll, blue foulard, and saddle-leather braces, and had been posed in a clubby atmosphere: mahogany-paneled room, high-backed leather chair, carved leather-topped desk. On the desk were an antique hourglass, brass nautical instruments, a blue-shaded banker's lamp, and a cut-crystal inkwell. Baronial oil portraits hung in the background. I could almost smell the sealing wax.

Under the letter was a fountain pen signature, elaborate and illegible. The photo caption identified him as Gregory Graff, Esq., Chief Consulting Officer of New Frontiers Technology, Limited, headquartered in Greenwich, Connecticut. The letter was concise but friendly, just this side of preachy. Extolling the virtues of vitamins, exercise, balanced nutrition, self-defense, and meditative relaxation. What Graff called the "New Age Actualization Life-style for Today's Striving Man and Woman." The second paragraph was a pitch for this month's New Products, offered at special discount for those who ordered early. The facing page was an order form complete with an 800 number and the assurance that "purchase specialists" were standing by to take calls twenty-four hours a day.

The catalogue was divided into sections marked by blue-tabbed index pages. I turned to the first. "Body and Soul." An assortment of iron-pumping gizmos that would have done the Inquisition proud, demonstrated by the sculpted couple on the cover, followed by nirvana-nostrums for the post-exhaustion wind-down: massage oil, air-purifiers, wave machines, white-noise simulators, little black boxes that promised to change the atmosphere in any home into one that stimulated "alphawave meditation." An electric "Tibetan Harmony Bell, re-creating one developed centuries ago in the Himalayas to capture the unique harmonies and overtones of high-altitude wind currents."

Section Two was "Beauty and Balance." Organic cosmetics, high-fiber cookies and candies, little yellow bottles of beta-carotene powder, lecithin capsules, bee pollen, zinc lozenges, water-purifying crystals, amino-acid combos, something new called "NiteAfter 100" that claimed to repair physiological damage wrought by "the 3 Deadly P's: pollution, pigging-out, and partying." Pills for sleeping soundly, for waking up cheerful, for enhancing "personal power during business meetings and power lunches." A mineral concoction that claimed to "restore psychophysiological homeostasis and enhance individual tranquillity"—presumably during bathroom breaks.

Next came "Style and Substance." Clothing and accessories in exotic hides and brushed steel. A programmable, self-locking and -opening "Briefcase With a Brain"; pseudo-antique accoutrements "conceived for the 21st Century and beyond"; pre-distressed aviator jackets; Mega-Sweat Personal Sauna warm-up suits, a symphony in nylon, latex, Teflon, down-fill, napa-lamb, and cashmere.

Four was "Access and Excel," which seemed to translate to geegaws the world had done quite well without till now. Voice-activated car starters, self-cooling oven mitts, motorized bagel slicers, chamois microwave covers, everything mono-grammable for a modest extra charge. I zipped through and was about to close the catalogue when the title of the last section caught my eye: "Life and Limb."

A study in style-conscious paranoia. Bugging devices, hidden tape recorders, phone-tap detec-tors, infrared cameras and binoculars for "turning your adversary's night into your day." Privacy Locks for conventional phones. Direct-link phones in hot-line red ("Take control of Ma Bell. Talk only when you want and to whom you want"). Polygraphic "stressmeters" camouflaged as transistor radios that promised to "unscramble and digitalize the double and multiple meanings in other people's communications." Voice-modi-fiers, footstep-triggered attack dog tapes ("Choose from 345D. Doberman, 345S. Alsatian Shepherd, or 345R. Rottweiler"). Ultra-thin paper shredders that fit into an attaché case. Cameras that looked like pens. Radios that looked like pens. Packets of dehydrated "Survival Cuisine." A reprise of the water-purifying crystals. When I got to the New Age Graphite-Handled Swiss Army Knife with Mini-Surgical Array, I closed the cata-logue.

"Very interesting." I held it out to Burden.

He shook his head. "Keep it, Doctor. My compliments. You've been receiving it for five months but haven't ordered anything yet. Perhaps a closer look will change your mind."

The catalogue went into my jacket pocket.

I said, "Quite an eclectic collection."

He responded with all the hesitation of a rodeo bull let out of the stall. "My brainchild. I was in the army just after Korea. Cryptography and decoding and computer technology—the infancy of the Computer Age. After discharge I went to Washington, D.C., and worked for the Census Bureau. We were just starting to computerize—the old days of clunky mainframes and IBM cards. I met my wife there. She was a very bright woman. Mathematician. Master's degree. I'm self-taught, never finished high school, but I ended up being her mentor. All those years working with statistics and demographic patterns, we got a good fix on shifting population masses, trends, how people in different regions and social strata differ in their purchasing patterns. The predictive power of residential variables. When ZIP codes came into being it was beautiful—such simplification. And now the new sub-codes make it even easier."

He sat down in one of the secretary chairs, made a half whirl, and spun back.

"The beauty of it, Doctor—of the informational age—is that things can be done so simply. When I left public service, I adapted my knowledge to the business world. Given my excellent typing skills combined with programming ability, I'm a corporation to myself—don't even need a secretary. Just a few toll-free lines, several free-lance operators working from home stations, and a few privately contracted printers in various locations around the country. I interface with all of them by modem. No inventory or warehousing costs—because there's no inventory at all. The consumer gets the catalogue and makes his or her choice. The operators take the order, communicate it immediately to the manufacturer. The manufacturer sends the product directly to the consumer. Upon delivery confirmation, the manufacturer's billed for retail markup—my fee for facilitating."

"Electronic middleman."

"Yes. Exactly. The advanced state of my technology allows me to be extremely flexible. I can add and delete products based on sales performance, alter copy, and produce highly focused mail-outs within a twenty-four-hour period. I've even begun experimenting with an automated operator system—pretaped messages combined with voice-activated pauses: The tape waits until the consumer's finished talking, then talks back in perfectly modulated, grammatical, regionless English. So one day I may not need any employees at all. The ultimate cottage industry."

"Who's Graff?"

"A model. I got him through a New York agency. You'll notice he's designated as Chief

Consulting Officer—a title that's meaningless from a legal point of view. I'm the President and Chief *Executive* Officer. I went through hundreds of photos before picking him. My marketing research told me exactly what I was looking for: youthful vitality combined with authority—a beard works very well for the latter, as long as it's short and neat. The mustache implies generosity. The surname *Graff* was chosen because upscale consumers respect anything Teutonic—regard it as efficient, intelligent, and reliable. But only up to a point. A forename like Helmut or Wilhelm wouldn't have done. *Too* German. Too *foreign*. 'Gregory' scores high on the likability scale. All-American. Greg. He's one of the boys, with Teutonic ancestry. A great athlete, smartest boy on the block—but someone you like. My research shows that many people assume he has a graduate degree—usually law or an M.B.A. The button-down shirt communicates stability; the tie, affluence; and the suspenders provide a flair—creativity. He's a man you believe in, instinctively. Aggressive and goal-oriented but not hostile, dependable but not stodgy. And concerned. Humanistic. Humanism is important to my target consumers—feeling charitable. Twice a year I give them the option of donating one percent of their total purchase to a selection of charities. Gregory's an excellent fund-raiser. People reach

deep into their pockets. I'm thinking of franchis-
ing him."

"Sounds very well thought-out."

"Oh, it is. And very lucrative."

Emphasizing the last word to let me know he
meant megabucks. A cottage industry tycoon.

That didn't mesh with the worn carpet, the
thirty-year-old furniture, the dirty Honda. But I'd
met other rich men who didn't care to show it. Or
were afraid to show it and hid behind a Just Plain
Folks facade.

Right now he was hiding something else.

I said, "Let's talk about Holly."

He looked surprised. "Holly. Of course. Is
there anything else you need to know about me?"

The naked narcissism threw me. I'd thought
his self-absorption was a means of delaying painful questions. Now, I wasn't sure.

I said, "I'm sure I'll have lots of questions
about all your family members, Mr. Burden. But
right now I'd like to see Holly's room."

"Her room. Makes sense. Absolutely."

We left the office. He opened a door across
the hall.

More notepaper walls. Two windows, covered by Venetian blinds. A thin mattress lay on
the floor, parallel to a low wooden bedframe. The
mattress had been slit open in several places, the
ticking peeled back, the foam scooped out in
handfuls. A crumpled ball of white bed sheet lay

rolled in one corner. Nearby was a pillow that had also been slit and sat in a pool of foam chunks. The only other furniture was a pressed-wood three-drawer dresser below an oval mirror. The mirror glass was finger-smudged. The dresser drawers were pulled open. Some clothing—cotton undergarments and cheap blouses—remained inside. Other garments had been removed and piled on the floor. Atop the dresser sat a plastic clock radio. Its beaverboard back had been removed and it had been gutted, parts spread across the wood.

"Compliments of the police," said Burden.

I looked past the disarray, saw the sparseness that had pre-existed any police intrusion. "What did they take with them?"

"Not a thing. They were after diaries, any sort of written record, but she never kept any. I kept telling them that but they just went in and pillaged."

"Did they say you were allowed to clean it?"

He fingered his eyeglasses. "I don't know. I suppose they did." He bent and picked a piece of foam from the floor. Rolled it between his fingers and drew himself up a bit.

"Holly used to do most of the cleaning. Twice a year I'd bring a professional crew in, but she did it the rest of the time. She liked it, was very good at it. I guess I'm still expecting her to . . . walk right in with a dustrag and start tidying."

His voice broke and he walked quickly to the door. "Please excuse me. Take as long as you like."

I let him go and turned my attention back to the room, trying to conjure the place as it had been when Holly had been alive.

Not much to work with. Those white walls—no nails or brackets, not a single hole or darkened square. Young girls typically used their walls as plaster notebooks. Holly had never hung a picture, never tacked a pennant, never softened her life with rock-poster rebellion or calendar imagery.

What had she dreamed about?

I kept searching for some sign of personal imprint but found none. The room was cell-like, assertively barren.

Did her father realize this wasn't right?

I recalled the back room, barren except for his toys.

His own place of refuge, cold as a glacier.

Emptiness as a family style?

Daughter as charwoman, handmaiden to the cottage tycoon?

The room began to close in. Had she felt it too? Living here, sleeping here, feeling her life drift by?

Ike—anyone who cared, who'd taken the time to care—might have been seen as a liberator. Prince Charming.

What had his death done to her?

Despite what she'd become—what she'd *done*—I felt for her.

I heard Milo's voice in the back of my head. *Getting mushy on me, pal?*

But I wanted to believe that if Milo were to come to this place, he'd feel something too.

The door to the closet was partially ajar. I opened it and looked in. The poison/perfume of camphor. More clothing—not much of it, mostly casual knits, T-shirts, sweaters, a couple of jackets. The pockets had been slit, the linings shredded. Faded colors.

More heaps of clothing on the floor.

Bargain-bin quality. Daughter of a tycoon.

Above the clothes pole were two shelves. The lower one bore two games. Candy Land. Chutes and Ladders.

Preschool amusements. Had she stopped playing at the age of six? Apart from that, nothing. No books, no fan magazines, no stuffed animals or mugs printed with fatuous phrases. No clear-plastic things that snowed when you turned them upside down.

I closed the closet door and turned back to the ravaged room, tried to picture the way it had looked before the police had come. The damage made it seem more human.

Cot and a dresser. Blank walls. A radio.

The word *cell* kept flashing.

But I'd seen jail cells that looked more inviting.

This was worse. Punitive.

Solitary confinement.

I had to get out of there.

18

Burden was back in his office, sitting at one of the computer workstations. I wheeled one of the secretary chairs into the center of the room and sat down. He touch-typed rapidly for a few moments before looking up, dry-eyed.

"So. What's the next step, Doctor?"

"Holly didn't seem to have many interests."

He smiled. "Ah, the room. You're thinking I isolated her. For some ulterior motive."

Exactly what I'd been thinking, but I said, "No. Just trying to get a picture of the way she lived."

"The way she lived. Well, it wasn't like *that,* believe me. Though I can understand your thinking it was. I've done my reading on child psychology. So I know all the theories of child abuse. Isolating the designated victim in order to maximize control. But that had nothing to do with us. Not even remotely. That's not to say we're . . . we *were* social butterflies. As a family or individually. Our pleasures have always been solitary. Reading, good music. Holly loved music. I always encouraged discussions of current events, various cultural debates. Howard, my firstborn, took to that. Holly didn't. But I always tried to provide the same sorts of things other children seemed to like. Toys, games, books. Holly never showed any interest in any of it. She hated to read. Most of the time the toys stayed in the box."

"What did she do for fun?"

"Fun." He drew out the word as if it were foreign. "Fun. For *fun,* she talked to herself, created fantasies. And she *was* inventive, I'll grant her that. Could take a piece of string or a rock or a spoon from the kitchen and use it as a prop. She had a terrific imagination—genetic, no doubt. I'm highly imaginative. However, I've learned to channel it. Productively."

"She didn't?"

"She simply fantasized, went no further with it."

"What were her fantasies about?"

"I have no idea. She was a demon for privacy, liked to close her door tight even when she was very young. Just sit on the floor or on her bed, talk and mumble. If I prodded her to get fresh air, she'd go out into the backyard and settle down on the grass, and start in doing exactly the same thing."

I said, "When she was younger, did she rock back and forth or try to hurt herself?"

He smiled like a well-prepared student. "No, Doctor. She wasn't autistic—not remotely. If you talked to her she'd respond—if she felt like it. There was no echolalic speech, nothing psychotic. She was just very self-sufficient. From an amusement standpoint. She made her own *fun*."

I watched the constantly blinking phones and self-shifting computer images. His fun.

"And she never kept any sort of diary?"

"No. She hated paper—threw everything out. Hated clutter, was a bug on neatness. Probably another example of genetics. I plead guilty to that kind of precision."

He smiled, not looking guilty at all.

I said, "I saw only two games in her closet. What happened to all the toys and the books?"

"When she was thirteen she did a massive housecleaning, took everything out of her room except for her radio and her clothing, and piled it up in the hall—very neatly. When I asked her what she was doing, she insisted I get rid of it. So, of course, I did. Gave it to Goodwill. There was no arguing with Holly when she made her mind up."

"She didn't want anything to replace what she'd gotten rid of?"

"Not a thing. She was quite happy with nothing."

"Nothing but Chutes and Ladders and Candy Land."

"Yes. Those." A split-second flinch. I snared it as if it were a moth.

"How old was she when she got those two games?"

"Five. They were bought for her fifth birthday by her mother."

He flinched again, forced a smile. "You see, we've got an insight already. What do you make of it? An attempt on her part to cling to the past?"

His tone was clinical, detached—the classic intellectualizer. Trying to turn the interview into a chat between colleagues.

I said, "I'm not much for interpretation. Let's talk about her relationship with her mother."

"A Freudian approach?"

Trying to keep any edge out of my voice, I said, "A thorough one, Mr. Burden."

He didn't say anything. Turning slightly, he tapped his fingers on the keyboard. I waited, watched the letters and numbers on the monitor do their freeway crawl.

"So," he finally said, "I guess this is what people in your field would call active listening? A strategic silence. Holding back to get the patient to open up?" He smiled. "I read about that too."

I spoke with deliberate patience. "Mr. Burden, if this is uncomfortable for you, we don't have to continue."

"I want to continue!" He sat up sharply, without grace, and his glasses slid down his nose. By the time he'd righted them he was smiling again. "You'll have to excuse my . . . I suppose you'd term it *resistance*. This whole thing has been . . . very difficult."

"Of course it has. That's why there's no reason to cover everything at once. I can come back another time."

"No, no, there'll be no better time." He looked away from me, touched the keyboard again. "Can I offer you something? Juice? Tea?"

"Nothing, thanks. If the things I've brought up are too hard for you to discuss right now, perhaps there's some topic *you'd* like to get into?"

"No, no, let's stay on track. Bite the bullet. Her mother. My wife. Elizabeth Wyman Burden. B. 1930, D. 1974." He tilted his head back, gazed at the ceiling. "An exceptional woman. Deductive and intuitive and extremely talented—musically talented. She was very adept at the viola da gamba. Howard played the modern viola, seemed quite promising but dropped it. I helped Elizabeth develop her abilities. She complemented me beautifully."

He twisted his mouth, as if searching for the right expression, settled on regret. "Holly was nothing like her, really. Nothing like me either, really. Both of us, Betty and myself, are—were—highly intelligent. That's not a boast, simply a descriptive statement. As a couple, we were intellectually oriented. As is Howard. I saw early that he had a gift for mathematics and tutored him intensively—not remedial tutoring; he was always an excellent student. *Supplementary* tutoring, so that he wouldn't sink to the level of the public school system—be dragged down to the lowest common denominator."

"The school wasn't meeting his needs?"

"Not by a long shot. I'm sure your experience has shown you the entire system's oriented toward mediocrity. Howard thrived on what I gave him, stayed on the math track. He's a graduate actuary, passed all ten exams the first time, which is almost unheard of. Youngest man in the state to do so. You should speak to him about Holly, get his point of view. Here, I'll give you his number. He lives out in the Valley."

He turned back toward his desk, took a small piece of paper out of a drawer, and scrawled on it.

I put it away.

He said, "Howard's exceptionally bright."

"But Holly wasn't much of a student?"

He shook his head. "When she got C-minuses it was because of teacher charity."

"What was the problem?"

He hesitated. "I could spin you some yarn about poor motivation, being bored in class, never finding her niche. But the truth is she simply wasn't very intelligent. An IQ of eighty-seven.

Not retarded, but the low end of the normal range."

"When did you have her tested?"

"At age seven. I did it myself."

"*You* tested her?"

"That's correct."

"Using what test?" I said, expecting some sort of quick-and-easy questionnaire lifted from a self-help book.

"The Wechsler Intelligence Scale for Children. It's the test of choice, isn't it? The most extensively validated?"

"The Wechsler's an excellent test, Mr. Burden, but it requires quite a bit of training in order to administer and score it properly."

"Not to worry," he said, with sudden cheer. "I trained myself. Read the manual carefully and boned up on a number of related articles in psychology journals. Then I practiced on Howard—he took to it like a duck to water. Scored one forty-nine, top tenth of a percent, I believe."

"The Wechsler's not supposed to be sold to laymen. How'd you get hold of it?"

Sly smile. "Not thinking of filing a complaint, are you, Doctor?"

I crossed my legs casually, returned the smile, and shook my head. "You must be pretty resourceful."

"Actually," he said, "it was painfully simple. I filled out an order blank at the back of one of the

psychology journals, sent in my money, put a
Ph.D. after my name, enclosed a card from my
business at the time—'Demographics, Incorpo-
rated. Applied Social Research.' It must have
sounded sufficiently psychological to the company, because a week later the test came, parcel
post."

Flaunting his duplicity. But then, why would
someone who made his living hawking Tibetan
Harmony Bells and personal power pills shy away
from a bit of self-serving subterfuge?

"I did a fine job of testing," he said. "More
thorough than any school psychologist would have
been. And I took the trouble to retest her twice. At
ages nine and eleven. The results were almost
identical—eighty-seven and eighty-five. No outstanding deficits or marked strengths, no imbal-
ance between Verbal and Performance scores. Just
a general dullness. My theory is that she experienced some sort of intrauterine trauma that affected her central nervous system. Perhaps due to
her mother's advanced age—Betty was thirty-nine
when she conceived. In any event, there had to be
some kind of brain damage, didn't there? It might
have been worse but for our unique situation."

"What do you mean?"

"Given *average* heredity, she might very well
have turned out truly retarded. With Betty and me
as parents, she was given a genetic boost into the
Dull Normal range."

I said, "Do you have her testing profile?"

"No. I threw it all out years ago. What would have been the point?"

"Did you ever consult a specialist about her learning problems?"

"In the beginning I gave the school a chance to come up with something—saw the usual assortment of civil service flunkies. Counselors, special education teachers, whatnot. Holly didn't fit into any of their classification groups—too smart for Educable Mentally Retarded, too dull for a normal classroom, no discipline or management problems that would have qualified her for Educationally Handicapped. They had conferences—those types love to have conferences. Sat there and talked down to me with their jargon—thought they could hide behind jargon because I didn't have a degree after my name."

"Would there be any records of those conferences?"

"No. I demanded they destroy them. I'm in the information business. I know how records can come back to haunt. They tried to protest—some stupid regulation—but I prevailed. Sheer force of personality. They were such a weak-willed bunch, so dull themselves. Endless talk, no action. I realized early on that I was on my own; any meaningful remediation would have to take place at home. So I washed my hands of them. It's the same way I feel about that policeman Frisk. That's why I took the initiative to call you. I know you're different."

The second negative reference he'd made to the school. I said, "Did you discuss your feelings about the school with Holly?"

He gave me a long stare. Searching. Illuminated by unwelcome insight.

"Doctor, are you trying to say I planted hatred in her mind?"

"I'm trying to get a picture of how she felt about the school."

"She hated it. She must have. It represented failure to her. All those years of incompetence and insensitivity. How else could she have felt? But she wasn't about to kill anyone because of that."

He gave a derisive laugh.

I said, "What kinds of remedial things did you do?"

"Gave her my personal attention—when she'd accept it. Sat down with her every evening after dinner and walked her through her homework. Tried to get her to concentrate, tried to bribe her—what you'd call operant conditioning. That didn't work, because she really didn't want anything. Eventually I did get her reading skills and math levels to a point where she could function in the real world—simple instructions and computations, road signs. She wasn't interested in—or capable of—any higher abstractions."

"How was her attention span?"

"Just fine for things she was interested in— cleaning and straightening, listening to pop music on her radio and dancing to it when she thought no one was looking. Non*existent* for things she didn't care about. But isn't that true of anyone?"

"Dancing," I said, trying to picture it. "So her physical coordination was okay?"

"Adequate. Which is all anyone needs for the dances they do today." He flapped his arms and made a grotesque face. "Betty and I used to dance seriously. Long-forgotten baroque and classical terpsichore—gavottes, minuets. Steps that really required virtuosity. We were quite a pair."

Drifting back, inevitably, to self-congratu- lation. Feeling as if I needed a thick rope to tug things back to Holly, I said, "Did you ever con- sider medication—Ritalin or something similar?"

"Not after I read up on the effects of long- term amphetamine usage. Stunted growth. An- orexia. Possible brain damage. The last thing Holly needed was *more* brain damage. Besides, she wasn't hyperactive—more on the lethargic side, actually. Preferred to sleep late, loll in bed. I'm an early riser."

"Did she have periods of emotional depres- sion?"

He dismissed that with a wave. "Her mood was fine. She just lacked energy. At first I thought it might be nutritional—something to do with blood sugar or her thyroid. But all her blood tests were normal."

Blood tests. Half-expecting him to answer that he'd punctured her vein himself, I said, "Did your family doctor have any suggestions when he gave you the results?"

"Never had a family doctor. Never needed one. I took both of them, Howard and Holly, to the Public Health Service for their blood work. For their immunizations too. Told the civil servants there that I suspected some kind of contagious infection. It's their responsibility to check that kind of thing, so they were forced to do it. I figured I might as well get something back for my tax dollars."

Genuine glee at dissembling. How much of what he told me about anything could be believed?

"Who managed their childhood diseases? Where did you take them when they had fevers and needed antibiotics?"

"They were very healthy children, rarely ran high fevers. The few times they did, I brought it down with aspirin, fluids—exactly what a doctor would tell me to do. The couple of times they needed penicillin, they got it from the Health Service. Measles passed them by. Chicken pox and mumps I managed according to the books— genuine medical books. The *Physician's Desk Reference*. I can read instructions as well as any doctor."

"Self-sufficiency," I said.

"Exactly. In some quarters, that's still considered worthwhile."

Trumpeting his achievements had made his Mr. Peepers persona fade completely. He looked belligerent, flushed, somehow bigger, huskier. A bantam cock swelling as he scanned the barnyard for rivals.

Changing the subject, I said, "There's quite an age difference between Holly and Howard."

"Eleven years. And yes, she was an unplanned child. But not an un*wanted* one. When Betty learned she was pregnant, she was surprised but happy. And that's saying a lot, because she wasn't a healthy woman—bleeding ulcers, irritable bowel syndrome. I don't know if you're familiar with that, but she suffered from problem flatulence, very bad chronic pain. Nevertheless, she carried on like a trooper, nursed Holly for eleven months—exactly the time we'd allotted to Howard. She was an excellent mother, very patient."

"How was Holly affected by her death?"

"Quite severely, I'd assume."

"Assume?"

"Assume. With Holly there was no way of knowing how she really felt about anything, because she didn't talk, didn't express herself very well."

"Did she attend the funeral?"

"Yes, she did. I had one of the mortuary attendants watch over her in a room off the chapel during the service and when we went out to the grave. Afterwards I sat down with her and explained what had happened. She stared at me, didn't say anything, cried just a bit, and then walked away. Out to the lawn. To sit. Spin her fantasies. I let her do it for a while, then took her home. A couple of times I heard her crying at night, but when I went in she stopped and rolled away and refused to discuss it with me."

"How did you explain to her what had happened?"

"I told her her mother had been very sick. She knew that—she'd seen Betty take to bed. I said she'd gone into the hospital to be treated for her stomachaches but that the doctors had been stupid and made mistakes and they'd killed her with their stupidity and we'd have to go on without her and be strong. That we were still a family and would carry on as a family."

"Your wife's death was due to medical malpractice?"

He looked at me as if I were in the "dull normal" range. "The woman had a nonfatal condition, Doctor. She *bled* to death on the operating table, in the presence of a full surgical team."

"Did you pursue it legally?"

He gave a sharp, mocking laugh. "I talked to a couple of attorneys, but they wouldn't take the case. Supposedly it wasn't cut and dried enough, given her prior medical history. The truth was, they had more than their share of whiplashes. They didn't want to bet their contingency fees on something that required some real research. I suppose I could have found some ambulance chaser to take it on, but at the time I had other things on my mind. Two children to raise, a business to run—I was doing all direct-mailing back then, still building up my lists. Much more labor-intensive than it is today. So I needed all my energy for that."

"It must have been a difficult time for you."

"Not really. I attacked it systematically, kept everything organized. Howard stayed on the straight-A track." He stopped. "Still, I suppose the way Holly turned out was partly my fault."

"Why do you say that?"

"I have an impressive array of intellectual skills and talents but I wasn't successful in communicating them to her—in getting her going on some sort of goal-oriented program. She persistently shut me out and I allowed it, because I didn't want to be cruel. So perhaps I was too kind." He shrugged. "Of course hindsight is always twenty-twenty, isn't it?"

Luxuriating in bogus confession.

Despite my aversion to snap diagnoses, a diagnostic label kept creeping into my mind:

Narcissistic personality disorder. Pathological egotism.

It fit. Even with the way he'd chosen to make a living. *Beauty and Balance. Access and Excel.* The catalogue was a paean to narcissism. I was willing to bet he'd put his brainchild ahead of his children. Put himself ahead of everyone and everything.

I tried to imagine what it would have been like to be one of his children, and my sympathy for Holly climbed another rung.

"So," he said, "we seem to be doing well. What else can I help you with, Doctor?"

"How did Howard and Holly get along?"

"Very well—no fights."

"Did they have much to do with each other?"

"Not much. Howard was busy with his activities—studies, extracurricular clubs—and Holly stayed in her room. That's not to say he didn't love her—he was always concerned about her, if a bit baffled."

"How's he holding up?"

"Like a trooper."

"Is he married?"

"Of course. Has a big house in Encino, south of the boulevard. One lovely daughter, sharp as a tack. They're all holding up like troopers. Go visit them, see for yourself. You really should, now that I think about it. Do speak with Howard."

Sounding urgent.

Go talk to my intelligent child. The one that came out good.

I said, "What about friends?"

"Holly? No, she didn't have any. When she was very young I remember a few neighborhood children coming over. They made noise and bothered my work and I had to shoo them outside. But eventually that stopped. Holly wasn't much for group play."

"When did it stop?"

He thought about that. "What you want me to say is that everything changed after her mother died, right? But in terms of the friend situation, I'm afraid I can't be that definite. In fact I'm almost certain she lacked playmates well before Betty's death. She wasn't much of a playmate herself, liked to go off on her own and leave her little guests in the lurch."

"What about when she got older? Did she make any school chums?"

"None. She didn't like anything related to school, wanted to drop out when she was fifteen, nagged me to allow her to take the equivalency test. I knew she'd fail it and refused to let her, but she kept on me—she could be quite stubborn when she set her mind on something. Finally, when she was sixteen, I agreed. She took it. And failed."

"Did that bother her?"

"Not really. Neither of us was surprised. I made her stick it out at Pali until she graduated—

at least get the paper. Not that she'd earned it, but the ninnies just kept passing her through. Typical civil service approach—take the path of least resistance."

"What did she do after graduation?"

"Stayed home. Listened to her radio—the pop music, and talk shows. She could play it twenty-four hours a day. I assigned her household chores: straightening, cleaning, doing simple paperwork. She enjoyed doing things for me."

Free live-in help. Convenient. Some men's idea of a wife. "Did she make any recent acquaintances? Since graduation?"

"How could she? She never went anywhere."

I said, "I've been told she was friendly with a delivery boy from Dinwiddie's Market. Isaac Novato."

His jaw set and he moved forward on his chair. "Where did you hear about this supposed friendship?"

"I was told he was someone she knew, they were seen talking."

"Talking. Well, that's possible. The boy delivered groceries to our home. Every week. Holly let him in and gave him his tip, so I suppose they might have talked as part of the transaction. What else did you hear?"

"That's about it."

"Is it? Well, I doubt they were actually friends. Not that it would bother me if they had been. No doubt you know he's black. Unlike others in this neighborhood—in this country—I consider race irrelevant. I judge a person by his accomplishments, not the concentration of melanin in his skin."

Given that credo, I wondered how he'd judged his daughter.

He said, "You seem skeptical."

"Not at all."

"Novato was treated decently in this house. Feel free to ask him."

"That's not possible," I said. "He's dead."

"Dead?" The shock froze his face, thawing gradually but not completely, leaving him with a distant look in his eyes. First reaction I'd seen out of him that I was certain was spontaneous.

"When did he die?"

"Last September."

"September. Come to think of it, I don't recall seeing him for a while."

"Did Holly show any signs of being upset around that time?"

"Upset? No, not that I noticed. How did he die?"

"He was murdered."

"Oh, my. By whom?"

"It's unsolved. The police think it was some sort of drug deal gone bad."

"The police . . . Do they think there's some connection to Holly?"

"No. It just came up when they traced her former acquaintances."

"Acquaintances," he said. "One thing I can guarantee you is that Holly had *nothing* to do with drugs."

"I'm sure she didn't."

"She had nothing to do with shooting at children, either." Pause. "But what if she got . . . caught up in something? If Novato got her into something."

"Such as?"

"Some kind of corruption."

He closed his eyes. A long silence passed and his face lost expression; taking his self-absorption under wraps. One of the laser printers spewed paper. Some of it fell to the floor. He ignored it, finally opened his eyes.

"Anything else?" he said, still sounding preoccupied.

"The police said it was your rifle she took to the school. Did she know how to shoot?"

"Not at all. She hated weapons. My firearms collection was the one part of the house she refused to clean. So that whole theory is nonsense."

"She was found with the rifle."

"That doesn't make her a murderer. She could have been lured there, convinced to take the Remington with her."

A flight of wishful thinking rapid enough to make my nose bleed. I said, "Lured how?"

"I don't know. Yet. But this Novato situation gives me something to chew on. Perhaps one of his gang friends had something to do with it."

"There's no evidence he was involved with gangs."

"In this city, drugs mean gangs."

Another long silence.

I said, "When did you notice the rifle was missing?"

"I didn't, but that means nothing. I rarely looked at the collection—I'd lost interest in it."

"Where do you keep the collection?"

He got up and took me back out into the hall. The door next to Holly's room opened to a deep cedar closet lined with gun racks on three walls. The racks were empty. The floor had been vacuumed. The space smelled of machine oil and tarnish.

"The police took all of it," he said. "Every piece. For *analysis*. I'm supposed to get it back soon. But you can bet it will take plenty of wrestling with red tape."

I counted eight slots on each of the three racks. "Nice size collection."

"All long guns. Antiques, for the most part. Flintlocks. Black powder. In nonfunctional condition. I bought the lot as an investment when I was being discharged from the service. An old army acquaintance needed quick cash. They've performed quite nicely as investments, though I never bothered to sell because, frankly, I don't need the money."

Thinking of Holly's poor marksmanship, I said, "What about the Remington?"

"What about it?"

"Was it a collector's item too?"

"No, just a run-of-the-mill Remington. Legal and registered."

"For hunting?"

He shook his head. "Used to hunt but haven't since I was a boy. I was an excellent shot—won marksman's ribbons in the army—but I had no reason to pursue it any further. The rifle was for personal protection."

I said, "Did you have some brush with crime that led you to arm yourself?"

That amused him. "No, this was an ounce of prevention. Where I grew up—rural Wisconsin— guns are a part of any household, just like salt and meat and butter. No doubt you advocate gun control."

"Why do you say that?"

"Being liberal—most mental health people are liberal, aren't they? Stubborn believers in the basic goodness of humanity. In any event, I'm not apologetic about keeping arms, and the suggestion that somehow I'm to blame for what happened is absurd. Besides, Holly never shot at anyone—

never would, never could. She didn't know how to handle firearms. That's why none of what they're saying makes sense. Unless she was corrupted."

"The night before the shooting," I said, "did you hear her leave the house?"

"No," he said. "I go to bed early. I'm an extremely sound sleeper."

"Does the house have an alarm system?"

"Yes," he said. "Though you'll notice there's no console pad in the entry hall. My system's a good deal more subtle."

"Did Holly know how to operate it?"

"Of course. She wasn't imprisoned."

"And she switched it off before she left?"

"The alarm never went off, so obviously she did. But she switched it on again—it was set when I woke up. I had no idea she'd left."

"Was that typical of her when she left at night?"

"Leaving at *night* wasn't typical."

"Mr. Burden, Holly was seen taking walks around the neighborhood at night."

More genuine surprise. "Well . . . she may have stepped out from time to time—to chase away a cat, or take some air. But by and large she stayed in her room. She had everything she needed right here."

His stare was fierce. He looked at his watch. "I suppose that's it for today."

A statement, not a question.

I said, "Sure."

He walked me to the door.

"So," he said, "How're we doing? What do you think?"

"We're doing fine."

He took hold of my sleeve. "She was an innocent, believe me. A *naïf*. IQ of eighty-seven. You, more than anyone, know what that means. She lacked the intellectual capacity to plot. And violence wasn't in her nature—I didn't raise her that way. She'd have no reason to shoot anyone. Certainly not children."

"Would she have reason to shoot a politician?"

He shook his head, exasperated. "I can't help but feel, Doctor, that you're still not grasping who she was, the way she lived. She never read the papers, never cared a whit about politics or current affairs or the outside world. She slept late, listened to her radio, did her dances, cleaned the house. Scrubbed it until it sparkled. At the proper time, she prepared simple meals for both of us—cold food. I did all the cooking when cooking was called for. She *liked* her routine. She found comfort in it."

He removed his glasses, held them up to the entry light and peered through them.

"It won't be the same without her. I'll be doing those things for myself now."

* * *

During the time I'd spent there, the sun had set and I walked out into darkness. It enhanced the feeling of having been away for a long time. Having been on another planet.

An unsettling man. The portrait he'd painted of his daughter was bleak. But instructive.

Living in a cell.

Talking to herself.

Scrubbing everything spotless.

Not autistic, but aspects of her behavior had an autistic flavor: self-absorption to an extent that implied mental disorder.

Creating her own world. Like father, like daughter.

But he'd willed his isolation. Channeled it *lucratively*. The New Age Entrepreneur.

Had she encased herself in a bubble only to be trapped within? A victim of genetic insult? Environmental accident? Some incalculable combination of both?

Or had she taken on her father's life-style of her own free will?

Had she been capable of free will?

She enjoyed doing things for me.

Had the purveyor of gadgets manufactured himself a housecleaning robot—efficient, mechanical, like some high-priced toy out of his catalogue? Adapted her inadequacies and pathology to his needs?

I've done my reading on child psychology . . .

know all the theories of child abuse . . . She wasn't
imprisoned. . . .

A little too quick on the draw?

Or was I just letting clinical guesswork get the better of me because he wasn't a likable man?

I reminded myself he was a victim, wanted to feel more sympathy, not the resentment that had grown within me during my incarceration in that cold, empty house.

I realized I was thinking of him, instead of Holly. Taken in by his narcissism.

I forced myself back to the main subject.

Whatever her motivations, an image of Holly Lynn Burden had emerged from the murky ground of the interview.

Early childhood loss.

Repressed anger.

Mental confusion.

Low intelligence.

Low achievement.

Low self-esteem.

Social isolation.

A young woman with no external life and a flood of unknown fantasies swimming through her head.

Dark fantasies?

Stir in a parental attitude that disparaged authority. Disparaged all schools, and one school in particular.

Add a sprinkling of new friendship, snipped

cruelly by violence. Buried rage that buds anew. And grows.

Night walks.

Guns in a closet.

Mahlon Burden couldn't have come up with a better profile of a mass murderer had I dictated it to him.

A profile of a time bomb, ticking away.

19

I got home to a dark, empty house. Over the last few months—the post-Robin months—I'd worked hard at learning to consider that soothing. Worked hard under the tutelage of a kind, strong therapist named Ada Small. Ever the conscientious pupil, I'd applied myself, gaining an appreciation for the value of solitude—the healing and peace that could come from moderate doses of introspection. Not that long ago, Ada and I had agreed to cut the cord.

But this evening, solitude seemed too much like solitary confinement. I switched on plenty of lights, tuned the stereo to KKGO, and cranked up the volume even though the jazz that blared out was some new wave soprano-sax stuff in a bloodcurdling-scream-as-art-form mode. Anything but silence.

I kept thinking about my meeting with Burden. The shifting faces he'd shown during the course of the interview.

The shifting attitudes he'd displayed toward his daughter.

There'd been an introductory display of grief, but his tears had dried quickly in the sanctuary of his computer womb, only to be followed by a shallow lament: *I'll be doing those things for myself now.*

He might have been discussing the loss of a cleaning woman.

Once again I told myself not to judge. The man had been through hell. What could be worse than the death of a child? Add to that the way she'd died—the public shame and collective guilt that even someone like Milo was quick to assign—and who could blame him for retreating, gathering whatever psychological armaments he had at his command?

I let that rationalization settle for a while.

His behavior still bothered me. The detachment when he'd talked about her.

An IQ in the Dull Normal range . . .

It was as if her weaknesses, her failure to be *brilliant*, had been a personal insult to him.

I imagined a Burden family crest. Crossed muskets over a field of Straight A's.

A man used to having his way. She'd upset his sense of organization, had been an affront to his *system.*

Using her to clean house. Prepare *cold food.*

Some sort of punishment? Or simply an efficient allocation of resources?

Yet at the same time, against all logic, he was proclaiming her innocence.

Contracting me for . . . what? A psychological whitewash?

Something didn't fit. I sat struggling with it. Finally told myself to stop taking my work home. Once upon a time I'd been good at following that dictum. Once upon a time life had seemed simpler. . . .

Suddenly the music was ear-shattering. I realized I'd blocked it out. Now I could barely stand it and went to switch stations. Just as I touched the dial, the saxophonist quit and some Stanley Jordan guitar wizardry came on. Good omen. Time to push all thoughts of the Burden family from my mind.

But my mind was no different from anyone else's: It abhorred a vacuum. I needed something to fill the space.

Call Linda. Then I remembered her restlessness. Needing to *breathe*. I'd learned the hard way not to crowd.

I realized I was hungry, went into the kitchen and took out eggs, mushrooms, and an onion. Jordan gave way to Spyro Gyra doing "Shake Her." I cracked eggs, chopped vegetables in tempo. Paying attention in order to get it just right.

I fried up an omelet, ate, read psych journals,

and did paperwork for an hour, then stepped onto the skiing machine and pretended I was crossing some snow-filled meadow in Norway. Midway through the fantasy, Gregory Graff's bearded visage appeared through the sweat-haze, urging me to work harder. Reciting a list of brand-new products that could maximize my performance. I told him to fuck himself and huffed away.

I got off a half hour later, dripping and ready to sink into a hot bath. The phone rang.

Milo said, "So how'd it go?"

"No big surprises. She was a girl with lots of problems."

"Homicidal problems?"

"Nothing that overt." I gave him a brief rundown on what Burden had told me.

He said, "Sounds like she led like a great life." I thought I detected sympathy in his voice. "That's all the father knows about Novato?"

"That's what he says. You learn anything new?"

"Called Maury Smith at Southeast. He remembered the case—said it was still unsolved, one of many. He wasn't working on it actively because no leads had turned up. There was definitely some of that attitude Dinwiddie had picked up—just another dope burn. He did wake up a bit when I told him it might be related to something on the West Side and he agreed to meet with me tomorrow for lunch and pull the file. I also got the address of the landlady—Sophie Gruenberg. He remembered *her* pretty vividly. Said she was an old commie, really hostile to the police, kept asking him how he could stand being a black *cossack*. That sounded so inviting I thought I'd drop in on her tomorrow morning."

"Care for a ride-along?"

"I don't know," he said. "Do pinkos relate well to shrinks?"

"Hell, yes. Marx and Freud bowled together every Tuesday at Vienna Lanes. Freud got strikes; Marx fomented them."

He laughed.

"Besides," I said, "what makes you think she'll relate to a *white* cossack?"

"Not just any cossack, m'lad. This one's a member of a *persecuted minority*."

"Planning on wearing your lavender uniform?"

"If you put on your feather boa."

"I'll go digging in the attic. What time?"

"How's about nine."

"How's about."

He came by at eight-forty, driving an unmarked Ford that I'd never seen before. Sophie Gruenberg's address was on Fourth Avenue, just north of Rose. A short stroll to the beach but this wasn't Malibu. It was a cold morning, the sun lurking like a mugger behind a grimy bank of undernourished, striated clouds, but zinc-nosed pedestrians were already tramping down Rose, headed for the ocean.

The business mix on Rose proclaimed Changing Neighborhood. In Venice, that meant business as usual; this neighborhood never stopped changing. Designer delis, gelato parlors, and cubbyhole trendtiques shared the sidewalk with laundromats, check-cashing outlets, serious-drinking bars, and crumbling bungalow courts that could be emptied by scrutiny from the Immigration Service. Milo turned right on Fourth and drove for a block.

The house was a one-story side-by-side duplex on a thirty-foot-wide lot. The windows were covered with iron security bars that looked brand-new. The walls were white stucco with red-painted wood trim under a brick-colored composition roof. The front lawn was tiny but green enough to satisfy the Ocean Heights Landscape Committee, and backed by a large germinating yucca plant and a nubby bed of ice plants. Dwarf iceberg roses lined a concrete path that forked to a pair of front stoops. The two doors were also red-painted wood. Brass letters designated them "A" and "B."

A white ceramic nameplate that said THE SANDERS had been nailed just beneath the "A." Unit B was marked with something else: A white poster taped to the door, bearing the legend

MISSING. REWARD!!! in bold black letters. Under that a photo-reproduction of an old woman—chipmunk face wizened as walnut meat, surrounded by a frizzy aura of white hair. Serious face, borderline hostile. Large, dark eyes.

Below, a paragraph in typescript:

SOPHIE GRUENBERG, LAST SEEN 9/27/88, 8 P.M., IN THE VICINITY OF THE BETH SHALOM SYNAGOGUE, 402½ OCEAN FRONT WALK. WEARING A BLUE-AND-PURPLE FLORAL DRESS, BLACK SHOES, CARRYING A LARGE BLUE STRAW HANDBAG.

D.O.B.: 5-13-16
HT: 4'11"
WT: APPROX 94 LB.
MENTAL AND HEALTH STATUS: EX-CELLENT

FOUL PLAY SUSPECTED

A $1000.00 REWARD HAS BEEN OF-FERED FOR INFORMATION LEADING TO THE WHEREABOUTS OF MRS. SOPHIE GRUEN-BERG. ANYONE POSSESSING SUCH INFOR-MATION SHOULD CONTACT BETH SHALOM SYNAGOGUE.

The address of the synagogue was reiterated

at the bottom of the page, along with a phone number with a 398 prefix.

I said, "September twenty-seventh. When was Novato killed?"

"The twenty-fourth."

"Coincidence?"

Milo frowned and rapped the door to Unit B, hitting it hard enough to make the wood rattle. No answer. He rang the bell. Nothing. We walked over to A and tried there. More silence.

"Let's try around back," he said. We peeked into a small yard landscaped with a fig tree and little else. The garage was empty.

Back on the sidewalk, Milo folded his arms across his chest, then smiled at a small Mexican boy across the street who'd come out to stare. The boy scampered away. Milo sighed.

"Sunday," he said. "Hell of a long time since I've spent Sunday in church. Think I can get partial points for synagogue?"

He took Rose to Pacific, headed south for a couple of blocks, and hooked right onto an alley that ran parallel with Paloma. Still no sunshine but the streets and sidewalks were a moving meat market; even the crosswalks were jammed.

The unmarked car inched through the crowd before turning into a pay parking lot on Speedway. The attendant was a Filipino with hair down to his waist, wearing a black tank top over electric-blue

bicycle pants and beach sandals. Milo paid him,
then showed him a badge and told him to park the
Ford where we could get it out fast. The attendant
said yessir and bowed and stared at us as we
departed, eyes full of curiosity, fear, resentment.
Feeling the stare at my back, not liking it, I
savored a tiny taste of what it was like to be a cop.

We walked toward Ocean Front Walk, making our way past street peddlers hawking sunglasses and straw hats that might last a weekend,
and stands selling ethnic fast food of doubtful
origin. The crowd was clearance-sale thick: multigenerational Hispanic tribes, shambling winos
who looked as if they'd been hand-dipped in filth,
mumbling psychotics and retro-hippies lost in a
dope haze, Polo-clad upscalers side by side with
rooster-coiffed high-punk roller skaters, assorted
body-beautiful types testing the limits of the anti-
nudity ordinance, and grinning, gawking tourists
from Europe, Asia, and New York, overjoyed at
having finally found the real L.A.

A kinetic human sculpture, a quilt patched
together with every skin tone from Alpine vanilla
to bittersweet fudge. The soundtrack: polyglot
rap.

I said, "The Salad Bowl."

"What?" said Milo, talking loudly to be
heard over the din.

"Just muttering."

"Salad bowl, huh?" He eyed a couple on

roller skates. Greased torsos. Zebra-skin loincloth and nothing else on the man, micro-bikini and three nose rings on the woman. "Pass the dressing."

Splintering park benches along the west side of the promenade were crammed with conclaves of the homeless. Beyond the benches was a strip of lawn planted long ago with palm trees that had grown gigantic. The trunks of the trees had been whitewashed three feet up from ground level to provide protection from animals, four-legged and otherwise, but no one was buying it: The trunks were scarred and maimed and gouged, crisscrossed with graffiti. Past the lawn, the beach. More bodies, glistening, half-naked, sundrunk. Then a dull-platinum knife blade that had to be the ocean.

Beth Shalom Synagogue was a chunky single story of tan stucco centered by aqua-green double doors recessed under a wooden plaque that bore Hebrew writing. Above the plaque was a glass circle containing a leaded Star of David. Identical stars floated above the arched windows on either side of the doorway. The windows were barred. Flanking the building to the north was a three-story drug rehab center. To the south was a narrow brick apartment building with two shopfronts on the ground floor. One space was empty and accordion-grated. The other was occupied by a souvenir shop entitled CASH TALKS, THE REST WALKS.

We walked to the front of the synagogue. Inside the entry alcove, a poster identical to the one we'd just seen on Sophie Gruenberg's door had been taped to the wall. Below that was a small bulletin board in a glass-fronted case: corrugated black surface with movable white letters, informing the religiously curious of the times for weekday and Sabbath services. The sermon of the week was "When Good Things Happen to Bad People"; the deliverer, Rabbi David Sanders, M.A.

I said, "Sanders. Unit A."

Milo grunted.

The doors were decorated with a pair of dead-bolt locks and some kind of push-button security affair, but when Milo turned the knob, it yielded.

We entered a small linoleum-floor anteroom filled with mismatched bookcases and a single wooden end table. A paper plate of cookies, cans of soda pop, a bottle of Teacher's whisky, and a stack of paper cups sat atop the table. A wooden panel door was marked SANCTUARY. Next to it, on a metal stand, stood a battered brown leather box filled with black satin skullcaps. Milo took a cap and placed it on his head. I did the same. He pushed open the door.

The sanctuary was the size of a master suite in a Beverly Hills remodel—more of a chapel, really. Light-blue walls hung with oil paintings of biblical scenes, a dozen rows of blond-wood bench pews bordered either side of a central linoleumed aisle layered with a threadbare Persian runner. The aisle culminated at a large podium faced with another six-sided star and topped by a fringed throw of blue velvet. Behind the podium was a pleated velvet curtain sided by two high-backed chairs upholstered in the same blue plush. Dangling over the podium was a cone of red glass, lit. A pair of tall thin windows toward the front of the room allowed in narrow beams of dusty light. The rear was couched in semidarkness. Milo and I stood there, half-hidden by it. The air was warm and fusty, overlaid with kitchen aromas.

A fair-complected bearded man in his late twenties stood behind the podium, a book open before him, addressing a front-row audience of four, all elderly. One man, three women.

"So we see," he said, leaning on his elbows, "the true wisdom of the Ethics of the Fathers lies in the ability of the *tana'im*—the rabbis of the Talmud—to put our lives in perspective, generation after generation. To teach us what is important and what isn't. Values. 'Who is rich?' the rabbis ask. And they answer: he who is satisfied with his portion. What could be more profound? 'Without manners, there is no scholarship. Without scholarship, no manners.' 'The more meat, the more worms.' " He had a soft, clear voice. Precise enunciation. Some sort of accent—my guess was Australian.

"Worms—oh, boy, is that true," said the sole male student, using his hands for emphasis. He sat in the midst of the women. All I could see of him was a bald head wisped with white and topped by a yarmulke, just like the one I was wearing, above a short, thick neck. "Worms all the time—all we got now is worms, the way we let society get."

Mutters of assent from the women.

The bearded man smiled, looked down at his book, wet his thumb with his tongue and turned a page. He was broad-shouldered and had a rosy-cheeked baby face that the dirty-blond beard had failed to season. He had on a short-sleeved blue-and-white plaid shirt and a black velvet skullcap that covered most of his tight blond curls.

"It's always the same, Rabbi," said the bald man. "Complication, making things difficult. First you set up a system. To do some good. Till then you're okay. We should always be looking to do good—otherwise what's the point, right? What separates us from the animals, right? But then the problem comes when too many people get involved and the system takes over and all of a sudden everyone's working to do good for the *system* instead of vice-a-versa. Then you got worms. Lots of meat, lots of worms. The more meat, the more worms."

"Sy, I think what the rabbi means is something different," said a plump woman on the far right. She had fluffy blued hair and heavy arms that shook as she used her hands for emphasis. "He's talking about materialism. The more foolish things we collect, the more problems we get."

"Actually, you're both correct," said the blond man in a conciliatory tone. "The Talmud is emphasizing the virtue of simplicity. Mr. Morgenstern is talking about procedural simplicity; Mrs. Cooper, material simplicity. When we complicate things, we drift further away from our purpose on this planet—getting closer to God. That's precisely why the Tal—"

"It happened with the IRS, Rabbi," said a woman with a thin, birdlike voice and a cap of dyed-black hair. "The taxes. The taxes were supposed to be for the people. Now it's people for the taxes. Same with Social Security. *Moishe Kapoyr.*" Twist of a wrist. "Upside down."

"Very true, Mrs. Steinberg," said the young rabbi. "Oftentimes—"

"Social Security, too," said Mr. Morgenstern. "They make like Social Security is something we're stealing, the young puppies, so they shouldn't have a new BMW each year. How many years did I work and contribute, like clockwork, back before BMWs were enemy airplanes? Now, they make like I want charity, bread out of their mouths. Who do they think baked them the bread in the first place? From trees it fell?"

The young rabbi started to comment but was drowned out by a discussion of the Social Security system. He seemed to accept it with practiced good nature, turned another page, read, finally looked up and saw us, and stood up straight behind the podium.

He raised his eyebrows. Milo gave a small nod of acknowledgment.

The rabbi left the podium and walked toward us. Tall, built like an athlete, with a sure stride. His students—old enough to be his grandparents—turned their heads and followed his path. They saw us. The synagogue grew silent.

"I'm Rabbi Sanders. Can I help you, gentlemen?"

Milo flashed the badge. Sanders examined it. Milo said, "Excuse the interruption, Rabbi. When you're through we'd like to talk to you."

"Certainly. May I ask about what?"

"Sophie Gruenberg."

The baby face braced itself, as if for pain. A child in a doctor's office, anticipating the needle. "Do you have news for us, Officer?"

Milo shook his head. "Just questions."

"Oh," said Sanders, looking like a prisoner who'd had his sentence delayed but not commuted.

"What?" said one of the women at the front. "What is it?"

"Cops," said Morgenstern. "I can always

tell. Am I right?" Seen front on, he was thick, with doughy features, shaggy eyebrows, and meaty workingman's hands that he waved as he talked.

I smiled at him.

He said, "I can always tell. Those yarmulkes are sitting there like they're ready to fly off."

Four faces stared at us. A quartet of antique masks scored by time but strengthened by experience.

Rabbi Sanders said, "These gentlemen are indeed police officers and they're here to ask questions about Sophie."

"Questions," said the plump woman, Mrs. Cooper. She wore spectacles, a white sweater buttoned to the neck, and a string of pearls. The blued hair was precisely marcelled. "Why more questions, now?"

"All we've gotten from the police is questions," said the hand-waving Morgenstern. "No answers—no meat, lots of worms. How long's it been? What, month and a half?"

The women nodded.

"You think there's a chance?" said Mrs. Steinberg, the black-haired woman. The hair was cut in bangs and bobbed. The face below it was chalk-white and thin and had once been beautiful. I pictured her in a Roaring Twenties chorus line, doing high kicks. "Even a little bit of a chance that she could still be alive?"

"Hush, Rose," said Mrs. Cooper. "There's always hope. *Kayn aynhoreh, poo poo poo.*" Her soft face quivered.

Morgenstern regarded her with a look of exaggerated scorn. "What's with this *aynhoreh* business, my dear? The evil eye? Superstition—*stupid*stition. What you got to have is rationality, the rational mind. Dialectics, Hegel and Kant—and of course the Talmud, excuse me, Rabbi." He slapped his own wrist.

"Stop joking, Sy. This is serious," said the black-haired woman. She looked at us, pained. "Could she possibly be alive, Officers? After all this time?"

Five faces, waiting for an answer.

Milo took a step backward. "I'd like to hope so, Ma'am," he said. To Sanders: "We can come back and discuss this later, Rabbi."

"No, that's all right," said Sanders. "We were just about to conclude. If you wait a minute, I'll be right with you."

He went back behind the podium, said a few more words about values and proper perspective, dismissed the class, and returned to us. The old people lingered near the front of the synagogue, huddling in discussion.

"Refreshments out in front, people," said Sanders.

The huddle buzzed, then broke. The women hung back and Mr. Morgenstern came forward,

the designated quarterback. He was no more than
five three, blocky and firm-looking. A toy truck of
a man in khaki work pants and a white shirt under
a gray sweater vest.

"You got questions," he said, "maybe *we* can
answer them. We knew her."

Sanders looked at Milo.

Milo said, "Sure. We'd appreciate any information."

Morgenstern nodded. "Good you agreed," he
said, " 'cause we voted on it—the people have
spoken. That should be respected."

We reassembled near the podium. Milo stood
in front of it. Sanders took a seat and pulled a briar
pipe out of his pocket.

"Tsk, tsk, Rabbi," said the woman who
hadn't yet spoken. Big-boned, no makeup,
brushed-steel hair tied in a bun.

"I'm not lighting it, Mrs. Sindowsky," said
the rabbi.

"Better you shouldn't do anything with it.
What do you need problems on the lips for? More
meat, more worms, right, Rabbi?"

Sanders blushed and smiled, cradled the pipe
in one hand and touched it longingly, but didn't
put it in his mouth.

Milo said, "I want to be straight with you
people. I've got absolutely nothing new to tell you
about Mrs. Gruenberg. In fact, I'm not investigat-

ing her case and I only came here because her disappearance may be related to another case. And I can't tell you anything about that one."

"Such a deal," said Morgenstern. "You must be fun at swap meets."

"Exactly," said Milo, smiling.

"What can we do for you, Officer?" said Rabbi Sanders.

"Tell me about Mrs. Gruenberg. Everything you know about her disappearance."

"We told everything to the police already," said Mrs. Cooper. "She was here, left, and that was it. Poof. Gone." The heavy arms rippled. "After a couple days the police agreed to talk to us and they sent a detective down who asked questions. He filed a missing persons report and promised to keep in touch with us. So far, nothing."

"That's because," said Morgenstern, "they got nothing. They had something, would this man be here, asking us to go over it again? How they gonna give you what they don't have?"

Milo said, "Do you remember the name of the investigating detective?"

"What investigating?" said Morgenstern. "He took a report—that was it."

"Mehan," said the rabbi. "Detective Mehan from Pacific Division."

"Which division you from?" said Morgenstern.

"West L.A.," Milo said.

Morgenstern winked and said, "Silk stocking detail, eh? Lots of stolen BMWs."

Rabbi Sanders said, "Detective Mehan did more than just file a report. He examined her . . . Sophie's house. I know because I let him in. We, my family and I, were—are—her tenants. We live side by side, kept each other's keys. Detective Mehan went into her unit and found no evidence of any crime being committed. Everything was in order. He also checked with her bank and found out she hadn't made any large withdrawals recently. And she hadn't asked the post office to withhold or forward mail. So it seemed to him she hadn't planned to take a trip. He thought she might have gotten lost somewhere."

"Impossible," said Mrs. Steinberg. "She knew Venice like the palm of her hand. She would never get lost. Right?"

Nods.

"True, but who knows?" said Mrs. Cooper. "Anything can happen."

Vulnerable looks. Long silence.

"Ahh," said Morgenstern. "All guesses. Including the bank stuff—you ask me, that means nothing. Sophie was a crafty one—she never told anyone what she was thinking or doing. Never trusted anyone—especially the capitalist bankers. So how much would she keep in bank accounts?

The big bucks? Or just *narrishkeit* small change?
Maybe she kept her serious cash somewhere else."

"Where would that be?" said Milo.

"I don't know," said Morgenstern. "She
didn't tell no one, you think she'd tell me? I'm just
guessing, same as you. Maybe in the house, under
the bed, who knows? She had her ideas. Maybe
she was saving up, waiting for the next revolution.
So maybe she took that and left, and you wouldn't
know nothing from nothing by checking with any
banks!"

The old man's color had risen.

Milo said, "So you don't know for a fact that
she kept large amounts of cash around the house."

I knew what he was thinking: dope.

"No, no," said Morgenstern, "I don't know
nothing. Which puts me in the same club with
everyone else. She wasn't a *personal* person,
know what I mean? Didn't let on what she was
thinking or doing. So I'm just saying, checking
the banks doesn't mean nothing as far as logical,
rational thinking goes. A person could keep cash
and just decide to leave—am I right?"

Milo said, "You've got a point."

"He throws me a bone," said Morgenstern.
But he looked pleased.

Mrs. Sindowsky said, "Tell him about the
pictures?"

"Oh," said the rabbi, looking uneasy.

"What pictures?" said Milo.

"Detective Mehan went to the morgue and took pictures of any . . . senior citizens who'd been . . . any unidentified victims that matched Sophie in age. He brought them to me to look at. He put out some bulletins, called some other police departments—Long Beach, Orange County—and asked if they had any unidentified . . . people. None were Sophie. Thank God."

Four echoing *Thank God*'s.

Sanders said, "In all fairness, he seemed to be thorough—Detective Mehan. But after three weeks had passed without her showing up, he told us there was a limit to what he could do. There was no evidence of any crime being committed. The choice was to wait or hire a private detective. We talked about doing that—the detective—made a few calls to agencies. It's very expensive. We asked the Jewish Federation to consider funding. They wouldn't approve a detective, but they did agree to the reward."

"Those skinflints—to them it's chump change," said Morgenstern.

Milo said, "Can you think of any reason she'd just leave?"

Blank looks.

"That's the point," said Mrs. Steinberg. "There'd be no reason for her to leave. She was happy here—why would she just leave?"

"Happy?" said Mrs. Sindowsky. "You ever see her smile?"

"All I'm saying, Dora," said Mrs. Steinberg, "is that after all this time maybe we have to assume the worst."

"Feh," said Morgenstern, shaking a thick fist. "Always with the gloom and doom. Chicken Little. The smog's falling."

"I've lived," said Mrs. Steinberg, drawing herself up, "through plenty. I know the way things are."

"Lived?" said Morgenstern. "And what've I been doing? Hanging on the wall like an oil painting?"

Milo looked at Mrs. Steinberg. "Besides the amount of time she's been gone, do you have any reason to assume the worst?"

All eyes focused on the black-haired woman. She looked uncomfortable. "It just doesn't make sense. Sophie wasn't the type to wander off. She was a very . . . regular person. Attached to her house, to her books. And she loved Venice—she'd lived here longer than any of us. Where would she go?"

"What about relatives?" said Milo. "She ever mention any?"

Rabbi Sanders said, "The only family she talked about were her brothers and sisters killed by the Nazis. She talked a lot about the Holocaust, the evils of fascism."

Mrs. Sindowsky said, "She talked a lot about politics, period."

"Tell the plain truth," said Morgenstern. "She was a Red."

"So?" said Mrs. Cooper. "That's some sort of crime in this free country, Sy? Expressing political views? Don't make to them like she was a criminal."

"Who says it's a crime?" Morgenstern retorted. "I'm only stating facts. The plain truth. What she was, was what she was. Red as a tomato."

"What does that make me?" said Mrs. Cooper.

"You, my darling?" said Morgenstern. "Let's say pink." Smile. "When you get excited, maybe a nice shade of fuchsia."

"Ahh," said the plump woman, turning her back on him and folding her arms under her bosom.

Milo said, "The poster says she disappeared around here. How did that happen?"

"We were having an evening social," said the rabbi. "A couple of weeks after Rosh Hashanah— Jewish New Year. Trying—"

"Trying to rejuvenate community spirit," Mrs. Sindowsky broke in, as if reciting from a lesson book. "Get a little action going, right, Rabbi?"

Sanders smiled at her, then turned to Milo. "Mrs. Gruenberg showed up but left after a short while. That was the last anyone saw her. I assumed she'd gone home. When the mail started piling up at her door, I got worried. I used my key and let myself into her unit and saw she was gone. I called the police. After forty-eight hours had passed, Detective Mehan agreed to come down."

"And the last time you saw her—at the social—was around eight?"

"Eight, eight-thirty," said Sanders. "That's only an estimate—the social began at seven-thirty and ended at nine. She wasn't there during the last half hour. We pulled up chairs and had a discussion. So she left some time before eight-thirty. No one's really sure."

"Did she bring a car or come on foot?"

"On foot. She didn't drive, liked to walk."

"It's gotten kind of tough around here to be walking at night," said Milo.

"Good of you to notice," said Morgenstern. "Days aren't so wonderful either."

"She wouldn't have worried about that?"

"She certainly should have," said Mrs. Steinberg. "With all the nogoodniks and lowlife hanging around, taking over the neighborhood—all the drugs. We used to enjoy the beach. You come around here during the week, Officer, and you won't see us taking the sun like we used to. All of us used to walk, to swim—that's why we moved here. It was paradise. Now when we go out at night, we take a car, in a group. Park it back on Speedway and walk to the *shul*, marching like a battalion of soldiers. On a nice summer night, a late sunset, maybe we'll take a longer walk. Still all together—as a group. Even then we feel nervous. But Sophie never joined in any of that. She wasn't a joiner. She lived here a long time, didn't want to admit things had changed. You couldn't talk to her—she was stubborn. She walked around like she owned the neighborhood."

"She liked to walk," said Sanders. "For exercise."

"Sometimes," said Morgenstern, "exercise isn't so healthy."

Mrs. Cooper frowned at him. He winked at her and smiled.

Milo said, "Rabbi, you lived next to her. What was her state of mind during the last few days before she disappeared?"

"The last few days?" said Sanders. He rolled his pipe in his palm. "Truthfully, she probably was very upset."

"Probably?"

"She wasn't one to express emotions openly. She kept to herself."

"Then why do you say she was upset?"

Sanders hesitated, looking first at his students, then Milo.

"There was," he said, "a crime. Someone she knew."

"What *crime*?" said Morgenstern. "*Say* it. A *murder*. Drugs and guns, the whole shebang.

Some black boy she was renting to. He got shot, over drugs." He squinted and his eyebrows merged like mating caterpillars. "Aha! *That's* the big secret you can't tell us about, right?"

Milo said, "Do you know anything about that?"

Silence.

Mrs. Sindowsky said, "Just what we heard from the rabbi here. She had a tenant; he got shot."

"None of you knew him?"

Shakes of heads.

"I knew *of* him but not *him*," said Mrs. Cooper.

"What did you know?"

"That she'd taken in a boarder. Once I saw him on his little motorbike, driving home. Nice-looking boy. Very big."

"There was plenty of talk," said Morgenstern.

"What kind of talk?" Milo said.

"A black kid—whadya think? Was she putting herself in danger." Morgenstern looked accusingly at the women. They seemed embarrassed. "Everyone's nice and liberal," he said, "till it comes to putting the mouth where the money is. But Sophie was a Red—it was just the kind of thing she'd do. You think he got her into some kind of trouble, the kid? Keeping his dope money in the house—they came to get it and got *her*?"

Milo said, "No. There's no evidence of that."

Morgenstern gave him a conspiratorial wink. "No evidence, but you're coming around asking questions. The plot thickens, eh, Mr. Policeman? More meat, more worms."

Milo asked a few more questions, determined they had nothing else to offer, and thanked them. We left, replacing our skullcaps in the leather box on the way out, walked a ways up Ocean Front, and had a cup of coffee at a teriyaki stand. Milo glared at the winos hanging around the stand and they drifted away, like sloughing dead skin. He sipped, running his gaze up and down the walk-street, letting it settle on the synagogue.

After a few moments all four old people came out of the building and walked off together, Morgenstern in the lead. An elderly battalion. When they were out of view, Milo tossed his coffee cup in the trash and said, "Come on."

The dead bolts on the synagogue's doors were locked. Milo's knock brought Sanders to the door.

The rabbi had put a gray suit jacket over his shirt, had his pipe in his mouth, still unlit, and was holding an oversized maroon book with marbled page-ends.

"A little more of your time, Rabbi?"

Sanders held the door open and we stepped into the anteroom. Most of the cookies were gone and only two cans of soda remained.

"Can I offer you anything?" said Sanders. He slid the book into one of the cases.

"No thanks, Rabbi."

"Shall we go back in the sanctuary?"

"This is fine, thanks. I was just wondering if there was anything you hadn't felt comfortable discussing in front of your students."

"Students." Sanders smiled. "They've taught me a good deal more than I've taught them. This is only a part-time job. Weekdays I teach at an elementary school in the Fairfax district. I conduct services here on weekends, give classes Sundays, run an occasional social evening."

"Sounds like a full schedule."

Sanders shrugged and adjusted his yarmulke. "Five children. Los Angeles is an expensive city. That's how I came to know Sophie—Mrs. Gruenberg. Finding affordable housing's impossible, especially with children. People in this city don't seem to like children. Mrs. Gruenberg didn't mind at all, even though she wasn't very . . . grandmotherly. And she was very reasonable about the rent. She said it was because we—my wife and I—had ideals, she respected us for them. Even though she herself had no use for religion. Marxism was her faith. She really was an unregenerate communist."

"She generally pretty vocal about her political views?"

"If one asked her, she'd speak her mind. But she didn't go about volunteering them—she wasn't a gregarious woman. Quite the opposite. Kept to herself."

"Not a joiner?"

Sanders nodded. "I tried to get her more involved in the synagogue, but she had no interest in religion, wasn't at all sociable. Truthfully, she wasn't the most popular person. But the others do care about her. They all look out for one another. Wanted to dip into their own pockets in order to hire the private detective. But none of them can afford it—they're all on pension. Detective Mehan told me it would probably be a waste of money, so I discouraged it, promised to bring it to the Federation again. Her vanishing has really frightened them—they're slapped in the face by their own helplessness. That's why I'm glad you returned when they were gone. Talking about Ike could only upset them more. That is what you want to talk about, isn't it?"

"Why'd Detective Mehan feel it was a waste of time?"

Sanders lowered his gaze and bit his lip. "He told me—and this is something I haven't told them—that it didn't look good. The fact that she hadn't made plans to leave meant there was a good chance she'd met up with foul play. The fact that her apartment was in order meant it had taken place on the street—as she walked home. He said that if she'd gotten lost and wandered away or had a stroke, she would have turned up by three weeks. One way or the other. He said private detectives could find people, but weren't much use discovering bodies."

He looked up. Blue eyes still. Jamming the pipe in his mouth, he bit down so hard his jaws bunched and the beard bristled.

Milo said, "She's your landlady. Is there a mortgage on the building?"

Sanders shook his head. "No, she owns it free and clear—has for several years. Detective Mehan found that out when he checked into her finances."

"What about other bills that come in? Who pays them?"

"I do. It doesn't come out to much—just utilities. I've also been collecting all her mail. What looks like a bill, I open and pay. I know it's not perfectly legal to do that, but Detective Mehan assured me it would be all right."

"What about your rent check?"

"I've opened an interest-earning account, deposited the October and November checks in there. It seemed the best thing to do until we learn . . . something."

"Where do you keep her mail, Rabbi?"

"Right here, in the synagogue, under lock and key."

"I'd like to see it."

He said, "Certainly," put his pipe in his jacket pocket, and went into the sanctuary. We watched him unlock a cabinet in back of the podium and draw out two manila envelopes, which he brought back and handed to Milo. One was marked SEPT/OCT.; the other, NOV.

Milo said, "This is all of it?"

"This is it." Sad look.

Milo opened the envelopes, removed the contents, and spread them out on the ledge of the bookcase. He inspected each piece of mail. Mostly flyers and computer-addressed bulk mail. *Occupant* appearing more frequently than her name. A few utility bills that had been opened and marked *Paid,* followed by dates of payments.

Sanders said, "I was hoping there'd be something personal, to give us a clue. But she wasn't very . . . connected to the outside world." His baby face had grown sad. Stuffing one hand in his pocket, he groped until he found his pipe.

Milo slid the mail back in the manila envelopes. "Is there anything else you want to tell me, Rabbi?"

Sanders rubbed the bowl of the pipe against his nose.

"Just one thing," he said. "And Detective Mehan filed a report on it, so you should have a record of it somewhere. The old people don't know this either—I didn't see any point in telling them. A few days after she disappeared—that was a Tuesday; this happened sometime over the weekend—burglars broke into the house. Into both our places. My family and I were out of town, at a school retreat in the city. Detective Mehan said it was probably a drug addict looking for things to sell. A coward: he'd watched the house—staked us out—waited until we were gone, and moved in."

"What was taken?"

"As far as I could tell, what he took from Sophie was a television, a radio, a silver-plated samovar, and some inexpensive jewelry. From us, even less—we don't have a television. All he got from us was some flatware, a ritual spice box and candleholder, and a tape recorder I use for teaching Hebrew. But he made a mess. Both units were in a shambles—food taken out of the refrigerator and thrown around, drawers opened, papers scattered. Detective Mehan said it showed signs of a disorganized mind. Immaturity—teenagers, or someone on drugs."

"What was the point of entry?"

"Through the back doors. I've since had new locks put on and bars on the windows. Now my children look out through bars."

He shook his head.

"The material loss was trivial," he said, "but

332   JONATHAN KELLERMAN

the feeling of violation—and hatred. The way the food was strewn about seemed so spiteful. And something else . . . that made it seem . . . personal."

"What's that, Rabbi?"

"He—the addict or whoever—wrote on the walls. In red paint that he took from the garage— the same red paint I'd just used a week before to paint the windows. It resembled blood. Hateful stuff—anti-Semitism. Profanities—I had to cover my children's eyes. And something else that I found very strange: *Remember John Kennedy!* Several exclamation points after the word *Kennedy*. Which doesn't make any logical sense, does it? Kennedy was anti-racist. But Detective Mehan said if he'd been crazy on drugs, he couldn't be expected to make sense. So I suppose that would explain it."

He frowned, chewed on the pipe some more.

Milo said, "You don't like that explanation?"

"It's not that," said Sanders. "It's . . . nothing tangible. Just a feeling my wife and I have had. Since Ike. Since Sophie. As if we're in jeopardy—someone's out there, intending to harm us. Despite the locks and the bars. Not that there ever is anyone, when I actually look, so I suppose it's nerves. I tell myself this is simply the way America is—learn to get used to it. But my wife wants us to move back to Auckland. That's New Zealand. Things were different there."

"How long have you been in L.A.?"

"Just since July. Before that, we lived in Lakewood, New Jersey. I studied at a seminary there, did have occasion to visit New York City, so I guess I should have been prepared for urban life. But in California I expected things to be more . . . relaxed."

"The term is *laid back,* Rabbi. Unfortunately, for the most part it's a facade."

"Seems to be."

"Since the break-in, have you and your family had any other problems?"

"Nothing, thank God."

Milo reached into a coat pocket, drew out the photo he'd taken from Dinwiddie, and held it in front of the rabbi's baby face.

"Yes, that's Ike," said Sanders. "Did his death have anything to do with Sophie?"

"Nothing as far as we know, Rabbi. What can you tell me about him?"

"Not much at all. I barely knew him. We passed each other a few times—that was all."

"How long had he been living here before he was killed?"

Sanders shook his head. "I don't know. My feeling was it had been for a while."

"Why's that?"

"They—he and Sophie—had a . . . comfortable relationship. As if they'd settled in with each other."

"They get along pretty well?"

"Seemed to." Sanders put his pipe in his mouth, then removed it. "Actually, they debated quite a bit. We could hear it through the walls. To be frank, she was a cantankerous old lady. But she and Ike did seem to have a certain . . . not rapport—I'd call it ease. He did chores for her, gardening, brought her groceries—I believe he worked at a grocery store. And the fact that she had him living with her, right in the apartment, would imply a great deal of trust, wouldn't it?"

"Any reason for her not to trust him?"

Sanders shook his head. "No, I didn't mean that at all. The racial thing has no personal relevance for me. But it is unusual. The old people have had bad experiences with black men—they tend to fear them. Not that there was any reason to fear Ike. From the few contacts I had with him he seemed a very good chap. Polite, pleasant. The only thing I did find unusual about him was his interest in the Holocaust."

"Unusual in what way?"

"The fact that he was interested in it at all. Someone his age, not Jewish—it's not a common interest, don't you agree? Though I suppose living with Sophie made it not that unusual. It was a favorite topic of hers—she may have passed it along to Ike."

"How do you know he was interested in it?"

"Because of an occurrence, last summer,

about a week after we'd moved in. I ran into him
in the garage. I was unpacking boxes and he'd just
driven in on his motor scooter. He was carrying a
huge armful of books and he dropped them. I
helped him pick them up. I noticed a title—
something about the origins of the Nazi party. I
opened it and saw from the bookplate that it had
come from the Holocaust Center—over on Pico,
in West L.A. So had the others I picked up. I
asked him if he was doing a school paper and he
smiled and said no, it was a personal research
project. I offered to help him if he needed it, but
he just smiled again and said he had everything he
needed. I thought it unusual, but I was pleased.
That someone his age would take an interest. Most
people his age have no idea what happened fifty
years ago."

"What did he and Mrs. Gruenberg used to
argue about?"

"Not arguments, in the sense of quarreling.
When I said debates, I meant discussions."

"Loud discussions?"

"Lively discussions, but we couldn't make
out the words—we weren't listening. Knowing
Sophie, though, my assumption would be politics."

"Any idea what Novato's political views
were?"

"None whatsoever." Sanders thought for a

moment. "Officer, do you suspect a political connection to . . . what happened?"

"No evidence of that either, Rabbi. How was Mrs. Gruenberg affected by Novato's death?"

"As I said before, I assumed she was upset. But I didn't see much of her reaction, because she stayed in her unit and didn't come out much after it happened. In retrospect, I realize that was odd—she used to be out in the yard hanging laundry, or taking her walks around the neighborhood. I only found out about the murder because another policeman—a black man whose name I don't remember—came by the house and asked me a few questions. About Ike. Did he use drugs? I told him, not to my knowledge. Who did he hang around with? I'd never seen anyone. Then he asked me about Sophie. Did *she* use drugs? Did she buy expensive things that she couldn't seem to afford? That, I laughed at. But when he—the black detective—told me why he'd come, I stopped laughing. After he left, I went over to Sophie's unit and knocked on the door. She didn't answer. I didn't want to violate her privacy, so I left her alone. I tried the next day, but she still didn't answer. I started to worry—with an old person, anything can happen—but I decided to wait a while before using my key. Shortly after, I saw her come out, walking toward Rose Avenue. Looking angry. Very grim. I went after her, tried to talk to her, but she just shook her head and kept walking. The next time I saw her was here at the synagogue. She came to the social. Given her state of mind, that surprised me. But she kept to herself, avoiding people. Walking around the room, looking all around, touching the walls, the seats. Almost as if she were seeing it all for the first time."

"Or the last," said Milo.

Sanders's eyes widened. He held the pipe with two hands, as if it had suddenly grown heavy.

"Yes, you're right," he said. "That could have been it. Seeing it for the last time. Saying goodbye."

20

When we got back to the pay lot, the Ford was in easy-exit position. The Filipino attendant stopped traffic on Speedway to let us out. Milo didn't acknowledge the courtesy.

I said, "Swastikas on cars, hate messages on walls. What do you think?"

He said, "I think the world's a kind and compassionate place," and nudged the car through the pedestrian jumble. The pedestrians weren't feeling cooperative today. Milo cursed as he inched forward, but his heart wasn't in it.

I said, " 'Remember Kennedy.' It doesn't make much sense. Unless it was a warning, not a tribute. As in, remember what happened to Kennedy—we'll get you too."

"Who's warning who?"

I said, "I don't know," and grew silent.

He smiled. "Starting to see evil everywhere? Sounds like a peace officer's perspective."

"Speaking of peace officers, this Mehan a good cop?"

"Very good."

"Think he and Smith ever compared notes?"

He gave me a sharp look. "What is this, the Police Review Board?"

"Just wondering."

"Wondering what? If one arm of the octopus knows what the other's doing? Usually not. But what if Mehan and Smith did put their heads together. What would they have ended up with? *Double* dead ends."

I said, "The dope thing might have led them somewhere. Smith was thinking in that direction—the rabbi said he was asking if Gruenberg had been involved in drugs. Not that that seems likely."

"Why not?"

"Little old dope granny? She sure wasn't living the life-style."

"Alex, most likely Smith *was* just fishing—working with what he had, which in this case was close to zero. But the way things have turned, you can't eliminate anyone. All the money to be made—it's loony tunes out there. We're getting old ladies packing their supp-hose with the stuff; people cuddling sweet little babies, the bunting's crammed full of white powder; cripples using false limbs. And Gruenberg's profile doesn't contradict a dope granny—she had radical political views, which means she might not have been so reluctant to buck the establishment. She keeps to herself, doesn't like company, and has Novato bunking in with her—some kid out of nowhere, with no ID, no past, and she's got him living in the same unit with her. A black kid. Even for Venice, that's strange—you saw how the other oldsters thought so. Then, just a few days after he's snuffed, she's gone. Maybe he was a commie too—that was the connection between them. Maybe the two of them had some political thing going. Hell, maybe that's where the dough went."

"Cash for the cause?"

"You want to speculate, I'll speculate."

I thought about it as he wrestled with the steering wheel and finally got back on Pacific. "Milo, if Gruenberg was involved in the dope scene, she could have made someone mad, and run out of fear. Or maybe the people she was afraid of got to her first. What if she'd ended up with a cash-flow or a dope-flow problem, and the break-in at her place was someone looking to collect?"

"Maybe," he said. "But the other thing you've got to consider is that junkies *are* prime opportunists. The posters could have tipped them off that she was gone; her place was vacant, a perfect target. The bottom line is, all of this is just head-tripping—we don't know shit."

A block later I said, "Could Holly have been

involved with them—Gruenberg and Novato's cabal?"

"*Cabal*? An old lady, a bag boy, and a retarded kid who isn't on anyone's subversive list? Not much of a cabal."

"She wasn't retarded—"

"Okay, just stupid. Same difference."

"I didn't say it was a competent cabal. Two of them are dead and one's missing. But maybe Holly's shooting at Massengil was politically motivated."

"If it was Massengil she was shooting at."

"If."

Milo came to a short stop at Washington Boulevard.

"Too weird, Alex. Got a headache." He drove into a self-serve gas station with a mini-mart at the back of the lot. I waited in the Ford as he purchased a packet of aspirin. Before he returned to the car, he went to the pay phone and stayed there for a while, popping tablets, feeding quarters and talking, the receiver tucked up under his chin. Making two calls.

When he came back, he said, "Mehan's out of town, two weeks' vacation, no one knows where any of his files are, they'll get back to me."

"Who was the second call to?"

He looked at me. "What a *sleuth*! I tried the Holocaust Center, wanted to leave a message for someone I know there. Got a tape, they're closed Sundays."

"That's right," I said. "They know you. You helped them trace that Nazi scientist—the one the army protected."

"Good old Werner Kaltenblud, president of the Poison Gas Club. Bastard's still alive in Syria, living like royalty, unrepentant. I've got a more recent connection to the Center. Last year someone painted swastikas on the side of the museum building they're putting up. Not my usual thing, but they called me because of Kaltenblud. Then it hit the news and the brass took over. ATD."

"Frisk?"

"No. The asshole who preceded him, but same old story: TV crews and politicos making speeches—Gordon Latch, in fact."

"How about Massengil?"

"Nope. Not his district."

"Maybe not his area of interest, either."

"Could be. It was a real circus, Alex. ATD playing *I Spy,* asking lots of clever questions, filing lots of paper, but they never bothered to surveill. Next week there were broken windows and an arson fire in one of the trailers out back in the construction site. We never found out who did any of it. So much for my credibility. But maybe I've still got enough good-will residue for them to think back and try to remember something about this Novato kid. Something more than his library card."

He turned left on Washington, driving parallel with the Marina. A different kind of crowd here. White slacks and deep tans and aggressive little foreign cars. The boulevard was lined with new construction—mostly low-rise designer office buildings festooned with reminders of an architectural heritage that had never existed, and nautical theme restaurants draped with BRUNCH! and HAPPY HOUR! banners.

"Pretty, huh?" said Milo. "The good life reigns."

He drove a couple of blocks, turned off on a street that dead-ended a block later. Small houses, in varying stages of gentrification. Cars lining the street, no people. He parked in front of a hydrant, left the motor running, got out, and opened the trunk.

He came back carrying a shotgun. Clamped it to the dashboard, barrel-up, and pulled the car out onto the street.

I said, "Where to?"

"Somewhere not so pretty."

He got back on Washington, took it to the Marina Freeway, switched to the 405, wrestled with the airport jam for a while, and got off on Imperial Highway heading east. Bordering the off-ramp were the broad gray lots of shipping terminals, import-export companies, and customs brokers, and a four-story self-storage facility that looked like the box an office building would come in. A red light halted us at the intersection of La Cienega and Imperial, and we waited it out, staring at the colossal truncated bulk of the unfinished Century Freeway: hundred-foot concrete dinosaur legs supporting a six-lane slab that ended in mid-air and was fringed with curling steel veins—a messy amputation.

The green arrow appeared and Milo turned. The terrain deteriorated rudely to a block of scabrous one-story buildings on a dry-dust lot. A pool hall, a liquor store, and a bar advertising "nude table dancers," all plywood-boarded and choked with graffiti. Even sin couldn't flourish here.

But a block later there were signs of revitalization. Weekly-rate motels, auto shops, car dealerships, wig stores, and run-down apartments. Several beautifully kept churches, a couple of shopping centers. The sprawling campus of Southwestern College. And for color, the Golden Arches and its rainbow-hued clones—modular fast-food setups so clean and unscarred they might have been dropped into the neighborhood just minutes before by some clumsy Franchise Stork.

Milo said, "Taking the scenic route."

I said, "Long time since I've been down here."

"Didn't know you'd ever been down here.

Most folks of the fair-pigment persuasion never find the opportunity."

"Grad school," I said. "First year. I was a research assistant on a Head Start program trying to increase the reading skills of ghetto kids. I took an interest in one of the children—a very bright little boy named Eric. I visited him a couple of times at home—I can still picture the place. He lived on Budlong, near 103rd. Nice-looking building, not at all what I expected for the area. Widowed mother, the father had been shot in Vietnam. Grandma helping out—place was neat as a pin. Lots of pressure from both Mom and Grandma for Eric to get A's, become a doctor or a lawyer."

"How old was he?"

"Five."

Milo whistled. "Long ways to med school."

"Fortunately he had the brains for it."

"What happened to him?"

"I followed him for a couple of years—phone calls, Christmas cards. He was still getting A's. And starting to develop bad stomachaches. I was going up to San Francisco for my internship. Referred the mother to a good pediatrician and a community mental health center. After that, we just kind of lost touch. He'd be college age by now. Amazing. I have no idea what happened to him. Guess that makes me your typical superficial do-gooder, huh?"

Milo didn't say anything. I noticed he was driving faster than usual. Two hands on the wheel. As we zipped eastward, the business establishments grew smaller, sadder, rattier, and I noticed a certain consistency to their distribution: check-cashing outlets, rib joints, nail palaces, liquor stores. Lots of liquor stores. Thin dark men lounged against filthy stucco walls, holding paper bags, smoking, staring off into space. A few women in shorts and rollers sashayed by and caught whistles. But for the most part the streets were deserted—that much South Central and Beverly Hills had in common. A quarter mile farther, even the liquor stores couldn't make it. Plywood storefronts became as common as glass. Movie theaters converted to churches converted to garbage dumps. Vacant lots. Impromptu auto graveyards. Entire blocks of dead buildings shadowing the occasional ragpicker or stray child. More young men, glutted with time, starved of hope. Not a white face in sight.

Milo turned left on Broadway, drove until 108th, and made a right. We passed an enormous, windowless brown brick fortress.

"Southeast Division," he said. "But we're not meeting him there."

He drove for another few miles, through silent residential blocks of tiny, characterless bungalows. Ocher and pink and turquoise texture-coat competed with the angry black-and-Dayglo tangle of gang scrawl. Dirt lawns were surrounded by sheets of chain link. Undernourished dogs scrounged through the trash that lined the curbs. A quick turn took us to 111th. Another led us into a cracked-asphalt alley lined with an alternating band of garage doors and more chain link.

A group of black men in their early twenties loitered midway down the alley. When they saw the Ford cruising toward them, they stared defiantly, then sauntered away and disappeared into one of the garages.

Milo said, "Strictly speaking, this isn't Watts—that's farther east. But same difference."

He turned off the engine and pocketed the keys, then unclasped the shotgun.

"This is where it happened," he said. "Novato. You want to stay in the car, feel free."

He got out. I did the same.

"Place used to be a major crack alley," he said, looking up and down, holding the shotgun in one hand. "Then it got cleaned up—one of those neighborhood group things. Then it got bad again. Depends what week you're here."

His eyes kept moving. To each end of the alley. To the garage doors. I followed his gaze and saw the pock and splinter of bullet holes in stucco and wood—malignant blackheads among the graffiti blemish. The ground was struggling clumps of weeds, garbage, used condoms, cellophane packets, empty matchbooks, the cheap-jewelry glitter of foil scraps. The air stank of dog shit and decomposed food.

"You tell me," said Milo. "Can you think of any reason for him to come down here except for dope?"

The sound of a car engine from the north end of the alley made both of us turn. Milo lifted the shotgun and held it with both hands.

What looked like another unmarked. A Matador. Sage-green.

Milo relaxed.

The car nosed up next to the Ford. The man who got out was about my age, medium-sized and trim, very dark, cleanshaven, with a medium Afro. He wore a banker's pin-striped gray suit, white button-down shirt, red silk tie, and glossy black wing-tips. Square-jawed and straight-backed and very handsome, but, despite the good posture, tired-looking.

Milo said, "Maury."

"Milo. Congratulations on the promotion."

"Thanks."

The two of them shook hands. Smith looked at me. His face was beautifully shaved and fragrant with good cologne. But his eyes were weary and bloodshot under long thick lashes.

Milo said, "This is Dr. Alex Delaware. He's a shrink, called in to work with the kids at Hale School. He was the one who discovered the connection between the Burden girl and your guy.

Been a department consultant for years but had never done a ride-along. I thought Southeast might be instructive."

"Doctor," said Smith. His grip was very firm, very dry. To Milo: "If you wanted to be instructive, how come you didn't give him his own shotgun?"

Milo smiled.

Smith took out a pack of Marlboros, lit one, and said, "Anyway."

Milo said, "Where exactly did it go down?"

"Far as I can remember," said Smith, "just about exactly where you're parked. Hard to recall with all the shootings we get around here. I brought the file—hold on."

He went back to his car, opened the passenger door, leaned in, and pulled out a folder. Handing it to Milo, he said, "Don't show the pictures to the doctor here unless you want to lose yourself a consultant."

"That bad?"

"Shotgun, from up close—you know what that does. He must have put his hands up in a defensive reflex because they got shredded to pieces—I'm talking confetti. The face was . . . shotgun stuff. Barely enough blood left in him by the time the crime-scene boys arrived. But he was dope-positive all right. Coke and booze and downers—regular walking pharmacy."

Milo thumbed through the folder, his face

impassive. I moved closer and looked down. Sheets of paper. Lots of typewritten police prose. A couple of photos taped to the top. Living color. Long-view crime-scene shots and close-ups of something lying face-up on the filthy asphalt. Something ragged and wet that had once been human.

My stomach churned. I looked away but struggled to remain outwardly calm.

Smith had been watching me. He said, "I guess you guys see that stuff—medical school and all that."

"He's a Ph.D." said Milo.

"Ph.D.," said Smith. "Philosophy doctor." He stretched his arm down the alley. "Any ideas about the philosophy of a place like this?"

I shook my head and smiled. As Milo read, Smith kept checking the alley. I was struck by the silence of the place—a sickly, contrived silence, like that of a mortuary. Devoid of birdsong or traffic, the hum of commerce or conversation. I entertained postnuclear fantasies. Then all at once, noise intruded with all the shock and harshness of an armed robber: the scream and wobble of an ambulance siren from afar, followed by high-pitched human screams—an ugly duet of domestic violence—from somewhere close. Smith gave a distasteful look, glanced at Milo's shotgun, opened his suit jacket, and touched the butt of the revolver that lay nestled in his shoulder holster. Then silence again.

"Okay. Let's see. Ah, here's the toxicology," said Milo, flipping pages. "Yeah, the guy was definitely fried."

"Deep-fried," said Smith, sniffing. "Why else would he be down here?"

Milo said, "One thing I wonder about, Maury. The kid lives in Venice. Ocean Front's a pharmacy in its own right—why bother coming down here?"

Smith thought for a moment and said, "Maybe he didn't like the brand they were selling locally. People do that now—get picky. The businessmen we're dealing with nowadays are into packaging and labeling. Dry Ice, Sweet Dreams, Medellin Mouton—choose your poison. Or maybe he was a businessman himself—selling, not buying, came here to collect something the boys over in Venice weren't providing."

"Maybe," said Milo.

"Why else?" said Smith. "Anyway, don't lose too much sleep over it. If I wasted my time trying to second-guess junkies and wet-heads, might as well nail my foot to the floor and run in circles all day." He puffed on his cigarette.

Milo said, "Yeah, saw your stats on the last report."

"Grim," said Smith. "Wholly uncivilized."

He smoked and nodded, tapped one wing-tip

and kept looking up and down the alley. The silence had returned.

Milo returned the file to him. "Not much in the way of background on him—no priors, no history, no family."

"Phantom of the opera," said Smith. "Sucker came right out of nowhere, no files on him anywhere. Which fits if he was an amateur businessman. They're getting crafty. Organized. Buying phony paper, moving around a lot, hiding behind layers, just like the corporations do. They've even got subsidiaries. In other cities, other states. Novato told his landlady he was from somewhere back east—that's as specific as I got. She forgot exactly where. Or didn't want to remember."

"Think she was lying?"

"Maybe. She was something, that one— flaming commie, didn't like cops, wasn't shy about telling you. Being with her was like being back in the sixties, when we were the enemies. Before *Miami Vice* made it hip to oink."

Smith laughed at his own wit, smoked, and said, "Nice to be hip, right, Milo? Take it to the bank, try to get a loan."

Milo said, "She tell you *anything*?"

"Diddly. It was all I could do to get her to let me in her house. She was real uppity. Actually called me a *cossack*—asked me how did it feel to be a black cossack. Like I was some kind of traitor to the race. *You* get anything out of her?"

"Couldn't," said Milo. "She's gone. Disappeared four days after Novato got hit. No one's seen or heard from her since."

Surprise widened Smith's weary eyes. He said, "Who's on the case?"

"Hal Mehan out of Pacific. He's on vacation, back in two weeks. From what I can gather, he did the usual missing-persons stuff, found out she hadn't packed or taken money out of the bank. Followed it for a couple of weeks and told her friends to hire a P.I. or forget about it. Told her neighbor it looked like foul play out on the streets."

Smith's foot tapped faster. "Mehan know about Novato?"

"The friends say they told him."

Smith said, "Hmm." His eyes half-closed.

Milo said, "Yeah, I know, he coulda told you. Shoulda. But the bottom line is you didn't lose anything. He dead-ended, moved on to greener pastures. The next-door neighbor saved her mail—I just had a look at it. Not much of it, just junk and a few bills."

Smith continued to look perturbed. "Who are these friends of hers? No one in the neighborhood seemed to know much about her. Only one who knew anything at all was the guy next door, some kind of English rabbi. He the one who saved the mail?"

Milo nodded. "Just spoke to him. The friends were a few old folk she knew from temple. Acquaintances more than friends. According to them she wasn't sociable, kept to herself."

"That's true," said Smith. "Man, that was some little old battle-ax."

"They also said she didn't have any family. Same as Novato."

Smith said, "Think that means anything?"

"Who knows?" said Milo. "Coulda been misery loving company. Two loners finding each other."

Smith said, "Black kid and an old white woman? Some company. Or maybe the two of them were up to something, huh? When I went around there on the Novato thing, saw how hostile and radical she was, how she didn't even want me to come *inside*, I asked around about her being involved in a dope thing. Asked the neighbors about people coming in and out at weird hours, fancy cars parked outside—the usual thing. No one knew anything."

"No one still does," said Milo. "There's one other thing you should know. A few days after she was gone, someone burglarized her place. The rabbi's too. Took small stuff, trashed everything, wrote nasty stuff on the walls."

"What kind of nasty stuff?"

"Anti-Semitic. And something about remembering John Kennedy, in red paint they'd stolen from the garage. That jibe with any of the gang stuff you've been seeing?"

Smith said, "Kennedy? No. There's some punk band—the Dead Kennedys. That's all that comes to mind." He thought. "If they got the paint right there, doesn't sound like they came to paint."

"Could have been just an opportunist junkie," said Milo. "Asshole got caught up in the intruder high and got artistically inspired."

Smith nodded. "Like a shitter." To me: "There're these guys break into houses, steal stuff, and dump a load on the floor. Or the bed. What do you think of that, psychologically? Or philosophically?"

"Power trip," I said. "Forbidden fruit. Leave a signature someone'll remember. Same as the ones who ejaculate. Or eat all the food in the fridge."

Smith nodded.

"Anyway," said Milo, "just thought you should know about all this."

"Thanks," said Smith. "In terms of a dope thing, I ran Novato through NCIC, the moniker files, DEA, called every smart narc in the Department as well as the Sheriff's guys. Nothing. The kid had no name in the business."

"Maybe he was a newcomer," said Milo.

"Trying to move in on someone and it got him dead."

"A newcomer," I said. "Novato. I'm pretty sure that's Spanish for 'novice.'"

Both of them looked at me.

I said, "Latin name on a black kid. It could be an alias."

"El Novato, huh?" said Smith. "Well, it's not a moniker—least not one of the ones we've got on file. Guess it could be an alias." He enunciated and put on a Spanish accent. "El Novato. Kind of like El Vato Loco. Sounds like something out of Boyle Heights, but this bro was black."

"Anything left of the fingers to print?" said Milo.

Smith shook his head. "You saw the pictures."

"How'd you ID him?"

"Wallet in pocket. He had a driver's license—that's it—and a business card from the place he worked at, some grocery. I called his boss, asked him about any family to notify. He said he didn't know of any. Later, after no one had claimed the body, I called the boss again, told him if he wanted, he could claim it, give it a decent burial."

"Spoke to him, too," said Milo. "He cremated it."

"Guess that's a decent burial," said Smith.

"Doesn't make much difference one way or the other when you're that way, does it?"

More screams from down the alley. The same two people tearing at each other with words.

Smith said, "I'll probably be back in the near future, pick up one of *their* bodies. Anything more you want to know about Novato?"

Milo said, "That's all that comes to mind, Maury. Thanks."

"Far as I'm concerned, Milo, good riddance. If he was a businessman on top of doping, and getting hit slowed his business, I'm even happier. One less piece of shit to keep track of."

Smith dropped his cigarette and ground it out with his heel.

"How well did the Burden girl know Novato?"

"They were seen talking to each other. Probably means nothing. I'm just following the chain wherever it leads. If there turns out to be a connection, I'll call you in."

"Yeah," said Smith. "That'd be real nice. Meantime, how about you remember me when the West L.A. roster opens up. I put in an application last year—no vacancies. Wouldn't mind getting over to civilized territory. Catch a little breathing time between homicidal incidents. Your promotion, you could have some say in it, right?"

"That kind of thing gets handled higher," said Milo, "but I'll do my best."

"Appreciate it. Could use some civilization."

"So he was a doper," I said, after Smith had driven away. "So much for Dinwiddie's expertise."

"Wishful thinking," said Milo, "does strange things to the old judgment quotient."

He avoided the streets on the way back, getting on the Harbor Freeway and taking it through the downtown interchange into the West Side of town. Neither of us said much. Milo seemed eager to get away.

I got to Linda's apartment at eight. She came to the door wearing a black silk blouse, gray jeans, and black western boots. Her hair had been done up, fastened by a silver comb. She had on large silver hoop earrings, blush that accented her cheekbones, more eye shadow than I'd seen before, and a look of reserve that forced its way through her smile. I was feeling it, too—a reticence, almost a shyness. As if this were a first date: everything that had happened two nights ago had been a fantasy, and we needed to start from scratch.

She said, "Hi, right on time," took my hand, and led me inside. There was a bottle of Chablis and two glasses on the coffee table, along with dishes of sliced raw vegetables, crackers, dip, and cubes of cheese.

She said, "Just a nip before dinner."

"Looks great." I sat down. She took a place beside me, poured wine, and said, "How about a toast?"

"Let's see. Things have been pretty nuts lately. So how about: to boredom."

"Hear, hear."

We touched glasses and drank.

She said, "So . . . what's new?"

There was plenty to tell her: Mahlon Burden in his natural habitat, Novato and Gruenberg. Savaged cars. Neo-Nazis in suburbia, a crack alley . . .

I said, "Let's honor the toast for a little while."

She laughed and said, "Sure."

We munched vegetables, drank some more.

"Got something to show you," she said, got up, and crossed the room toward her bedroom. The jeans showed off her shape. The boots had very high heels and they did something to her walk that convinced me two nights ago had been real.

She came back with a boom box. "Amazing the sound you can get from one of these."

She set it up on the coffee table, next to the food. "Takes cassettes and compact discs."

Looking like a kid on Christmas morning, she set the control on battery, pressed EJECT, and

handed me the compact disc that slid out. Kenny
G: *Silhouette*.

She said, "I know you like jazz—saxophone.
So I thought this might be right. Is it?"

I smiled. "It's great. That was really nice of
you." I popped the disc back in and pressed PLAY.

Sweet soprano sounds filled the small apartment.

She said, "Umm, that's pretty," and sat back
down. We listened. After a while I put my arm
around her. During the brief dead time between
the first and second cuts on the disc, we kissed.
Gently, with restraint—a deliberate holding back
that was mutual.

She pulled away, said, "It's good to see
you."

"Good to see you too." I touched her face,
traced her jawline. She closed her eyes and sat
back.

We stayed locked in a lovely inertia. Kenny
G did his thing. It seemed a personal serenade.
After the fourth cut, we forced ourselves up and
left.

We went to the galleries, taking in the newer
places on La Brea, looking at lots of bad art, a few
experiments that succeeded. The last gallery we
visited was brand-new and a surprise—older stuff,
by L.A. standards. Early twentieth-century works
on paper. I found something I wanted and could

afford: a George Bellows boxing print, one of the minor ones. I'd missed getting one from the same edition at an auction last year. After some deliberation I bought it and had it wrapped to go.

"Like the fights?" she said as we left the gallery.

"Not in the flesh. But on paper it makes for good composition."

"Daddy used to take me when I was little. I hated it, all the grunting and the blood. But I was too afraid to tell him." She smoothed her hair, closed her eyes. "I called him today."

"How'd it go?"

"Easier than I thought. His . . . wife answered. She was kind of cool. But he actually sounded happy to hear from me. Agreeable— almost too agreeable. Old. I don't know if it's because it's been such a long time or he's really aged that much. He asked me when I was coming back for a visit. I beat around the bush, didn't give him a straight answer. Even if I wanted to go back, so much else is going on right now. By the way, I confirmed your parents' group for tomorrow. Should be a good turnout—" She stopped herself. "Ah, the toast. Viva boredom."

"Forget the toast if you feel like it."

"I don't feel like it," she said, and put her arm around my waist.

We got to the car. I put the print in the trunk and drove to a place on Melrose: Northern Italian food, seating inside and out on the patio. The night breeze was kind—the sort of caressing warmth that keeps people moving to L.A. despite the phoniness and the madness—and we chose outside. Small lacy trees in straw-covered pots separated the patio from the sidewalk. White lattice partitions had been set up around groupings of tables, affording the illusion of privacy.

The waiter was a pony-tailed recent acting-class graduate playing the part of Solicitous Server and he recited what seemed like an endless list of specials with the hubris of a memory course graduate. The lighting was so dim—just a single covered candle on each table—that we had to lean forward to make out the menus. We were hungry by now and ordered an antipasto, seafood salads, two kinds of veal, and a bottle of Pellegrino water.

Conversation came easily but we stayed faithful to the toast. When the food came, we concentrated on eating. Solicitous wheeled the dessert cart tableside and Linda chose a monumental cream and hazelnut thing that looked as if baking it required a building permit. I ordered a lemon ice. When she was halfway through the pastry, she wiped cream from her lips and said, "I think I can handle reality. Okay if we ditch the boredom pledge?"

"Sure."

"Then tell me about the Burden girl's home. What was the father like? Can you talk about it?"

"In terms of confidentiality? Yes. One of the conditions I gave him was that anything I learned could be passed on to you, to the kids, or to the police. But I didn't learn anything earth-shattering. Just confirmed what I suspected."

"How so?"

I gave her a synopsis of my visit. She said, "God, he sounds like a real jerk."

"He's different, that's for sure."

"Different." She smiled. "Yes, that's much more professional than *jerk*."

I laughed.

She said, "See why I wouldn't make a good therapist? Too judgmental. How do you do it, keeping your feelings from getting in the way?"

"It's not always easy," I said. "Especially with someone like him. While interviewing him I realized I didn't like him, resolved to keep that in the forefront of my mind. Which is what you do. Be aware of your own feelings. Stay aware. Put the patient's welfare first, keeping yourself in the background. Like an accompanist."

"You consider him your patient?"

"No. He's more of a . . . consulting client. The way the court would be, in a custody evaluation. Not that I'm going to be able to tell him what he wants to hear: that she was innocent. If anything, she fits the profile of a mass murderer pretty closely. So my hunch is I'll probably get fired fairly soon. It's happened before."

She put half a hazelnut in her mouth and chewed. Some tension—the intensity—had returned to her face.

I said, "What is it?"

"Nothing. Oh, heck, I just keep thinking about my car. It was the first thing I bought myself when I had money. It looked so sad when they towed it away. They say it'll live, but surgery will take at least a month. Meanwhile, I've got a rental. If I'm lucky, the district won't hassle me when it comes time to divvy up."

She pushed her fork around on her dessert plate. "The thing that keeps bugging me is: Why *my* little clunker? It was parked on the street with all the others. How'd they know who it belonged to?"

"Someone probably saw you in it."

"Meaning someone was watching me? Stalking me?"

"No," I said quickly. "I doubt we're talking about anything that sophisticated. More likely someone spotted you, knew you were associated with the school, and decided to strike out."

Opportunism. I knew why the word had leaped into my mind. All this exposure to politics. Ugliness.

"So you think it was someone local?" she said.

"Who knows?"

"Stupid punks," she said. "I won't let them dominate my life."

A moment later, she said, "So what's my next step? Start toting a gun?" She smiled. "Maybe not such a bad idea after all. Like I told you, I'm a crack shot."

"Hope I stay on your good side."

She laughed, looked down at what remained of her dessert. "Want any of this? I'm full."

I declined, called for the check, and paid Solicitous. As we got up from the table I noticed simultaneous movement from a table on the other side of the lattice. As if we were sitting next to a mirror. The synchrony was so strong that I actually gave a second look to make sure we weren't. But it was two other people—the vague outlines of a man and a woman. I thought nothing of it as we headed toward the car, but as I drove away from the curb, another car pulled out right behind us and stayed on our tail. I felt my chest tighten, then remembered the similar fantasy I'd had just a few days ago. The paranoia that had caused me to pull off Sunset into the service station.

Brown Toyota. What appeared to be two people. A couple. Absorbed with each other. Now another couple, right behind us, but from the spacing of the headlights, this car was larger. A midsized sedan. No flicker.

Okay. Definitely not the same car. Nothing odd about two couples leaving a restaurant at the same time. And heading this way on Melrose was the logical route for anyone living west of Hancock Park.

Ease up, Delaware.

I looked in the rearview mirror. Headlights. Same ones? The glare prevented me from seeing who was inside.

Ridiculous. I was letting all the talk of plots and counterplots go to my head.

"What's wrong?" said Linda.

"Wrong? Nothing."

"All of a sudden you're all tensed up. Your shoulders are all crunched."

The last thing I wanted to do was feed her anxiety. I consciously relaxed, tried to look more casual than I felt. Snuck another glance in the rearview mirror. Different set of headlights, I was pretty sure. A caravan of headlights, stretching for blocks. Typical weekend jam-up on Melrose . . .

"What is it, Alex?"

"Nothing. Really." I turned off Melrose onto Spaulding and pulled a therapist switcheroo: "How about yourself? Still thinking about the car?"

"Got to admit I'm a little edgy," she said. "Maybe we should have stuck to the boredom pledge."

"Don't worry," I said. "I can get you bored again, really quick." I cleared my throat and put on a whiny, pedagogical tone: "Let's talk educational theory. The topic of the day is, ahem, curriculum adjustment. Macro- and micro-variables of a variety of contemporary text offerings that contribute to greater, ahem, student participation while holding constant class size, budgetary factors, and the, ahem, cement/asphalt ratio of the surrounding play areas in a suburban school prototype, as defined by—"

"All right, I believe you!"

"—the Harrumph-Pshaw Educational Coercion Act of 1973—"

"Enough!" She was laughing hard.

I looked in the mirror. No headlights. Stretched my arm across the seat and touched her shoulder. She scooted closer, rested a hand on my knee, then removed it. I put it back.

She laughed and said, "Now what?"

"Tired?"

"More like wired."

"Want to help me hang the print?"

"That kind of like 'come up and see my etchings'?"

"Same general idea."

"Hmm."

"Hmm what?"

"Hmm yes."

I squeezed her shoulder, drove home feeling relaxed. Except for the two dozen times I checked my rearview mirror.

* * *

"I love everything about this place," she said, stretching out on the leather sofa and undoing her hair. "The view, the pond—it's simple but you've done a lot with it. Feels bigger than it is. How long have you been living here?"

"Almost seven years."

"Out here that just about makes you a homesteader."

"Got the wagon train out in back," I said, holding up the Bellows. "How does this look?"

"Little to the left." She got up. "Here, I'll hold it. You take a look for yourself."

We exchanged places.

She said, "What do you think?"

"Perfect."

I measured, hammered the nail, hung the print, straightened the frame. We returned to the sofa and looked at it.

"Nice," she said. "That's a good place for it."

I kissed her without restraint. Her arms went around me. We clinched till we lost breath. Her hand settled on my fly. Gently squeezing. I began unbuttoning her blouse, got two buttons loose before she said, "Whoa," and lifted her hand.

"Something the matter?"

She was flushed and her eyes were shiny. "No, nothing . . . It's just . . . every time we get together, we just *do* it? *Bam*?"

"Not if you don't want to."

The white lashes fluttered like down. She took my face in her hands. "You really that chivalrous?"

"Not really. But all that talk about your being a crack shot has me worried."

She laughed. Turned serious just as quickly. "I just don't want it to be . . . easy come, easy go. Like everything else in this town."

"That's not for me either."

She looked uncertain, but kissed me again. Deeply. I got into it.

She squirmed.

I backed off. She pulled me closer, held me to her. My heart was racing. Or maybe it was hers.

"You want me," she said, as if amazed at her own power.

"Oh, yeah."

A moment passed. I could barely hear the gurgle of the pond.

"Oh, what the heck," she said, and put her hand back.

21

I heard her get up the next morning at six. She had dressed and was drinking coffee at the kitchen table when I came in half an hour later.

"Blue Monday," she said.

"Feeling down?"

"Actually, not one bit." She gazed out the window. "Really love this view."

I filled a cup and sat down.

She looked at her watch. "When you're ready, I'll take a ride back to my place. I want to get to school early, set up your parents for today's group."

"How many do you expect?"

"About twenty. Quite a few are Spanish-speaking. I can be your translator but it means I've got to clear my desk first."

"Sounds good."

"Do you think you'll need more than one session?"

"Probably not. I'll be available for individual follow-ups."

"Great."

Both of us talking shop, skirting the personal as if it were a dead animal in the middle of the road.

I drank a little more coffee.

She said, "Want any breakfast?"

"Nope. You?"

She shook her head. "How about a rain check, then? I'm a pretty good breakfast cook—nothing Cordon Bleu, just down-home integrity and high quantity."

"I look forward to making you prove it."

Her smile was sudden, white, dazzling.

We touched hands. I drove her home.

During the drive she looked out the window a lot and I sensed more pulling away—a reaffirmation of her ability to take care of herself. So I dropped her off in front of her building, told her I'd see her at eleven, put gas in the Seville, and used a pay phone at the station to call my service for the messages I'd neglected to pick up yesterday. Just one, from Mahlon Burden, reminding me to call his son and reiterating Howard Burden's business number.

Just after nine I called Encino.

A female voice said, "Pierce, Sloan, and Marder."

"Howard Burden, please."

Her tone became guarded. "One moment."

Another female voice, louder and nasal: "Howard Burden's office."

"I'd like to speak with Mr. Burden."

"Whom shall I say is calling?"

"Dr. Delaware."

"May I ask what this is about, Doctor?"

"A personal matter. I was referred by Mr. Burden's father."

Hesitation. "One moment."

She was gone for what seemed like a long time. Then: "I'm sorry. Mr. Burden's in a meeting."

"Any idea when he'll be free?"

"No, I don't."

"I'll give you my number. Please ask him to call me."

"I'll deliver the message." Frosty tone. Letting me know a call-back was about as likely as world peace. I thought I understood her protectiveness.

"I'm not with the press," I said. "His father is pretty eager for me to talk with him. You can call Mr. Burden Senior and confirm that."

"I'll give him the message, sir."

Another roadblock at the entrance to Ocean Heights. When I saw the pair of squad cars, my hands went clammy.

But this was a smaller police presence than on the day of the sniping—just two black-and-whites, an equal number of uniformed cops standing in the middle of the street, chatting with each other, looking relaxed.

They refused to answer my questions and had a few of their own. I spent a long time explaining who I was, waiting for them to call the school and verify it with Linda. She couldn't be reached. Finally, after showing them my psych license and med school faculty card and tossing in Milo's name, I was allowed through.

Before I walked back to my car I tried again. "So what's going on?"

The cops looked amused and annoyed at the same time.

One of them said, "Show time, sir." The other hooked his thumb toward the Seville and said, "Better be getting going."

I drove off, speeding up Esperanza. The school was ringed with vehicles and I had to park more than a block away. More cop cars, along with bland-looking sedans that might have been unmarkeds, media vans, at least three white ultrastretch Mercedes. And spectators—a few of the locals, standing in front of their homes. Some looked sour—the put-upon resignation of picnickers invaded by ants. But others seemed pleased, as if waiting for a parade.

I walked on, wondering what had brought

them out. What "show time" meant. Then I heard it, as I got closer to the school grounds. A relentless drumbeat. Synthesizer trills over a walking bass run.

Carnival sounds. A rock-and-roll carnival. I wondered why Linda hadn't mentioned anything to me.

Directly across from the school entrance, a local stood blocking the sidewalk. Thickset older man in plaid madras pants and white Ban-Lon golf shirt, smoking a cigarette and flicking ashes onto the sidewalk. Flicking in the direction of the school. As I approached, he stopped and stared. Dry-ice squint, raw-pork complexion.

"Morning," I said. "What's all the hubbub?"

He peered at me, flicked, and said, "Some *singer*." His tone of voice said he placed that one rung above pimp on the occupational ladder.

"Which one?"

"Who knows?" He took a drag. "First they force themselves on us; then they bring in their jungle music."

He gave me a challenging look. I walked around him and crossed the street. His cigarette flew by me, landed on the macadam, throwing off sparks.

The fence around the schoolyard was laced with orange and silver streamers, hung so densely I couldn't see inside. The gate was locked. A school policeman was at the front door to the

school building, along with a husky black man
with Rasta dreadlocks and a patchy, blemishlike
beard. The black man wore white sweat pants and
an orange T-shirt that said THE CHILLER TOUR!
MEGA-PLATINUM! in metallic letters. He held a clipboard in one hand, a set of gold-plated keys in the
other. As I got closer, the school cop retreated.

Dreadlocks said, "Name."

"Dr. Delaware. Alex Delaware. I work at the
school."

He looked at the clipboard, ran his finger
down a page. "How do you spell thot, mon?" His
enunciation was precise.

I told him. He turned a page and his brows
compressed, pulling forward several twists of hair.
"Delaware. As in the state?"

"Exactly."

"Sorry, mon, I don't see anything like thot."

Before I could reply, the door swung open.
Linda stormed out. She'd changed into a cheerful-
looking yellow dress but didn't look happy.

"Stop hassling this man!"

The school cop and Dread turned to stare at
her. She came down the steps, took my arm,
pulled me past them. Dread said, "Mo'om—"

She held up a warning finger. "Uh-uh, don't
say a word! This man works here. He's a famous
doctor! He has a job to do and you're getting in the
way!"

Dread pulled at a lock and grinned. "Sorry,

mo'om. I was just looking for his name—no offense intended."

"No *offense*?! I gave your people his name! They promised me there'd be no hassle!"

Dread smiled again and shrugged. "Sorry."

"What the heck do you think this is anyway? Some disco club?" She glared at the school cop: "And what about *you*! What the heck are you *here* for—just here to keep him *company*?"

Before either of them could answer, we were inside. She slammed the door behind us.

"Jesus! I just knew that was going to happen!" She was still gripping my arm as we speed-walked down the corridor.

I said, "What's going on?"

"*DeJon Jonson* is what's going on. He's chosen to honor us with a personal appearance. For the sake of the poor victimized children."

"The Chiller himself?"

"In all his spangled glory. And his *entourage*. Groupies, roadies, press agents, an army of bodyguards—clones of Mr. *Reggae* out there. And a whole bunch of unclassifieds who look as if they should be shipped off to drug rehab. Not to mention every TV, radio, and newspaper hack in town and a dozen pencil-pushers from the Board who haven't seen the inside of a schoolyard since Eisenhower."

She stopped, straightened her dress, patted her hair. "And of course, our dear Councilman

Latch—it was he who arranged the whole thing."

"Latch?"

She nodded. "Wifey-poo's show biz connections, no doubt. She's here, too, patting the kids' heads and wearing a rock that could pay for all our school lunches for a year."

"Diamonds on a revolutionary?"

"California revolutionary. What my dad used to call Cadillac Commies. Lord save me from Monday morning surprises."

"No one told you?"

"Nope."

"So much for his hearing me."

"What's that?"

"Latch. The time he dropped in to play his harmonica. I talked to him about keeping things predictable. He told me he'd *heard* me—I'd given him food for thought."

"Oh, he heard it all right. He just chose to disregard it."

"When did you actually find out?"

We resumed walking. She said, "One of the pencil-pushers left a message on my machine last night at ten. I had the poor manners to be out with you, didn't pick up until this morning. Which gave me a heck of a lot of time to prepare, right? I managed to get to Latch just a while ago, told him this could be disruptive. He didn't process that at all, said getting a star of DeJon's *caliber* wasn't something that came up every day; this was a coup for the kids."

I said, "Coup for him. Tape a few thousand feet of happy-face video for the next campaign."

She made a taut, throaty sound, like a mama bobcat warning hunters away from the lair. "You know, what gets me the most is that Sunday call from downtown. That's got to be a historical first. Ordinarily I can't even get them to take a message during working hours. Ordering textbooks, begging for funds for field trips—everything takes forever. Molasses Standard Time. But for this, they can move like rockets."

I said, "Rock and roll never dies. You even got your guard back."

She gave a disgusted look. "You should see the production they've put together. Crew from the record company arrived at seven, along with carpenters from the district. They set up a big stage out on the yard in one hour *flat*. P.A. system, all those streamers, the works. They even printed up a *schedule*—do you believe that! Orange print on silver satin paper, must have cost a fortune. Everything laid out by the minute: Latch makes a speech; then DeJon does his thing, throws paper flowers at the kids, and is whisked off to a waiting limo. It actually says that—*Whisked Off. To Waiting Limo*. The whole darned thing gets filmed for the evening news and probably used on DeJon's next rock video. His flunkies came into the classrooms and distributed release forms for the kids to take home."

I said, "Mega-platinum and the Nobel Peace Prize too. With all this excitement, what's the status of the parent group?"

"The parents are all here—though I had a heck of a time getting Jonson's yahoos to understand they needed to be let through without a body search. I had to watch the door all morning. 'Course, once Latch's people realized who they were, they laid out the red carpet—snapped their pictures with Latch, gave them front-row seats for the show."

"How'd the mothers react to that?"

"Confused, at first. But they got into it pretty quickly—celebrities for an hour. Whether they'll be in a receptive state for talking about problems, I don't know. I'm sorry."

I smiled. "Not receptive even for a *famous doctor*?"

She colored. "Hey, to me, you're famous. The kind of fame that matters."

We reached her office. As she unlocked it, she said, "Alex, I know it's the same old question, but what's the psychological effect of something like this on the kids?"

"Let's hope they'll have some fun, get back to their routine in a day or so, and move on. The main risk you run is that they'll get so overstimulated that they experience a case of the morning-after blues once the hoopla dies down. I used to see it a lot when I worked at the hospital. Celebrities would blow in for photo-op visits with poor little sick kids, then disappear just as suddenly, and the kids would be left with their pain and disease and a sudden silence on the wards that was really . . . harsh. It was due to the shift in arousal—decompression. I started to think of it as the psychological bends."

"I know what you mean," she said. "We see the same kind of thing after an all-day field trip. They're supposed to be having fun but they fall apart."

"Exactly," I said. "It's why so many birthday parties end up in tears. Another thing to consider is that all this excitement and strangers—politicians, the press—could cause them to remember the last time things got so excited around here."

"The sniping? Oh, boy."

"Some of them may flash back to it, get anxious all over."

"Terrific," she said. "What do I do?"

"Keep an eye out for anxiety reactions—especially among the younger ones. When things quiet down, try to get them back to a routine. Maintain discipline but be flexible. They may need to talk about the concert, talk out the excitement—and any fear they're experiencing. If any persistent reactions develop, you know where to find me."

"You're becoming a fixture here, Doc."

I smiled. "Ulterior motives."

She smiled back, but looked low.

"What is it?" I said.

"I'm supposed to be in charge, but I feel . . . irrelevant."

"This is a one-shot deal, Linda. By tomorrow you'll be back in control. But yeah, it stinks. They should have told you."

She gave another sad smile. "Thanks for the support."

"Ulterior motives."

This time her smile was untarnished.

She took my hand and led me inside the office, locked the door behind us, threw her arms around me, and kissed me hard and long.

"There," she said. "My own contribution to overstimulation."

"Acknowledged," I said, catching my breath. "And appreciated."

She kissed me again. We went into her inner office. The music from the schoolyard pounded through the walls.

"Here's the list of parents," she said, handing me a sheet of paper.

I took it. The music stopped. An amplified, reverberating voice took its place.

She said, "Let the games begin."

*   *   *

We stood at the back of the yard, looking out over hundreds of heads, watching Gordon Latch.

He stood behind a lectern at the center of the stage, brandishing his harmonica. The lectern was polished walnut embossed with the city seal. The stage was heavy lumber, elevated and backed with a thirty-foot wall of black silk that looked like a patch on the clear blue eye of the sky. Lots of sound equipment but no instruments. No musicians either. Just the press, crowding around on all sides, filming, talking into tape recorders, jotting. And a small army of hulking types in orange T-shirts patrolling with walkie-talkies. Some of the Beef Brigade stood on stage, others down at spectator level. From the way they glared and scanned the crowd, they could have been guarding the crown jewels.

Latch grinned and waved, puffed a couple of high notes into the mike, and said something about celebrating life. His words echoed across the schoolyard and died somewhere out on the spotless streets of Ocean Heights. A row of ten folding chairs had been set up to the left of the podium. Eight of them were occupied by middle-aged men and women in business suits. Except for the sound gear and the Orange Men lurking behind them, it could have been a middle-management seminar.

Sitting in the two seats closest to the podium were Bud Ahlward, in the same brown suit he'd worn the day he'd shot Holly Burden, and a thin, attractive woman with taffy-colored wedge-cut hair, a deeply tanned face, and a jawline so tight it looked like a seam.

Mrs. Latch. The former Miranda Brundage. Looking at her attire reminded me the sixties were ancient history. Or maybe they'd never happened at all. She had on a two-piece black leather outfit with padded shoulders and gold lamé appliqué, diamond earrings, and the rock Linda had mentioned—a solitaire on a chain that, even at this distance, reflected enough light to brighten a ballroom. Her legs were well shaped, sheathed in gray silk, crossed at the ankles, her feet encased in spike-heel thonged affairs that had to be handmade Italian. She alternated between gazing out at the audience and looking up at her husband.

Even at this distance she looked bored, almost defiantly jaded. I thought I remembered that she'd once wanted to be an actress. Either she had no talent or wasn't bothering to fake it.

Latch held forth in echoplex eloquence:

". . . so I told DeJon [jon . . . jon . . . jon] you're someone everyone looks up to [to . . . to . . . to]. Your message is positive, a message for today, and the kids at Hale need you!"

Applause line.

Latch stopped and waited.

The kids didn't get it, but the suits and the

orange gorillas did. The sound of twenty pairs of hands clapping was feeble.

Latch beamed as if it had been an ovation at the National Convention, removed his welfare glasses, and loosened his tie. His wife's affection for high style hadn't rubbed off: He had on a rumpled tan corduroy suit, blue chambray shirt, and navy knit tie.

"DeJon said *yes!*" Up-raised fist.

"The school board said *yes!*" Punching air.

"So *we* put it to*geth*er for *you!*" Both hands raised. Dual victory V's.

". . . So here he is, boys and girls of all ages: the *Chiller,* the ultimate *Crowd-Thriller,* De*Jo-on Jonson!*"

Power chords tumbled out of the speakers like avalanche boulders: rumbling, deafening, threatening, finally picking up melodic content and terminating as a sustaining organ tone—a fugue performed by an E. Power Biggs on acid. A hailstorm of guitar chords shattered the silence. Thunderous drums. Hissing cymbals. The suits on stage looked stricken but kept their places. The orange T-shirts marched toward them and touched the backs of their chairs. As if choreographed, the bureaucrats in the suits got up and filed off the stage. Miranda Latch and Ahlward hung back, she applauding with aerobic fervor that seemed disconnected to the ennui in her eyes.

Latch left the podium and took her hand.

Waving to the audience, the two of them walked off the stage. Ahlward trailed, looking bored, one hand inside his jacket.

The three of them took seats in the front row, amid a group of plainly dressed women—my group. The mothers were all applauding. I couldn't see their faces.

The music got louder. Linda grimaced.

I said, "One sec," and made my way toward the front of the assembly, weaving past news crews and camera gear.

Finally I got close enough to see. Hundreds of faces. Some blank, some puzzled, some burnished with excitement. I glanced over at the front row. The mothers looked intimidated but not unhappy. Instant celebrity.

Latch noticed me. Smiled and continued snapping his fingers in time with the beat. Bud Ahlward followed his boss's glance, let his eyes settle on me, then looked away. Miranda was snapping her fingers too. For all the fun she was having it might have been physical therapy.

I returned my attention to the kids. The volume of the music continued to climb. I saw one little girl—a first grader—slap her hands over her ears.

I moved forward to get a better look. The little girl's eyes were squeezed shut and her mouth was trembling. A blast from the speakers and she burst into an open-mouthed wail rendered silent by the din. No one noticed. All eyes, including those of her teacher, were fixed upon the stage.

I went back to Linda and managed, with gestures and shouts in her ear, to communicate what was happening. She looked over at the little girl, who was crying harder. Then she nudged me and pointed. A couple of other kids in the lower grades were looking unsteady, holding their ears too. More tears.

Linda gave a furious look and stomped forward, elbowing cameramen and orange bruisers until she reached the little girl's teacher. She talked behind her hand, pointed discreetly. The teacher's mouth formed an O. Looking chastened, he turned his attention back to his class.

I counted about six or seven children crying by now, four of them kids I recognized easily because they were in the high-risk group. Linda saw them too. She went over to each of them, bending low, patting heads, talking in their ears. Taking their hands and offering them the choice of leaving.

Four headshakes, three nods. She removed the nodders from the group, herded them past the press clutch, back into the school building.

I followed her. It took me a while to get into the building. Linda was halfway down the main corridor, sitting on the floor in a circle with the three children. Smiling, talking, holding a hand puppet and making it talk in a high-pitched voice.

The children were smiling. No distress that I could see.

I took a few steps forward. She looked up.

"Look, kids, it's Dr. Delaware."

"Hi," I said.

Shy waves.

"Anything you guys want to ask Dr. Delaware?"

Silence.

"Looks like everything's under control, Dr. Delaware."

I said, "Great, Dr. Overstreet," and went back outside.

Though the music was louder, the stage was uninhabited. Not a musician in sight, not even a synthesizer wizard. I realized this was going to be a lip-sync exhibition. Prefab passion.

Nothing happened for several seconds. Then what appeared to be a huge orange flame burned its way through the black backdrop. Gasps from the audience. As the flame got closer, it turned into an oversized sheet of heavy satin, trailing along the stage. Beneath the satin was movement—a swelling and pulsating as the sheet shimmered forward. Like a gag horse, minus head or tail. Cheap trick, but eerie.

The sheet bumped and grinded its way center stage. Organ crescendo, cymbal crash, and the sheet dropped, revealing six more huge men, bare-chested and wearing orange tights and silver jackboots. Three blacks, on the left, scowling under broom-bristles of straightened yellow hair. On the right, a trio of Nordic types in royal-blue Afros.

The six of them spread their legs and assumed wrist-gripping iron-pumper poses. Between them appeared a very tall, very skinny man in his mid-twenties, with skin the color of India ink, Asian eyes, and orange Jheri-curled past-the-shoulders hair that looked as if it had been braised with axle grease. Wide shoulders, the hips of a prepubescent boy, rubbery limbs, a Modigliani neck, and the terminal-illness cheekbones of a *Vogue* model.

He wore electric-blue goggles in tiger-hide plastic frames that were wider than his face, a tight silver silk jumpsuit embroidered with orange thread and festooned with costume sapphires in baroque patterns. His hands were encased in fingerless blue satin weight-lifter's gloves; his feet shod in silver high-tops with orange laces.

He snapped his fingers. The musclemen retreated, satin sheet in hand.

The music picked up pace. Jonson pranced, knees high like a drum majorette, did a Nijinsky leap, shot off a flurry of tap-dance pyrotechnics, and ended with a split that transformed him into an inverted silver T and made my groin hurt vicariously.

Then, sudden quiet topped by a high-pitched

hum from the speakers. A few of the older kids were out of their seats, bouncing and clapping and calling out, "DeJon! DeJon! Do 'Chiller'! 'Chiller'! DeJon! DeJon!"

The orange-haired man scissored himself upright and smiled feverishly. Went pigeon-toed and knock-kneed, shimmied, squatted, did a backwards double somersault followed by a headstand and some rapid hand-walking, then jumped back to his feet, flexed each bicep, and bared his teeth.

The music resumed: a modified reggae beat supercharged by a string-popping funk riff.

His teeth parted and his mouth opened wide enough for a tonsil display. A very whispery tenor oozed out of the speakers.

> *When the night moves in,*
> *And creepies crawl,*
> *And thingies creep,*
> *Over castle walls,*

Gasp. Hand to mouth. Look of exaggerated fear.

That's when I'm real.
That's when I live.
I'm your party man,
Got so much to give.
Cause I'm a chiller. Love your chiller.
Baby I'm your chiller. Got to love your chiller.
Sweet kind of chiller. Got to kiss your chiller.

Seductive leer. Change of tempo to a manic two-four almost drowned out by shouts and applause. Jonson belly-danced, jumped back, raced forward, skidded to a stop at the edge of the stage, rolled his eyes. When he lip-synced again, his whisper had turned into a raspy baritone:

And when the snakes of wrath
Meet the toads of fire,
And scorpions waltz
Across the pyre,
That's when I breathe.
That makes me whole.
I'm here to love
Your mortal soul.
Cause I'm a chiller. Love your chiller . . .

Charming.

I searched for signs of anxiety among the children. Many of them were rocking and bopping, singing along, shouting out Jonson's name. Taking it the way it was meant to be taken—as a sound-wave gestalt, the lyrics irrelevant. It went on for another minute. Then a rain of orange and silver flowers appeared out of nowhere, butterfly-delicate. The musclemen reappeared with the orange sheet and Jonson was whisked offstage. The whole thing had taken less than two minutes.

Latch got back onstage and mouthed inaudible thank-yous over the cheers. The press surged past him, taking off in the direction of the sheet. Latch stood there, abandoned, and I saw something—a spoiled, peevish look—creep onto his face. Just for a second. Then it was gone and he was grinning again and waving, his wife and Ahlward by his side.

Things had gotten wild out in the cheap seats. The kids were pelting each other with flowers; teachers struggled to line them up. I looked back at the front row and saw my mothers standing alone, confused. The Latches and Ahlward stood nearby, surrounded by young-scrubbeds like the ones I'd seen the day of the sniping. Lots of congratulations from the troops. Latch getting what he needed, soaking it up while maintaining a TV face. No one made any attempt to talk to the mothers.

I started making my way over, waiting for whole classes to pass, getting my insteps trampled by tiny feet. Camera crews were pulling up cable, creating tripwires, and I had to watch where I stepped. When I was a few feet away, Latch saw me, grinned, and waved. His wife waved too; Pavlov would have given her an A. Ahlward remained stolid, one hand in his jacket.

Latch said something to him. The redheaded man walked over to me and said, "Dr. Delaware, the councilman would like to speak with you."

"Gee whiz," I said.

If he heard me he didn't let on.

22

I followed him, but at the last moment I veered away and went to the mothers. Latch's face took on that same deprived-brat look. I wondered how long it had been since he *had* been told no.

The women looked deprived too. Of their bearings. A few held paper flowers, seemed afraid to throw them away.

I walked up to them and introduced myself. Before they could reply, a voice behind me said, "Dr. Delaware. Alex."

No choice but to turn. The councilman had regained his camera happy-face. But his wife had gotten tired of wearing hers. She'd put on sunglasses—copper-and-gold designer originals with a lavender-blue tint. The two of them were standing together but seemed far apart. Ahlward and the dress-for-success bunch hung back several yards.

Latch held out his hand. "Good to see you again, Alex."

"Councilman."

"Please. *Gordon*."

The inevitable pressing of flesh. He pumped hard enough to draw water.

I turned back to the mothers, smiled, and said, "One minute, please," in my basic Spanish.

They smiled back, still confused.

Latch said, "Alex, I'd like you to meet my first wife, Miranda." Chuckling. Her smile was murderous.

"Randy, this is Dr. Alex Delaware, the psychologist I told you about."

"Pleased to meet you, Doctor." She gave me four fingertips and retracted them quickly. Her formality seemed defiant. Latch gave her a quick, nervous look, which she ignored. Up close she seemed smaller, brittle of voice and bone. And older. Her husband's senior by a good five years. Betrayed by her skin. The rich tan and well-applied makeup failed to mask the fine wrinkles and liverish blotches. Her mouth was wide and had a nice, sensual curve to it but had started to pucker. Her nose was skinny and short with large nostrils—probably rhinoplasty. Her chin was marred by a sprinkle of pocks. Her diamonds were flawless but made her look washed-out in contrast.

Latch said, "Randy's always had an interest in psych. We both have." He put his arm around her. She tensed and smiled at the same time.

She said, "That's true, Doctor. I'm a people

person. We're organizing—Gordie and I—a mental health committee for the district. Concerned citizens reaching out to help the mentally ill. I'd be privileged if you'd join our advisory committee."

I said, "I'm flattered, Mrs. Latch, but my time's pretty committed right now."

Her smiled evaporated and her lower lip curled—another spoiled child. A little girl used to guilt-tripping Daddy. But she replaced it almost immediately with an inch of charm-school tooth-flash. "I'm sure it is," she said airily. "But if you change your mind—"

"Let us know, Alex," said Latch. He spread his arms over the yard. "Pretty fantastic, wasn't it? The kids really got into it."

I said, "He puts on quite a show."

"It's more than a show, Alex. He's a *phenomenon*. A natural resource, one of a kind. Like the last golden eagle. We were lucky to get him—it was a coup. We owe it all to Randy." Squeezing his wife's shoulder again and jostling her. She dredged up yet another smile.

"The healing power of music," said Latch. "We should have more shows, at other schools. Make it a regular thing. Give the kids a positive message. To raise their self-esteem."

Snakes of wrath. Toads of fire.

I said, "The show was pretty intense, Gordon. Some of the children were frightened."

"Frightened? I didn't notice."

"A handful, mostly younger ones—all the noise, the stimulation. Dr. Overstreet took them inside."

"A handful," he said, as if calculating electoral impact. "Well, that's not too bad, considering. Put enough kids together anywhere and a few are bound to get uptight, right?"

Before I could answer he said, "Guess that means another lecture on coordination, huh? How about letting me off? Dr. Overstreet already read me the riot act before the concert."

I looked back at the mothers and said, "It's been good talking to you, Gordon, but I've really got to be going now."

"Ah, your parents group—yes. I know about it because when I saw how uncomfortable they looked, I went up to them, found out who they were. We made sure to see they felt at home."

Slightly different from the way Linda had told it.

I said, "Great."

He stepped closer and put his hand on my shoulder. "Listen, I think what you're doing is great. I didn't have a chance to tell you that, last time. Looking at the whole family as a unit. Bringing your treatment to the community. We used to do that up at Berkeley. It was called street psychiatry back then and we were constantly being accused by the psychiatric establishment of being subversive. What it boiled down to, of course, was that they were threatened by challenges to the medical model. No doubt you've experienced that somewhere along the line, too. Being put down by M.D.'s?"

I said, "I try to stay out of politics, Gordon. Good to meet you, Mrs. Latch."

I turned to leave. He kept his hand on my shoulder and held me back. A cameraman strolled by. Latch smiled and held it. I saw my reflection in his glasses. Twin reflections. A pair of unfriendly, curly-haired guys eager to be rid of him.

"You know," he said, "I never did get around to coming back—to talk to the kids."

"Not necessary," I said. "I'd say you've done enough."

He tried to read my face, said, "Thanks. It was quite an experience putting it together on such short notice. Dr. Overstreet's gripes notwithstanding."

I stared at him. The twins in the glass looked mean, which suited me just fine. I said, "Ah, the tortured life of a modern-day saint. Which network did you call first?"

He paled, and his freckles stood out. His expression was that of a guy with new white bucks who's just stepped in fresh dog shit. But he kept smiling, looking out for cameras, put his arm around me, and drew me away from his wife. To an observer we might have been buddies sharing a smutty joke.

Over his shoulder I saw Ahlward, motionless, watching.

When we were out of earshot, Latch lowered his voice. "We live in a cold world, Alex. Adding to the cynicism level isn't a virtue."

I shrugged out of his grip. "What can I say, Gordon? Sometimes it just comes with the territory."

I turned my back on him and went to do my job.

I led the mothers into the building, realizing I had no idea where the group session was going to be held. Nothing like a few minutes of wandering the building to engender confidence in the therapist. But just as we approached Linda's office, she stepped out and took us to the end of the hall and through a set of double doors I'd never been through before. Inside was a wood-floored half-gym. I realized it was the room I'd seen that first day, on TV: children huddled together on the hardwood floor, the cameras moving in with surgical cruelty. In real life the room looked smaller. TV had the ability to do that—inflate reality or crush it to insignificance.

Plastic folding chairs had been arranged in a circle. In the middle was a low table covered with paper and set up with cookies and punch.

"Okay?" said Linda.

"Perfect."

"Not the coziest environment, but with Jonson's people taking over all the empty classrooms, it was all we had."

We seated the women, then ourselves. The mothers still looked frightened. I spent the first few minutes passing out cookies and filling cups. Making the kind of small talk that I hoped would let them know I had a personal interest in their children, wasn't just another authority figure pulling rank.

After explaining who I was, I talked about their children—what good kids they were, how strong, how well they were coping. Implying, without being patronizing, that children that robust had to have loving, caring parents. For the most part they seemed to understand; when I got blank looks I had Linda translate. Her Spanish was fluent and unaccented.

I called for questions. They had none.

"Of course, sometimes," I said, "no matter how strong a child is, the memory of something frightening can come back—in bad dreams. Or wanting to hold on to Mama more, not wanting to go to school."

Nods and looks of comprehension.

"If any of that has happened, it doesn't mean there's anything wrong with your child. That kind of thing is normal."

A couple of sighs of relief.

"But bad memories can be . . . helped. Cured." Using the C-word they'd tried to drum out of me in grad school. Linda said, *"Mejor. Curado."*

Several of the women leaned forward.

"Mothers," I said, "are a child's best helpers—the best teachers of their children. Better than doctors. Better than anyone else. Because a mother knows her child better than anyone. That's why the best way to cure a bad memory is for the mother to help the child."

"What can we do?" said a girlish-looking woman with thick black eyebrows and long coarse black hair. She wore a pink dress and sandals. Her English was barely accented.

"You can let your children know it's okay to talk about being afraid."

She said, "Gilberto, when he talks he gets more afraid."

"Yes, that's true. In the beginning. Fear is like a wave."

The long-haired woman translated.

Puzzled looks all around.

I said, "At first, when a child meets something that scares him, the fear grows, like a wave. But when he goes into the water and swims—gets used to the water—the wave grows small. If we pull the child away when the wave is high, he never sees that, never learns how to swim and remains afraid. If he gets a chance to feel strong, in control, that's called coping. When he copes, he feels better."

More translation.

"Of course," I said, "we have to protect our children. We never throw them right into the water. We *stay* with them. Hold them. Wait until they are ready. Teach them to conquer the wave, to be stronger than the wave. With love, and talk, and playing games—giving *permission* to the child to swim. Teaching him to swim first in the small waves, then the bigger ones. Moving slowly, so the child is not frightened."

"Sometimes," said the long-haired woman, "it's not good to swim. It's dangerous." To the others: "*Muy peligroso.* Sometimes you can drown."

"That's true. The thing is—"

"*El mundo es peligroso,*" said another woman.

The world is dangerous.

"Yes, it can be," I said. "But do we want our children afraid all the time? Never swimming?"

A few headshakes. Doubtful looks.

"How?" said a woman who looked old enough to be a grandmother. "How can we make it *not* be dangerous?"

All of them looking at me, waiting. For my next words of wisdom. A cure.

Fighting back feelings of impotence, I said

the things I'd planned to say. Offered small remedies, situational tinkering. Baby steps across a vast, cruel wasteland.

Afterward, when Linda and I were alone in her office, I said, "What do you think?"

"I think it went fine."

I was sitting on the L-shaped sofa and she was picking dead leaves off a potted devil ivy.

"The thing that bugs me," I said, "is that basically they're right. The world they live in is dangerous. What could I tell them? Pretend it's Dick-and-Jane territory and go merrily skipping along?"

"You do what you can, Alex."

"Sometimes that doesn't seem like much."

"Hey," she said, "what is this, role reversal? When *I* told *you* the same thing, you gave me a nice little speech about making a difference on an individual level."

I shrugged.

She said, "C'mon, Doctor. Moping doesn't become you."

She came around behind me and placed her hand on the back of my neck. Her touch was cool and soothing. "Why so low all of a sudden, anyway?"

"I don't know. Probably a combination of things." *Things* that seemed out of context but had stuck in my mind. Snapshots in a homicide file, a little boy who'd be college-age by now. *Things* I didn't want to talk about.

I said, "One thing that gets to me is knowing Latch will come out of this smelling sweet. He buttonholed me after the show, trying to play Mr. Sensitive Guy in front of his wife. I let it ride for a while, tried to get through to him that this impulsiveness isn't what the kids need. That some of them had actually gotten scared by the concert. He couldn't have cared less. I half-expected him to rip open his shirt and have on one of those *you've-obviously-mistaken-me-for-someone-who-gives-a-shit* T-shirts underneath. So I lost my cool, let on that I knew all he cared about was making political points. That got a rise out of him. So now I'm a bipartisan loudmouth. I've made fast friends on both sides."

She began massaging my neck. "So you're not a politician. Good for you. He's slime. He deserved it."

"His wife just might agree with you. I got the distinct impression theirs isn't the ultimate love match."

"Know what you mean," she said. "He introduced me to her, and I did pick up on a certain lack of warmth on her part. Maybe she's got on one of those T-shirts herself. Under the designer duds. Did you see that rock?"

"Power to the people," I said.

"Serves him right if she hates him—for marrying money. Serves both of them right. Darned Cadillac Commies." She laughed. "I just hate it when Daddy's correct."

A moment of silence while her fingers kneaded my neck. Then she said, "Daddy. He's *my* wave, you know. I'm still figuring out what to do about him: Can I ever forgive him? Can there ever be anything good again—any *family*?"

"You'll figure it out."

"You're pretty sure about that, huh?"

"Sure I'm sure. You're a smart kid. Your instincts are good."

"Smart kid. That so?" She put her face next to mine. "My *instinct,* right now, is to do something lewd in this office."

"Like I said . . ."

"However," she said, standing, "my better *judgment*—my superego—reminds me I've got work to do and a faculty meeting in twenty minutes."

I said, "Aw, shucks," and got up.

She pulled me to her and we embraced.

"You're a sweet, sweet man," she said. "And I'm glad you let me see you in a down mood, that you trusted me enough not to be Mr. Perfect."

I kissed her neck.

She said, "Whatshername was crazy to let you go." Then she tightened in my arms. "God, what a stupid thing to say. My mouth is really running—"

I silenced her with another kiss. When we broke apart, I said, "I want to see you tonight."

"I've got homework."

"Skip it. I'll write you a note."

"Bad *influence*."

"I certainly hope so."

23

I was home by four and picked up three messages. None from Howard Burden, one from his father inquiring whether Howard and I had connected yet, and a couple of throwaways from people wanting to sell me things I didn't need. I put those aside and returned the last one—from a Superior Court judge named Steve Hupp, with whom I'd worked on several child-custody cases. I reached him in chambers. He wanted me to consult on a custody battle between a famous entrepreneur and a famous actress.

"I do all the famous ones, Alex," he said. "Particularly wonderful people, these two. She claims he's a psychopathic coke-sniffing pederast; he claims she's a psychopathic coke-sniffing nymphomaniac. For all I know they're both right. She's got the kid in Switzerland. They'll pay your expenses to fly over there and evaluate. You can work in some skiing while you're over there."

"Don't ski."

"Buy a watch, then. Or start a bank account. You'll earn plenty on this one."

"Attorneys on retainer?"

"Both sides. It's been going on for over a year."

"Sounds like a real mess."

"Truthfully? It is."

"Thanks, but I'll pass, Your Honor."

"Thought you would. But if you have a change of heart, let me know. You can change the names, write a screenplay, and get rich."

"So can you, Steve."

"I'm doing it," he said. "Got a script making the rounds right now at Universal—noble jurist takes on the system. Perfect for Michael Douglas. Things turn out right, I'll be off the bench and on the set." He laughed. "Right. Meanwhile, onward to stem the ever-rising tide of marital discord— you should see our dockets. How come people are so screwed up anyway, Alex?"

"How should I know?"

"We sent you to school to know that kind of stuff."

"Maybe it's poor water quality, Steve. Or not enough dietary fiber."

At 4:45, I called Mahlon Burden. His machine answered and I told it I was still trying to reach Howard. Then I phoned Pierce, Sloan, and

Marder and waited as the receptionist put me through to Howard Burden's office.

A man's voice answered, low-pitched and sluggish. "Burden. Speak."

"Mr. Burden?"

"Yeah, what is it?"

"This is Dr. Alex Delaware. I called before."

"Yeah, I know who you are."

"Is this a bad time?"

"It's always a bad time."

"Your father suggested I talk to you. About Hol—"

"I know what it's about."

"Let's set up an appointment then—"

"How much is he paying you?"

"We haven't discussed that."

"Uh-huh. Doing the charity circuit? You a Schweitzer protégé?"

"I know you've been through a lot and—"

"Cut," he said. "Dump the script and be straight. You want to talk about Holly? I'm gonna be here all night anyway, you might as well be my coffee break. You show up anytime before, say, ten-thirty, you can have ten minutes."

Not much. But I sensed that ten minutes with this one would be interesting. "Where are you located?"

He rattled off an address in the sixteen-thousand block of Ventura Boulevard. Heart of Encino. At this time of day, getting over the Glen

into the Valley would take at least half an hour,
add another twenty minutes braving the slog on
Ventura, and I figured I'd be able to make it within
an hour. Returning to the city would be faster. My
date with Linda was for eight-thirty. Ample time.

I said, "I'll be there within the hour."

"Like I said, ten-thirty. Ten minutes."

Encino had been built up since the last time
I'd been there. It always seemed that way with
Encino. Pierce, Sloan, and Marder: Consulting
Actuaries. "Benefits and Pension Specialists" occupied the top floor of a narrow, seven-story pink
limestone and mirrored-glass rectangle squeezed
between a medical building with a Thai restaurant
on the ground floor and a Rolls-Royce/Jaguar/
Land Rover dealer.

The lobby was layered with rust-colored
granite. There were two elevators on the south
wall, both of them open. I rode up alone, stepped
into a long hallway carpeted in gray plush and
papered in white vinyl textured to look like trow-
eled plaster. Track lights shone overhead. Map-
plethorpe flower photos in Lucite frames lined the
walls, looking disturbingly visceral in such a
passionless place.

The main entrance was at the north end of the
corridor, through a floor-to-ceiling wall of glass
lettered in gilt that listed the partners of the
actuarial firm and informed the uninitiated that

Pierce, Sloan, and Marder had branches in San Francisco, Chicago, Atlanta, and Baltimore. I counted twenty-two partners in the L.A. office. Howard Burden's name was fourth from the top. Not bad for a thirty-year-old with poor manners.

Watch those value judgments, Delaware. Maybe, but for grief, he was the Prince of Charm.

On the other side of the glass the reception area was brightly lit. And empty. The door was bolted by a heavy slab of polished brass. I knocked, felt the glass tremble. Waited. Knocked again. Waited some more. Knocked harder.

So much for my ten minutes. Nothing like a drive into the Valley at rush hour to get the old juices flowing.

Just as I turned to leave, one of the elevator doors opened and a man stepped out. He was corpulent and walked with a flat-footed waddle. Fortyish, five-eleven, totally bald on top, thin brown hair fringing the sides, florid skin, a bushy brown mustache carelessly trimmed. Sixty extra pounds, all of it soft, most of it hanging over his belt. Gold buckle on the belt that glinted as he approached. Long-sleeved white shirt, double-pleated navy slacks, black loafers, a blue tie patterned with lavender squares and loosened at the neck. All of it expensive-looking but it seemed as much a costume as DeJon Jonson's getup—as if someone had dressed him up.

He huffed toward me, using his arms the way

race-walkers do, carrying a ring of keys in one hand, a wet-looking sandwich wrapped in cellophane in the other. Under the cellophane, a wilted pickle clung to the sandwich for dear life.

"You Delaware?" His voice was deep, slightly hoarse. He rattled his keys. The chain had a Mercedes-Benz logo. His neck was furrowed and sweaty. There was a grease spot on the pocket of his shirt, just under the HJB monogram.

I'd been expecting someone who looked ten years younger. Trying to hide my surprise, I said, "Hello, Mr. Burden—"

"You said an hour. It's only been"—he raised the sandwich hand and flashed a gold Rolex Oyster—"forty-eight minutes."

He walked past me and unlocked the brass bolt, letting the glass door fly back at me. I caught it, followed him to the right of the reception desk and around the walnut wall. Behind it was another ten yards of gray carpet. He stopped at double doors. Gold letters on the left one said:

HOWARD J. BURDEN, A.B., M.A.

FELLOW, SOCIETY OF ACTUARIES

He pushed it open, race-walked through an outer office and into a large walnut-paneled room. Not much wood showed through; the walls were blanketed with diplomas, certificates, and photographs. The desk was heavy-looking, very shiny and inlaid with elm burl bordered in ebony. The desk top was shaped like the letter P and piled high with books, magazines, mail, interoffice envelopes, tilting piles of papers. Behind it was a high-backed blue leather chair; behind that, a credenza. In the center of the credenza was an IBM PC; on either side of the computer, more clutter.

Above the credenza a plate-glass window offered a northern view: the high-rise profile of Ventura Boulevard dipping past housing tracts and mini-malls and the stone-colored ribbon of the 134 Freeway, vibrating like an enervated nerve fiber. Then onward, toward the brown expanse past Sylmar that stretched to the base of the Santa Susana mountains. The mountaintops had begun to fade into evening. Wisps of cinnabar and silver from the west alluded to a glorious sunset that had never quite made it. Smog pigments. Pollution art.

Howard Burden saw me looking, drew the drapes, and sat down behind the desk. Shoving papers aside, he began unwrapping his sandwich. Corned beef and sauerkraut on rye, the bread half-sodden.

I looked for somewhere to sit. The two chairs opposite his desk were filled with documents. So was a long blue leather chesterfield couch running perpendicular to the window. Some of the stacks looked ready to topple. The muddle and disarray lent the room a frantic but human energy—so different from his father's sterile sanctum. I permitted myself some sidewalk psychoanalysis.

Burden liberated the sandwich and took a big bite, not bothering to swallow before saying, "Just throw some of that shit on the floor."

I cleared one of the chairs and sat down. He continued to eat, using a paper napkin to dab at the sauerkraut juice that trailed down his chin. I glanced over at the photos on the wall. Burden and a pleasant-looking blond woman with a penchant for sleeveless knit tops, white slacks, and Top-Siders. *She* appeared to be around thirty; in some of the shots he looked like her father. About half the photos also featured a little girl of around five. Dark-haired. Eyeglasses on her, too. Something familiar . . .

Happy family poses. Smiles that seemed genuine. Disneyland. Sea World. Universal Studios. A water park. Miniature golf. The three of them in frog hats, both parents hugging the little girl. She, clutching an all-day sucker. Eating ice cream cones together. The little girl in a school play, dressed as an elf. Graduating from kindergarten in a miniature cap and gown. I realized what had struck me about her. She resembled the driver's license picture Milo had shown me. A young Holly with something to smile about.

I said, "You have a lovely family."

He put down his sandwich and crumpled his napkin in a pudgy fist.

"Look," he said, "let me lay my cards on the table right now: I'm doing this under *duress*. My father is a complete and total asshole. I don't *like* him, okay? Any bullshit he may have handed you about him and me having anything in common is bullshit, okay? So the fact that you're working for him puts you immediately on my shit list. You've got to work your way off, which I doubt is possible because you're *high* on the list. The only reason I agreed to see you is because he was calling the fucking office ten times a day, bugging the shit out of my secretary. And when *she* wouldn't put him through, hounding Gwen—my wife—at home. I knew if I didn't give him his way, he'd drop in, the way he did before, making an ass out of himself, embarrassing me. Six years I've been here, three promotion parties plus an open house, and he never showed up. We haven't goddam *talked* in five years; Amy hasn't seen a *birthday* gift from the bastard. Now all of a sudden he wants something, here he is."

"When was this? His showing up?"

"About a month ago. I was in a meeting. He waltzed right past the secretary, came in here, sat and waited and played his goddam chamber music on a cassette deck for an hour. Anyone else, she would have called Security and had him thrown out on his ass. Which would have been okay with me. But she didn't know that. All she knew was that he's her boss's father—what the fuck can she do? So she let him stay and when I got here, he made like it was nothing—he fucking *invades* me and it's *nothing*."

"What did he want?"

"Had I seen Holly recently? Did Holly seem upset to me? As if he gave a shit, ever cared about how anyone *felt*. I told him I had no idea. He tried to press me. I told him I had no idea. Doing the old broken-record routine. Finally he got the point but he just kept hanging around. Trying to make conversation, wasting my time. Pretending we were just buddy-buddy. Good old *Dad*. So now when he calls, ten fucking times, here and at my house, tells me *you're* gonna call, I should meet with you, give my insights about Holly—*insights*—what's my choice? Say no and have another visit? He's a fucking *badger,* never listens, never gives an inch. My blood pressure's no good under the *best* of circumstances, so I opt to see you, okay? So let's do our ten minutes, say we did it, and get it the hell over with, okay?"

He opened his mouth wide and clamped it shut on the sandwich, tore off a piece like a lion working at raw meat.

"The other thing you need to understand," he said, "is that I don't like psychiatrists or *psychologists* in the *first* place. I think what you people do is total *bullshit*—taking money from neurotic suckers and pretending to be their friends. As if you'd continue to smile and say uh-huh if the checks stopped coming. Pretending it's *science,*

pretending you *know* something. I read tons of
psychiatric reports, all the time—insurance
bullshit. I consult to *major* corporations, advising
them on the cost/risk patterns of setting up different kinds of health-care systems. Three *guesses*
who the biggest abusers are?" He pointed at me,
the Grand Inquisitor. "Hundred-and-fifty-buck-
an-hour bills for *adjustment* reactions, *stress* syndrome, all kinds of ambiguous crap. Workers'
comp rip-offs. My standard advice to companies
is, Stay away from mental health benefits. Corruption's the name of the game: company plan
pays for in-patient care, tons of employees get
hospitalized. Switch over to outpatient benefits,
and all of a sudden every local shrink becomes a
big fan of office therapy. Funny thing about that,
huh? Real *scientific*."

"You're right," I said. "That kind of thing
goes on all the time and it stinks."

He pulled the sandwich away from his mouth
and hefted it like a football. For a moment I
thought he was going to throw it at me. "That
supposed to *disarm* me? Convince me you're a
righteous guy?"

"I'm not trying to convince you of anything,"
I said. "Fact is, I don't even know what I'm doing
here."

"You're here because Mahlon Burden manipulated you here."

"Guess that makes two of us who have trouble telling him no."

His fingers tightened around the sandwich, turning it into something misshapen and doughy. Sauerkraut and juice leaked out and plopped onto the desk. He picked up a shred of pickled cabbage and put it in his mouth. Chewed absently and licked the edges of his mustache and suddenly looked lost. A sad, soft, fat kid, left out of the game once again.

"I'm sorry," I said. "I know this is a shitty time for you and I don't want to make it worse. We've both been manipulated. There's no need to go on."

"I *blame* him," he said.

"For Holly?"

"For Holly, for everything. For this." Pinching a roll of fat. "For my mother. She should have been taken to the hospital as soon as she started bleeding and shitting blood—the toilet bowl was white and she turned it red. I still remember that. I'll never forget it. *Everything* was coming out of her. She was in pain. Any idiot could have seen she needed medical attention, but as usual *he* knew best, told her all she needed was bed rest, to take it easy. He didn't take her in until she passed out."

"Why?"

"He doesn't like doctors, doesn't trust them.

Can always do better himself. Can do anything better than anyone."

His face was heated, greasy with sweat, scowling and squinting like that of a prizefighter taking punishment. Punished by his rage.

"As far as I'm concerned," he said, "he fucking *killed* her. I was sixteen, should have had a driver's license, should have been able to drive her to the hospital myself. But he wouldn't let me learn to drive until I was eighteen. Said I wasn't *mature* enough. He kept Holly waiting until she was nineteen."

His eyes bulged and his soft belly shook. His fists were big and meaty and the sandwich was no more than a dough-ball. He looked at it and dropped it in the trash.

I said, "He told me a different story about your mother. Routine surgery gone wrong. Medical malpractice."

"The only malpractice was his. *Spousal* malpractice—too bad you can't sue for that. By the time they got her to the operating room, she'd lost too much blood and her electrolytes were all screwed up. She went into shock and never came out. I know, because I used my connections a couple of years ago to pull her chart."

He slammed his fist down on the desk.

"Sure he told you a different story. He lies. Without blinking. Tells you one thing one minute, then denies he said it a minute later. Or maybe to him it's not a lie—maybe he really believes the bullshit he spins for himself. I don't know. Even after all these years I don't know. And I don't give a fuck. What I do know is that he's a selfish asshole who cares only for himself and is into power trips—total control. He has to control everyone and everything. Call the shots. When I lived at home I was a prisoner: The way I dressed, what I ate, everything had to pass his fucking muster. Moving out was like being reborn."

"What about Holly?"

"My sister was the worst kind of prisoner."

"Solitary confinement."

He looked startled.

I said, "It's the phrase that came to me when I saw her room."

His eyes moistened. "Yeah. A fucking life sentence. At least I had the ability to get myself out of there. She didn't—no skills. She's—*was*— one step above retarded. Which was perfect for *him*. Soon as she finished high school, he fired the maid, used Holly to clean the house."

"Did Holly object?"

"Holly didn't object to anything."

"Was he ever . . . inappropriate with her?"

His eyebrows rose. "What do you mean?"

"Sexually inappropriate. Overtly abusive."

He shook his head. "You guys have that on the brain." Then his face tensed with anger. "Why? Do you know something?"

"No," I said quickly. "Nothing at all."

"Then why'd you ask that?"

I phrased my words carefully. "They lived an isolated life, which is consistent in abuse situations. He used her as a cleaning woman. It seemed almost . . . marital."

"Don't go smearing us," Burden said. "We've been through enough."

"I wasn't planning to—"

"Let me make one thing clear: If my name or the name of anyone in my family shows up in any report you write for him or anyone else, I'll fucking sue you with the full weight of this corporation behind me. And if you mention anything to *him* that gets *him* hassling *me*—about anything—I'll personally take it out of your hide. I may look like some fat fuck, but I can bench-press two hundred, okay?" He raised his shoulders and pounded the desk for emphasis. "That clear?"

I said, "I'm not writing anything up. And I came here to talk about your sister, not you."

That shook him. He rolled his knuckles on the desk, gorillalike, then sank low in his chair. Several moments passed before he spoke.

"Before you showed up I told myself I was going to give you diddly, maintain my dignity, and here I go pushing the me-buttons." He gave a sick smile. "God, I'm turning into him."

"I doubt it," I said, looking pointedly at the photos on the wall. "What you've created for yourself looks a hell of a lot different from what you grew up with."

He covered his eyes with one hand. "They're the best," he said in a choked voice. "I can't let this affect them."

"I understand."

"Do you? Do you know what it's like for a six-year-old to walk out of her house and have reporters scream at her? To have kids at school taunt her about her aunt shooting at children? I had to move both of them out of town. I was just thinking about bringing them back. I can't let this change them—can't let *him* into our lives."

"Of course not," I said. "The narcissism would be destructive."

He nodded. "That's exactly what my therapist called him. Narcissistic personality disorder— sees himself as the center of the world. Like a three-year-old who's never grown up. Incurable— I shouldn't expect him ever to change. My choice was either learn to accept him or stay away from him. At first I thought I could learn, get some kind of casually friendly thing going. But after I met Gwen and her family, saw the way families *should* be, it made me realize what he'd done to all of us. How truly *fucked* he'd been. It made me hate him more."

I listened to all of it, but two words rang in my ear: *my therapist.*

Burden saw my incredulous look, smiled, and shrugged.

"Mine's different," he said. "One of the good ones. Straight shooter. I started seeing him back in college—the counseling center. I was having stomachaches, thought I was going to die the way my mother did. He was doing volunteer work, never earned a cent. Took him two years to fix me up; then he booted me out into the real world. He's retired now. Lives down in Del Mar, plays golf. Once in a while I get down there. Dr. George Goldberg."

I didn't recognize the name.

"He didn't know you either. I called him and asked him about you. He asked around, looked you up, said your credentials were good, you seemed to have a decent reputation. Otherwise I wouldn't have agreed to see you, blood pressure or no blood pressure."

"Did Dr. Goldberg ever meet your father?"

"No. The bastard never knew I was seeing anyone—otherwise he would have done something to stop it. Or take it over. Now he's hired *you*. Pretty funny, huh? Sweet fucking ironies of life."

"I don't know what he told you," I said, "but I'm not working for him, haven't taken a penny from him, and don't intend to. I got involved because the police asked me to help the kids at the school cope with the aftermath of the sniping."

He said, "Yeah, the kids. How're they doing?"

"They're doing all right, but the idea of a total stranger—a girl—shooting at them is still baffling to them. So when your father offered me the chance to learn something about Holly, I took it."

"Holly," he said. He stared at his desk and shook his head. "I know what she did was evil. If my kid had been out in that yard I'd have wanted to kill her myself. But I still feel sorry for her. I can't help it."

"That's understandable. Do you have any idea *why* she did it?"

He shook his head. "I've been racking my brain—Gwen and I both have. I mean, Holly was weird—she was always weird. But never violent. Not that I knew her well—so many years between us, we never had a damn thing in common. Never had any kind of a relationship. She didn't cling the way other little sisters do—she always went her own way, doing her own thing. And *he* was always comparing us—holding me up to her as an example, driving a wedge between us."

"What was her own thing?"

"Sitting in her room listening to the goddam radio and dancing in circles. Crazy-looking. I used to be embarrassed about her. She was . . . dull. I didn't want anyone to know she was my sister." He gave a sick smile. "Now it's out, huh?"

I smiled and nodded.

He said, "Gwen has four brothers. She's very close to all of them. She couldn't understand how a brother and sister could be total strangers. Then when she met *him,* she understood—how he kept us separate, always had. To control us. The hell of it is that recently, we were trying to change things. Gwen initiated it. She invited Holly over, tried to get to know her better. Also to get Holly away from him. Gradually. Out of her shell. She was willing to put the time into Holly. In some ways, what's happened has been harder on her than me."

"You had Holly over to your house?"

"Yes. Just a few times—maybe three or four."

"When was this?"

"This summer. August, September. We made sure to invite her when he was gone. He travels a lot, visiting his suppliers. The business is his fucking life—his real kid. That fucking asshole Graff he created—his own personal Frankenstein doll. We knew if he found out he'd try to fuck it up, and on top of that, Gwen refuses to have him anywhere near Amy. We didn't even want to call, because for all we know, he's got the phones tapped—he's a real gadget freak, loves all that paranoid high-tech stuff. Still reliving his spook days in the army—"

"He was a spy?"

"Some sort of Intelligence work. Supposedly. He'd hint around at it, then if I asked him, refuse to talk about it. 'I can't get into that, Howard.' Sadistic. Always on a fucking power trip."

"He told me he was in cryptography, demographics."

"Like I said, he lies. Maybe he made all of it up, was a fucking latrine cleaner. Anyway, Gwen drove by the house until she caught Holly out in front, taking out the garbage. She tried to strike up a conversation, told Holly to call us next time he was out of town. A few weeks went by—we didn't think she'd follow through. But then she did. We had her over for Sunday dinner. Turkey. Chestnut stuffing. One thing I did remember is she'd always loved turkey."

"How'd it go?"

"It wasn't a bundle of laughs, if that's what you mean. Not much conversation. Holly mostly sat and listened to the three of us talk, watched Amy play with her dolls, never joined in much. Then we put on music and she danced a little; she wasn't very graceful. But then she and Amy started to do it together. And they danced the next few times she came over. Amy's very bright—she was the one leading Holly. The two of them actually seemed to be getting along well, like peers. Amy's a very kind child—she'd never make fun. She knew Holly was strange, but she never said anything about it, just danced with her. Gwen and I both thought we were making some progress, but then Holly stopped calling. Just like that. We couldn't figure out why, said to hell with him and tried phoning, got his fucking machine. So Gwen started driving by again, waited for a time when his car was gone, and knocked on the door. Holly answered. Gwen said she looked terrible—haggard, as if someone had died. Gwen tried to talk to her, but she shut her out, kept wringing her hands and talking nonsense."

"What kind of nonsense?"

"Saying stuff over and over again. Gibberish. *Wanna see.* Or *wanna say. Wanna see too.*"

"T-O-O?"

"Or maybe it was T-W-O—who gives a fuck? Doesn't make much sense either way, does it? Gwen tried to get her to explain, but Holly got agitated and ran back inside the house. Gwen followed her in. Holly had gone to the gun closet, pulled out a rifle. *That* freaked Gwen out. She left in a hurry and called me. We talked about it, figured Holly had had some kind of breakdown. Her grabbing the gun really had us worried—she'd always hated his guns, never went near them. We called the police, anonymously. Told them a disturbed person had access to firearms and gave them the address. They asked if the disturbed person had either been certified disturbed or had actually threatened someone with the gun. We said no. They said then they couldn't do anything unless we went to Recognizance Court and convinced the judge she was a danger to herself and others. Even then all we could get would be a seventy-two-hour hold. And *he* was sure to fight that. So we ended up doing nothing. Because of Amy. We didn't want her exposed to any craziness. To courts and shrinks and *him*. And we stopped trying to get closer to Holly."

"When did this happen—grabbing the gun?"

"Last month. A couple of weeks before . . ."

He hung his head. "So what happened is no big surprise, is it? She was obviously having violent thoughts and no one took them seriously. I keep wondering if I could have prevented it."

"Not likely," I said. "Did you tell the police any of this?"

"What the hell for? Drag my family into more shit? Get my name in the papers again? Besides, the guy they sent down looked like a fucking actor, couldn't have cared less."

"Lieutenant Frisk?"

"Yeah, that was him. I remember thinking what an asshole. Trying to stare me down, obviously considered himself hot shit. Kept harping on was she a member of any subversive groups. That's a laugh, huh? Holly joining the fucking Red Brigade." He shook his head. "No, we haven't talked about it—the guns—to anyone. Gwen still can't talk about it—any of it. She's convinced it's her fault. Here she is, the kindest person who ever walked this earth, and she's blaming herself."

I said, "The kind ones always do. Maybe you and she should take a trip down to Del Mar."

Risking his anger by giving advice.

But he said, "Maybe," in a defeated voice. "I wish there was some way to turn back the clock. I know it's a fucking cliché, but it would make life a helluva lot easier, wouldn't it?"

He covered his face again, gave a loud sigh.

I said, "Do you remember when it was that Holly stopped calling?"

"September. Late September."

Right after Ike Novato's murder.

Terrible. Haggard. As if someone had died.

I said, "Did she have any friends?"

"None that I ever saw."

"Did she ever mention the name Novato?"

He moved his hand from his face. "No. Who's that?"

"Someone who may have been a friend. He delivered groceries for Dinwiddie's market. We know he and Holly had at least a few casual conversations."

"Is that what he says?"

"He doesn't say anything. He's dead."

"How?"

"Murdered, last September. Just around the time Holly started pulling away from you."

"Murd—Oh, Jesus. You think that's what tipped her over?"

"It's possible."

"You're saying this Novato meant something to her?"

"Maybe. Your father says no—"

"What he says means fucking diddly-squat. Who is—was—this Novato? What kind of person."

"People who knew him say he was a nice kid. Smart, black. Ted Dinwiddie thought highly of him. He was Dinwiddie's delivery boy."

He smiled. "Black. That makes sense. Back in high school, Ted Dinwiddie used to be our local flaming radical. Now he's a businessman, probably feeling guilty about it. Hiring a black kid is something he would have done. And felt nervous about. The anxiety would have assuaged his guilt."

He was silent for several moments, seemed to be lost in memories. Before the silence could curdle, I said, "What are your father's political views?"

"I don't know that he has any. He's a fucking Mah*lon*icrat. Worships himself—fuck everyone else."

"When Holly came over did she ever talk politics?"

"Nothing. Like I told you, she barely said

anything at all. Why? What's this all about? Who
killed Novato?"

"It's unsolved."

"How'd it happen?"

I considered how much to tell him. When I
didn't answer right away, he moved forward and
said, "Look, I've opened myself up to you.
Maybe I'll feel better for it tomorrow, maybe not.
But the point is, I didn't hold back and I don't
really know you from shit. So if you've got
something to tell me, something I can bring home
to Gwen, help her make sense of it, I need to know
it. I fucking *deserve* it."

I told him about Novato's death in the alley
and Sophie Gruenberg's disappearance. Mentioned nothing of Smith's suspicion that the two of
them had been involved in dope. Talked about
Gruenberg's radical politics and resurrected my
theory that Holly had been motivated by some sort
of twisted political impulse. Aiming at Massengil.
I had nothing to back that up, but the therapist in
me had taken over; I wanted to make Burden feel
better.

It worked.

He thought for a long time, then said, "It
makes it a little easier to take. That she wasn't
going for the kids. That in some crazy, fucked-up
way she had a goal. Friends. People who cared
about her."

He turned away, looked at the images of his

wife and his daughter. "We wanted to be her friends. That was the whole point. To get to know her, reconnect. Make up for lost time—salvage something. But you can't do that, can you? It just doesn't fucking work that way, does it?"

24

Ten minutes had stretched to more than an hour. When I got up to leave, Burden was so subdued he looked drowsy, and the hand that I shook was wet and limp. I left him at his desk and walked to the elevator.

Outside, the air had stayed warm, and though it reeked of exhaust, I was happy to draw it into my lungs. Happy to get away from the hatred and rage that had filled his office like swamp gas.

I thought I understood, now, why Mahlon Burden had been so eager for me to speak with his son. Howard had shut him out; the two of them had no communication. But if Howard talked to me, I could pass along what I learned to the old man.

Shrink as modem.

That's my main talent. . . . I do know how to put things together.

And Howard had talked; I'd learned a lot

more than I'd expected. But nothing I was going
to report to Burden.

I reviewed it as I drove: Holly had deteriorated psychologically shortly after Ike Novato's
death. Handled the rifle she'd ultimately taken to
the storage shed . . .

*Wanna see, wanna say. Wanna see or say
too.*

Or was it *two?*

See two *what?*

Probably just gibberish, not worth interpreting.

What relationship, if any, was there to Novato's death? Gruenberg's disappearance?

I began to doubt if I'd ever really understand
what had led Holly to that shed.

Nothing like that feeling of competence . . .

As I turned back onto the Glen, I was
determined to put all of it out of my mind. Think
good thoughts. Think about Linda. About kissing
her.

I got home at seven-forty. She arrived an
hour later, wearing a pink dress and sandals, her
hair loose and sun-gold.

The first kiss was long and deep and I felt as
if I was giving myself over to it completely. But
when it ended she said, "You feel tense. Everything okay?"

"Just a little tired. And hungry. Still up for Mexican?"

"You bet. My treat."

"Not necessary."

"Don't worry." She rubbed my shoulder. "When we do Spago, you'll pay."

Just as we made it to the door, the phone rang.

She said, "Go ahead."

I took it in the living room.

"Alex? It's me." Robin's voice.

"Oh. Hi."

"Hi. You all right?"

"Sure. Fine. How about you?"

"Fine. I'm just waiting for some glue to set, thought I'd call and touch base."

"I appreciate that. How're you?"

"Great. Real busy."

"As usual."

"As usual."

Linda had taken out her compact and was looking in the mirror.

Robin said, "So."

"So."

Linda looked up. I smiled at her and she smiled back.

"Alex, is this a . . . bad time?"

"No. I was just on my way out."

"Anywhere special?"

"Dinner."

"Hey," she said, "feel like picking up a pizza and dropping by? For old times' sake?"

"That would be . . . difficult."

"Oh," she said. "Going *out* going out."

"Uh-huh."

"Oh. Sorry. I'll let you go. 'Bye."

I said, "Wait. Is everything really okay with you?"

"Great. Really. And there's someone 'round these quarters too. Nothing cosmic at this point, but the indicators are good."

"I'm glad."

"Okay," she said. "I just wanted to touch base. Glad you're okay. Be well."

"Take care of yourself."

"You, too."

" 'Bye."

" 'Bye."

Linda said nothing as we walked out to the car. I drove to Sunset, cruised past the 405 Freeway on-ramp, listening to Miles Davis. A few moments later, she turned down the radio and said, "Her?"

I nodded.

"You didn't have to rush things for my benefit."

"No sense in dragging it out."

"Okay."

I said, "It's over, but we're still dealing with some of the . . . friendship residue."

"Sure. Makes sense." A moment later: "She's beautiful."

"What do you mean?"

"I found a picture of her. This morning, in your library. Face down on one of the book-shelves."

"Oh?"

"Don't be mad," she said, "I wasn't snoop-ing."

"I'm not mad."

"What happened is, I woke up early, thought I'd get something to read, and found it while I was looking through your books—at least I assume it's her. Long curly hair, kind of rusty-colored? Really good figure? Beautiful wide dark eyes? The two of you standing in front of some kind of lake?"

The lagoon at U.C. Santa Cruz. I remem-bered the trip—the motel we'd stayed at. Rumpled sheets. Walks in the mountains . . .

"It's an old picture," I said. "I didn't know I still had it."

"Nothing wrong if you had kept it on purpose."

"I'm not one for souvenirs."

"I am," she said. "I've still got pictures of Mondo in one of my scrapbooks. Before every-thing went bad. What does that say about me—psychologically?"

"Uh-uh." I shook my head. "Off duty. No out-of-the-office interpretations."

"You don't have a proper office."

"Need I say more?"

She smiled. "Anyway, she is beautiful."

"She is. And it's over."

"You said that already."

"Got in the habit of saying it," I said. "Trying to convince myself. It eventually worked."

"Would you hate me if I asked how and why?"

"*How* is, she went on a trial separation that stretched to something permanent. I fought it, tried to persuade her to come back. By the time she'd changed her mind, I'd changed mine. *Why* is, she felt I was smothering her. Overpowering her. She'd grown up with an overpowering father, needed to stretch her wings, try things out by herself. I'm not trying to make it sound corny or clichéd. There was validity to it."

"And now she wants you back."

"No. Like I said, it's just the friendship residue."

Linda didn't answer.

We drove for a while.

"Smothering," she said. "I don't see you that way at all."

"I'm not the same guy I was a year ago. The whole thing made me take a good look at myself."

"Not that I'd like that myself," she said. "Being smothered."

"Somehow, I don't see you as smotherable."

"Oh?"

"You fought for your stripes a long time ago, Linda. No one's going to take them away from you."

"Think I'm pretty tough, do you?"

"In a good way. I think you can handle yourself."

She put her hand on the back of my neck.

"Ooh, even tighter. Sorry for making you talk about it. What a Nosy Nancy I am."

"Nosy Nancy?"

"It's a regionalism."

"From what region?"

"My apartment. There—I got you to smile. But this *neck*—it's like hardwood." She moved closer, began kneading. I felt her warmth and her strength, coming from those soft hands, the ones I'd thought passive when I first met her.

She said, "How's that?"

"Fantastic. I'd trade dinner for about an hour of it."

"Tell you what," she said. "First we pig out on Mexican food, then we return to either your place or mine, I give you a real Texas massage, and then you can smother me. You just forget about all the ugliness and the complications and you smother me to your little heart's content."

It ended up being my place. We were in bed

when the phone rang. Lying naked in the darkness, listening to Gershwin's own rendition of *Rhapsody in Blue*, holding hands.

I said, "Jesus, what time is it?"

"Twenty after eleven."

I picked up the receiver.

Milo said, "Hi."

"What's up?"

"From the nuance of irritation in your voice, might I infer that this is a bad time?"

I said, "You just keep getting better and better at the old detecting game."

"Someone with you?"

"Uh-huh."

"Blondie, I hope?"

"None of your—"

"Good, it's her I want to talk to. Put her on."

Puzzled, I handed the receiver to Linda. "It's Milo. For you."

She said, "For me?" and took it. "Hello, Detective Sturgis, what is it? . . . Oh. You're sure? . . . That's great. How did you . . . Oh. That was lucky. . . . You think so? Okay. Sounds interesting . . . I guess. If you really think so . . . Okay, I'll be there. Thanks."

She reached across me and hung up the phone. Her breasts grazed my lips. Reflexively, I nibbled. She pulled away and said, "Want to go for a ride?"

* * *

A street named Fiesta Drive. No fog tonight. In the moonlight, the magnolias looked like paper cutout trees.

The house was tidy-looking, no different from any of the others on the block. An Oldsmobile Cutlass was parked in the driveway; behind it, the low, black cigar of a Firebird Trans Am. On the Firebird's rear bumper was a sticker with the call letters of a heavy-metal radio station and another that said LIFE IS A BEACH.

The front door smelled of fresh paint. The bell chimed out the first seven notes of "Battle Hymn of the Republic." A worried-looking, heavyset woman in her fifties opened the door on the fifth note. She had on moss-green slacks and a white blouse and was barefoot. Her round face was pale under a crown of baby-blue hair rollers. Her jawline had lost the battle with gravity.

Linda said, "I'm Dr. Overstreet."

The woman trembled and said, "I'm . . . They're . . . Won't you come in. Please."

We stepped into a living room identical in size and trim and layout to the one in the Burden house. This one was painted buttercup-yellow with contrasting white moldings and furnished with a skirted floral chintz sofa and matching chairs, a brown corduroy recliner, golden-maple end tables, and shiny white ceramic lamps. Prints of plein-air landscapes and still lifes favoring fruit and fish hung on the walls, along with a bronze Zodiac wheel and an old Christmas wreath. The fireplace had been bricked up and painted white. A model schooner fashioned of rough-edged copper sheeting and brass wire sat on the hearth.

A dark-complected man with sharp features sat on the recliner, but he wasn't relaxed. He had thinning black hair, whitening at the temples, a drawn lantern-jawed face that sagged—orienting downward as surely as a dowsing rod. He wore a T-shirt and gray slacks under a plaid Pendleton robe, terry-cloth slippers on white, blue-veined feet. His arms rested on the sides of the recliner, the hands clenching and unclenching.

Milo stood across from him, to the left of the sofa. A boy of around sixteen or seventeen sat right below him. The boy was big, in a soft, bulky way, with thick, formless white arms extending from the rolled sleeves of a pea-green patch-pocketed T-shirt. Around his pudgy wrists were nailhead-studded leather bands. His black jeans were tucked into chain-heeled Wellington boots. A massive stainless-steel death's-head ring dominated his left hand. His right hand shielded his face. What little I could see of his countenance was puffy, not yet fully formed, under dark hair cut close to the scalp. Fuzzy approximations of sideburns ran down cheeks speckled with pimples, and dipped an inch below his earlobes. He didn't look up at our entrance, just continued to do what he'd obviously been doing for a while: crying.

Milo said, "Evening, Dr. Overstreet and Dr. Delaware. These are the Buchanans, Mr. and Mrs."

The man and woman gave miserable nods.

"And this is Matthew. He did the artwork on your car."

The boy cried louder.

His father said, "Cut that the hell out. At least face up to it and don't be a coward, goddammit."

The boy continued to cry.

Buchanan shot up and walked to the couch, a big, soft man. He took hold of the boy's wrists and yanked them away. The boy bent low, tried to bury his face between his knees. His father reached under and forced his head upward, gripping him by the jaw.

"You look at them, goddammit! Face up to it, or it'll be even worse for you, I promise."

The boy's face was pasty and snot-smeared, his mouth lopsided and grotesque in his father's grasp. He clenched his eyes shut. Buchanan swore.

Mrs. Buchanan took a step toward her son. Her husband's eyes warned her off. His hand tightened. The boy yelped in pain.

"Easy," said Milo. He touched Buchanan's

arm. The man stared at him furiously, then backed off.

"Sit down, sir," said Milo gently.

Buchanan returned to the recliner, drawing his robe around him and looking away from the rest of us.

Milo said, "Matt, this is Dr. Overstreet. Principal of the Hale school, but you probably know that, don't you?"

The boy stared at Linda, terrified, then clamped his eyes shut.

Linda said, "Hello, Matthew."

The boy buried his face again.

His father whipped around and said, "Say it!"

The boy mumbled something.

Buchanan was up in a flash. His right arm shot out and the boy's head snapped back.

Mrs. Buchanan cried out.

Milo said, "That's enough! Sit down!"

Buchanan put his hands on his hips and stared at Milo. "I want him to say it."

"Pete," said his wife.

Her husband pointed a finger at her. "*You* keep the hell *out* of this!"

"Mr. Buchanan," said Milo, "let's not make things worse than they are. Why don't you just sit down?"

"I'da been listened to in the first place," Buchanan said, "there'da been no trouble. He *did*

it. He's got to face *up* to it—no more *coddling*."
He tried to stare down Milo, gave up and glowered
at his wife.

Milo said, "You're absolutely right, sir. Face
up is exactly what he needs to do. So let's give him
a chance to do that."

Buchanan looked at his son. "Say it!"

The boy choked out a "sorry" between sobs.

"Sorry, *ma'am*!" barked his father.

"Sorry, ma'am."

"He really is," said Mrs. Buchanan, looking
at Linda. "He's never done anything like this
before and never will again. We're *all* so sorry."

"Stop apologizing, for God's sake," said her
husband. "What in hell do *we* have to apologize
for? Except maybe for your coddling him, giving
him everything he whines for so he's never had to
take any goddam responsibility for himself."

"Pete, please."

"Don't Pete please me!" said Buchanan.
"Just stop getting in the way and let me handle this
the way it should have been handled a long time
ago." He extended a pair of big white hairy fists.

His wife bit her lip and turned away. The boy
had stopped crying long enough to follow the
parental skirmish.

Buchanan Senior turned his back on him and
approached Linda. His lip was quivering and I
noticed that one eye drooped lower than the other.
"Ma'am, I've got a President's last name. I

believe in this country. A *deep* belief. We've got soldiers in our family going way back, generations. I did my time in Korea, active duty, got the papers to prove it. So we sure don't encourage any Nazi talk around here. He musta picked it up on that crap he plays all the time—rock videos. Which is long gone from this house, that's for sure."

An angry look over his shoulder.

The boy covered his face again.

"Don't you dare when I'm talking to you!" shouted his father. "Face *up,* goddammit!"

He turned and moved toward his son. Milo got between them. "I'm going to have to insist that you sit, sir. *Now.*"

Buchanan tightened, then let out breath.

Milo's face was a police mask.

Buchanan muttered, then returned to the recliner, picked up the previous day's newspaper from an end table, and pretended to be interested in the sports section.

His wife's heavy face was ripe with humiliation.

Milo said, "Dr. Overstreet, if you want to press charges, I'll have Matt arrested and taken in."

The boy started crying again. His mother followed suit.

Mr. Buchanan looked at both of them with revulsion.

Linda walked over to the sofa and studied the boy. He tried to avoid her gaze, sniffled, and wiped his nose with his sleeve.

She said, "Why, Matt?"

Fidget. Shrug.

"That's important for me to know. Before I decide what to do. Why'd you do it?"

The boy mumbled something.

Linda said, "What's that?"

"Don't know."

"You don't know why you demolished my car?"

Shrug.

"What'd you use?"

"Crowbar."

"Did you know it was my car?"

Silence.

"C'mon, Matt. You owe me."

Nod.

"You knew it was my car?"

"Yeah."

"Why'd you want to hurt me? Have I ever done anything to you?"

Shake of head.

"Then why?"

"The school."

"What about the school?"

"Bringing the . . . them in."

"Who?"

"The niggers and beaners. Everyone said you

were bringing them in to take over the neighbor-hood."

"Everyone? Who's everyone?"

The boy shrugged. "Just people."

Buchanan broke in. "He didn't hear that here. Not that I approve of what you've done, but we stick with the law, go our own way and don't make trouble for others. And we don't talk gutter talk. I work with the colored—we get along just fine."

"What kind of work do you do, Mr. Buchanan?"

He named an electronics company. "Line supervisor. Got seventy-five people under me, plenty of them Mexicans and colored. He didn't hear that kind of gutter talk here." To his son: "Did you!"

The boy shook his head.

"It's the goddam rock videos," said his father. "And that car—he never shoulda had it. Too damn babyish to wipe his own nose. Look at you!"

Mrs. Buchanan left the room and came back with a box of tissues. She pulled one out and handed it to her son.

He swabbed his nose.

His father said, "Congratulations, smart guy. That Trans Am is history."

"Dad—"

"Shut up!"

Linda said, "Matt, let me get this straight.

You resent me because you think I'm trying to take over your neighborhood by bringing in kids from other neighborhoods. So you smashed up my car."

Nod.

"How'd you know it was my car?"

The boy said, "Seen you." Barely audible.

"Was anyone else with you?"

Shake of the head.

"Did anyone else know you were going to do this?"

"No."

"You just did it yourself."

Nod.

"Why'd you paint a swastika on the car?"

Shrug.

"Do you know what the swastika stands for?"

"Kinda."

"Kinda? What does it stand for?"

"Germans."

"Not Germans," said his father. "Nazis. Your grandfather fought them."

Linda said, "Why'd you paint a swastika?"

"Dunno. Just being kinda . . ."

"Kinda what?"

"Rad. Bad. Like the Angels."

"Hell's Angels?"

"Yeah."

"Christ," said his father.

Linda said, "What were you doing up so late, Matt?"

Buchanan glared at his wife and said, "Good goddam question."

The boy didn't answer.

Linda said, "Matt, I asked you a question and I expect an answer."

"Cruising."

"With a crowbar?"

No answer.

"Why'd you have a crowbar with you?"

"To do it."

"To smash my car with?"

Nod.

Buchanan said, "Talk, goddammit."

"Yeah," said the boy.

"So you'd planned to smash my car."

Glance at his father. "Yeah."

"For how long?"

"I dunno—few days."

"Why a few days? What gave you the idea?"

"Her . . . the shooting." The boy sat up straighter, doughy face brightening. "It just showed how fu— how trashed everything was, the ni— the black kids and the Mexes. It just showed how ruined everything was and it was the school's fault." Turning to his father: "That's what *you* and she said."

Mrs. Buchanan put her hand to her mouth.

"Oh, Christ," said her husband, blanching. "You goddam little moron! People have opinions— this is America, for Christ's sake! You express an opinion—you're supposed to speak your mind.

That's what democracy is. Otherwise it might as well be Russia. But you don't go around destroying private *property* for Christ's sake!"

He turned to Linda. "Listen, ma'am, you'll be paid every last penny for your car. That Trans Am is going to the used-car dealer tomorrow and every last penny we get from that will go for *your* car and you've got my word on that."

"Good. I expect payment within a week," said Linda. "But that's not enough."

The boy stared at her, petrified.

"Please," said Mrs. Buchanan, "don't make him go to jail. He's—"

"Not jail," said Linda. "Too easy. I want more out of him. Some real repentance." To Matt: "Where do you go to school?"

"Pali."

"Junior?"

"Sophomore."

"What time do you get off?"

"Two."

"He's in limited academic," said his mother.

"By two-thirty I want you over at my school. Helping out."

"How?" said the boy.

"Any way I want you to help. One day you might be scrubbing some graffiti off a wall. Another day you might be working the Xerox machine. Or writing an essay."

The boy flinched.

"Don't like to write, Matt?"

"He's had trouble," said his mother. "Dyslexia."

"Then it'll be especially helpful for him."

"Yes, it will," said Mrs. Buchanan. "Yes, it surely will. We do appreciate it. Thank you, ma'am."

"Detective Sturgis," said Linda, "I'm willing not to press charges if Matt here cooperates and ends up being a big help to me. On one condition. If he screws up, can I still press them?"

"Absolutely," said Milo. "I'll keep the file open, make sure he gets the max, all felonies, tried as an adult." To Matt: "We're talking heavy jail time, son."

"He'll cooperate," said his mother. "I'll see that he—"

Linda said, "Matt? You understand what's going on?"

"Yeah— yes. Ma'am. I will. I . . . I'm really sorry. It was dumb."

"Then I'm willing to give you a chance."

Mrs. Buchanan poured out copious thanks.

Mr. Buchanan seemed to sag in his chair, looking older, smaller, the strain of macho pretense lifted from tired shoulders.

He said, "You're one lucky camper, mister. And you haven't heard from me, yet."

25

Outside at the curb, Milo said, "I had nothing to do tonight. Went driving. Saw his car circle the block real slowly, about nine-thirty, slow down further when he reached the school. Third time he came around I decided to put the cherry on my roof and stop him. He had the crowbar right there on the seat. Dumb kid. He nearly browned his pants when he saw me."

Linda said, "You heard the mother—all those school problems."

"Just like Holly," I said.

"But they didn't know each other," Milo said. "I worked him over on that with extreme thoroughness. He has no record, no membership in any gangs or groups. So it looks like this is the only mischief he's been into—or caught at."

Linda's back was to him. He raised an eyebrow, wanting to know how much I'd told her.

I gave a tiny shake of my head, said, "Maybe you nipped a criminal career in the bud."

"His career wouldn't have lasted long—the dumb ones are the ones we catch. Anyway, time to be shoving off. Sorry for waking you but I thought you'd want to know."

"I did," she said. "I'm glad you called. Do you think I did the right thing?"

"Seems as good an option as any. The juvenile system takes over on something like this, we're talking stern lecture. Maybe. If you got a real kick-ass judge, a week at the honor farm and exposure to some people he doesn't need to be exposed to. But if he screws up again, let me know. I can always pull a few fast ones, procedurally speaking, and scare the bejesus out of him."

Linda said, "Okay. And thanks again."

He said, *"Bon soir,"* saluted, and walked off.

"Good man," said Linda.

"No argument there."

We went back to my place and found we were too wound up to sleep. I located a deck of cards in a kitchen drawer and we bored ourselves with a few hands of poor-attention-span gin, finally turned off the lights and dozed, lying close to each other.

The next morning, I drove her back to her apartment and went up with her. She changed into a lilac-colored suit, picked up her rental car in the subterranean garage, and drove to school. I ran a few errands, then drove there myself. Bits of streamers still clung to the chain link. Otherwise the grounds were quiet—almost ghostly. Morning-after blues.

I waited in Linda's office while she checked to see if any adjustment problems had cropped up in the aftermath of the concert. A few teachers reported some unruliness, but nothing they couldn't handle. At noon I stopped in with those teachers and, having convinced myself everything was going smoothly, left.

At 1:00 P.M., Mahlon Burden called. "Any progress, Dr. Delaware?"

"I met with your son last night."

"Excellent. And?"

"He had nothing new to offer about Holly, but he did say you visited him about a month ago. You were concerned about her."

Pause. "Yes, that's true. I knew Howard had been . . . sneaking her over to his house. He and his wife thought I didn't know, but of course I did. Since they were spending more time to-gether, I thought he might be able to tell me why she'd been looking sad."

"Sad?"

"Withdrawn. Uncommunicative. More than usual."

"When did that start?"

"Let me think back—late September or the beginning of October. I remember because my fall catalogue had just gone out. Excuse me for not mentioning it when you were at the house, but with everything that's been going on—the memories—it slipped by. I haven't been functioning at full capacity."

"Did you suspect her contact with Howard was causing the withdrawal?"

"I didn't suspect anything, Doctor. I was simply trying to develop hypotheses. Now, of course, you've provided me with one. The death of the black boy. That occurred late September. He and Holly may have been closer than I thought. What else do you know about him other than that he was a drug user?"

"Some people who knew him doubt he was a drug user."

"People?"

"Ted Dinwiddie."

"Ted Dinwiddie." Burden gave a small laugh. "Not exactly an Einstein, that one. Howard used to do his homework for him. Where was Novato killed?"

"South L.A."

"South L.A. Before the riot we used to call it Watts—never could understand that, people burning down their own homes, fouling their own nests. Did your detective friend mention which gang he belonged to?"

"There's no evidence he belonged to any gang."

"In this city, drugs means gangs," he said. "Or at least that's what they say. What else can you tell me about him?"

"That's it."

"All right, then. What's next on our agenda?"

"Mr. Burden, I haven't learned anything that would vindicate Holly. And to be honest, I don't see myself moving in that direction."

Pause. "That's very disappointing, Doctor." But he didn't sound disappointed. Or surprised. "Have you considered talking to members of Novato's family—delving into his background?"

"He was from back east, didn't have family out here. And frankly, Mr. Burden, I don't see that as being helpful in terms of what you want."

"Why's that, Doctor?"

"There just doesn't seem to be any connection to Holly."

Silence on the other end.

"I'm sorry," I said. "I don't see anywhere to take the evaluation that would fulfill your needs."

He said, "I'm sorry you feel that way. Why don't you come over again? The two of us can put our heads together, develop some hypotheses."

"Maybe in a while," I said. "I'm a little tied up now."

"I see," he said. "But you're not closing the door?"

"No," I said. "The door's never closed."

"Good." Pause. "Quite a ruckus down by the school yesterday. Papers said Councilman Latch brought in a rock singer to entertain the children. Making political hay?"

"Bales of it."

"Why not?" he said. "Seize the moment. Next thing you know, they'll be dancing on my daughter's grave."

An hour later Milo called and I told him of my meeting with Howard Burden, described the mental deterioration Howard had seen in his sister after Novato's death. Her holding the rifle. *Wanna see two.*

He said, "What'd she wanna see two of?"

"No idea."

"Hmm," he said. "How 'bout wanna see two people dead? Massengil and someone else."

"Latch?"

"Could be," he said. "Two shitbirds with one stone. Talk about your civic responsibility. Or maybe she was planning to do Massengil at the school, head off somewhere else for victim number two. It's not unusual for these nutcases to have elaborate plans—delusions. But I don't have to tell *you* that, do I? Anyway, all this does is firm up the lone-assassin picture, puts her hands on the weapon a good two weeks before the shooting— shows premeditation. She was mentally shaky to begin with, got stressed out by Novato's death,

became unglued, spent a month and a half building up anger, going to the gun rack, getting the
feel of the thing. Then, boom. How'm I doing—
psychologically?"

"Good enough."

"It's not gonna sound too good to Daddy."

"I just spoke to him, put him on hold."

"Till when?"

"Indefinite."

"Didn't have the heart to cut him off?"

"I've got nothing to offer him," I said. "But
for all I know, his defenses are about to come
tumbling down. I wanted to go easy."

"Thought you didn't like the guy."

"I don't, but that doesn't alter my responsibility. Besides, the guy's pathetic—got nothing
left in the way of family. His son hates him—it's
obvious he just wanted me to talk to him because
there's no communication between them. So I
went easy."

"Interesting," said Milo.

"What is?"

"Having a job where you've got to be watching yourself all the time, caring about people's
feelings."

"Part of your job too."

"Sometimes," he said. "But mostly the people I care about are dead. Speaking of which, I got
in touch with Santa Monica College. Novato did

register for summer session, but he dropped out after a week."

"Long enough to get his name listed at the Employment Center."

"That's what I thought too. Probably why he registered in the first place. No ID, no references, would have been hard to find a job."

"Dinwiddie would have liked the student thing. He yearns for school days."

"My question," Milo said, "is why Novato would want a low-paying job if he was selling dope."

"A cover? Smith said they were getting sophisticated."

"Maybe. Be that as it may, I don't know that any of it is worth pursuing. My source at the Holocaust Center flies in from Chicago this afternoon. Got an appointment down there at five— that's the last thing I'm gonna do on it. Ever been there?"

"No."

"You should see it. Everyone should."

"I'm free at five."

"You drive."

Scaffolding and an enclosed wooden perimeter marked a construction zone next to a two-story building made of white brick and black marble.

"That's the museum," said Milo. "House of Tolerance. They just broke ground last month."

Traffic was congested for a half-block radius around the site. Motors groaned, clay dust billowed, hammer thuds and saw whines rose above the combustive groan of idling engines. A hard hat in an orange vest stood in the middle of Pico, directing a crane as it backed up onto the boulevard. A female traffic cop whistled and white-gloved a steadily building herd of autos into submission.

Milo leaned toward the center of the Seville and looked in the rearview mirror. A moment later he looked again.

I said, "What is it?"

"Nothing." His eyes swept back and forth.

"Come on, Milo."

"It's nothing," he said. "A while back I thought someone might be on our tail. It's probably nothing."

"Probably?"

"Don't get in an uproar." He sat back.

"Where'd you see it?"

"Just before Motor, near Fox Studios. Probably my imagination—there doesn't seem to be anyone back there now, but it's too stacked up to be sure."

"Maybe it wasn't your imagination. I've had the same feeling a couple of times the last week."

"That so?"

"I also put it down to imagination."

"Probably was."

"Probably?"

"Like I said, Alex, don't get in an uproar. Even if there was someone, most likely it was the Department."

"Why do you say that?"

"The car. Plymouth sedan. Flat gray, black-wall tires, radio antennae. Except for the narcs and all their confiscated hot rods, the Department hasn't discovered special effects."

"Why would the Department be following us?"

"Not us. *Me.* Maybe I stepped on someone's toes. Got big feet." He wiggled his brogans.

I said, "Frisk?"

He shrugged. "Yeah, I suppose. It's Kenny's type of game, but it could be anyone. My persona's never that grata."

"But what about the ones who followed me? Guilt by association?"

"Ones? How many were there?"

"Two, both times. First in a brown Toyota, then some kind of sedan. Male and female the second time, I think."

"Sounds kind of imaginative for the Department. When and where'd it happen?"

"Both times were at night. Coming out of restaurants. The first time I was by myself, in Santa Monica. The second was this past Sunday night, with Linda. Melrose near LaBrea."

"How long did they stay with you?"

"Not long." I told him about driving into the gas station to avoid the brown Toyota.

He smiled. "Flashy move, Double-0-Seven. They show any signs of noticing you after you pulled into the station?"

"No. Just drove right by."

"What about the second time?"

I shook my head. "I pulled off onto a side street and they were gone."

"Doesn't sound like much of a tail," he said. "And no similarities to the one I just saw. This was one guy—male Cauc, standard issue. And he didn't just stay right on our tail. He hung back— the way they teach you in cop school. That's what caught my eye—the spacing. Professionalism. A civilian would have missed it. *I* could have easily missed it. Even now, I'm not sure it wasn't some guy just happening to be driving by. If the Department was bothering to run a two-man tail, chances are the second guy would have been in another car, doing an A-B. Your guys, on the other hand, were obvious as hell—you saw 'em, didn't you? Which leads me to believe they weren't tailing you. So all in all, I'd vote for imagination, Alex."

"Yours is real, mine's baloney?"

"Just keeping a sane perspective," he said. "Mine's probably baloney too."

He sat back, made a show of stretching his legs and yawning.

The crane was finally gone and we advanced.

As I turned the corner, Milo checked out the cars that sped by.

"Nothing," he said. "Forget the whole thing."

We parked in the visitor's lot in back of the center and walked around to the front entrance. After passing through a metal detector, we signed in with a plainclothes guard in an open booth. He was young, sharp-featured, with cropped black hair, a strong chin, and hard eyes.

Milo showed ID and said, "We're here to see Judy Baumgartner."

"Wait, please," said the guard. Some kind of accent. He stepped back several feet and made a call.

"Israeli," said Milo. "Since the swastikas, they use ex-secret-service guys as security. Very stubborn. They can be a real pain in the ass to deal with, but they get the job done."

The guard returned to the counter. "She'll be a few minutes. You can wait up there." He pointed to a short, open flight of stairs. Above it was a landing backed with a black-and-white mural of wide-eyed faces. Frightened faces. It reminded me of the TV broadcast the day of the sniping.

Milo said, "How about we look at the exhibit?"

The guard shrugged. "Sure."

We took the open stairs down to the basement level. Dark hallway, the sounds of typing and ringing phones. A few people traveled the corridor, purposeful, busy.

To the right of the stairs was a black door marked EXHIBIT in small steel letters.

"Temporary," he said, "until the museum's done."

He opened the door to a room about thirty feet square, paneled gallery-white, gray-carpeted, and very cool. Photo blowups lined the walls.

Milo began walking. I followed.

The first picture: storm troopers kicking and beating elderly Jews on the streets of Munich.

The second, stolid-looking citizens marching with placards:

> RAUS MIT
> EUCH DRECKIGE
> ## JUDEN!

I stopped, caught my breath, went on.

A jackbooted, peak-capped soldier, not more than nineteen or twenty, using tin snips to cut the beard of a terrified grandfather as other soldiers look on in glee.

The shattered and defaced storefronts of post-Kristallnacht Berlin. Swastikas. Posters in crude gothic lettering.

Gutted buildings. Shattered faces.

A triptych midway down the first wall made me stop even as Milo kept walking. A winter scene. Forest of monumental conifers atop gently rolling snow dunes. In the foreground a row of naked men and women huddled in front of trench graves; some still held shovels. Dozens of emaciated physiques, caved-in chests, shriveled genitals. Victims obscenely bare amid the frosty beauty of the Bavarian countryside. Behind the prisoners, a dozen SS men armed with carbines.

Next photo: the troopers raise weapons to shoulder. An officer holds a baton. Most of the diggers keep their backs turned, but one woman has shifted to face the soldiers, screaming, open-mouthed. A dark-eyed, black-haired woman, her breasts shrunken, her pubic thatch a dark wound in white flesh.

Then: bodies, heaps of them, filling the trenches, merging with the snow. One soldier bayonets a corpse.

I forced myself to move on.

Close-ups of barbed wire—iron fangs. A sign in German. A shred of something clinging to the fangs.

Snarling dogs.

A blowup of a document. Columns of numbers, straight margins, beautifully printed, neat as an accountant's ledger. Opposite each column, hand-scripted words. *Bergen-Belsen. Gotha. Buchenwald. Dachau. Dortmund. Auschwitz. Landsberg. Maidanek. Treblinka.* Opposite each

name, a number code. Body count. So many
digits. A horrific arithmetic . . .

More snowy-white images: bleached bones.
Piles of them. Femurs and tibias and finger bones
white as piano keys. Pelvic cradles stripped raw.
Yawning rib cages. Scraps and fragments rendered
unidentifiable.

A mountain of bones sitting on a base of dust
and grit.

An incomprehensible Everest of bones, landscaped with jawless skulls.

My stomach lurched.

Another enlarged document: multisyllabic
German words. A translating caption: PROCESSING
PROCEDURES. The final solution.

Compulsively detailed lists of those bound
for the refuse heap:

Jews. Gypsies. Subversives. Homosexuals.

I looked over at Milo. He was across the
room, his back to me. Hands in pockets, hunched
and bulky and predatory as a bear out on a night
forage.

I kept walking, looking.

A display case of Zyklon B poison-gas can-
isters. Another containing a shredded striped uniform of coarse cloth.

Little children in cloth caps and braids,
herded onto trains. Bewildered, tear-streaked.
Tiny hands reaching out for mother love. Faces
pressed against a train window.

Another group of children, in spotless school uniforms, marching beneath a swastika banner, giving a straight-armed salute.

Black gallows against a cloudy sky. Bodies dangling from them, their feet barely touching the ground. A caption explaining that the scaffolding had been specially constructed with short drops, so that death, from slow strangulation, was prolonged.

Guard towers.

More barbed wire—spooling miles of it.

Brick ovens.

Pallets of charred, caked matter.

Fat complacent cats licking at a pile of it.

Tiled laboratories that resembled autopsy rooms. Sinks full of glassware. Humanoid things on tables.

A paragraph describing the science of the Third Reich. Ice-water experiments. Eye-color experiments. Artificial-insemination experiments. Cross-species breeding experiments. Benzine injections to harden the arteries. "Surgery" without anesthesia to study the limits of pain tolerance. Twin studies. Dwarf studies. Authoritative-looking men in white coats, bearing scalpels like weapons.

Rows of graves outside a "sanitarium."

Milo and I had come face to face. When I saw the moisture in his eyes, I realized mine were wet too.

My throat felt as if it had been stuffed with dirt. I wanted to say something but the thought of speaking hurt my chest.

I turned away from him and dried my eyes.

The gallery door opened. A woman came in and said, "Hi, Milo. Sorry to keep you waiting."

Cheer in her voice. It jolted me like an ice-water bath.

She was in her mid- to late forties, tall and slim, with a long neck and a smallish oval face. Her hair was short, gray, and feathered. She had on a silk print dress in mauves and blues, and mauve suede shoes. Her badge said J. BAUMGART-NER, SENIOR RESEARCHER.

Milo shook her hand. "Thanks for seeing me on short notice, Judy."

"For you, anything, Milo. If I look a wreck, it's from sitting at O'Hare for four hours waiting to take off. Place is a zoo."

She looked perfectly put together.

Milo said, "This is Alex Delaware. Alex, Judy Baumgartner."

She smiled. "Good to meet you, Alex."

Milo said, "He's never been here before."

"Well then, a special welcome. Any impressions?"

"I'm glad I saw it."

My voice was strained. She nodded.

We left the gallery and followed her down the hall to a small room furnished with four gray metal desks arranged in a square. Three of them were occupied by young people—two females and a male of college age—poring over manuscripts and notating. She greeted them and they said hi and went back to work. The walls were filled with bookcases of the same gray metal. A cardboard box sat atop the unoccupied desk.

Judy Baumgartner said, "There's a meeting going on in my office, so this will have to do."

She sat behind the desk with the box. Milo and I pulled up chairs.

She pointed to the box. "Ike's stuff. I had my secretary go into the library card catalogue and pull everything he'd checked out. This is it."

"Thanks," said Milo.

"I've got to tell you," she said, "I'm still pretty shaken. When I got the message in Chicago that you needed to see me, I thought it was going to be something about hate crimes or maybe even some progress on Kaltenblud. Then when I got back and Janie told me what you wanted . . ."

She shook her head. "He was such a nice kid, Milo. Friendly, dependable—*really* dependable. That's why when he stopped showing up for work, I was really surprised. Tried to find the number he'd given me when he applied to volunteer, but it was gone. Must have gotten thrown out. Space is at a premium—stuff gets thrown out all the time. I'm sorry."

Milo said, "He worked here?"

"Yes. Didn't Janie tell you?"

"No. All I knew was he'd checked out books, done some research."

"He did research for me, Milo. For over two months. Never missed a day—he was one of my steadiest ones. Really dedicated. His suddenly dropping out bothered me—it wasn't like him. I asked the other volunteers if they knew what had happened to him but they didn't. He hadn't made friends—kept to himself. I tried to get a number for him but he wasn't listed. Finally, after a couple of weeks of his not showing up, I put it down to impetuous youth. Figured I'd overrated his maturity. I never expected . . . never knew. How'd it happen, Milo?"

Milo told her about the shooting, told her it had taken place in a dope alley but left out the toxicology report.

She frowned. "He sure didn't seem like a druggie to me. If any kid was lucid and straight, it was Ike. Unusually straight—almost too serious for his age. He had a really . . . crisp mind. Still, people can maintain, can't they?"

"When did he start volunteering?"

"Late April. Walked in off the street and announced he wanted to help. Good-looking kid, fire in his eyes—passion. He reminded me of the way students used to be during the sixties. Not that I greeted him with open arms. I wanted to make sure he was stable, not just caught up in some impulsive thing. And frankly, I was taken by surprise. We don't get much interest from non-Jewish kids, and with all the black-Jewish tension lately, the last thing I expected was a black kid wanting to do Holocaust research. But he was really sincere. On top of being smart. A very quick study, and that's hard to find nowadays. The gifted ones all seem to stay on the career track, get rich quick. The ones like those three"—she pointed to the other desks—"are the exception."

"Did they know Ike?"

"No. They just started. Fall interns. The summer group consisted of three students from Yeshiva University in New York, one each from Brown and NYU, and Ike. From Santa Monica College. All the others went back for fall semester. Ike didn't hang out with them. Kind of a loner, really."

"You said he was friendly."

"Yes. That's odd, isn't it, now that you mention it. He *was* friendly—smiled a lot, courteous, but he definitely kept to himself. When Janie told me what had happened, I thought back, realized how little he'd told me about himself during the interview: He'd arrived a few months earlier from back east, was working and going to school. He told me he loved history, wanted to be a lawyer or a historian. He kept steering the conversation away from personal things and toward substance—history, politics, man's inhumanity to man. I was so taken by his enthusiasm that I went along with it, didn't ask very many personal questions. Do you think he was hiding something?"

"Who knows?" said Milo. "There's no record at all of his application?"

"No, sorry. We dump tons. Anything to avoid the paper-glut."

"Wish I had the luxury," he said. "By now I dream in triplicate."

She smiled. "Be thankful you don't deal with the federal government. After years of haggling, the Justice Department's finally started turning over names of old Nazis who're still living here. They all lied on their visa applications and we're processing to beat the band—meeting with federal prosecutors in the various cities, filling out *mountains* of forms, trying to persuade them to move faster on drawing up deportation papers. That's what I was doing in Chicago: trying to sock it to a kindly old geezer who runs a bakery on the South Side—best pastry in town, free samples to all the local kiddies. Only problem is, forty-five years ago that geezer was responsible for gassing eighteen hundred kiddies."

Milo's face got hard. "Gonna nail him?"

"Gonna try. Actually, this particular case looks good. Of course there'll be the usual outcry from his family and friends: We've got the wrong guy; this one's a saint, wouldn't hurt a fly; we're only persecuting him because of his noble anti-communist background—Moscow's behind all of it, you see. As if the Russians would give us the time of day. Not to mention a whole bunch of mewling from the nonconfrontational wimps who think human nature's basically pure and bygones should be bygones. And, of course, straight-out anti-Semitic garbage from the revisionist morons—the it-never-happened-in-the-first-place-but-if-it-did-they-deserved-it crowd. Your basic neo-Bundists."

"Neo-who?"

"Bundists." She smiled. "Sorry for being esoteric, I was referring to the German-American Bund. It was a big movement in this country, before World War II. Passed itself off as a German-American pride society, but that was just a cover for American Nazism. Bundists were big in the isolationist movement, agitated against U.S. involvement in the war, used the America First cover to press for mandatory sterilization of all refugees—that kind of thing. But they weren't just a tiny fringe group. They held rallies at Madison Square Garden for thousands of people, complete with swastika banners, Brown Shirt marches, 'The Horst Wessel Song.' Ran paramilitary training camps—two dozen of them, with bunkhouses for 'storm troopers.' Their goal was to set up a German-speaking colony—a Sudetenland—in New York State. First step toward an Aryan

America. Their leaders were paid agents of the
Third Reich. They published newspapers, had a
press service, a book publishing company called
Flanders Hall. Got support from Charles Lind-
bergh and Henry Ford—the Bundesführer, a man
called Fritz Kuhn, was a Ford Motors chemist—
and plenty of politicians too. They interfaced with
Father Coughlin, Gerald L.K. Smith, lots of other
loonies. But after Pearl Harbor, their leaders were
rounded up for espionage and sedition and sent to
prison. It put a damper on the movement but didn't
kill it. Extremism's like that. A recurrent cancer—
you need to be always looking out for it, cutting it
away. Nowadays it's skinheads, revisionists . . .
the Holocaust never happened. They thrive on
economic hardship—tried to exploit the farmers'
problems a few years back. The latest thing is
Odinism. Some sort of ancient Norse religion.
They reject Christianity because it evolved out of
Judaism. Then there's this other group that claims
to be the real Hebrews. We Jews are subhuman,
the spawn of Eve and the snake. Farrakhan says
the same kind of thing—white separatists showed
up at one of his rallies and donated money."

"Nutso," said Milo.

"But dangerous. We're working overtime
keeping an eye on them all."

"Was Novato involved in investigating any of
them?"

"No. We keep the volunteers away from that

kind of thing—too dangerous. I'm up to two death threats a week. He did library work: reshelving, working on the index catalogue. I'd call down with a list of references and ask him to get them for me. Sometimes I'd send him to outside libraries—UCLA or Hebrew Union College. Or over to the Federal Building to pick up some documents. He had a motorcycle, which made him perfect for that. Mostly what he did was read—on his own time. Sat in the library until closing time, then took stuff home with him."

She looked down at the box. "I glanced through it. Seems to be mostly Holocaust history. The origins and structure of the Nazi party and neo-Nazi groups. At least that's what he checked out. We've got a very comprehensive civil rights collection, and we put together an entire section on black slavery. But he didn't check out any of that. I was surprised. Which just reminds me how easy it is to stereotype—you've got to fight it constantly. Still, it's the first time I can remember a black kid focusing exclusively on the Holocaust. There was something about him, Milo. A naïveté—an optimistic sincerity—that was really touching. You just knew that in a couple of years he was going to get disillusioned and lose some of that. Maybe even all of it. But in the meantime it was nice to see. Why would anyone want to kill him?" She stopped. "Pretty dumb question coming from me."

"It's always a good question," Milo said. "It's the answers that stink. Did he ever mention any family or friends?"

"No. The only time he got even remotely personal was toward the end of his . . . Must have been early September. He came into my office to deliver some books, and after he put them down he kept hanging around. I didn't even notice at first—I was up to my elbows in something. Finally I realized he was still there and glanced up. He looked nervous. Upset about something. I asked him what was on his mind. He started talking about some pictures he'd come across while cataloguing—dead babies out of the crematoria, Mengele's experiments. He was really affected. Sometimes it just hits you, out of the clear blue—even after you've seen thousands of other pictures, one will set you off. I encouraged him to talk, get it all out. Let him go on about why, if there was a God, He could let those things happen. Why did terrible things happen to good people? Why couldn't people be kind to one another? Why were people always betraying one another— *brutalizing* one another?

"When he was through I told him those were questions humanity had been asking itself since the beginning of time. That I had no answers, but the fact that he was asking them showed he was one cut above the crowd—had some depth to him. The wisdom to question. That the key to making the world a better place was to constantly question, never accept the brutality. Then he said something strange. He said Jewish people question all the time. Jewish people are deep. He said it almost with a longing in his voice—a reverence. I said thanks for the compliment, but we Jews don't have a monopoly on either suffering or insight. That we'd swallowed more than our share of persecution, and that kind of thing did tend to lead to introspection, but that when you got down to it, Jews were like everyone else—good and bad, some deep, some shallow. He listened and got this strange smile on his face, kind of sad, kind of dreamy. As if he were thinking about something else. Then he turned to me and asked me if I'd like him better if he were Jewish.

"That really threw me. I said I liked him just fine the way he was. But he wouldn't let go of it, wanted to know how I'd feel if he were Jewish. I told him we could always use another bright penny in the tribe—was he thinking of converting? And he just gave me another strange smile and said I should be flexible in my criteria. Then he left. We never talked about it again."

"What did he mean, 'criteria'?"

"The only thing I can think of was that he was considering a Reform or Conservative conversion. I'm Orthodox—he knew that—and the Orthodox have more stringent criteria, so maybe he was asking for my approval, asking me to be flexible in my criteria for conversion. It was a strange conversation, Milo. I made a mental note to follow up on it, try to get to know him better. But with the workload it just never happened. Right after that, he stopped showing up. For a while I wondered if I'd said the wrong thing, failed him in some way."

She stopped, laced her hands. Opened a desk drawer, pulled out a pack of cigarettes, lit one, and blew out smoke.

"So much for quitting. My first all week. Talking about this isn't good for my willpower. Since I got your message I've been wondering if there was something he was asking from me that I didn't give. Some way I could have—"

"Come on, Judy," said Milo. "Dead-end thinking."

She held the cigarette at arm's length. "Yes, I know."

Milo took it and ground it out in an ashtray.

She said, "Been talking to my husband?"

"It's my job," he said. "Protect and serve. Got a few more questions for you. Hate groups. Anything new on the local scene?"

"Not particularly, just the usual fringies. Maybe a slight upswing in incidents that seems to be related to the situation in Israel—a lot of the printed material we've been seeing lately has been emphasizing anti-Zionist rhetoric: Jews are op-pressors. Stand up for Palestinian rights. A new hook for them since the U.N. passed the Zionism-is-racism thing. Basically a way for them to sanitize their message. And some of the funding for the worst anti-Semitic literature is coming from Saudi Arabia, Kuwait, and Syria, so I'm sure that's got something to do with it."

"Who'd be breaking into houses and painting anti-Semitic slogans on the walls?"

"That sounds kind of adolescent," she said. "Why? Are you getting a lot of that? If you are, we should know about it."

"Just one incident. At the place Ike used to live and the apartment next door. His landlady was Jewish and the next-door neighbor's a rabbi, so it probably has nothing to do with Ike."

"Milo," she said, "you don't think he was killed because of his work here?"

"Nothing points to that, Judy."

"But you're not ruling it out. You're here because you have at least some suspicion he might have been killed because of his race."

"No, Judy," he said, "I'm a long way from that."

"Kennedy," I said softly.

It was the first time I'd spoken since we entered the room. Both of them stared at me.

"Yeah," said Milo. "There is something else. Along with the anti-Semitic stuff, they wrote, *Remember John Kennedy!* That make any sense to you?"

"Could," she said, "depending on which John Kennedy you're talking about."

"What do you mean?"

"If they scrawled John *F*. Kennedy that wouldn't make much sense. But there was another John Kennedy. Confederate veteran. Lived in Pulaski, Tennessee, and started a social club for other Confederate veterans called the Ku Klux Klan."

I said, "Punks who know history?"

Milo didn't say anything.

We left, taking along the carton of books Ike Novato had checked out.

I said, "What do you think?"

Milo said, "Who the hell knows?"

"Seems to me it's starting to smell more like politics than drugs. Both Novato and Gruenberg have a strong interest in Nazis. Both get killed. Someone breaks into their apartment and paints racist slogans."

Milo frowned, rubbed his face. Then his beeper went off.

I said, "Want me to find a phone?"

"Nah, I'll call from your place."

He did and put down the phone. "Gotta go, fresh d.b. Don't worry—nothing to do with Nazis. Paraplegic in a rest home on Palm—looks like natural causes."

"How come the D-Three goes out on some-thing like that?"

"One of the attendants pulled my guy aside and told him the paraplegic had been pretty healthy the day before—and this wasn't the first funny death they'd had there. Place was full of health code violations, patients getting beaten, sitting in their own shit, not getting their medi-cine. Owner of the home is politically connected. My guy got nervous. Wanted to know *procedure*. Procedure is I go out there and play nursemaid."

He walked to the door. "Got any plans for tonight?"

"Nothing."

He pointed at the carton of books. "Got time for some reading?"

"Sure."

"There's a lot of stuff there. You might wanna check first for notes in margins, underlin-ing, that kind of thing. Barring that, maybe a trend in the kind of books he chose—a subpattern, something more specific than just an interest in Nazis. Depending on how complicated it gets over in Palms, I'll try to get back tonight, see if you've come up with anything."

"Am I being graded?"

"Nah, it's pass/fail. Just like real life."

26

Mahlon Burden had left a message at four.

"He said to tell you," the operator said, "that he's free to pick up where the two of you left off. Any time."

"Thanks."

"He sounded kind of eager," she said. "Burden. Why's that name familiar?"

I told her I had no idea, hung up, finished a long-overdue report, then sat down with the carton of books at seven o'clock.

The first volume I picked up was an English translation of *Mein Kampf*. I flipped the pages, found no notes in the margins or underlining.

The second book was entitled *This Must Not Happen Again: The Black Book of Fascist Horror* by Clark Kinnaird. Large print, small press, publication date of 1945.

Flipping through these pages revealed a note in the margin of page 23. The adjoining text read:

"Unless it is understood that the Germans

made their heinousities as well as their war profitable they are incomprehensible."

What followed was a description of the financial benefits the Nazis had reaped from the racial laws that allowed them to confiscate Jewish property. Next to it, someone had neatly printed in pencil:

"Same old story: power and money, no matter what wing."

I turned more pages, found no more notes. Just a clearly written chronology of World War II and lots of pictures, the same kinds I'd seen in the Exhibit Room. I got caught up in the horrors and was still reading at nine-fifteen, when Milo returned.

He said, "Anything?"

"Not yet. How was the rest home?"

"Nothing overly weird, homicide-wise. Despite what the attendant said, the patient did have a history of respiratory problems. Have to wait on the coroner for a definite cause of death."

He gave a disgusted look. "Place was a real Disneyland—all those empty eyes. Remind me to amend my will: First signs of infirmity, have me taken out to the desert and shot. You hungry?"

"Not really." I held up the book.

"Hey," he said, "if I only took nutrition when life was pretty, I'd goddam starve to death."

We drove to a sushi bar on Wilshire near Yale. It had been a while since we'd been there and the place had undergone a redecoration: pine bar and shoji screens and samisen music thrown over for purple and black velvet walls, smoked mirrors, laser-art rock posters, and a sound system that would have done DeJon Jonson proud. Same chefs, but new costumes—black pajamas and headbands. They brandished their knives and shouted greetings over the disco beat.

Milo looked at them and said, "Reminds me of the fucking Cong."

"Wanna try someplace else?"

He scanned the array of raw fish at the bar and shook his head. "Comestibles still look good. I'm too tired to go hunting."

We took a table as far away from the noise as possible, ordered hot sake and ice water and lots of food. He finished quickly, called the waitress back, and ordered more shrimp and yellowtail. Just as it arrived, he said, "Oh, shit."

"What."

"Beeper just went off."

"I didn't hear it."

"That's 'cause it didn't make a sound. I've got it on Silent/Vibrate—I can feel it buzzing in my pocket. Rick insisted on it—same one he's got. So when we go to the *theater*, we won't be offensive to the other *theater*goers. 'Course, the last time we went to the *theater* was back in '85."

I said, "Sounds like something out of Burden's catalogue. Pretty high-tech for the Department."

"What Department? Rick bought it. Promotion gift." He wiped his mouth and got up. "Be back in a sec. Don't touch my shrimp."

But he was gone for a lot longer than a sec, and when he came back he looked very grim.

"What is it?"

"Two more d.b.'s. Double homicide." He stuffed a piece of shrimp in his mouth, threw money on the table, and loped away fast.

I caught up with him. "What's the rush? Thought you were off duty."

"Not for these." We were out on the sidewalk. He ran faster. Passers-by stared.

"What is it, Milo? More nursemaiding?"

"Oh, yeah," he said. "Nursemaiding like crazy. One of the d.b.'s used to be Samuel Massengil."

The address was on Sherbourne just south of Olympic, a block from Beverly Hills. A maple-lined street of well-kept older two-story duplexes and newer apartments. Quiet neighborhood, solidly middle class. The blinking lights of police cars were visible a block away, a vulgar intrusion.

Milo's ID got us through fast. A uniformed officer directed us to one of the duplexes on the west side of the street: white, Spanish style, wrought-iron grillwork, tasteful landscaping. A yellow Fiat Spider was parked in the driveway under an arched porte-cochere. It had reflector vanity plates that read CHERI T. Crime-scene tape had been stretched across the stucco arch that led to the duplex's ground-level entry. Next to the arch was a large oleander, pruned to tree shape, in full pink bloom.

A young black cop with a long bony face came out of the house. When he saw Milo he touched his hat and said, "Burdette, sir. I'm the one you spoke to."

Milo said, "What do we know, Burdette?"

Burdette looked at me. His eyes filled with questions but he kept them there. "Two bodies out in back, both male cauc, possible gunshot wounds to the head. Definitely d.b. but we called the ambulance anyway—quiet, no siren, just like you said. One's the assemblyman; the other I don't know—ID may be in the pockets but we haven't touched them."

"Probable gunshot wounds?"

"That's what it looks like. The light's not real great out there and we didn't want to get too close, mess up the scene. There's copious pooling blood near both heads and I didn't see any slash marks or bludgeon wounds. Also, the witness . . . the party reporting heard gunshots."

"You're sure it's *him*?"

"Yes, sir. I'd know that face anywhere, and the P.R. confirmed it."

"Where is the P.R.?"

"Inside. Ground floor."

"Name?"

Burdette pulled out a pad and shined a flashlight. "The name on her license is Cheryl Jane Nuveen. Female black, black and brown, five six, one fifteen, DOB four/eight/fifty-three. This address. No wants or warrants. But some or all of it might not be righteous."

"Why's that?"

"She's a pro."

"A hooker?"

Burdette nodded. "High-priced but it's fairly obvious once you see the setup. She's shook up but streetwise. After she answered the first few questions and confirmed that d.b. one was *him*, she refused to talk until she could call her lawyer."

"She put in that call yet?"

"Not yet. I told her to wait. Wanted to keep things as quiet as possible—just like you said. We Mirandized her but didn't pump her."

"Good," said Milo. "Before she clammed up, you get any story from her on what happened?"

"She called it in on nine-one-one. Said she thought there'd been shots fired in her backyard, *thought* she saw two guys down. The dispatcher gave it to us as a possible ADW, shots fired, Code Two high. We expected a prowler situation, but when we got here—"

"Who's *we*?"

"Ziegler and me." Burdette crooked a thumb at a stocky white officer standing guard at the curb.

"When'd the call come in?"

"Ten-oh-four. We were over at Patricia and Pico on a traffic stop, possible deuce, dropped that and got here at ten-twelve, did a careful search, saw who d.b. one was, the way both of them were dressed—it was obvious this was no prowler situation. Then when we went inside and saw her setup and her demeanor, we put two and two together. Also, the fact that the assemblyman's car was parked back there and hers was in the drive-way meant he was probably visiting her—I figure he wanted to keep his car off the street just in case someone recognized it. When I laid that out for her she admitted he'd been up there, he was a john. That's when she shut up and asked to change her clothes. We didn't let her, wanted to preserve the scene."

"Why'd she want to change?"

"All she had on was a robe over . . . probably nothing."

"Why didn't she change before you got here?"

"Good question, sir. Maybe she was shook up—she actually looked pretty shook up."

"Despite being streetwise."

"Yes, sir."

"Anyone else live with her?"

"No, sir. It's her place—she owns the whole building. Upstairs is rented to an artist, but she says he's in Europe."

"Hooker as landlady," said Milo. "The high-priced spread. Blood wouldn't be routine for her the way it would for a street gal. Okay, I can see her shook up. What else?"

"We Mirandized her like I said, called you, then called in for assistance in order to be able to secure the crime scene like you instructed. We used a restricted band to keep it quiet, no mention of d.b. one's identity. Eight-L Five-Code-Sixed us—that's Martinez and Pelletier. Pelletier's in there with her now—we figured a woman might keep her calmer, no allegations of sexual stuff, maybe even get something out of her information-wise. But we agreed no one would pump her until you got here. Eight-Oh-Twenty-three got here just a few minutes after—that's who you saw blocking the street."

"Any indication she was more than the P.R.?"

"No, sir, nothing obvious."

"Any intuition on that?"

"Intuition?" Burdette chewed on the word. "Well, sir, she did call it in right away—bodies were still warm when we got here. So if she's the shooter she's not a very bright one. We didn't see any gun in the house but we haven't really searched. I guess anything's possible."

"What's her demeanor?"

"I'd call it upset, sir. Pretty scared. Not shifty or . . . guilty, if that's what you mean."

"You did good," said Milo. "Techs and coroners?"

"On their way."

"Okay, let's take a look back there."

Burdette glanced at me again.

Milo said, "This is Dr. Delaware. He's a psychologist consulting to the Department—the schoolyard sniping. We were having a meeting on that when your call came in—that's his Caddy out in front. Have someone move it to a less conspicuous spot, okay?" To me: "Give him your keys, Doc. You come with me."

I handed the keys to Burdette. He said, "Just straight past the car and through the driveway. We taped off a radius."

"Gimme your flashlight," said Milo.

Burdette gave it to him and left, swinging my key ring.

We walked under the porte-cochere and into the backyard, which was small and square and backed by a flat-roofed double garage with old-fashioned wooden hinge doors. Most of the ground area had been paved with concrete. A narrow strip of lawn on the north side sported a peach tree and a T-shaped metal pole designed to hold a clothesline. There was no outdoor lighting, but light from a shaded rear window and a floodlight on the roof of the duplex next door combined to pour a tallowy wash over the southern part of the property. Some of the light flowed onto a late-model Chrysler New Yorker.

Next to the car were two bodies lying belly down, limbs splayed, heads twisted to the side. A tape line had been run around them. They'd fallen close together on the concrete—perhaps two feet separated them. Their legs overlapped, creating a human V, and had the loose but contorted posture unique to pre-rigor corpses and rag dolls. Both were dressed in suits—one gray, one that appeared tan in the night light. The left trouser-leg of the one in tan had ridden up, revealing a thick white slab of hairless calf that shone like polished ivory. Rorschach splotches extended from both heads.

Keeping his distance, Milo swept the flashlight over the yard, focused it on the faces.

"Him, all right. Puffy from hemorrhaging— bullet probably danced around in there. Looks like an entry back here, top of the neck. Straight to the medulla oblongata. It was probably fast. Same shot on number two, a little higher, also clean. Someone came from there, back of the car, side of the garage, caught 'em by surprise and bang bang. Close range, looks very pro. Hey, Alex, look at this. This who I think it is?"

His beam had rested on the face of the

tan-suited body. Corpulent, white bearded, suety cheeks compressed against the cement. Santa Claus with glassy, sightless eyes under swollen lids.

"Dobbs," I said.

"Well," he said, "you figured they had some kind of extraprofessional relationship. Now we have an idea what it was."

He retracted the flashlight, shook his head. "Talk about your house calls."

Maintaining his distance, Milo diagrammed, took notes, measured, searched for footprints and thought he saw some on the other side of the Chrysler, near the northern corner of the garage.

"Wet grass there," he said. "And dirt. Low fence to the neighbor's yard. Easy escape route. We might be able to get a cast."

"Good hiding spot, too," I said.

He nodded. "Like a goddam duck blind. The light from next door doesn't carry this far. They walk out to the car, feeling nice and mellow. Pop pop."

He continued examining the yard. The coroner, ambulance, and crime-scene van showed up within seconds of one another, and the area was engulfed in frantic activity. I retreated to the porte-cochere and waited as Milo gave orders, asked questions, pointed, and scribbled.

When he finally walked away from the action, I stepped out.

He looked at me as if he'd forgotten I was there.

"Getting plainclothes out to both their offices, make sure this isn't related to some kind of Watergate situation. I've gotta talk to Ms. Nuveen. Why don't you go home? I'll catch a ride to your place."

I said, "The press will be showing up soon. Don't you think I'd be less obtrusive if I stayed with you?"

"If you leave right now you'll be real unobtrusive."

I said, "Promise to behave good, Mr. Policeman."

He hesitated. "All right, come with me. And as long as you're there, keep your eyes open and make yourself useful."

The living room had maroon-lacquered walls and cream-colored marbleized molding, a dark-beamed vaulted ceiling, and a thermostat set at eighty. The decor was African safari transposed upon someone's idea of a Paris salon: zebra and tiger skins layered over high-gloss herringbone hardwood, elephant-leg occasional table, lots of cut crystal, porcelain, and cloisonné, overstuffed chairs upholstered in a black-and-maroon floral chintz, a pair of carved ivory tusks sharing space on the quasi-quatorze coffee table with a stack of art books, art nouveau lamps with beaded shades, heavy brocade drapes with gold hems tied back from black wooden shutters, a green marble mantel bearing a collection of millefleurs and linenfold paperweights, and everywhere the smell of musk.

She sat in one of the chairs, looking younger than indicated by her driver's license birthdate— late twenties would have been my guess. Her skin was the color of mocha ice cream, her eye shadow iridescent peacock-blue. The eyes below them were wide-set and active. She had long slim brown legs, narrow feet ending in pearly-pink toenails, full lips glossed a soft pink, a tight jaw, and straightened hair the color of red clay that hung past her shoulder blades. Her kimono was royal-purple Thai silk patterned with jade-green dragons, buttonless and very short, held together with a green sash. No matter how many times she tightened the sash, the robe kept coming loose and revealing a healthy mocha chest. She crossed and uncrossed her legs a lot, smoked an ultra-king-size Sherman tinted to match the robe, and fought to keep from trembling.

"Okay, Cheri," said Milo, handing her a *faux* malachite phone. "Go ahead, call your lawyer. Tell him to meet you downtown, at Central Booking."

She bit her lip, smoked, looked at the floor.

"Downtown." Her voice was soft, slightly nasal. "Haven't seen that place in a long time."

"Bet you haven't, Cheri. Come a long way since Imperial Highway. Or was it Sunset and Western?"

She didn't answer.

He said, "Got to hand it to you—this is some place. Self-made woman." He put the phone down and picked up a Lladro figurine. Victorian lady with a parasol.

He spun the parasol and said, "Spain, right?"

For the first time she looked at him. With fear. Wondering how long something that delicate could survive between those thick fingers.

He put down the figurine. "Who's your decorator?"

"Me. I did it myself." Defiance and pride made her sit up a bit straighter.

"Creative, Cheri."

She pointed to the art books. "I read lots of stuff. *Architectural Digest*."

He lifted the phone again and held it out to her. She made no effort to take it.

"Call him, Cheri. Then we'll take you down. Hey, your hands are shaking, babe. Tell you what, give me the number and I'll dial it for you. How's that for personal service?"

She took a deep drag on the purple cigarette. "Why?"

"Why what?"

"Why're you leaning on me, talking about downtown?"

"It's not just talk, Cheri. It's real."

"Real." She dragged again, coughed, touched her bosom, tugged the sash. "Real. This is what I get for doing my civic duty. Moment I saw it I called."

He said, "I appreciate that, except now instead of acting civic you're clamming up and demanding your lawyer, which is more like *perp* behavior. So now I'm wondering what you have to hide, and now I have to take you downtown to be extra careful to cover my butt."

She hugged herself, rocked, smoked, crossed her legs. "They treated me like a perp right off, read me Miranda."

"That's for your sake, Cheri."

"Yeah, everyone's out to do me a favor." She waved the cigarette, created sinuous smoke streams.

Milo cut through the smoke with his finger. "Sherms. Usually when we see those they're in evidence bags. Spiked with Dust."

"Not my thing," she said. "I live healthy."

" 'Course you do," he said. "But let me ask you, what's the chance once we start going over this place—and we are going to go over it—that we don't find *something*? Roach under the bed, little speck of hash, maybe some 'ludes or poppers to make a party go smoother. Something one of your guests accidentally dropped and the cleaning woman just happened to miss—you do have a cleaning woman."

"Twice a week," she said.

"Twice a week, huh? Things *do* have a way of accumulating between cleanings."

"Listen," she said, "all there is, is pills. Valium. Legal. Prescription—fact, I could use one right now."

"Not now, Cheri. We need you lucid—clear."

"I know what *lucid* means. Don't think I'm no woodhead."

"Perish the thought. Woodheads don't usually end up owning the building." He jiggled the phone. The clapper hit the bell and gave off a dull ring.

She said, "You find anything funny in there, I don't know a single thing about it."

"It's your responsibility, Cheri. You own the whole building."

She muttered something.

Milo said, "What's that?"

No answer.

"Go on, make the call, or give me the number so I can call."

She was silent.

"Anyway," he said, "the dope we're gonna find might keep you in lockup for a while, but it's the least of your problems. Let's not forget those two gentlemen out back."

She shook her head. "Nuh-uh. I don't know a thing about them—about what happened."

"You knew *them*."

"Professionally, that's all."

"Professionally," said Milo. He lifted a satinized purple business card from a cloisonné holder. "Cheryl Jane Nuveen. Recreational *Counselor*. Recreation, huh? Sounds like shuffleboard on deck."

The cigarette dangled from her fingers, dripping ashes onto the zebra skin.

Milo said, "Enough small talk. What's the lawyer's number? Got to be a five-five exchange, right? Beverly Hills. Or Century City. Two hundred, two-fifty an hour. I figure the initial tab's gonna run you three, maybe four thousand, minimum. And that's only filing the papers. Once we book you, the meter really starts running—"

"Book me on what? Calling nine-one-one?"

"—and those guys like retainers, don't they? Got payments on the Mercedes, keep the account going at Morton's. Meanwhile you've got no *recreation* to counsel and your own payments keep coming. What's the mortgage on this building you own, couple of thou a month? Meanwhile, you're in storage with girls from the old neighborhood—they're gonna be real happy to see someone made good, owns the whole building. They're gonna relate very friendly to that."

She raised her voice: "Book me on *what*?"

"My turn to ask questions. Your turn to shut up or answer."

She stabbed a crystal ashtray with her cigarette. Kept stabbing after the glow had died. "Nothing to answer about."

"Two bodies in your backyard and nothing to answer about?"

She rolled her eyes. "I told you I don't know about that."

"You knew *them*."

"Professionally."

"Who else besides you knew they were coming here tonight to play?"

"No one."

"No one?"

"That's right. I'm discreet—my business is based on it."

"No one," said Milo, "except the guy you called tonight in order to set 'em up."

Her mouth dropped open. "Oh, no—oh, no—no way you're gonna—"

"Cute deal, Cheri. You give him time to get away, then call nine-one-one and play good citizen: you *think* there's been a shooting. You *think* there's maybe two guys—prowlers—lying out dead in your backyard."

"That's the truth! I mean, about not knowing

they were dead. How'm I gonna know they were dead or not? You think I'm gonna go out there to feel a pulse!"

"Making it sound as if they were strangers."

"What's the diff? I called, didn't I?"

"Who else knew they were here, Cheri?"

"No one. I told you—"

"Too bad," he said. "Officers Burdette and Pelletier told me you weren't gonna be helpful, but I decided to keep an open mind. Looks like—"

"Burdette? That the house nigger with the attitude? That boy was *rude* to me, gave me that look—that . . . that . . ."

"Patronizing look?"

"Yes," she said, "*Patronizing*. He was *extremely* patronizing. To the *nth*. Had an attitude. Like he was some King Hoohah and I'm some little sister who's stepped out of line, it's his job to knock me down. And the other one, she's nothing but a diesel dyke—staring at my attributes whenever she got the chance. You guys shouldn't be hiring perverts."

"Attributes?" said Milo.

"Yeah." She bent low in illustration, threw back her shoulders, suddenly confident again. She smiled at Milo, received a blank stare in return, and switched her attention to me.

Her smile was inviting and though I knew it was artifice, I had to look away to keep from reciprocating. When I did, she cursed under her breath.

Milo said, "Okay, we'll take you downtown. You make the call from there. Get ready for a little nostalgia, Cheri. Sucking in AIDS breath in a holding cage full of five-dollar strawberries while getting your *attributes* checked out."

She looked at me again, spread her legs slightly while keeping them crossed at the ankles. Confirming Burdette's assessment of what was— or wasn't—under the kimono.

I looked away again.

She said, "Okay. Fuck the lawyer. I didn't do a thing wrong—don't need to buy him another Mercedes. Give me one of those polygraphs. Crank it up—I've got nothing to hide."

Milo said, "Polygraphs can't stand up to smooth criminals. Anyone comfortable with lying can pass."

Anger mottled her face like a rash. "So what the fuck do you *want*?"

"Just straight talk, Cheri. How you hooked up with Massengil and Dobbs in the first place. How long it's been going on—*everything* that's been going on. And everything connected to what happened tonight."

She smiled through the anger. "Everything, huh? Sure your little policeman's heart can take it?"

He hooked a finger at me. "Case it can't, he knows CPR."

"Okay," she said, crossing her legs again. "You pitch, I'll catch."

Milo said, "Let me make sure I'm getting this clear. You're saying you want to talk about the events of this evening—December 6, 1988? Give a statement of your own free will, no attorney present?"

"Uh-huh." She gave a wide smile full of big, perfect, milk-white teeth. Ran her tongue between them, sat up straight, touched her bosom.

"Yeah. Yes. Sure I'll talk. To *you*. Cause you *are* the King Hoohah. You're the real thing, chief, that's for sure. And Cheri doesn't go for *facsimiles*."

27

She said, "Sacramento—that's the begin-ning."

She put another cigarette in her mouth. Milo lit it for her.

She smoked for a while.

Milo said, "Sacramento."

"Yeah. That's where I met him. I had a place there. My own place, smaller and not as quality as this one, but my own, also."

Milo said, "Always been an independent, have you, Cheri?"

Her mouth tightened. "Not always. But I learn. I pride myself on that—learning from my mistakes."

"How long ago?"

"Three years ago."

"Where?"

"O Street, right up near the Capitol."

"Doing your bit for good government?"

"You bet. More of them woulda took more of what I gave, there'd be less strife, believe me."

"Where you from originally?"

"Here. Inglewood."

"How'd you get up to Sacramento?"

"I was in San Francisco first—three years. Moved 'cause I wanted things more quiet. And something I could do myself. Someone told me politicians were always wanting it—you had a seller's market."

"Recreation."

She smiled. "Yeah. Being close to the action meant they could make their speeches in the morning, drop by for a lunchtime party, and go back to their speeches with a smile on their faces."

"They," said Milo. "How many others besides Massengil?"

"Lots, chief. It's a company town. Not that fearless leaders was all I did. You had your doctors and your bankers, like any other place. But being there in that place, you did see lots of political types—aides, lobbyists, administrative assistants, all that shit. You learn to talk like them after a while."

"Fun bunch?"

She grimaced. "Not hardly. I mean, they were free with the buck—expense accounts. But as a group, they had inclinations. If you know what I'm saying."

"I don't."

"Kinky," she said, as if talking to an idiot. "Mostly for tying-up. Bondage. Always wanting to be tied up or tying me up. Nearly every one of them. Got so when I took one on that I knew was political, I had the neckties and the ropes all ready. A few of them even wanted to be . . . embarrassed. Dirty stuff. Never seen so many people wanting to tie or to be tied. All horny about who was in *charge*. Then you'd turn on the TV, see those same faces you just saw all wrinkled up or wearing a leather mask, crying and pleading not to spank 'em, even though that's what they really wanted—you'd see 'em giving speeches on the TV, going on about law and order, the American way, all that shit. Meanwhile, you're knowing their idea of law and order is being hog-trussed."

She laughed, filled her lungs with smoke. "Don't it just make you want to run out and vote?"

Milo smiled. "Massengil a tyer or a tyee?"

"Tyee. Liked to have his arms and legs all bound up, so tight the blood was cut off. Then he'd stretch out and make me do all the work. Then afterwards, which was quick—with most of them it's real quick"—she snapped her fingers— "I had to snuggle next to him like I was his mama and he'd latch onto my bubbies and talk like some little kid. Baby talk. Oogum snoogums for Mr. Law and Order."

She laughed again, but looked uneasy.

"Real disillusioning," she said, "isn't it.

High and mighty types running things, and what
they really are is whining, bubby-sucking babies.
Then, of course, there's cops—"

"He ever get racial?"

"What do you mean?"

"Make racist comments? Want to set up some
racist fantasy?"

"Nope," she said. "Just the tying and the
oogum talk."

"How'd you meet him?"

"Through the other one."

"Dobbs?"

"Uh-huh. He's a doctor—psychiatrist. Liked
to pretend this was all medical. Sex therapy. I
should think of myself as his therapy *assistant*."

"When'd you first meet Dobbs?"

"My last year in Frisco."

"How?"

"Had this girlfriend of mine who got into the
therapy thing—took a course or something and got
this piece of paper saying she was legal. A
surrogate. Dobbs taught the course, offered her a
job. Used to send her people—patients—have her
kick back some of the money to him. She made
good, but he made better. Then when she moved
out of town because her ex was threatening her,
she gave him my name. I moved down to Sacramento and he started sending the people to me."

"Even though you're not legal."

She smiled, "But I'm good, chief. I can be real patient—real thera*peu*tic when I have to."

"I'll just bet you can, Cheri. What other politicians did Dobbs send you besides Assemblyman Massengil?"

"Just him," she said. "It's like they were special buddies."

"What kind of special buddies?"

"Not fags or anything. Sometimes a couple of closet fags will use me to get into theirselves—doing a double and then accidentally one of their things brushes up against the other thing and we got a brand-new picture. But not them. They just used to show up, together. Like Sam needed Fatso to lead the way, and Fatso got off on setting things up."

"He never sent anyone else to you?"

"Not down here."

"What about Sacramento?"

"Okay, a couple. But after I did a little business with him, I didn't want to do any more."

"Why not?"

"He was a pig is why not. With Lorraine he'd taken fifty-five percent. With me he was wanting sixty. *Finder's fee.* He said I needed him—his being involved made it legal. Threatening me." She shook her head and rubbed one knee. "I went indy to get greedy pigs *off* my back. Told him bull*shit*, my being involved made it illegal for him and he had a lot more to lose than I did if the shit

hit the fan. So we settled on twenty percent. Couple of months later, I had enough of my own business going, anyway. Taking a hundred percent. Didn't want none of his, even with twenty percent, and told him so."

"How'd he react to that?"

"Made a face but didn't argue. And kept seeing me. With Sam. Sam had a thing for me."

"Was he ever a client himself?"

"Once in a while."

"Tyer or tyee?"

She shook her head. "All he wanted was wham-bam, Oh Jesus, oh Jesus!, roll his fat butt off, and fall asleep. Mostly he was a watcher—couple of times I caught him peeking through the door when I was with Sam. That gave me the creeps, but I didn't say a thing. Didn't cost me anything."

"Where's your trick book?"

"No trick book." She tapped her coiffure. "Everything's in here."

"How about your calendar?"

"No calendar either. Each day passes I tear it up in little pieces and flush it down."

"We're gonna tear the place apart, Cheri."

"Tear all you want. There's no book. And don't ask me to give you names—otherwise I *will* go downtown and suck AIDS breath."

"Who knew Massengil was coming here?"

"No one knew. No one knew about anybody.

That's my specialty—discreetness. And with him I was extra-careful, 'cause he was so nervous about being caught, wouldn't even leave his car out on the street. When he had an appointment, I cleared my calendar all day so they wouldn't be running into anyone."

"Considerate."

"Fuck considerate," she said. "I charged 'em for time lost."

"Speaking of that, what kind of tariff are we talking about?"

"Four hundred an hour." Wide smile. "More than my lawyer makes and I didn't have to pass any bar tests."

"Cash?"

"Nothing but."

"How often did Massengil see you?"

"Three or four times a month."

"What was the schedule?"

"What I told you—tying up, nuzzling bubbies, sometimes I'd feed them dinner. Then they'd leave and I had the whole night to myself, watch Johnny Carson."

Milo said, "That's not what I meant by schedule, Cheri. Which days of the week did they show up? What routine?"

"No routine. I'd get a call from Sam—or from Fatso—day or two before. Clear the calendar and they'd come by and we'd have a little party."

"Always the two of them?"

"Always." She turned thoughtful. "Maybe they *were* fags, really wanting to do a little dick-rubbing . . . I don't know. I just know they never got into that here."

"No schedule," said Milo.

"No."

"So how'd anyone know they were here?"

"Beats me. Maybe somebody followed 'em."

"Followed 'em here and just waited, huh?"

She shrugged.

Milo said, "How'd the shooter know to wait for them to come out—know that the two of them wouldn't be spending the night?"

"Not my thing," she said, "spending the night. No one spends the night."

"Who'd know that, besides you and your tricks?"

She was silent.

He said, "You're gonna have to give us that book, Cheri."

"I keep telling you there is no book."

Milo sat back and crossed his legs. She smoked, touched her hair, rocked her foot. Finally she said, "I give you that, I'm finished."

He said, "C'mon, Cheri. Two bodies out in back, one of them a public figure? You're finished anyway."

She smoked in silence some more. Pulled something out of an eyelash.

"Book's in the bank. Safe deposit box."

"Which bank?"

"I give it to you, you gonna help me move? Get me outa here safe, help me get my equity out of the building, plus keep my kid safe?"

"Where's the kid?"

"Inglewood, with my mom."

"How old?"

"Nine. Real smart, gotta great voice, sings in church."

"What's his name?"

"André."

"André. I'll do what I can for you and André."

"Do what you can, huh? That's politician talk, chief—just another way of saying *fuck you*."

"Got a place to move?"

"Somewhere conservative. Uptight. Conservative folks get the horniest. Need an outlet."

"Like the folks up in Sacramento."

"Just like."

"Why'd you move from there to L.A.?"

"We're back asking questions?"

"That's right. Why the move, Cheri?"

"It was his idea."

"Dobbs's or Massengil's?"

"Sam. The *Assemblyman*. He really had a thing for me—a *taste* for me. Get a *taste* for something sweet and it's like drugs, you never get enough."

"Three or four times a month isn't much of a fix."

"He's . . . he was old. What I gave him lasted. He really got off on it."

"Why'd he want you to move down here?"

"Said he didn't like having me so close to his workplace—Sacramento was a small town, loved gossip. Someone might find out. He found this place for me—some kind of special deal: The person died, left no will."

"Probate?"

She nodded. "He knew all about probates, had all these land records because of his job. Said I should jump on this one. It was a bargain—all I had to do was put up some cash."

"Did he help you with the down payment?"

"Not a penny. He would have, but I didn't need him, had plenty of my own. I flew down here, saw the place, saw what I could do with it, and figured, why not? My place up there had appreciated, built up equity. Now I got at least a hundred and sixty equity on this one, maybe more."

"What did he want in return?"

"*Me. When* he wanted me. Clearing my calendar so he didn't bump into no one—no one would know."

"No one except Dobbs."

"That's right."

"Was Massengil aware that Dobbs was a peeper?"

"Don't think so. Usually he had his eyes closed, all screwed up. But who knows? Maybe they had a little buddy-game going. I don't try to get into their heads. I'm somewhere else when I'm doing it."

"Four hundred an hour," said Milo. "Three, four times a month. Nice chunk of cash-outlay."

"He never complained."

"Management consulting," I said.

She looked at me. "Consulting. Yeah, I like that—that's class. Maybe I'll use that instead of Recreational Counselor."

Milo said, "Tell me about tonight. Exactly the way it happened."

She chain-lit another cigarette. "What happened is that they came here at nine-thirty, did their things—"

"Both of them?"

"This time, yeah. Piggy took sloppy seconds—he liked it that way, wouldn't let me wash. And then I gave them something to eat. The Colonel. Legs and breasts and cole slaw and biscuits. Leftovers from the night before, but they ate it like it was fancy French cooking. Standing up, in the kitchen. Drank two cans each of my Diet Pepsi. Then they paid me and split. Money's in my undies drawer—go check. Twelve hundred— twelve ones. New bills. I said to Sam, 'What'd you do, honey, just print it?' He liked that, laughed, and said, 'That's my job. I'm on the Finance Committee.' After they were gone and I put the money away, I went into the bathroom, turned on the shower. To clean off, get them outa me. While the water was running I heard it— almost *didn't* hear it 'cause of the water, but I did. Bang bang. I know that sound. Like a fool I looked out the window, saw them lying there, him running away. Like a fool I called and did my civic duty and now I'm sitting here talking to you, chief."

Milo said, "Who's *him*?"

"The shooter."

"One guy?"

"One's all I saw."

"What'd he look like?"

"All I saw was his back—running behind the garage. There's a low fence behind there. He probably got in that way—got out too. Rotten wood—I been meaning to put in a new one. You check, you'll probably find some kind of footprint. There's gotta be footprints 'cause it's muddy back there, got a leaky sprinkler, the water settles. Someone had to leave footprints. You go on and check and see if I'm telling it straight."

"Tell me more about the shooter."

"Nothing more to tell. Dark clothes—I think. It was dark. I dunno."

"Age?"

"Don't know—probably young. He moved like he was young. Not like an old fart. I seen plenty of old farts move, believe me."

"Height?"

"Not too tall or too short that I noticed. I mean, nothing hit me as being one way or the other—it was dark."

"Weight?"

"Same story, chief. There was nothing special about him. Just a guy—I saw his back. It's too far to see good. Go look for yourself through that window. And dark. I keep it that way, so people can park and get out without no one seeing 'em."

"What did his face look like?"

"Never saw a face. Can't even tell you if he was black or white."

"What color were his hands?"

She thought. "Don't recall. Don't know if I even saw hands."

"Average height and weight," said Milo, reading from his notes. "Probably young."

"That's it—if I could tell you more, why wouldn't I?"

"Black clothing."

"Dark clothing. What I mean is, nothing shined out, like a light-colored shirt or anything, so it was probably dark."

"What else?"

"That's it."

"Doesn't add up to much, Cheri."

"You think I'm gonna chase after him to get a closer look? I was stupid to look in the first place. Soon as my brain cleared and I realized what was happening, I dropped to the floor. Only reason I looked in the first place was I got caught by surprise. I mean, this was not what I expected to happen."

She closed her eyes, held the cigarette with one hand, her elbow with the other. The robe came loose, exposing heavy, black-nippled breasts, between them an inch of mocha sternum.

Milo said, "How do I know for sure you didn't finger them for the guy, Cheri?"

Her eyes opened, very wide. " 'Cause I *didn't*. Why would I do that and get myself all involved—do it in my back*yard*?"

"For the money."

"Got enough money."

"No such thing."

She laughed. "True. But I didn't. Give me the poly. I'm not that smooth."

She let the robe open wider. Milo reached over and closed it, placed her hand on the outer flap, and said, "Anything else you want to tell me, Cheri?"

"Just get me outa here. Outa L.A. With André."

"We'll be checking everything out and if you're being righteous, I'll be righteous with you. Meanwhile, I do want you to call your attorney

and tell him to meet you over at West L.A.
Division. You'll be driven over there and wait for
me. It'll take me a while to get over there. When
I do, you'll repeat the statement you just gave me
in front of a video camera."

"TV?"

He nodded. "Tonight you're a star."

She said, "The names I'll give you—what's
in the book. But I won't do that on tape."

"Fair enough, long as you're straight."

"I will be. Bet on it."

"I don't bet much on anything anymore,
Cheri."

"This time you can, I swear it." She crossed
her heart.

He said, "What's your attorney's name?"

"Gittelman. Harvey M. Gittelman."

"Even though you gave this of your own free
will in front of a witness, I want Mr. Gittelman
with you when we tape. He can shoot his mouth
off all he wants, raise two-hundred-buck-an-hour
objections. I get paid overtime, and I got nothing
to go home to. After we're finished you'll be
released in his custody and asked to stay in town
for as long as we need you. If you make any
attempt to leave town, I'll put you in Sybil Brand
as a material witness and André will miss his
mama. You're not gonna want to stay in this
place, what with the way the lab boys are going to
tear it apart and the way your neighbors are gonna

relate to you after the shit hits the fan—which it will. Soon. So it's okay for you to stay somewhere else, long as I know where it is and long as it's in the county. You want to do business in the new place, keep up the mortgage, that's fine with me too. Got it?"

"Got it. I swear it. But no business. Business means people, and people are problems. I need a vacation."

"Up to you." He stood.

She said, "When can I sell this place? Get my equity out?"

"If it turns out you're not involved in the shooting I can clear it for you pretty soon—a month or so. If you're fucking with me, I'll tie it up for years. Not that it'll matter, where you'd end up."

She crossed her heart again. "I'm not fucking with you. God's truth. All I want is my equity."

She started to get up.

He said, "Sit there. Don't move. I'm gonna call Officer Pelletier back and she's gonna watch you while you get dressed. We'll want that kimono to analyze. She'll also put bags on your hands until one of the techs comes in and does a paraffin test. That'll tell us if you've fired a gun lately—or worked with industrial-strength fertilizer."

"Been working with plenty of shit," she said. "But not that kind. And no gun. Bet on it."

"You'll also be printed so we can run you through NCIC. Any outstanding wants or warrants, better to tell me now."

"Nothing. Bet on that too."

"One thing I will bet on," he said. "You've got half a dozen monikers."

"Not that many. And I haven't used them in a long time."

"Give 'em to me anyway."

She ticked off her fingers. "Sherry Nuveen, with an S, like the wine. Sherry Jackson. Cherry Jackson, with a C. Cherry Burgundy. Cherry Gomez—that's when I had a spic on my back. He made me take his name, like we were married."

"Nuveen your given name?"

She shook her head. "Mom's second husband's name. I took it when I was seven. Then he left."

"What's the name on your birth certificate?"

"Jackson. Sheryl Jane Jackson. With an S. DOB four/eight/fifty-three, just like the license says. I look younger, don't you think?"

"You look great," he said.

She beamed. "Clean living."

He said, "What's the license plate stand for? On the Fiat. Cheri T."

She smiled again. Batted her lashes and laid down a few more mascara tracks. Vamping in order to maintain composure.

"T is for *Tart*," she said. "Cherry *Tart*.

Cause that's what I am. Sweet and juicy and filling."

When we were just outside the front door I said, "Think she's innocent?"

"Innocent?" He smiled. "You should see the way she's got the guest bedroom set up. It's a bondage museum—Marquis de Sade would feel right comfy. But of the shooting itself, probably. She's right—why would she set them up on her home territory, then phone it in? That's in terms of setting it up. In terms of her being the shooter herself, what's the motive? Sometimes, in a whore situation, passions do get out of hand and someone gets hurt. But it's usually the whore who's the victim and it's usually messy. This was neat. Planned. Very cold. Also, I had the tech look alongside the garage and he says it does look like fresh footprints. His educated guess is a man's running shoe, medium size. None of which will mean shit if she flunks the paraffin test and we find the gun in her undie drawer. I'll be putting her through her paces all night and most of the morning, see if I can get anything more out of her."

"Dark clothes," I said. "It's also the way Holly was dressed when she camped out in the storage shed."

"So what're you saying? Back to the cabal? Roving bands of teenage ninja assassins?"

I said, "Anything's possible."
He didn't argue.

He got my keys back from Burdette and found out where the Seville was parked. Then he told Pelletier—a five-foot blonde with a pixie chin—to bag Sheryl Jackson's hands and take her back to the station. As we left the duplex, a couple of other West L.A. detectives showed up. He told me to stay put, went over to them and filled them in, giving them instructions about searching Jackson's apartment and ordering them not to talk to the press until he'd finished reinterviewing her.

A few spectators had come out on the sidewalk. Uniforms kept them at a distance. Several vans with TV station logos had pulled up to the barricade. Reporters and camera crews were milling around, setting up lights.

Milo said, "After me, the deluge."

We began walking to the Seville. A sports-car rumble sounded down the block and a peacock-blue Pontiac Fiero with three antennas sprouting from the roof sped to the barricade, backed up at a noisy twenty miles per, and parked at the curb.

Lieutenant Frisk got out, took in the scene, spotted us, then came forward in a smooth, loose stride. He was wearing a shawl-collar black tuxedo with a pleat-fronted, wing-collared shirt, scarlet tie, and matching handkerchief. As he came toward us, I saw a woman get out of the Fiero—young, tall, fashion-model figure, cover-girl face, long dark frizzed hair. Her black taffeta cocktail dress showed off gleaming shoulders. She looked around, glanced in the little blue car's side mirror, and glossed her lips. One of the uniforms waved to her. She didn't see it or else ignored it, primped some more, and got back in the car.

"Sergeant," said Frisk.

"Evening on the town, Ken?" said Milo.

Frisk frowned. "Is the victim's identity verified, Detective?"

"Yeah, it's him. The other one's Dobbs, the psychologist who looks like Santa."

Frisk turned his attention to me. "What's *he* doing here, Detective?"

"He was with me when the call came in. No time to drop him off."

Frisk looked as if he were struggling to bring up gas. "C'mere, Sergeant."

The two of them walked a few yards away. The beam of a streetlamp allowed me to see them clearly. Frisk pointed at Milo and said something. Milo answered. Frisk pulled out a pad and pen and began writing. Milo said something else. Frisk kept writing. Milo ran his hand over his face and spoke again. Frisk looked irritated but continued writing. Milo talked, rubbed his face, bounced on the balls of his feet.

Frisk put the pad away and said something

that made Milo's face darken. He kept talking, wagged a finger. Milo wagged back.

Their body language grew progressively combative—hands fisted, faces thrust forward, chins extended like bayonets. It reminded me of my boxing print. Milo used his size to advantage, looming over Frisk. Frisk defended by rising on the balls of his feet, doing lots of tight, jabbing things with his hands. They began talking simultaneously—talking over each other, competing for air space. Other policemen were starting to notice, shifting their attention from the crime scene to what was happening under the lamppost. I could see Frisk's neck muscles straining; Milo's arms were down now, stiff at his side, his hands still rolled into fists.

Frisk made a conscious effort to relax, smiled, and gave a dismissive wave. Milo shouted something. He must have sprayed Frisk with spit, because the younger man stepped back several paces, yanked his red handkerchief from his pocket, and wiped his face. Frisk smiled again and spoke. Milo flinched as if he'd been slapped. His fingers opened, curled, and tightened. Frisk's turn to rock on the balls of his feet. Subtly, but eagerly, like a hungry welterweight. For a moment I was certain they were going to come to blows. Then Frisk turned heel and stomped away.

Milo watched him go, knuckling his chin. Frisk called a uniformed cop over, talked rapidly, began pointing at the murder duplex. The cop nodded and crossed the street to the building. The dark-haired young woman stepped out of the Fiero again. Frisk whipped his head in her direction and gave her a hard look. She got back in the car.

I looked over at Milo. He was staring at the growing hubbub near the barricade, a frightful look on his face. I stayed in place, catching curious glances from cops. Finally Milo saw me and waved me over.

"Get me the hell outa here, Alex."

The Seville was parked facing south. I drove away from the crime scene, got on Olympic, heading west. We didn't talk all the way to Beverly Glen. As I turned off, he said, "The slick fuck."

"What'd he do, take over?"

"Oh, yeah."

"He can do that? Just like that?"

"Just like that."

"That mean he suspects it's political?"

"He doesn't suspect *shit*. *No* one knows shit—it's too *early* to know shit, goddammit. What it means is that he sees it as a goddam juicy one. More TV time, chance to wear another fancy suit. Kenny do love his press conferences."

"Kenny," I said. "Out on the town with Barbie—there's a real Kenny and Barbie."

"That's *Mrs*. Kenny. The adorable, spoiled Kathy. Assistant Chief's favorite daughter."

"Oh."

"Oh."

I drove quickly up the Glen, reached the bridle path that leads to the house, and turned onto it. Though the view out the passenger window was solid black, Milo was staring at it, rubbing his face.

I said, "Did he do anything else to piss you off?"

"To piss me off? Nah. Just implied that you and I had a romantic thing going—gave a dirty little smile and told me I should think twice before bringing my *friends* to crime scenes. When I asked him to clarify that, he said I knew what he meant. I kept bugging him. Finally he let it out: People of my *ilk* were ill-*suited* for security cases. Ill-suited for guarding the public safety."

I blew out air. "Okay. So it's the same old limited thinking. Not the first time, won't be the last." But I couldn't help thinking it was the same thing he and I had suspected about Dinwiddie and Ike.

He grunted.

I said, "Is it safe to ask you what you think?"

"About what?"

"Massengil. Whodunit. Think there's any relationship to Holly? Or Novato and Gruenberg?"

"Who the hell *knows,* Alex? What're you trying to do, make me feel downright impotent?"

I said nothing, pulled up in front of the house.

He said, "All right, what's on your mind?"

"Maybe someone avenged her."

"Who? Daddy?"

"I wasn't thinking of him. Why? Do *you* suspect him?"

"I don't suspect anything, Alex. Haven't had time to suspect. It's not even my fucking case anymore so why should I *bother* to suspect? But if you're talking revenge, revenge is usually a family thing. And you told me Burden's a nut."

"Not a nut. Narcissistic."

"Revenge is pretty narcissistic, isn't it? Playing God, power over life and death. You told me yourself he's a control freak. Bragged about being good with guns."

I thought about that. "Planning to talk to him?"

"I'm not talking to anybody. Per the slick fuck."

"You can't challenge him?"

He didn't answer and I regretted asking.

I said, "Permit me a bit more theorizing?"

"Stop asking permission as if I'm some sort of prima donna and just spit it out."

"When I mentioned revenge, I was thinking of something else. The cabal. Other members. Setting out to avenge her. And carry out the assignment that she failed to complete."

"Assignment? Alex, if you were serious about political assassination, would you *assign* someone like her to do it?"

"Granted we're talking the amateur hour," I said. "But competence isn't always the rule of thumb for those kinds of groups, is it? Look at the Symbionese Liberation Army."

"Ye olde Crispy Critters," he said. "Yeah, those guys weren't too swift."

"But they got famous, didn't they? Which is what amateurs are after. High profile and a romantic death."

"If death is romantic, I'm a fucking poet."

"Holly had a dreary life, Milo. No present, no future. Belonging to a fringe group could have given her purpose. Going out in a blaze of glory might not have looked bad at all."

"You're saying she was on a suicide mission?"

"No. But she might not have worried about the risks."

"A group thing, huh?" he said. "Back to the ninjas. So who killed Novato and disappeared Gruenberg?"

"Maybe that *was* a dope thing. Or maybe it was the opposition. Right-wing radicals."

"*Two* groups of assholes?"

"Why not? Now that you mention it, it brings to mind something I just read scribbled in one of Novato's books: 'Same old story: power and money, no matter what wing.' Maybe what he was referring to was political extremism—and he was becoming disillusioned."

Milo said, "KKK assholes versus commie scumbags? Very colorful. But before you get carried away, don't forget that what happened tonight could have had nothing to do with politics—just some jealous john. This could all be related to Cheri. Guys get attached to these girls—it happens more than you'd imagine. Or maybe it *was* political but had nothing to do with Holly, or Novato, or Gruenberg. Massengil was not Mr. Charm. Could be one of his disgruntled constituents set out to vote with his trigger finger."

"Not Mr. Charm," I said, "but popular enough to last twenty-eight years."

"So much for the incumbency advantage." A moment later: "I don't know, Alex. What's been going on is so weird I don't even want to apply logic, because when I do, I start doubting the *value* of logic. One thing you can take comfort in: Your hunch about there being something funny between Massengil and Dobbs was right on."

I said, "Sloppy seconds. Management consulting. Great way to launder Cheri's fees."

"What do you think about what she said—politicos and bondage?"

"Makes sense psychologically. Like you once said, politicians mainline power. For some of them, sex would be just another dominance game.

What would be interesting to find out is who else, either here or in Sacramento, was aware of Massengil's kinks. Who besides Dobbs knew Massengil was carrying on with Cheri. And maybe there were other Cheris. The guy Massengil slugged in the Assembly—DiMarco—would be someone to talk to. What if he found out about it and leaked it—another kind of revenge. Or took a more direct route."

"Shot them himself?"

"Burr shot Hamilton. White shot Milk and Moscone."

"Shit," he said. "All sorts of ways to go. That's why I wanted to get her down to the station and lean on her some more. I tried to tell Frisk about it, tell him what needed to be done to keep the investigation clean. But he just cut me off. Said 'Thank you, Detective, everything's under control.' As in: Fuck you. I don't need your faggot ideas." Milo shook his head. "Fuck it, it's not my problem. I wash my hands of it. Hate press conferences anyway."

Saying it too loud and too fast; I wasn't sure I believed him. That he believed it himself. But this was no time to argue.

28

Linda had phoned and left a message at ten: *Just called to say hi. Be up until eleven thirty.*

It was close to one, and though I wanted to talk to her, I decided to do it in the morning.

I was wound up. Sensory overload. Not ready to tackle the kind of stuff Ike Novato had chosen to read about. TV would be reruns of movies that shouldn't have been produced in the first place, and hucksters pitching cellulite cures and eternal salvation. I did a half hour on the skiing machine, showered, then hobbled into bed and fell asleep.

I woke up thinking about the kids at Hale and called Linda at seven-thirty. She had already heard about Massengil's murder on the early morning newscast. The newscaster hadn't mentioned anything about a woman being involved. I told her about Sheryl Jackson.

"My God, what's happening, Alex?"

"I wish I knew."

"Could there be some connection with the sniping?"

"The way things are going, we may never find out." I recounted how Frisk had kicked Milo off the case.

"Another politician," I said. "This must be our year for them."

She said, "Year of the Rat. What should I do about the kids, Alex? In terms of Massengil?"

"The main thing to look out for is their attributing Massengil's death to something they did—or something they thought. Children—and the younger they are, the truer this is—sometimes equate thinking with doing. They have to be aware of Massengil's attitude toward them: They may have seen him on TV or heard their parents discussing what a bad person he was. If they wished him harm, or even death, they may get it in their heads that those wishes are what killed him."

"Step on a crack, break Mama's back."

"Exactly. Also, over the next few days the media will probably turn Massengil into some kind of hero. He's not going to seem like a bad guy anymore. That could be confusing."

"A hero?" she said. "Even with the hooker?"

"The fact that they haven't yet gone public with the hooker may mean they intend to keep that part of it under wraps. Frisk trades in secrets. He'd make a deal like that if it was in his best interests."

She paused, then said, "Okay. So I should make sure to disconnect their thoughts about Massengil from what happened to him."

"And from the sniping."

"Should I do it as an assembly or have the teachers handle it class by class?"

"Class by class to accomodate the different developmental levels. I can come over right now, if you'd like."

"No," she said. "Thanks anyway. But I'd like to try this myself. In the long run, I'm the one who'll have to deal with it."

"Makes sense," I said.

"But," she said, "I wouldn't mind seeing you after school."

"How about seven? Your place?"

"How about."

I made very strong coffee and squeezed grapefruit for juice—no doubt Mahlon Burden had a gadget that did it faster and cleaner—and, so fortified, turned on the eight o'clock news.

I tuned in midway through a film-clip retrospective of Massengil's career. Terms like "aggressive campaigner" and "veteran lawmaker" predominated. Sheryl Jackson remained unnamed. Dr. Lance Dobbs was described as a "prominent psychologist, management consultant, and adviser to the assemblyman." The Lesser Corpse. For all the public knew, he and Massengil had been playing poker.

The police were offering no theories as to the identity of the assassin(s) but were investigating "several leads." That from the police chief himself. A reporter's question about the sniping at Hale prompted a quick "At this time we see no connection, but as I said, gentlemen, all aspects of this tragedy are being looked into." Frisk stood in back of the chief, projecting the faithful-servant solemnity of a Vice Presidential candidate.

Cut to Massengil's tearful widow, a stout grandmotherly woman with wounded eyes under a bubble of white hair, sitting on a velvet divan being comforted by two of the assemblyman's four grown sons. The other two were flying in from Colorado and Florida. On the wall behind the divan were framed pictures. The camera closed in on one of them: Massengil throwing a grandchild up in the air. The baby looked terrified and delighted at the same time. Massengil's smile was ferocious. I turned off the set.

Postponing my next history lesson, I did chores and paperwork for a couple of hours, netted leaves out of the pond, and showered. But by eleven I was at the dining room table, facing Ike's books. Turning pages, searching for more marginal notes—to what end?

*At the very least you'll have your conscious-
ness raised, pal.*

A week ago I would have claimed a sterling
consciousness, in no need of raising. I was no
stranger to suffering—I'd spent half my life as a
receptacle for the misery of others. Walking the
terminal wards, dispensing words, nods, empathic
looks, strategic silences—the meager kindnesses
endowed by my training. Ending too many bleak
nights mired in the unanswerable *why is life so
cruel* ruminations that come with that territory.
The kind of questions with which you stop tortur-
ing yourself only when you realize there are no
answers.

But the horror of these books was different,
the cruelty so . . . calculated. Institutionalized
and efficient.

Homicide in service of the state.

Psychopathy elevated to patriotic duty.

Children shoved into boxcars under the ap-
proving eyes of soldiers not much older than
children themselves. Assembly-line tattooing.

The *processing* of humans as ore.

I'd intended to skim, but found myself reading. Found the time slipping away, until it was
noon, then past.

At two-thirty, I began a book on the Eichmann trial. A chapter toward the end presented
trial documents proving a deliberate plan to exter-
minate the Jews. Nazi records chronicling a con-

ference at German Interpol Headquarters in Berlin, convened by one Reinhard Heydrich on January 20, 1942, in accordance with a letter from Hermann Goering charging Heydrich with arranging a final solution. A secret conference attended by learned men: *Dr.* Meyer. *Dr.* Leibrandt. *Dr.* Neumann. *Dr.* Freisler . . .

The plan had been well thought-out, making use of data already collected by the previous mass murder operations of *Aktion* squads. Detailed statistics on the demographics of eleven million Jews.

The first stage would be mass evacuation under the guise of *Arbeitseinsatz*—the "labor effort." Those evacuees not liquidated by "natural causes" would be "treated suitably." The whole thing had the arrogant detachment of an academic conference, the participants conducting scholarly, high-minded discussions of optimal killing techniques. . . .

A secret conference, revealed to posterity only because Herr Eichmann, compulsive clerk that he was, had taken copious notes.

A conference held in the Berlin district known as Wannsee.

Wannsee.

Wanna see.

Wanna see? Wanna see too? Two?

My breath grew short and the ache in my jaw reminded me I'd been clenching my teeth.

I returned my gaze to the book. The pages before me were well thumbed, foxed to fuzz at the corners.

In the right margin the words had been penciled, in the neat, measured printing I'd come to know as Ike Novato's:

"Wannsee II? Possible?"

Several inches below that: "Crevolin again? Maybe."

Then a phone number with a 931 prefix.

The Fairfax district.

Wannsee II.

Crevolin. It sounded like a hair-replacement tonic. Or something made from petrochemicals.

Some kind of code? Or maybe a name.

I dialed the Fairfax number. A receptionist recited the call letters of one of the TV networks. Surprise slowed my response and before I could answer she repeated the triad of consonants and said, "May I help you?"

"Yes. I'd like to speak with Mr. Crevolin." Fifty percent chance of getting the gender right.

She said, "One moment."

Click.

"Terry Crevolin's office."

"Mr. Crevolin, please."

"He's out of the office."

"When do you expect him back?"

"Who is this, please?"

Not knowing how to answer that, I said, "A friend. I'll call back later," and hung up.

I dialed the Holocaust Center and asked for Judy Baumgartner. She came to the phone sounding cheerful.

"Yes, Alex, what can I do for you?"

"Milo asked me to look through Ike Novato's books. I just came across something Ike wrote in one of the margins and thought you might be able to explain it to me."

"What is it?"

"Wannsee Two. He wrote it in the margin of a chapter on the original Wannsee conference."

"Wannsee Two," she said, pronouncing it *Vahn-say*. "He never mentioned that to me. Strange that he should even know about that."

"Why's that?"

"Wannsee Two's pretty esoteric. Just a rumor, really, that circulated years ago—back in the seventies. Supposedly, there was a secret meeting between elements of the radical right and those of the radical left—white leftists who'd broken with the black militants and turned heavily racist. The alleged goal was to set up a national socialist confederation—plant the roots of a neo-Nazi party in this country."

"Sounds like the Bund, reborn."

"More like the Hitler-Stalin pact," she said. "The extremes crushing the middle. We checked it out, never found any evidence it had happened.

The prevailing wisdom is that it's apocryphal—one of those urban folk myths, like alligators in the sewer system. But chances are this particular myth got a little special help. The rumor began circulating just around the time of Cointelpro—the counterintelligence program the Nixon administration set up to sabotage radical movements."

"Where was this conference supposed to have taken place?"

"I've heard different versions, ranging from Germany to right here in the U.S. I've even heard claims that it took place on a military base—the confederation was supposed to have lots of members in the armed forces and in various police forces around the country. How's that for something to feed your paranoia?" Pause. "Wannsee Two. This is the first I've heard of it in a very long time. I wonder how Ike knew about it."

"His landlady was an old radical with an interest in the Holocaust," I said. "The two of them used to talk politics. She may have told him about Wannsee Two and he may have decided to research it."

"Well, given that, I can see why he'd pursue it. Blacks were a prime target of Wannsee Two. The way the story goes, one of the intentions of the confederation was to foment hatred between the minorities. Pit the blacks against the Jews—have the blacks *kill* the Jews, which would be easy because the Jews were passive wimps, ready to march into the ovens again. Once the blacks had served their purpose, they would be annihilated. Also a snap, because *they* were so gullible and stupid. And of course, when the cowardly Hispanics and Asians saw what was going on, they'd leave the country of their own accord—go back where they came from—and the borders of White America would be hermetically sealed."

"Sounds pretty nuts."

"So did Hitler, at the beginning. That's why we investigated the Wannsee Two thing as thoroughly as we've ever investigated anything. But we never came up with anything to support it."

I said, "There was something else in the margin. Crevolin. And a phone number. I called it and got the office of someone named Terry Crevolin, at one of the TV networks."

"I know Terry!" she said. "He works in development—screening scripts. He worked with us last year on our war-criminal special—*The Hidden*. We won an Emmy."

"I remember. Did Ike know him?"

"Not as far as I know, but I'm starting to see there were lots of things I didn't know about Ike."

"Could they have met at the Center?"

"No. Terry was just here a couple of times, for meetings. And that was last year, months before Ike showed up. Though I suppose there could have been a chance meeting if Terry dropped in without my knowing it. What exactly did Ike write in that book?"

"*Wannsee Two?*—the *two* in roman numerals—followed by the word *Possible?* Then *Crevolin again? Maybe.* And Crevolin's number. It could mean he tried to talk to Crevolin once— about Wannsee Two—hadn't been able to reach him, and was thinking of trying it again. Any idea why?"

"The only thing that comes to mind is that Terry used to be involved with the New Left— even wrote a book about it. I recall his mentioning that. He seemed kind of embarrassed and proud at the same time. I guess Ike could have seen him as a source, though how Ike would know that, I have no idea."

"A source on the New Left?"

"Maybe. Certainly not on the Holocaust. Terry wasn't especially knowledgeable about that until we educated him. You've really got my curiosity piqued. If you find out anything useful, please let me know."

I called the network again and got patched through to Crevolin's office. He was still out. This time I left my name and said it was about Ike Novato. Then I phoned Milo at the West L.A. station, planning to play Show and Tell. He wasn't in either. I called his home number, got Rick's recorded voice on a machine, and recited what I'd learned about Wannsee II. Saying it out loud made me realize it wasn't much: a dead boy's exploration of an urban myth.

I searched through the rest of Ike's books, found no more marginal notes or Wannsee references, and repacked them. It was close to six by the third time I called the network. This time no one answered.

Crevolin again?

Instead of implying Ike had been unsuccessful in reaching the network man, it might mean they'd talked and Crevolin hadn't given him what he wanted.

But why had Ike believed Crevolin would be helpful?

A New Left veteran. And author.

Perhaps Ike had gotten hold of Crevolin's book and found something interesting.

I looked at my watch. An hour until I was supposed to pick up Linda.

I called a bookstore in Westwood Village. The clerk checked *Books in Print* and told me no book by anyone named Crevolin was current and the store had no record of ever having stocked it.

"Any idea where I might get hold of it?"

"What's it about?"

"The New Left, the sixties."

"Vagabond Books has a big sixties section."

I knew Vagabond—Westwood Boulevard just above Olympic. Right on the way to Linda's.

A warm, cluttered place with the dusty, easy-browsing feel of a campus-area bookstore, the kind of place L.A. campuses rarely have. I'd bought a few Chandler and MacDonald and Leonard first editions there, some art and psych and poetry books. I looked up the number, called, waited ten rings and was about to hang up when a man answered:

"Vagabond."

I told him what I was looking for.

"Yup, we have it."

"Great. I'll come by right now and pick it up."

"Sorry, we're closed."

"What time do you open tomorrow?"

"Eleven."

"Okay. See you at eleven."

"It's pretty important to you?"

"Yes, it is."

"You a writer?"

"Researcher."

"Tell you what: come around through the back, I'll give it to you for ten bucks."

I thanked him, did a quick change, and left, picking up Westwood Boulevard at Wilshire and taking it south. I reached the back entrance to the bookstore by 6:25. The door was bolted. After a couple of hard raps, I heard the bolt slide back. A tall lean man in his thirties, with a boyishly handsome face framed by long wavy hair parted in the middle, stood holding a grimy-looking paper-back book in one hand. The book's cover was gray and unmarked. The man wore sneakers and cords and a Harvard sweat shirt. A tenor sax hung from a string around his neck.

He gave a warm smile and said, "I looked for a cleaner one, but this was all we had."

I said, "No problem. I appreciate your doing this."

He handed me the book. "Happy research."

I held out a ten.

"Make it five," he said, reaching into his pocket and giving me change. "I recognize you now. You're a good customer, and it's a ratty copy. Besides, it's not exactly one of our fast-movers."

"Bad writing?"

He laughed and fingered some buttons on the sax. "That doesn't start to describe it. It's self-published dreck. *Downright turgid* would be flat-tery. Also, the guy sold out."

I opened the book. The title was *Lies,* by T. Crevolin. I turned a page, looked at the name of the publisher. "Rev Press?"

"As in *o-lution*. Pretty clever, huh?"

He raised the sax to his lips, expelled a few blue notes and bent them.

I thanked him again.

He continued to play, blowing harder, raised his eyebrows, and closed the door.

* * *

I tossed the book into the trunk of the Seville and drove to Linda's.

We went to a place in the Los Feliz district that I'd gotten to know during my days at Western Pediatric. Small, Italian, deli case in front, tables in back. Ripe with Romano cheese and garlic sausage, olive loaf and prosciutto, a beautiful brine smell wafting up from open vats of olives.

I ordered a bottle of Chianti Classico that cost more than our dinners combined. Each of us finished a glass before the food came.

I asked how the children were handling Massengil's murder.

She said, "Pretty well, actually. Most of them didn't seem to have that clear a picture of who he was. It seems like a pretty remote experience for them. I dealt with the cause and effect thing. Thanks for getting me on the right track."

She filled my glass, then hers. "Catch the six o'clock news?"

"No."

"You were right about Massengil—they're turning him into a saint. *And* Latch's best friend."

"Latch?"

"Oh, yeah, center stage. Delivering a eulogy in Council chambers. Going on about how he and *Sam* had *enjoyed* their differences but through it all there'd been a mutual respect, an appreciation for the process of give-and-take, whatever. Then condolences to the widow, a formal proposal to make it a day of official mourning for the beloved leader. The whole thing sounded like a campaign speech."

"Beloved leader," I said.

"Everyone loves him now. Even the guy Massengil punched out—DiMarco—had nice things to say."

"Nothing like death to enhance the old public image."

"If his corpse were up for reelection, he'd probably win."

I raised my glass. "What a concept. Suicide as a campaign tactic. The possibilities are fascinating—like adding the post of Official Exhumer to the cabinet."

Both of us laughed. She said, "Lord, this is grisly. But I'm sorry, I just can't start liking him because he's dead. I remember how he used us. And what he liked to do with that call girl. Ugh."

I said, "Any mention of Dobbs through all of this?"

"Respected psychologist, consultant, et cetera."

"No mention of his working at the school?"

She nodded. "That was the respected psychologist part. They made it sound as if he'd been treating the kids all along—so much for an informed press. There were also a few questions about a possible connection to the sniping, but

Frisk brushed them off with doubletalk: every contingency being investigated, top secret, et cetera, et cetera. Not that any cops've been down to talk to us."

She licked her lips. "Then Latch goes out in front of City Hall, rolls up his sleeves, and lowers the flag to half-mast himself, looking real solemn. Twenty years ago he was probably burning it."

"People have short memories," I said. "He proved that by getting elected. He's gotten his foothold; now he's angling for respectability. The Great Conciliator. Combine that with the DeJon concert and the fact that it was his man who saved the day, and he'll probably go down as the hero in this whole thing."

She shook her head. "All the stuff they don't teach you in civics class. When you get down to it, they're all the same, aren't they? One big power trip, no matter what they claim they stand for."

No matter what wing . . .

She said, "What is it, Alex?"

"What's what?"

"All of a sudden you got this look on your face as if the wine was bad."

"No, I'm fine," I said.

"You didn't look fine."

Her voice was soft but insistent. I felt pressure around my fingers; she'd taken my hand, was squeezing it.

I said, "Okay. Ready for more weirdness?" I

told her about Ike Novato's research. Wannsee II. The New Confederation.

She said, "Crazies on both ends putting their heads together. What a lovely thought."

"The expert at the Holocaust Center doubts it actually took place. And if anyone would know, she would."

"That's good," she said, "because that is *too* weird."

We both drank wine.

I said, "How's Matt the car basher working out?"

"No troubles so far. I've got him doing scut stuff, wanted to show him who was boss right at the outset. He's really a meek little kid in an overgrown body. Pretty docile, no social skills. A real follower."

"Sounds like Holly."

"Sure does," she said. "Wonder how many of them like that are out there."

She let go of my hand. Touched her wine-glass but didn't raise it to her lips. Silence enveloped us. I heard other couples talking. Laughing.

"Move your chair," she said. "Sit next to me. I want to feel you right next to me."

I did. The table was narrow and our shoulders touched. She rested her fingers on my knee. I put my arm around her and drew her closer. Her body was taut, resistant. A tremulous, high-frequency hum seemed to course through it.

She said, "Let's get out of here. Just be by ourselves."

I threw money on the table, was up in a flash.

As far as I could tell, no one followed us home.

29

We fell asleep holding each other; by six-thirty the next morning we'd shifted to opposite sides of the bed. She opened one eye, rolled back to me, put her leg over my hip, fit me to her, eager for union. But when it was over, she was quick to get out of bed.

I said, "Everything all right?"

"Dandy." She bent, kissed me full on the lips, pulled away, and went into the shower. By the time I got there she was out, toweling off.

I reached out to hold her. She let me, but just for a moment, then danced away, saying "Busy day."

She left without eating breakfast. I sensed a reserve—a trace of the old chill?—as if the no-ugliness rule had sheltered us for a few hours, but at the expense of intimacy.

I showered alone, made coffee, and sat down with Terry Crevolin's book.

*   *   *

Downright turgid *would* be flattery.

The book was full of typos and grammatical errors. If editing had taken place I couldn't see it. Crevolin had a fondness for two-hundred-word sentences, random italics, creative capitalization, frequent references to "Ottoman manipulation," "mercantile demonics," "the new State-Management Bank," and quotations from Chairman Mao. ("In wars of national liberation, patriotism is applied internationalism.")

A sample sentence read: "None of the *existent* forms of conscious revolutionary rhetoric or *trans*-cultural *revolutionary activity* thus devised *by* the Labor Discipline and related Labor Vanguards as means of *eliminating* Commodityism and mercantile *demonics* seem so far able to self-defend against a steadily *diminishing* Proletarian Consciousness fermented by an *anarchic, carnivalous, mirror-gratifying,* and ultimately *dissipated* pseudo-Ideology concurrently *nurtured* by the Power Structure. . . ."

All that and pictures, too—photo-snippets culled from textbooks and magazines, some of them sloppily hand-colored in crayon. Headshots of Marx, Engels, Lenin, Trotsky, and for reasons I couldn't comprehend, Buddha, Shakespeare, and a rhesus monkey. Cloth-capped workers waiting in bread lines. Byzantine icons. Greek statuary. Dustbowl migrants with faces out of a Woody

Guthrie song. The Egyptian pyramids. Butterflies. Two pages of ancient weapons—maces, halberds, long swords. A Sherman tank.

I tried to make some sense of it, but the words passed through me without being digested—literary fiber. My eyes blurred and my head began to hurt. I flipped to the last chapter in hopes of finding a summation, some central message I could make sense of. Something that would tell me why Ike Novato had sought out the author.

What I found was a two-page spread of a crayoned mushroom cloud captioned BEAR LODGE, R.I.P., THE GREATS. On the next page was a photo-reproduction of a newspaper story from *The New York Times*. April 21, 1971. The word LIES! in large red letters had been hand-printed diagonally over the copy. The red letters were grainy. I read through them.

IDAHO BLAST THE RESULT OF RADICAL BOMB FACTORY ACCIDENT SAYS FBI

BEAR LODGE, IDAHO. — Federal and local law enforcement authorities in this rural logging community report that an enormous explosion that took place during the early morning hours was the result of the accidental detonation of a cache of high explosives stockpiled by left-wing radicals conspiring to carry out a program of domestic terrorism and violent political protest.

The explosion, described by witnesses as a "firestorm," occurred at 2:00 A.M. and totally demolished a former lumber warehouse and several vacant outbuildings a half mile outside Bear Lodge, in addition to setting off fires in surrounding heavily forested areas that took six hours to suppress. Structures within the town of Bear Lodge experienced shattered windows and minor wood and masonry damage. No Bear Lodge residents reported injuries but ten people in the warehouse are believed to have perished.

"The ground just started shaking. It felt like an earthquake," said Nellie Barthel, owner of the Maybe Drop Inn Tavern and Truck Stop in Bear Lodge, as she swept up broken bottles and glasses. "Or one of those sonic booms, but a lot louder. Then we saw the fire and smoke pouring into the sky from the east and we knew something had happened out there with those people at the old log depository."

Tax documents obtained in Twin Falls reveal that the titled owner of the warehouse, Mountain Properties, had leased the hundred-year-old clapboard building the previous August for a six-month period to an "M. Bakunin"— believed to be an alias alluding to 19th century Russian anarchist Mikhail Aleksandrovich Bakunin. "Bakunin's" stated purpose on the lease agreement was "storage of agricultural materials and food."

Employees and officers of Mountain Properties were not available for comment. However, residents of Bear Lodge (pop. 326) report increased activity in the vicinity of the warehouse during recent weeks, the "outsiders" hauling truckloads of fertilizer, sawdust, sugar and other materials along the quarter-mile service road leading to the four-story storage building.

"They must have bought the stuff somewhere else because they never came into town to shop," said Dayton Auhagen, a buckskin-clad trapper who sometimes camped in the now-charred forests surrounding the warehouse. Auhagen described the warehouse tenants as "not from anywhere around these parts. But they minded their own business and we minded ours. That's the

way it is out here. We're all individual-
ists."

Southern Idaho Regional FBI
Agent-in-Charge Morrison Stowe had
another view of the blast victims. "They
were political radicals suspected of acts
of urban terrorism or conspiracy to commit terrorism. The substances they were
stockpiling are all potential nitrating
agents and thus have a potential role in
the manufacture of nitroglycerine-based
explosives."

Although he declined to specify the
precise process of bomb manufacture,
Stowe did say, "It's not all that difficult.
During the last couple of years there
have been several manuals circulating
among the subversive underground:
bomb cookbooks that make do-
it-yourselfing sound easy. What they
don't emphasize sufficiently is that ni-
troglycerine is an extremely unstable
compound no matter how you cook it
up. Minute variations in heat or humid-
ity can set it off. We believe that's what
happened here. These individuals were
manufacturing bombs, an accidental
detonation occurred and they blew
themselves up."

Stowe added that while the force of

the blast was so great as to render identification of bodies virtually impossible, eyewitness accounts combined with a "careful and longstanding investigation" led the Bureau to believe that at least ten individuals perished in the blast, including two young children, and that no members of the group escaped. He listed the blast victims as:

Thomas Harrison Mader Bruckner, 29, of Darien, Connecticut. A Columbia University graduate, teaching assistant in sociology at the University of California, Berkeley, and founding member of the violent Weathermen offshoot of Students for a Democratic Society (SDS), Bruckner was scion of an old Colonial family whose members have included several congressmen and a signer of the Declaration of Independence.

Catherine Blanchard Lockerby, 23, of Philadelphia and Newport, Rhode Island. A former Columbia University psychology student and Weatherman, Lockerby is described as Bruckner's live-in companion and also the descendant of an affluent, socially prominent family.

Antonio Yselas Rodriguez, 34, of

San Juan, Puerto Rico and the Bronx, New York. A convicted forger and burglar, Rodriguez is wanted on an outstanding fugitive warrant for escape from the Rikers Island prison in New York where he was being held for trial on assault charges related to a December 1970 South Bronx bar brawl. He is termed a "major suspect" in several bombings attributed to the Puerto Rican separatist/extremist group, FALN.

Teresa Alicia Santana, 26, of the Bronx, New York, is Rodriguez's common-law wife and suspected FALN cell leader.

Mark Andrew Grossman, 24, of Brooklyn, New York. Former New York University political science student, Weathermen founder, and self-described "labor activist," Grossman was wanted for questioning related to attempted sabotage of several Eastern Seaboard power stations.

Harold Cleveland "Big Skitch" Dupree, 39, convicted murderer and armed robber, paroled from Rahway, New Jersey, state prison in October of last year. Dupree was an official of the Black Fist prison gang and suspected founder of the Black Revolutionary

Armed Forces, and was believed to be responsible for a string of armed car robberies in upstate New York.

Norman Samuel Green, 27, of Oakland, California. A former graduate student and teaching assistant in political science at the University of California, Berkeley, a former SDS official and antiwar activist, Green is believed to have been a prime force behind the "People's Park" riots and other student protests at the Berkeley campus. He is thought to be the "M. Bakunin" to whom the warehouse was leased.

Melba Tamara Johnson-Green, 28, of Oakland, California. Norman Green's wife and a former law student at the University of California, Berkeley, where she was a member of the Law Review before dropping out one semester short of graduation. An SDS member, an antiwar and women's liberation activist and a suspected recruiter for the Weathermen on the Berkeley campus.

Malcolm Isaac Green, 2, of Oakland, California, the Greens' son.

Fidel Frantz Rodriguez-Santana, 8

months, of the Bronx, New York, the
son of Rodriguez and Santana.

Asked why members of groups
such as the Black Revolutionary Armed
Forces and the Weathermen, which had
been known to have experienced significant ideological differences in the
past, had cooperated in assembling the
explosives cache, Agent Stowe said,
"Our information is that they were
trying a unity-is-strength approach.
All the major subversive groups have
fallen upon hard times. Successful prosecution and imprisonment of leaders
and exposure of their true goals have
decimated their ranks, and new recruits
are rare. The only ones left tend to
be hard-core, violent radicals. This
appears to have been a last-ditch effort
to establish a radical confederation in
order to disrupt society and damage
lives and property. Because of their
violent tendencies, it's no surprise
they ended up this way. Unfortunately,
the two children were innocent victims."

Facing the clipping was a poem surrounded on all
sides by a border of dozens of tiny Jesuses on
crosses.

BLACK LIES, WHITE LIES

blood on sawdust
rich and warm sweet with purpose
the splinters pierce martyrflesh
fascist sky ironred firered
uglysound
mycountrytis ofthee
mycountryrightorwrong they say
meanwhile spilling the sacramental blood
                              of
          righteous ones
       truth   the ultimate victim
in their game the ultimate game
win or lose
battle
not the war
my heart bleeds too
rich and warm
for
joe hill
sacco and vanzetti
che
leon
triangle fire girls
thirdworld saints
piglies   black and white
together
just the battle

because of red red
blood
power to the people!!!!

The last page was taken up by a photo, a group portrait of twenty or so people standing and kneeling in two rows in front of an ivy-covered brick building. The handwritten caption said, "Berkeley, Feb. 1969. Great bash. Even revolutionaries have to party."

Arms around shoulders. Smiling faces. The joy of camaraderie. A few pairs of marijuana eyes.

Several heads had been haloed in black crayon—five men, three women. Handwritten names above each.

Thomas Bruckner and Catherine Lockerby stood together in the center of the front row. He, pear-shaped and stooped in a faded work shirt and jeans, with limp brown shoulder-length hair and a thick drooping mustache that obscured the bottom half of his face. She, big, heavily-built, barefooted, wearing a batik muumuu, with her blond hair drawn back severely. Thin lips yielded reluctantly to mirth. Piercing eyes, strong jaw. In another place, another time, she might have matured to a horsey society woman.

Next to her stood "Tonio" Rodriguez, medium-sized and clean shaven, surprisingly clean-cut, his dark hair shorter than that of the others, side-parted. Button-down shirt and jeans.

Eyes hidden behind mirrored Highway Patrol sunglasses. Teresa Santana had her arm around him. She was very short, very thin, wore a black turtleneck and tight jeans. Her long black hair was parted in the middle, framing an oval face with fashion-model cheekbones, almond eyes, full lips. A miniature Joan Baez, but hardened by a life more brutal than show biz.

Mark Grossman and "Big Skitch" Dupree stood on the left side of the second row, only their faces visible. Grossman's was soft, childish, without much chin. He wore a huge blond Afro and fuzzy muttonchops that made him look out of focus. Dupree's Afro was more modest. He wore black-framed eyeglasses, had a square, asphalt-colored face and a full beard. No smile. Penetentiary wariness.

To the far right side of the second row were the haloed visages of Norman and Melba Green. Next to Melba was an unhaloed face that I recognized.

Roundish, freckled, an unruly mop of dark hair. Pinched features, round tortoise-shell eyeglasses—the kind the British welfare department used to distribute for free. A skimpy mustache and feathery Vandyke that had the pasted-on look of theatrical costumery. But take away the facial hair, add a few years, and it was the same man I'd run into in a classroom, playing a har-

monica. Same man I'd seen introducing a rock
star.

Even back then, Gordon Latch had worn a
politician's smile. I stared at his picture for a
while, creating hypotheses, running with them,
hitting brick walls, trying again, finally turning
my attention back to the Greens.

Norman Green had been very tall—from the
way he towered over the others, at least six three
or four. He had coarse dark hair, parted in the
middle and held in place with a leather thong.
Roman nose, thick dark eyebrows, long handsome
face, rendered Lincolnesque by a bushy, mus-
tacheless beard. Something about the face
familiar . . .

His wife was of medium height, which
brought the top of her head to his bicep. Black and
pretty but severe-looking, as if preoccupied. She
wore a collarless white blouse, ebony bead neck-
laces, and huge ebony hoop earrings. Haughty
smile. Fluffy Afro above a fine-boned oval face.
The carved-mask good looks of an African prin-
cess. Her face familiar too.

Black woman, white man.

It made me think of something. I turned back
pages, to the newspaper clipping.

*Malcolm Isaac Green, 2, of Oakland, Cali-
fornia.*

Seventeen years ago. Seventeen plus two.
The time-frame fit.

Hispanic name on a black kid.

I went into the library, scrounged until I found my Spanish-English dictionary.

Page 146: **novato** *m*. novice, beginner.

Flip to the English-Spanish side.

Page 94: **green** *adj*. verde; novato, inexperto.

I put the book down and got on the phone.

30

Still unable to reach Milo. Unable to get a bored desk officer at the West Side station to tell me where he was.

Where were the cops when you needed them?

I remembered Judy Baumgartner's account of her cryptic conversation with Ike. *Relax your standards.* If I was interpreting my dictionary correctly, that made sense. I phoned her again at the Holocaust Center. Her secretary informed me she was out of the office and was cagey about saying more. Remembering what Judy had said about death threats, I didn't push, but finally managed to convince the secretary that I was legitimate. Then she told me Judy had flown back to Chicago, wasn't expected back for three days. Did I want to leave a message? Thinking about what kind of message I could leave, I declined and thanked her.

As I hung up, I thought of someone else who'd be able to firm up my theory. I looked up

the number of the Beth Shalom Synagogue and
dialed it. No one answered. The directory yielded
three *Sanders, D.*, only one with no address listed
and a Venice exchange. I called it. A woman with
an accent similar to the rabbi's answered. Children's voices filled the background, along with
what sounded like recorded music.

"Rabbi Sanders, please."

"Who may I say is calling?"

"Alex Delaware. I met him at the synagogue
the other day. Along with Detective Sturgis."

"One moment."

Sanders came on saying, "Yes, Detective
Delaware. Any progress on Sophie?"

"Still an ongoing investigation," I said.
Amazing how easy that came . . .

"Yes, of course. What can I do for you?"

"I've got a theological question for you,
Rabbi. What are Orthodox Judaism's criteria for
determining if someone's Jewish?"

"Basically, there are two," he said. "One
must either be born to a Jewish mother or undergo
a proper conversion. Conversion is predicated
upon a course of study."

"Having a Jewish father wouldn't be
enough?"

"No. Only the Reform Jews have accepted
patrilineal descent."

"Thank you, Rabbi."

"Is that all?"

"Yes. You've been very helpful."

"Have I? Does your question have anything to do with Sophie?"

I hedged, repeated the open investigation line, thanked him for his time, and hung up. Tried Milo again both at the station and at home. At the former, the desk officer's boredom had progressed to torpor. Answering machine at the latter. I told it what I'd learned. Then I tried the network again.

"Mr. Crevolin's in a meeting."

"When will he be free?"

"I can't say, sir."

"I called yesterday. Dr. Alex Delaware? Regarding Ike Novato?"

"I'm sure he got your message, sir."

"Then how about we try to get his attention with a new message."

"I don't really—"

"Tell him Bear Lodge claimed *nine* victims, not *ten*."

"Barry Lodge?"

"Bear, as in the animal. Lodge as in Henry Cab—as in hunting lodge. Bear Lodge—it's a place. It claimed *nine* victims. *Not ten.*"

"One second," she said. "I'm still writing."

"You can also tell him that *apathy* claimed the tenth. Just a few months ago. Apathy and indifference."

"Apathy and indifference," she said. "Is this some kind of concept for a script? 'Cause if it is,

I know for a fact the fall season's completely
programmed and it's really not worth pitching
anything until they clear the board for the next
sweeps."

"Not a concept," I said. "A true story. And it
would never play on prime time."

She called me back an hour later to say "He'll
see you at four," unable to keep the surprise out of
her voice.

At five to four, I walked across a network
parking lot crammed with German and Swedish
cars. I was wearing a tan gabardine suit and
carrying my briefcase. A roving security guard in
his seventies took down my name and directed me
to a flight of metal stairs that led up to the second
floor of the bulky deco building. On the way, I
passed a canopied waiting area filled with hundreds of people lined up for tickets to the latest
late-night talk show. A few of them rotated their
heads to inspect me, decided I was nobody to be
concerned with, and turned their attention else-
where.

At the top of the stairs were double plate-
glass doors. The reception area was big as a barn:
thirty feet high, walls bare except for a giant
reproduction of the network logo on the south side
and, just below it, a door marked PRIVATE. The
floor was travertine tile, over which a surprisingly
shabby maroon area rug had been laid. In the
precise center of the rug was a rectangular glass

coffee table. Hard black leather sling chairs ran along both sides. On the far side of the room a young black security guard sat behind a white counter. To his left a white Actionvision monitor played some sort of game show. The sound was off.

I gave him my name. He opened a ledger, ran his finger down a page, turned to the next page, did more finger-walking, stopped, made a call on a white phone, listened, and said, "Uh-huh. Okay, yeah." To me: "Be a couple of minutes. Whyncha have a seat."

I tried to get comfortable in the sling chair. The glass table was empty—no magazines, not even an ashtray.

I said, "Nothing to read. That supposed to be a philosophical statement?"

The guard looked over as if noticing that for the first time, chuckled, and returned his attention to the monitor. A hefty woman in a print dress was bouncing up and down, embracing a male host who was trying hard to maintain a blow-dried smile. As the woman continued to hug him, the smile finally faded. The host tried to get loose. She held tight. Colored lights flashed in the background.

The guard saw me looking. "They turn off the sound. Don't ask me why—I just started. That's some kind of new show—*Fair Fight*, I think it is. Still trying to figure out exactly what

it's all about. What I *think* it is, is that you got to
insult your friends, give away their secrets, in
order to answer questions and win the big money."

The host finally pried himself free of the
hefty woman. She started bouncing again. The
name tag on her bosom fluttered. Despite her
bulk, she was firm as a canned ham. The host
smiled again and pointed and said something. In
the background a beauty-contest runner-up in a
black mini-dress spun something that resembled a
bingo bin. The camera closed in on numbers
incandescing along a giant roulette wheel rimmed
with flashing light bulbs.

The guard studied the screen, squinting.
"Tough to know what they're saying," he said. "I
figure a couple of more weeks on the job and I'll
be able to read lips."

I settled back and closed my eyes. At four-ten
the PRIVATE door opened and a young woman with
strawberry-blond hair stepped out. She wore a
sequined red T-shirt over black jeans and had a
reluctant, tired smile.

"Dr. Delaware? Terry can see you now." She
gave the door a shove and walked through, leaving
me to catch it. Treating walking as if it were an
athletic event, she took me past a half-empty
secretarial area to a short, bright hallway marked
by six or seven doors. The third door was open.
She said, "Here," waited until I went in, and left.

No one was in the office. It was a medium-sized room with an eastern view of more parking lot, tar-paper rooftops, intestinal twists of hammered metal ductwork, and the smog-softened contours of central L.A. The walls were gray grass cloth; the carpeting, tight-nap industrial tinted the dull aqua of a poorly serviced swimming pool. Floating in the center was a clear-plastic desk with matching chair. Perpendicular to the desk was an anorexic couch upholstered in slate-blue tweed. Facing the desk were two blue chairs with chrome legs. Warm and comfy as an operating room.

Three of the gray walls were unadorned. The one behind the desk was filled with color animation celluloids. *Cinderella. Pinocchio. Fantasia.* Given what Judy had told me, I hadn't expected political posters, but Disney took me by surprise. My gaze lingered on Snow White about to accept a poisoned apple from a gleeful crone.

A man came in, cupping his hand to his mouth and coughing. Forty or close to it, short, with a pallid, soft-featured face under a salt-and-pepper new-wave crew cut stiff with butch wax. One of the faces that had been in the group photo, younger, thinner, long hair. Second row, right, I thought. Shadowed by Norman Green's towering height.

He stared at me. There were sooty bags under his eyes. A gold stud sparkled in his left ear. He wore a baggy black bomber jacket over a gray silk

T-shirt, gray sharkskin trousers with pegged cuffs, black high-top Reeboks.

He sat down. The height of the apple in the Snow White cel was such that it appeared to sit atop his head.

William Tell in Melrose Avenue duds.

He said, "Terry Crevolin." Incongruous bass voice.

"Alex Delaware."

"So I've been told. Sit."

As I did, he got up and locked the door. Two silk T-shirts exactly like the one he was wearing hung on dry-cleaner's hangers from a hook on the back.

He returned to the desk, sifted through papers for a few moments, then said, "Yeah, you look like a doctor. What kind of doctor are you?"

"Psychologist."

"Psychologist. But you know about what plays in prime time."

I said, "I know Bear Lodge sure wouldn't. Too long ago and times have changed. No one cares much about a bunch of radical freaks blowing themselves up."

One of his eyes twitched. He looked at my briefcase.

We had ourselves a little staring contest. He was pretty good at it—plenty of practice, no doubt, with desperate writers pitching concepts. But I'd sat through tens of thousands of hours of therapy. On the doctor's side of the couch. Waited out every evasion known to mankind . . .

Finally he said, "I was given the impression you had something for me—a concept. If you do, let's hear it. If not . . ." Shrug.

"Sure," I said. "Here's a concept: adolescent search for identit—"

"It's been done."

"Not like this. My protagonist is a bright young kid, orphaned at a very young age. Good-looking, idealistic. Half-black, half-Jewish. His parents are political radicals who die under suspicious circumstances. Seventeen years later he tries to find out how and why. And ends up getting murdered for his efforts—set up in a phony drug bust. Lots of good stuff in between but probably too downbeat, huh?"

Something that could have been pain scuttled across his face. He said, "You've lost me."

"Ike Novato. *Novato* as in Spanish for novice. Novice as in *green*. The little boy who once belonged to Norman and Melba Green."

Crevolin inspected his nails.

I said, "He tried to see you this past summer, couldn't get through."

"Lots of people try to see me."

"Not about Bear Lodge."

He peered at a cuticle.

"Do lots of them get murdered, Mr. Crevolin?"

Some color came into his face. "Boy, this sounds pretty dramatic."

"He was murdered. Check it out for yourself. Last September. Drug deal gone wrong down in Watts. Funny thing is, though, people who know him say he never used drugs, had no reason to go to Watts."

"People," he said. "There's no way to know someone—to really know what goes on in someone's head. Especially a kid, right? The whole kick about being young is keeping secrets, right? Creating your own private world and keeping everyone else out of it. If you're really a shrink you should know that."

"Ike Novato's secrets were dangerous," I said. "They may have killed him. And his grandmother too. An old woman who lived in Venice named Sophie Gruenberg."

His mouth opened, then closed.

I said, "She disappeared a few days after he was killed. The police think someone disappeared her. They've got no leads, can't seem to connect any of it, think maybe there's a dope connection. But I'll just bet they'd love to talk to you."

He said, "Oh, shit."

I said, "Gruenberg to Green. Green to Novato. The family had a thing for name changes, but they kept the hue consistent. When did Norman Green change his?"

"He didn't. His old man did. For business.

The father was bourgeois; the mother didn't approve of the name change. After the old man died, she changed it back."

"But Norm didn't?"

"No. He liked the old man. Politically, he saw eye to eye with his mother. But she was hard to get along with. Abrasive. Emotionally, she and Norm weren't close."

His nostrils flared and closed. He rolled his lips over his teeth, chewed on a pinkie. "Listen, I'm sorry to hear all this. What's it got to do with me?"

Bad bluffer. Pinocchio would have laughed and lent him his nose.

I said, "I think you know. One family destroyed—three generations exterminated, because the wrong people got asked the wrong questions. Asking you might have been safer, but Ike couldn't get through."

He waved a hand frantically. "Don't lay that on me."

"You're laying it on yourself. You've never forgotten Bear Lodge. That's why you agreed to see me."

He slumped, ran his fingers through his spiky hair, checked the time on a wristwatch thin enough to fit through a coin slot.

I said, "Getting his message last summer brought back those memories full force. You probably considered seeing him. Your idealism may be long-buried under a heap of game shows but—"

He sat up. "I don't do game shows."

"—you're still a person of principles. Or so it's been suggested."

"Yeah? By who?"

"Judy Baumgartner at the Holocaust Center. She says you helped them get that documentary produced. She's the one who told me about your book."

His expression turned sour. He pulled something out of his jacket pocket. An orange lollipop that he unwrapped with stealth and haste, as if it were a forbidden pleasure. He jammed it in his mouth, sat back, hands folded across his belly, pacified.

"Principles, huh?"

"Why'd you turn him down?" I said. "Too painful opening old wounds? Or was it just inertia? All those meetings you take every day, you simply didn't have the energy to handle another one?"

He yanked out the lollipop, started to say something, gagged on it, and stood up, turning his back to me. He faced the rear wall, taking in his cartoon buddies.

I said, "Fairy godmothers and glass slippers. Would that life were so simple."

"You with the government?" he said.

"No."

"Show me some ID."

I took my driver's license, psychology license, and medical school affiliation out of my wallet and handed them to him. "Got major credit cards, too, if you want to see them."

He turned around, examined them, gave them back. "Doesn't really mean anything, does it? You could be who the papers say you are and still be government."

"I could but I'm not."

He shrugged. "And what if you are? Like you said, times have changed—no one cares anymore. What's my crime? Shifting gears into a survival mode? What's the penalty gonna be? Working at another network?"

I smiled. "How about working with game shows?"

He leaned forward. "Come on, level with me. What's this really about?"

"It's about what I told you. I want to ask you some of the questions Ike Novato never got to ask."

"Why? What's your connection to him? Were you his shrink?"

"No. I never met him. But I've been looking into the death of one of his friends. A young girl named Holly Burden."

I waited for a sign of recognition, got none.

I said, "Her family asked me to do a psychological autopsy. To try to understand why she died. That led me to Ike. He was one of the few friends she'd had. A confidant. I traced him back to the Holocaust Center, some books he checked out on racism. He'd written your name and number in a margin. Judy was certain he hadn't met you there, thought he might have tried to reach you because of your previous life."

I opened the briefcase and pulled out his book. "I bought this today, read the Bear Lodge story and saw the Berkeley picture. Figured out who Ike really was."

He sat down, put the lollipop back in his mouth and withdrew it quickly, as if it had lost its flavor. "Some literary masterpiece, huh? I was coming down from acid and mushrooms and Methedrine chasers when I wrote that. Flashing back and seeing God. One superstoked weekend, no revisions. I didn't even come up for air. Pulitzer Prize stuff, it ain't."

"Don't sell yourself short," I said. "It had a certain raw energy. Passion. The kind you probably don't experience much anymore."

"Look," he said, stiffening, "if you think you're going to come in here and lay all this guilt on me—for surviving—forget it. I've worked that through. With my own *psychologist*."

"I'm happy for you, Terry. Too bad Ike won't be working anything through."

We locked eyes again. Again, he broke first.

"A cave," he said. "That's where I ended

up—that's where I wrote the damned thing. In a *cave*, okay? You understand? That's how I was living after Bear Lodge. Like some *Neanderthal* because I had no rich daddy like so many of the others in the movement. No trust fund, nothing to fall back on when the dream ended. I couldn't get a serious job because I'd dropped out to fight the good fight after one semester. I had a D average, no skills to do anything other than march around and chant. And the market for chanters wasn't too hot after the dream died, unless you felt like doing some Hare Krishna free-lancing. I even tried that, but their bullshit got to me, their scams and their stinking incense. All *I* knew was picking fruit, digging ditches, stoop work—that's the kind of stuff I grew up doing. On a scrub lot that never went anywhere because *my* daddy couldn't compete with the big growers and died with more debts than good sense. I headed up the coast, picking my hands bloody, bunking with the illegals. I was in Yuba City when they started digging up all the *braceros* Corona had hacked up. The guy who'd bunked next to me had disappeared. Victim number twenty-three. That scared me outa there, up to Oregon. My cave. Picking plums by day, playing Neanderthal by night. Scared me into a clear head, too—no acid, no pills, not even hash or grass. No Betty Ford clinic, just me and the long nights and the creepy-crawlies. To help get through it, I started writing. The ultimate therapy, right? Abby had done it; Jerry had done it; why not me? The end result was that piece of stupidity you're holding in your hot little hands. The first draft was dull pencil on sheets of ledger paper I ripped off from the shift boss. At night, using a flashlight. Later, when I had a couple of bucks, I bought a notebook and some Bics. I wrote other stuff too. Poetry that sucked. Short stories that sucked. A TV script that sucked. *Comedy. Lots* of comedy. In order to laugh myself out of suicide. Same plot line, over and over: revolutionaries who work for IBM but can't quite hack the straight life. Ha ha funny, right? I convinced myself it was profound, convinced myself no one was out to kill me anymore and hitched down to L.A. Showered, shaved at the Union Station, bought a suit at the Salvation Army, walked all the way to this center of spiritual purity and tried to get my script read. Couldn't get a foot in the door, but downstairs there was a sign saying they were hiring pages. I faked a wholesome attitude, got the job. First money I earned was used to publish the piece of crap. First printing of three hundred copies, never went into a second. I peddled it to head shops on consignment, never saw a dime. Learned hippie entrepreneurs were the worst. Learned I wasn't going to be Mr. Bestseller—time to shift to another tack. So I worked. Every scut job the network offered me. Worked my way up to this. I won't bore you with the details."

"Sounds like the American dream."

"Hey, it's a free country. Really is. I learned that the hard way. Testing the system—starting at rock bottom and taking it to the limits. Which is more than most people ever do. That's not to say there isn't plenty that's rotten in the system, but what's better? The Ayatollah? The Chinese? So I'm here for the long haul, trying to get through each day, paying my mortgage. I know what I do every day isn't feeding starving orphans, it isn't heart surgery, but I try to get some quality through when I can, okay? It's no better or worse than anyone else's gig, right? Which is what I want now. To be like anyone else. *Blend* in, concentrate on Terry, learn to be self-centered. Drive a car with leather seats, sit in the Jacuzzi at night, listen to compact discs, and get philosophical. Just get through each day."

He pointed a finger at me. "I paid more dues longer than anyone else I know, so forget your guilt."

I said, "Your guilt isn't my concern. Other people paid dues too. The ultimate dues. Norm and Melba Green, the rest of the gang at Bear Lodge. I'm sure any of them would be happy to trade places with you."

He closed his eyes, rubbed his eyelids. "Oh, boy, everything comes back like a wheel, doesn't it."

I said, "You were part of the group, weren't

you? What made you decide not to show up the day of the big blast?"

"Decide." Eye twitch. "Who decided? It was an accident—*twist of fate.* If I read it in a script, I'd call it hokey."

"How'd you escape?"

"I was *babysitting.* Taking the kid to the doctor."

"Which kid?"

"Malcolm Isaac. He was sick."

"Why didn't his parents take him?"

"Because they were sick too. All of them were. Puking their guts out. Some kind of intestinal thing—diarrhea, fever. Something they ate— bad meat. I'd just come up the day before. There were two groups, you see. Two cadres. I was part of the second, brought communications from the second to the first. We were all supposed to get together in a week or so. I was a vegetarian back then. Didn't eat the meat. That saved me. Me and the other kid."

"Rodriguez and Santana's son? Fidel?"

"Fidelito," he said. "He was just a baby, too young for meat, on formula because Teresa couldn't nurse. So he was healthy too. Crawling around the warehouse, fat and happy. But Malcolm Isaac had it bad. Really high fever, diarrhea, crying in pain. Melba was worried about dehydration, wanted him to see a doctor, but she and Norm were too sick to take him themselves. So they asked me, and I did. Public health clinic in Twin Falls. Me and him and a bunch of loggers and Indians in the waiting room. They had a country-western station on and he was wailing over it, in pain. That didn't impress the nurses. They turned up the volume, made us wait. Porter Wagoner and Dolly Parton. Funny the things you remember, huh? I was holding him, wiping his forehead with alcohol pads, when I heard it—beep beep news bulletin breaking into the country music."

His own brow had broken out in sweat. He wiped it with the back of his sleeve. "Big explosion at a warehouse in Bear Lodge. No one else in the waiting room was even listening—they could care less. But to me it was like everything was caving in, like a big hole in the earth—everything just being vacuumed into it. Then the FBI guy comes on and starts talking about some bomb factory, lying through his government-issue teeth, and I knew someone had shafted them. Knew I had to run."

"There was no bomb factory?"

He gave me a disgusted look. "Right. Lard and sugar and horse manure and sawdust—we were making a *produce* nuke, right? If it was that easy, half the farms in America would've blown up before Ronnie Ray-gun screwed them over."

"Half the farms in America don't have igniting devices."

"Neither did we. The FBI stooge either made that up or planted it. The supplies we'd stockpiled were for *growing,* not destroying. Seeds, fertilizer. Organic fertilizer. The sawdust was for compost. The lard was for cooking and making tortillas—Teresa loved to make tortillas. The plan was to stockpile enough stuff to put together a decent-sized collective farm, big enough to be viable. A new Walden. We were gonna move in on government land that was going to waste just a few miles south—land that was ripped off from the Indians in the first place. The plan was to squat on it, liberate it, homestead it, plow, sow, then invite the Indians to join us in the establishment of a new collective *state.* We knew it wouldn't last—Tricky Dicky's Nazis would move in and overrun us. All we wanted was to last long enough to create something viable—for the press. The publicity would put us in a good light—the government destroying crops. What's more all-American than farming, right? So we'd be the good guys. Black and white and brown and red working together. The establishment would be seen as putting out all the negative energy. Too threatening, so they destroyed it."

"Who's they?"

"The government. Or some free-lance running dogs, working for the government. Someone had to have poisoned the meat, planted charges, waited until all of us were in that warehouse, puking, weakened, then blew it to kingdom-come. Some sort of remote-control detonator. Death knell for the dream."

"Collective farming," I said. "It's not exactly what comes to mind when you think of the Weathermen, FALN, the Black Army. People like Mark Grossman and Skitch Dupree."

"That's 'cause you've been programmed to think that way. Everyone in that warehouse— everyone in New Walden—was a *fugitive* from violence. We were sick of violence, sick of the way things had turned. Tonio and Teresa had just quit FALN. Skitch had taken a lot of crap for renouncing violence—even got shot at by Black Revo Army dudes because he changed his tune. Norm and Melba were the architects of the plan. They'd turned their heads totally away from vi- olence." He shook his head. "Bomb factory. Do you think Norm and Melba and Tonio and Teresa would have brought their kids into some *bomb* factory?"

People had brought their babies to Jim Jones. Sacrificed countless other innocents to other Mo- lochs. I didn't say anything.

He said, "I sat in that clinic waiting room, and I knew everything was over. I wanted to run. But Malcolm was hot as a skillet, needed to see the doctor, so I sat and waited and hoped no one could see I was ready to burst out of my skin. Finally we got seen by a nurse, after all that time. She gave me medicine, told me he'd probably be okay once the fever broke, to give him lots of fluids, come back in a couple of days. I left, walked around the corner, carrying him, kept walking until I found a car with the keys left in the ignition. Got in, laid him across the front seat, started it up, drove all the way through Nevada, into California. Stopped to buy apple juice and diapers, driving while holding a bottle to his lips. Hundreds of miles of nightmares, roads with no one else on them, him screaming for his mama, me constantly thinking someone was gonna get on my tail, gun us down. Made it all the way to L.A. before dawn."

"To Venice," I said.

He nodded. "Like I said, they'd never gotten along, she and Norm, but where else could I take him? I left him on the doorstep and split."

I opened his book, turned to the Berkeley picture, and showed it to him. "The other people—they were the second cadre?"

Another nod. "They were a hundred miles up the Snake River, negotiating for building materials. The plan was to build log cabins. They had bought the stuff from a logging contractor but got delayed trying to find some way to haul it down— Teamsters gave 'em grief, didn't want to deal with a bunch of goddam hippies."

"What'd they do after the explosion?"

"Disappeared. Mostly up to Canada."

He took the book. Gazed at it. Closed his eyes.

I said, "What happened to them?"

He opened his eyes and sighed. "These two"—he jabbed a finger—"Harry and Debbie Delage. They stayed up there—they were French Canadian. I think they're teachers in Montreal but I'm not sure, haven't had contact with them. With any of them."

The finger drifted. "Ed Maher and Julie Bendix went to Morocco, moved around, and then came back, got married, had a bunch of kids. I heard she died of breast cancer a couple of years ago. He's probably back east—his family had money. . . . Lyle Stokes got involved in this New Age crap—crystals and past lives. He's making a fortune. . . . Sandy Porter I don't know. . . . Gordy Latch married that fascist's daughter and became a scumbag politician. . . . Jack Parducci's a lawyer in Pittsburgh, joined the GOP."

He stared at the picture a while longer, closed the book, and gave it back. "Fuck nostalgia."

I said, "Who determined which cadre someone went into?"

"It wasn't anything formal, just kind of natural selection. The first cadre were the leaders—thinkers, theorists."

I said, "The second cadre fared a hell of a lot better than the first."

"What are you getting at?"

"Nothing you haven't wondered about your-self for seventeen years."

"You're wrong," he said. "I don't wonder about anything. Wondering's a dead-end street."

I said, "Why'd you choose Bear Lodge?"

"Randy Latch owned the property—her father had left it to her."

"She was Mountain Properties?"

"Behind a bunch of dummy corporations—trust fund stuff, tax shelters. Her old man set it up for her. That's why we pretended to lease it, so it would look businesslike, no one would dig into it."

"With those connections," I said, "didn't Latch aspire to first-cadre status?"

"He might have, but that wasn't a serious possibility. He was lots of noise, no substance. Not well respected. One of the reasons they kept him around was her money. After Bear Lodge, the two of them dropped out, reappeared as Jack and Mrs. Armstrong. Still lots of noise, no substance. The American public eats that up, right? No surprise he ended up doing what he's doing."

"Tell me about Wannsee Two."

He sat up straight. "Where the hell did *that* come from?"

"Ike Novato left some notes indicating he was researching it. He wrote it right above your name. He *wondered* about it."

Crevolin gave a sick look. "That's what he wanted to talk to me about? Hell, *that* would have been easy."

"Easy in what way?"

"Easy to answer. I could have told him the truth: Wannsee Two is government-issue drivel. Tricky Dicky Evil Empire Cointelpro disinformation tailor-made for John Q. Gullible. The government wanted to discredit us, so they planted bogus news items in the establishment press about us getting together with the neo-Nazi fringe—the old crapola about extremists on both ends being equivalent, Hitler and Stalin. Tarring us with the same brush as the KKK in order to isolate us, make us look bad. But in the end I guess it was just easier to blow us up—notice how you don't hear about Wannsee Two anymore. And there are plenty of right-wing racist assholes running around."

He shook his head, rubbed his temples. "Wannsee Two. I could have handled that in two minutes. *I* thought he wanted to get into personal stuff—his parents, raking up old memories."

"Could Sophie Gruenberg have been interested in Wannsee Two?"

"Doubt it. That old lady was too sophisticated to be taken in by that kind of crap."

"You knew her well?"

His headshake was vehement. "I only met her once. With Norm. But he talked about her. Said she was a revolutionary of the old stripe—

well-read, intellectual. Even though he didn't get along with her, he respected her intellect."

"You only met her once?"

He was silent.

I caught his eye.

He said, "Twice. When I returned to L.A.—doing my little network page gig—I checked in with her. To see how things were going."

"With Ike?"

"With the world." He twisted his lip between thumb and forefinger.

I said, "Did you really just leave him on the step?"

"You bet I did. It was all I could do to hide and wait until she took him in. Going there in the first place was a risk. I was totally freaked-out, wanted to get the hell out of town before the men in the gray suits came calling. I figured eventually someone would figure out I hadn't been blown up and try to finish the job."

He laughed. "No one bothered. All these years."

I said, "You mentioned the Feds' running dogs. Any suspects?"

"Sure," he said. "There were these weird trapper types skulking around in the forest. Mountain men—long hair, beards, homemade buckskins, eating grubs and whatever. Living off the land, like Redford in *Jeremiah Johnson*. We kind of did a mutual ignoring thing with them, but later, when I had time to think, I started to wonder. Because using them would have been a perfect government setup. We were naïve—we trusted anyone who looked counterculture. Crew-cut types sneaking around would have gotten us immediately paranoid, but *those* hairy fuckers we ignored. They'd been there before we got there, didn't seem to have any real interest in us. Also, we respected the way they were doing their own thing. Thought of them as hippies with guns and Bowie knives. Macho freaks. We were *jazzed* by the whole live-off-the-land bit—that's what *we* were aiming for. So it would have been easy for one of them to sneak in, plant the bombs, and sneak out. They were probably G-men or *agents provocateurs*—probably pushing paper in Toledo today. Which is punishment enough, right?"

The bitterness in his voice put the lie to his last statement.

I said, "Did you discuss any of these suspicions with Sophie Gruenberg the time you dropped by?"

"Didn't have to. Moment she closed the door she sat me down and started lecturing to me about how the explosion had been a government plot; Norm and Melba and the others were martyrs. No tears—she was very tough. Just anger. This hot rage that made it seem as if she was vibrating." He smiled. "She was a tough old lady. I could see her running a guillotine back in Bastille days."

"Where'd she send Ike to be raised?"

"What makes you think she sent him anywhere?"

"He'd just moved to L.A. a few months before his death, told people he'd been living back east. That makes sense. Someone as suspicious as Sophie might be nervous keeping the son of martyrs around in plain view."

"I don't know the details," he said. "When I asked about him, she said she'd sent him away to relatives. Said government people had come snooping around pretty soon after the blast, asking questions of the neighbors. She called them god-dam cossacks. Said if they found out she had him with her, they'd kidnap him or something, claim she was unfit and take him away. She said he needed to be in a safe place for a while. I took that to mean temporary, she was planning to bring him back, but I guess she could have kept him away the whole time."

"Any idea where these relatives lived?"

"She didn't say and I didn't ask. I kind of assumed it was Philadelphia because Norm was born there—the family used to live there."

"You only dropped in on her once?"

"That's it. She was part of what I'd put behind me. So was Malcolm Isaac. *That's* why I didn't see him—it wasn't just apathy. What would have been the point?"

His tension had lifted him out of his chair,

and his skin had turned waxy. His eyes kept moving, up and down, side to side, back at the cartoon characters. Everywhere but at me.

I said, "I understand."

"Do you? To understand you've got to know what it's like to be a hunted animal—mainlining adrenaline, looking over your shoulder, hearing things, seeing things. Peeing your pants, afraid to move, afraid not to move. Convinced every tree is a storm trooper, not knowing what's real and what's not, when that bullet's gonna come flying by, or the blade or the time bomb turning you into instant smog. By the time I dropped in on her, I'd finally managed to pull myself out of that insanity. Working at my page gig, renting a little bachelor apartment, going to the supermarket, the laundromat, the filling station. Eating Swanson TV dinners and hot dogs—no more macrobiotics, I was ready for some nitrite-cramming, like a real American. Doing regular-person stuff, so happy and grateful to be alive. I mean, I couldn't *believe* they weren't coming after me—couldn't believe they were letting me live and work and eat hot dogs and do my thing and no one was trying to blow me up."

He tugged at his cheeks, created a sad mask. "It took me a long time to get there. To realize no one cared about any of it anymore. The war was over; Nixon had gone down; Eldridge was marketing codpiece-pants; Jerry and Abby were doing

Wall Street, the talk-show circuit; Leary was asshole buddy with G. Gordon Liddy. Fascists were wearing long hair and beards, hippies going for crew-cuts. Boundaries blurring, all the old myths dead. Live and let live—bygones *were* bygones. It was *my* turn to live. I *worked* at living. Malcolm Isaac's call came at a bad time. I'd just gotten engaged to be married, was planning to go away with my lady. Real vacation, bring a little romance into my life—better late than never, right? We've since broken up, but at the time it looked liked forever, rice and flowers. I had my tickets in my hand when he called. Out the door. Last thing I wanted to deal with was the past—what would have been the point?"

"No point," I said.

"Gotta keep moving forward," he said. "No point in looking back. Right?"

"Right."

But a plain truth filled the space between us—unseen but corrosive.

No one had cared because he'd been second cadre all the way. Too unimportant to kill.

31

I pulled out of the network lot. This time someone followed me.

At first I wasn't sure, wondered if the time spent immersed in Crevolin's fugitive memories had made *me* paranoid.

The first hint of suspicion came at Olympic and La Cienega, just east of Beverly Hills, as I squinted into a platinum sunset glare that ate through my shades. A tan car two lengths behind me changed lanes the moment my eyes hit the mirror for the twentieth time.

I slowed. The tan car slowed. I looked back, trying to make out the driver, saw only a vague outline. Two outlines.

I slowed some more, received an angry honk for my efforts. I picked up speed. The tan car held back, stretching the distance between us. We cruised that way for a while, then hit a red light at La Peer. When things got moving again, I eased into the fast lane and put on as much speed as the crush would allow. The tan car continued to hold back, retreated into vehicular anonymity. By Doheny Drive, I couldn't see it anymore.

So much for high intrigue.

I tried to relax but kept drifting back to exploding warehouses. My imagination gorged itself on conspiracy theories until my head started to hurt. Then I noticed it again. Center lane, two lengths behind . . .

I managed to get into the center lane. The tan car moved out of it, into the fast lane, coming up on my left. Wanting a better view?

Making sure not to move my head, I snuck a peek in the mirror. Still there.

Traffic in the right lane was dragging a bit now. I squeezed into it, settled into the slower pace. Hoping for a view of my own. The vehicles that had been in back of me whizzed by. I kept an eye to the left, waiting for the tan car to pass. Nothing.

Rearview peek: gone.

Another light at Beverly. Behind me, again. Two lengths.

It took until Roxbury for me to get back into the fast lane. The tan car stayed with me, all the way to Century City.

The sun was nearly down. Headlights came on. The tan car became a pair of yellow spots, indistinguishable from hundreds of others.

The loss of visibility made me feel violated,

though I knew I was also less easy to spot. Anger took the place of fear. Felt a whole lot better than fear.

Practice-what-you-preach time, Doc.

Best-defense-is-a-good-offense time, Doc.

Just before Overland, I made a sudden move into the center lane, then the right, drove a block and made a quick turn onto a side street, just past a Ralph's market. Speeding a hundred yards, I doused my lights, pulled over to the side, and waited, the engine still running.

Residential street. Small nicely kept houses. Tall trees. No foot traffic. Lots of parked cars on both sides; my turn to blend in.

The first set of headlights from Olympic belonged to a gray Porsche 944 that zipped by at fifty per and pulled into a driveway at the end of the block. I made out the shape of a man with a briefcase. He disappeared into one of the bungalows.

Soon after came a Dodge Ram van with the logo of a plumbing company on the side, driving at moderate speed. It stopped at the next corner and turned right.

Then nothing for several minutes. I waited, almost ready to concede the afternoon to paranoia, when I heard an automotive hum coming from Olympic.

Heard but didn't see.

The side mirror revealed a faintly resolving

image, just a hint of chrome under streetlight: a car with its headlights off, making its way slowly toward me.

The hum grew louder.

I slumped low.

The tan car cruised by at ten per. Plymouth sedan. Not unlike the unmarked Milo used. Not unlike the car he'd thought had been following us on our way to the Holocaust Center.

Ten miles per. Slow cruise. The way cops cruise when they're looking for trouble.

My engine suddenly sounded deafening. They had to hear. I should have turned it off. . . .

But the tan car kept going, turned right, and disappeared. I pulled out, keeping my lights off, and went after it. Caught up just as it made another right turn. Tried to read the license plate, couldn't, got closer.

Not close enough to make out any details of the two people inside.

I nudged the accelerator, came just short of tailgating.

Switched on my lights.

Nonreflector plates, a number, two letters, four more numbers. I shot a mental snapshot, developed it just as the passenger swiveled sharply and looked back.

The tan sedan came to a sudden stop. I jammed on the brakes to avoid rear-ending it. For a moment I thought there'd be a confrontation, was prepared to back away. But the tan car peeled rubber and took off.

I let it go, preserving letters and numbers in my head until I got home.

Still no luck reaching Milo; where the hell was he? I called his house and got the machine again. Phoned the Cedars-Sinai emergency room and asked for Dr. Silverman. Rick was in the middle of surgery, unable to come to the phone. I called the machine again and recited the tan car's license number, explained why it was important to trace it as quickly as possible, and gave a summary of what I'd learned from Terry Crevolin. Talking to the damned thing as if it were corporeal, an old pal. Mahlon Burden would have been proud of me.

When I was through I phoned Linda at home.

"Hi," she said. "Have you seen it yet?"

"Seen what?"

"The Massengil stuff hitting the fan—right now, the six o'clock news. Call me back when you've had your fill of it."

The newscast was featuring the second assassination of the late assemblyman, this one not nearly as quick and clean as the ambush in Sheryl Jane Jackson's backyard. A photo of Massengil that could have been a mug shot. An old one of Cheri T in a corkscrew hairdo and white eye shadow that was. The jail photographer had preserved her looking like the hollow-eyed, switchblade-in-purse streetwalker she'd once been.

The gloating anchorwoman went on in a sultry voice about sex for hire . . . the *exact relationship* between the two victims and Jackson still being unclear . . . sex scandal . . . sex sex sex . . . Massengil's reputation as a law-and-order politician who'd campaigned against pornography . . . twenty-eight years in the state legislature advocating . . . sex . . . psychological adviser . . . sex . . .

She needn't have bothered talking. Pictures were still worth millions of words: Massengil open-mouthed and snarling, Dobbs's well-fed sanctimoniousness. Cheri's eyes, full of corruption and defiance.

Now an action shot. Ocean Heights. The Widow Massengil walking out of her front door to a waiting car, black-garbed, face and snowy bouffant hidden by veil and hands. Hobbling, hunched, in the protective grip of all four sons. Flashbulbs popping, microphones thrusting. The bereaved family fleeing with all the dignity of war criminals hustled to the tribunal.

The station's resident political commentator came on, wondering who was going to fill Massengil's unexpired term. Apparently a political technicality was operative: Since Massengil's death had occurred after the nominating period for

his next term, there would be no special election
and the remaining eight months of the term would
go fallow. In accordance with tradition, the widow
had been considered the most probable replacement, but today's disclosures made her an unlikely
contender. Faces of possible candidates flashed on
the screen. A deputy mayor I'd never heard of. A
former TV anchorman—with an obsession about
separating paper trash from the rest of the
garbage—who surfaced every few years to play
small-time Harold Stassen and was regarded as a
municipal joke.

Then Gordon Latch.

The resident commentator reported "inside
rumors" that Latch was considering running for
the vacated seat. Next came footage showing him
at his desk, fending off questions and letting the
viewing public know that "during difficult times
such as these we've all got to pull together and not
stoop to careerism. My heartfelt thoughts are with
Hattie Massengil and the boys. I urge all of you to
refrain from unnecessary cruelty."

I turned off the set and called Linda back.
"Had my fill."

She said, "I was no fan of his, but I hate the
way his poor family's being dragged through the
muck."

"Yesterday's hero, today's wet spot."

She said, "Why now? A day after? The
police knew right away."

I thought about that. "Frisk snatched the case away from Milo because of the glory potential. But maybe he had time to think about it, examine the facts, and realized it would be slow going. A glory case can be a double-edged sword: If he develops no suspects, he runs the risk of looking incompetent in the public eye. Shifting focus to a sex scandal buys him time—notice how there was no mention of the progress of the investigation."

"True," she said. "Just the S word."

"Over and over and over. Also, if Massengil was scum, the urgency to learn who killed him dims a bit, doesn't it? Maybe buys Frisk a little more public patience. Of course, another possibility is that it wasn't Frisk who leaked."

"Latch?"

"Makes sense, doesn't it? I've seen at least two instances where he seems to have been in touch with Massengil's itinerary, so maybe he's even got a mole on Massengil's staff and found out about Massengil's extracurricular activities. Not that he's the only candidate. Massengil had plenty of enemies up in Sacramento, no shortage of people who might have hated him enough to spit on his grave. Could be Latch just used the information—seized the opportunity and went from conciliator to contender. It fits his pattern: a talent for surviving and thriving on the misfortunes of others."

"Sounds like a scavenger," she said. "A vulture. Or a maggot."

"Dung beetle came to my mind," I said.

She laughed. "Well, now that we're into such appetizing images, have you had dinner yet? I'm in a cooking mood."

"Love to, but it's not a good night."

"Oh." She sounded hurt.

I said, "I want to see you. But . . ."

"But what, Alex?"

I took a deep breath. "Listen, I don't want to scare you but I'm pretty sure someone followed me this evening. And I don't think it's the first time."

"What are you talking about?"

"The night we had dinner on Melrose, I thought someone left the same time we did, followed us for a while. At the time I brushed it off, but now I don't think so."

"You're serious."

"Unfortunately."

"Why didn't you tell me that night? When you first suspected it?"

"I really thought I was letting my imagination get the better of me—there just didn't seem to be any point. Then Milo told me he'd spotted a tail when we were driving together. He thinks it was Frisk. Or someone else in the Police Department. One arm of the LAPD hydra trying to find out what another was doing. Milo's not the most popular guy in the Department."

She said, "Cops love doing that, going after one another. Paramilitary thinking. Destroy the individual. Daddy had all sorts of stories about officers he'd caught with their pants down. His eyes used to light up when he told them." Pause. "Why would they be following you?"

"Guilt by association. And don't worry about it—I'll have an answer soon. I got the license number of the car that followed me today. As soon as I reach Milo he'll be able to trace it."

"Don't worry about it, huh? But you're afraid to be with me tonight."

"It's . . . I just don't want to put you in any . . . jeopardy."

"From the police? Why would I be in jeopardy from them? All my parking tickets are paid up."

I said nothing.

She said, "Alex?"

I sucked in my breath again, mentally phrased my words while letting it out, and told her about all of it. Novato, Gruenberg, Crevolin, Bear Lodge.

When I was through she said, "Why didn't you tell me sooner?"

The chill.

"I guess I was being . . . protective."

"And what made you think I needed protect-ing?"

"It wasn't that," I said. "It had nothing to do with you. We were having good times together. I didn't want to . . . pollute them."

"So you kept me in the dark."

"Not out of any base motives—"

"Okay. Have a good evening."

"Linda—"

"No," she said. "Don't throw any more words at me. I've had enough of that. And don't worry about me. I'm a big girl. I don't need *protecting*."

She hung up. When I tried to call back, the line was busy. I checked with the operator and was informed that the phone was off the hook.

Alone, my thoughts drifted from misery to misery. Bomb factories. Cadres. Political conver-sions . . .

The common thread running through all of it: Latch.

I thought of the sanitation process that had transformed him from Hanoi Harry to public servant. Those years of seclusion with Miranda somewhere in the Northwest.

Years of seclusion after Bear Lodge.

Time and money and an easy smile. What else did a politician need in the eighties? But what would happen to the smile if the money stopped flowing?

Remembering Miranda Latch's demeanor at the concert, I wondered how long the spigot would stay open. Thought of someone who might be able to tell me.

Superior Court had been closed for hours, but I was pretty sure I had Steve Hupp's home number in my Rolodex. I went into the library and found it. A Pasadena exchange. A very young, very breathy female voice with a Scandinavian accent answered.

"Judge Hupp's residence."

"I'd like to speak with the judge, please."

"Who may I say is calling?"

"Alex Delaware."

"One moment."

A heartbeat later Steve came on.

"Hey, Alex, change your mind about Switzerland?"

"Sorry, no, *Judge* Hupp. How's the residence?"

"That's Brigitta, our *au pair*. Just brought her over from Sweden. She's not much on housework but she does like answering the phone—proud of her English. And her legs. Julie hates her guts. So, if you haven't had a change of heart, to what do I owe the pleasure?"

"I'd like a little favor—some information."

"What kind of information?"

"Whether or not a certain party has filed for dissolution recently. Does that violate any canons of ethics?"

"No, it's all public record, unless we seal the records on an individual—and we're reluctant to seal. There's really got to be a good reason for it. Not that we go around just giving out information. Why do you want to know?"

"It relates to a case I'm working on."

"Meaning you can't tell me."

"Well . . ."

He laughed. "Alex, Alex. Haven't you learned yet that one-way streets don't usually go very far? Okay, for you I'll do it. I remember all the nasty ones you helped me clear. What's the party's name?"

I told him.

"You're involved with *them*? I didn't know it had gotten that far. Didn't even know they had kids."

"What do you mean 'that far'?"

"Her attorney did a preliminary filing a couple of weeks ago. They've got a long way to go before custody comes up. I don't expect to see them in court for half a year. Think it'll be a dirty one?"

"Could be. Lots of money involved."

"All hers. But I don't see him asking for alimony. Wouldn't do much for the old public image, would it? Young man on the rise living off his wife's dole."

"He is on the rise."

"Oh, yeah. The talk around City Hall is he's *bored* with things there. Got his eye on the seat Massengil had the good manners to vacate, then onward to something congressional—as in D.C. Anyway, I'm glad you're involved. Maybe we can keep the shrapnel to a minimum."

"Hope so, Steve. Thanks."

"Sure. Any time. See you in court."

I felt edgy staying at home and decided to leave until I was able to reach Milo and find out who'd been in the tan car. Another drive up the coast seemed like a good idea. Just as I was out the door my service called.

"Dr. Delaware, tsk tsk," said an operator whose voice I didn't recognize. "You haven't called in for your messages since noon and there's a whole bunch of them."

"Any emergencies?"

"Let me see . . . hmm . . . no, it doesn't look that way. But Detective Spurgis—"

"Sturgis."

"Oh. Is that a *t*? I'm new here. Flo took it—can't read her handwriting. Okay, Detective *Stur*gis left a real long one. You want me to put it away or read it to you?"

"Read it, please."

"Okay, let's see . . . He said to tell you

things have climbed higher dash capital F capital E capital D. I guess that spells FED—at least that's the way Flo wrote it. Capital F, capital E, capital D. Or maybe it's a T. Things have climbed higher. FED. Or TED. But your name's not Ted, so I guess it's FED. Anyway, things have climbed higher dash FED. You'll be contacted. Sit tight. Got all that?"

"Got it. What time did he call?"

"Let's see . . . it says here five-thirty on the slip."

"Thanks."

"You sure do get some good ones, Dr. Delaware. You must have an interesting life."

32

I sat tight. The knock on the door came at 11:23. A double rap followed by a single punch of the doorbell.

"Who is it?"

"FBI, Dr. Delaware."

"Could I see some identification, please?"

"Certainly, Doctor. I'll hold it up to your peephole."

I looked through the hole, couldn't see much, even after switching on the landing light. "How about dropping it through the mail slot?"

Hesitation. Voices conferring in low tones.

"Sorry, Doctor, we can't do that."

Keeping the chain on, I opened the door a couple of inches.

"Here you go, Doctor." A hand holding a small leather case came forward. Gold badge on one side, picture ID on the other. The picture was of a man in his late twenties. Light-brown hair cut short with a right-hand side part. Full face, sharp features. HOYT HENRY BLANCHARD. SPECIAL AGENT, FEDERAL BUREAU OF INVESTIGATION, U.S. DEPT. OF JUSTICE.

I undid the chain and opened the door all the way. The life-sized version of the picture stood on the landing wearing a gray suit, white button-down shirt, and blue tie with a silver stripe. Six feet tall, narrow frame at odds with the heavy face. Square-lensed steel-framed glasses that made his eyes look indistinct. Behind him was a woman about his age. Dirty-blond pageboy, capuchin-monkey face, gold-rimmed eyeglasses.

Blanchard said, "This is Special Agent Crisp."

He and I shook hands.

Crisp didn't smile or extend her hand. She was short and long-waisted with chunky calves. Her outfit said *no time for small talk*: navy-blue two-piece suit with a high-necked white blouse, black leatherette purse big enough to hold a day's worth of groceries. Behind her glasses she had a tax auditor's eyes. Both she and Blanchard had the compulsive, suspicious look of accountants who've done time on the streets. Was the bureau still actively recruiting CPAs?

Blanchard said, "You're careful, Doctor. That's wise."

I said, "With all that's been going on . . ."

"Absolutely. Sorry for the hour."

"I was up."

He nodded. "So you got the message."

"I did. What can I do for you?"

"We'd like to interview you."

"About what?"

He permitted himself a brief smile. "Everything that's been going on."

I stood back. "Come on in."

"Actually," said Blanchard, "we'd prefer if you came with us."

"Where to?"

Crisp bristled at the question. At the fact that I was questioning them. The two of them looked at each other.

Another bland smile from Blanchard. "Sorry, Doctor. We're really not authorized to say *where* until you agree to come *with*—I know it's kind of a Catch Twenty-two, but that's the way it is."

"Information transfer regulations, sir," said Crisp. Her voice was husky. "In a security matter, we're not authorized to discuss it outside of the approved locus."

Blanchard glanced at her as if she'd talked out of turn. Gave me the kind of look common to good-natured parents of ill-behaved children. "We're not talking summons or a warrant or anything like that, Doctor. Meaning you're not obligated to accompany us. But it would be a big help to our Task Force."

"We can get a summons easily enough," said Crisp, as if to herself.

Good cop, bad cop? A reason for it, or just force of habit?

I said, "Is Detective Sturgis part of the Task Force?"

Blanchard cleared his throat. "Like Agent Crisp said, we're really not authorized to give out any information outside the approved locus— meaning a certain specific site—which is where we want to take you. Then we can clear everything up. But let's just say that your expectations vis-à-vis Detective Sturgis have a high probability of being met."

Crisp shifted her giant purse to the other shoulder.

I hesitated.

Crisp looked at her watch and glared.

Blanchard said, "Not to worry, Doctor. We're the good guys."

"No offense," I said. "But sometimes it's hard to tell."

His expression said he'd taken offense. But he stuck another smile on his face and said, "Guess it is."

Crisp tapped her watch and said, "Let's just come back tomorrow morning with paper, Hoyt."

Blanchard ignored her and said, "Tell you what, Doctor—how about we give you a number to call? Verify the Task Force."

"How about if I talk to Detective Sturgis myself?"

"That's fine in principle, but the problem is he's unavailable by phone—on radio alert, restricted band." He put his finger to his mouth and thought. "Tell you what—I can probably get him on the unit in our car." To Crisp: "Okay, Audrey?"

She gave a bored shrug.

Blanchard turned back to me. "Okay, we'll try. But Headquarters may not okay the communication; the lines have got to be kept clear at all times."

"High intrigue," I said.

"You bet." Smile.

Crisp was unamused.

"Okay, let's go down to the car," said Blanchard. "No. Even better, I'll go to the car and bring the unit up."

"Fine."

He turned and took a step down.

Crisp's purse slid off her shoulder and thumped on the landing.

I bent, picked it up, and gave it to her. Up close she smelled of cinnamon gum, had gravelly skin under pancake makeup.

"Thanks," she said. Finally a smile from those disapproving lips.

She used one hand to take the purse, drew back the other and touched her forehead, fixing hair that didn't need fixing. Then she lowered it and lunged forward suddenly. Hitting me very hard in the solar plexus, using a stiff-fingered karate punch that turned her hand into a dagger.

Electric pain. I lost breath, sucked air, clutched at my belly, and doubled over.

Before I could straighten, someone behind me—it had to be the smiling Blanchard—shoved a hand in the small of my back, rattling my kidneys, and slung an arm around my neck.

A blur of gray sleeve. Gray noose. Under the fabric, hard muscle pressing against my carotid.

My mind knew the right moves—heel on instep, elbows back—but my oxygen-starved body wouldn't obey. All I could do was flail and gasp.

The gray arm pushed upward, keeping the pressure on and rolling against my neck as if it were dough. Forcing its way under my chin, shoving my head back so hard it whiplashed. Clamping harder against the carotid, relentless.

Consciousness faded. I saw Crisp, watching. Amused.

Blanchard kept squeezing. I wanted to tell him what I thought of him—how unfair he'd been, pretending to be the good cop. . . .

My legs gave out. A heavy, oily blackness oozed up all around me . . . total eclipse of . . .

I came to in the back seat of a car—lying across it, my wrists bound behind me. I wiggled my finger, felt something hard—warm, not metal. Not handcuffs. I touched it again. Some kind of plastic tie. The kind the police use for quick trussing.

The kind that had always reminded me of garbage-bag fasteners.

I managed to sit up. My head felt as if it had been squeezed for juice. My throat was raw as tartare. An inside-of-the-seashell noise roared in my head and my eyes were out of focus. I blinked several times to clear them . . . to catch a view of passing terrain . . . establish bearings.

Blanchard was driving, Crisp up front, next to him. The car made a quick turn. I rolled, twisted my body, fighting to stay upright, and lost. I hit my head against the door panel. Sharp sting, then nausea ate its way into my gut—a reprise of the sucker punch.

My eyes slammed shut and I gave an involuntary groan.

"It awakens," said Crisp.

Blanchard laughed.

Crisp laughed back. No internecine conflict now. Two bad cops.

It felt as if we were moving very fast, but that could have been my head spinning. I fought down the queasiness, managed to pull myself up again.

I mouthed words, produced sound: "Wha . . . who . . ." My tonsils ached.

"It *talks,*" said Crisp.

"If it knows what's best for it, it will shut the fuck up," said Blanchard.

I pressed my face against the window glass. Cold and soothing. Outside, more greasy black.

Endless black.

Blind-from-birth black.

I felt a stab of vertigo, had to concentrate on not rolling back down, clawed at the seat with my bound hands and felt a fingernail rip.

I looked out the window again, barely able to keep my eyes open. My pupils felt as if they'd been dipped in glue and breaded with grit.

I closed them. The same flat black . . .

Ladies and gentlemen, tonight the part of Hell will be played by Absolute Darkness.

I bit my lip with frustration, flopped like a beached seal, rubbed my face against the door panel, happy to be chafed. Metal nubs where the handles should have been.

Low conversation from the front. More laughter.

I blinked some more. Opened my eyes and waited for them to accommodate to the darkness. Finally. But everything was still blurred. It hurt to focus.

I looked anyway. Searched for context.

Black turned to gray. Grays. Lots of them. Contours, shading, perspective . . . Amazing how many grays there were when you just took the time to look . . .

Dead streets.

"It observes," said Crisp. She turned and looked down at me. Her monkey face reminded me of a Stephen King book cover. "Want to know where we are, cutie?" she said. "The Valley. Feel like being a Valley Boy tonight?"

Bound but no blindfold.

They didn't care what I saw.

Garbage didn't fight back.

I shoved that out of consciousness, worked at staying lucid. Ignoring weak bowels, hammering heart, the drainpipe noise in my head.

Blanchard fed the car more gas and it surged forward. My eyes finally cleared. A darkened shopping center. A lazy streetlight casting a urine-colored glow over boarded-up businesses, cracked and missing signs, texture-coat walls sprayed with gang wisdom. An empty parking lot shot through with weeds.

Bad part of the Valley.

Blanchard made another series of quick turns that my eyes couldn't make out.

A sprinkling of signs.

CUIDADO CON EL PERRO. BONDED PREMISES . . . ELEMENT DEPOSITORY . . . KEEP OUT, THAT MEANS YOU!

Then a reflective orange diamond, gem-bright: PAVEMENT ENDS.

Blanchard kept going, onto a dirt strip that rocked the car, traveled for another few minutes before making a short stop at a padlocked sheet-metal gate.

Crisp got out, letting in more gas stink. I heard fiddling, rattling, rasp, and creak. She got back in and said, "Okay." The petrol smell lingered, as if it had saturated her clothing.

Blanchard drove through the gate. Crisp got out again, locked it, and returned. The car moved forward, across empty space, past several vehicles parked diagonally. VW bugs. I thought of Charlie Manson's apocalyptic dream: Veedubs converted to armored dune buggies—heavy artillery for the race war Helter Skelter was going to foment.

Blanchard slowed and pulled up in front of a bank of concrete. I made out metal-railed stairs, a platform. A loading dock. Behind it the outlines of a blocky, flat-faced structure—fifty feet of bulk unrelieved by architectural detail.

Light from the left—a low-wattage bulb surface-scratching the darkness like crayon relief. Dribbling illumination down on the top half of a grated door. To the right, a bigger door, triple-garage width, corrugated steel.

The smaller door opened. Three figures came out. Shadow people.

Blanchard turned off the engine. Crisp bounced out like a kid going to a birthday party.

The scuff of footsteps. The right rear car door opened. Before I could see their faces, my ankles were gripped and I was pulled down, slid out of the car. As I emerged, hands took hold of my body at the belt, under my armpits. Fingers digging in.

Grunts of effort.

I went limp. Make the bastards work.

As they carried me away, I caught a glimpse of the car. Tan, I thought. But I couldn't be sure in the darkness.

I was swung up and forward, sagging, butt scraping the ground.

Carried with all the care of a sack of spoiled meat.

Time to take out the garbage.

33

It took a while for them to get the small door open. I heard tumblers and clicks and machine whirrs—some kind of electronically driven combination lock. No one spoke. I was held fast by the limbs, trunk dangling, joints aching. Staring at trouser legs and shoes . . . Click.

Inside. Floor level. Cement floor. Cold, conditioned air—or maybe I was shivering for another reason.

I was carried by silent pallbearers through an aisle sided with high tan walls. Cardboard tan. Partitions. Plywood doors. A warehouse. Sectioned into cubbies. Unevenly lit. Patches of illuminated cement flooring followed by intervals of darkness that made me feel as if I'd disappeared.

Now into a larger area. My captors' footsteps echoing. Other footsteps now, softer. Distant. I had a sense of vast open space. Cold space.

Hell was a warehouse. . . .

Was this how lab animals felt, readied for air-freight?

Then other sounds: typewriter pecks. Computer bleeps. Scraping soles.

More cardboard. Boxes, stacks of them. I made out lettering. Black-stenciled. PRINTED MATERIAL. SPECIAL RATE. Lots of those. Then a few that said MACHINERY. FRAGILE.

A flash of yellow. I twisted to see what it was. A forklift. And another. Several smaller vehicles that looked like sit-down lawn mowers. But no gas stink here. Just the yeasty, respectable fragrance of fresh paper.

Lots of huffing and puffing from my bearers. My eyes raced past trouser legs. A few pairs of stockinged female calves. I began counting feet. Two, four, six, eight, ten . . . I craned upward, hurting my spine, wasn't able to make out faces.

The aisle angled to the left. My journey as hunting trophy continued for another twenty paces before coming to a sudden stop. Heavy breathing, locker-room sweat. The hands holding me lifted and twisted. All at once I was upright, arms still fastened behind me.

Coming face to face with Them.

Blanchard. Trying to smile while huffing.

Others. Ten of them. Younger. Clean-cut.

I knew them without knowing them. Had seen them at a school. Attending a shooting. Enjoying a concert.

Bright-eyed, then. Dead-eyed tonight. Faces set in the mire of obedience. As if the internal light in each of them had been switched off. Conservation of personality.

The other times, they'd dressed for success. They were dressed for something else tonight: black turtlenecks over black jeans and sneakers. The proper attire for an all-night wait in a storage shed. Or a backyard killing.

I said, "Hello, boys and girls. Take me to your leader."

It shook a couple of them out of their zombie reverie. They held on to me but retracted their heads, as if I'd just given off a bad smell.

It talks.

Blanchard stepped forward and backhanded me hard across the face. My head twanged from the blow. I focused away from the pain—from the fear. Looked past all of them. Narrow passageway created by ten-foot-high stacks of PRINTED MATERIAL cartons. Directly in front of me was a black wooden door. Something painted on it. A red circle containing a spearhead.

Someone stepped out from behind one of the cartons. Someone wiggle-walked toward me.

Beth Bramble in a long-sleeved black dress. Her hair was drawn back tight. Chromium thunderbolt earrings dangled from her earlobes.

I struggled to clear my throat and said,

"Mourning period over for the beloved leader?" It hurt to talk.

Blanchard hit me again. Bramble said, "Aw," the laughter back in her voice.

She came closer, making kissy-poo movements with her lips. She'd eaten something with a lot of garlic in it. It folded into her perfume—floral pizza.

She chucked me under the chin. Pinched me by the cheek Blanchard had slapped. Pinched it again, harder, twisted, and smiled.

Through the agony I said, "Secret agent time, Beth? Nothing like getting an inside track on the opposition."

She smiled, said, "Fuck you, darling," pinched me again, let her fingers drop down my shirtfront, then my fly. She lingered there, gave me a playful honk. Someone snickered. Bramble winked at the young ones, turned, and disappeared behind the cartons.

Blanchard knocked on the black door.

A muffled reply came from the other side.

Blanchard opened it, put his head in, and said, "He's here, D.F. Everything smooth as silk."

Another muffled answer.

I was shoved in, and the door slammed behind me.

The room wasn't much, maybe fifteen feet

square, poorly lit. Maroon linoleum floor worn through to the concrete slab in several spots, block walls painted institutional white, warped acoustical ceiling browned by moisture, sheet-metal ceiling vent that dumped out stale, frigid air.

In the center was a seven-foot olive-drab desk that had to be army surplus. Two green metal chairs sat in front of it. Extra chairs stood folded in one corner. On top of the desk was a black multiline phone and a short stack of papers weighted down by a tarnished artillery shell. Running against the left wall was a brown couch that looked thirdhand.

Bunker-nouveau? All that field-command drabness provided a nice sense of contrast with what covered the wall behind the desk. A flag big enough for City Hall. Black muslin bordered in red satin. In the center a red spear-in-a-circle motif.

Gordon Latch sat on the couch, wearing double-pleated ankle-pegged black slacks with narrow cuffs, black snakeskin boots with riding heels, and an oversized black silk shirt buttoned at the collar in the pseudo-nerd style favored by actors and dope dealers. The shirt had twin breast pockets with flaps, pearl buttons, and ostentatious epaulets. Chrome spears glistened from the lapel tips. His legs were crossed, his posture relaxed— the casual but calculated slump of an old favorite guest on a late-night talk show.

He tossed me a victory smile. The smile flickered. His triumph marred by something . . .

I looked over at the green desk and understood.

Behind it sat Darryl "Bud" Ahlward in a high-backed green leather swivel chair. His uniform was identical to Latch's but for rainbow splashes of battle ribbons over each breast pocket and a black leather shoulder holster from which a black gun butt protruded.

Gold spears on his lapels. Despite the generous tailoring of the shirt, his shoulders stretched the arm seams.

He sat very straight and very still, eyes static and changeless.

I turned back to Latch and said, "Nifty little role reversal. Still second cadre, huh, Gordon?"

Latch sat up straighter and started to speak. Ahlward shoved the words back down his throat with a quick look. Latch turned away from both of us, recrossing his legs and making a show of boredom.

I said, "So this is what the well-dressed storm trooper's wearing this season. What's the official greeting? *Sieg Heil Ciao*?"

Ahlward reached across his chest and took the gun out of his holster—a big black affair with a long barrel and a high-tech profile. He caressed it, then pointed it at me.

"Sit down."

I said, "Or is it Haberdashery *uber Alles*?"

Latch said, "Asshole."

I feigned puzzlement. "Let's see now, which one are you, Gordie? Goebbels or Goering? Must be Goering, 'cause it looks like you've got a little paunch sprouting under those baggies. And what about the charming Ms. Crisp? Is she doing Eva Braun in tonight's pageant, or is that Beth Bramble's role?"

Ahlward sighted down the barrel of the big black pistol. His left eye closed. I fought to keep my eyes open, staring straight ahead. Behind him.

Concentrating on the spear logo, glowing scarlet and ugly. Thinking of photos at an exhibit. A wintry day in Bavaria. Bodies collapsing into a ditch.

"You're a puzzling piece of turd," said Ahlward. "I've researched you. Always getting into things that aren't your business."

"For the last time," said Latch.

Ahlward said, "Show and Tell time, turd." Gestured with the gun.

I said, "Why should I bother?"

Ahlward smiled. "Because," he said. "Every second's precious. Everyone thinks they're immortal. Amazing the things creatures will do— how low they'll sink—to buy seconds."

I said, "Is that a fact?"

"Scientific fact. Toss a kike-creature in freezing water and watch him prolong his agony just to buy seconds."

"Toss a penny in the pool and he'll dive in voluntarily," Latch added.

Ahlward smiled and said, "They gasped like fish and screamed in Yiddish for mercy, even though they knew it was no use. Just kept going until they turned into Popsicles. Scientists are using it today. Hotshot research on hypothermia. Who knows? Maybe you'll end up benefiting mankind too."

"An entire new area of inquiry," said Latch. "Pain tolerance."

"So," said Ahlward. "You'll cooperate. What's the alternative?"

"The alternative is, I say fuck you."

Ahlward put his gun away and pushed a button on the phone. His reward was a single short ring. He picked up the receiver and said, "Now."

He sat back and folded his arms across his chest. Same stance I'd seen a few days ago. In a classroom.

A single knock sounded on the door.

Ahlward said, "In."

Two clean-cuts came in, grasping something big and white and limp under the arms. Both of them were husky, very young. One was blond and had bad acne. The other, dark-haired, with a wispy mustache.

Twenty years old, tops. They should have been beer-bashing. Trolling for cheap thrills.

They stood at attention, grim, pithed of soul.

The white thing between them was Milo, head lolling, heels dragging.

Dead weight. My heart did a high jump and landed in my gullet, choking off air. I moved forward. Ahlward snatched up the gun and said, "Stay."

Buy seconds.

I remained in place and looked at my friend.

He was barefoot and had been stripped down to his undershirt and trousers. The shirt was ripped and splotched with blood. His eyes were swollen shut, his lip split in a couple of places and blood-engorged. Worms of dried blood crawled all over his face, trailed down his chin and onto the shirt. One of his shoulders was exposed through a rent in the undershirt. Scraped raw and still weeping. Blue-maroon cabbage-shaped bruises blossomed along his arms. Despite his bulk, he looked small.

His head sank lower and bobbed. I saw more blood at the crown, crusting his hair. Where it hadn't been damaged, his skin, always pale, had the dirty-porcelain cast of the terminal ward.

But faint pumping movement under the shirt. Respiration.

He passed wind; a raw growl.

Latch chuckled. The boys in black grinned.

I said, "Milo." Louder than I'd intended; it made me sound desperate.

His face didn't change but something passed through the raw-liver lips. Half sigh, half retch; I couldn't tell if it was voluntary.

He sank again. The black-shirts tightened their grip. Eagle Scouts helping a drunk across the street, whether he wanted to cross or not . . .

Ahlward said to me: "Here's the way it's going to be. You're going to sit down right now and not give me any shit, or I'm going to walk up to your asshole buddy and hurt him while you watch. When he's no longer of any use, I'll blow his brains out, making sure lots of wet gray stuff lands right on your shirt. Then I'll cut the stuff with a fork and knife and feed it to you. Vomit it up, you'll eat vomit for dessert. One way or the other, you're going to get it all down. After that I'll hurt you. Take you apart—surgery—and make you watch it happen. Turn you into a fucking cartoon. You'll be the only one not laughing."

Shrugging with my arms behind me was painful. I sat down. "Well, if you put it that way, D.F. . . . D.F. Let's see—gotta be *Der Führer,* right? You guys have a thing for initials. D.F., L.D.—where's the harmonica, Gordon? Still playing requests? How about the old 'Horst Wessel Song,' or isn't that in your repertoire?"

Talking fast. To keep from shaking.

Ahlward gave his hand an impatient wave.

The Gestaposcouts began dragging Milo out of the room.

I said, "No. I want him here." Surprised at the assertiveness in my voice. Good clear sound, finally, shooting out of my aching throat.

Buy seconds; I half-expected to die.

But Ahlward looked amused. He held up a hand and the black-shirts stood still.

"You *want*."

"You want what I've got, D.F. What I want in return is seconds. Just like you said. For both of us."

"You *want*."

He got up and put his hands on his hips. He wore a narrow tooled black belt with a gold spear buckle. Hanging from the left side of his belt was a black leather sheath that dangled like an off-center codpiece. He slid something out of it. A hunting knife with a black haft and gold cross-piece. Wide, tapering, foot-long blade. Big enough for butchering large game. Outdoorsman's knife . . .

He turned it, examined the blade, then lowered it and held it parallel to his right leg. Then he came from around the desk with remarkable speed and stood in front of me.

"You *want*," he said.

Smiling was as easy as chewing ground glass. "Got to play the few cards I've got, D.F."

His pink eyebrows arched. "You think you have *cards*?"

"I know I do. The only reason you brought me here is because I have something you want—information. You need to find out how much I know, who I've talked to. About Bear Lodge. Wannsee Two."

"Three," said Latch.

A silencing look from Ahlward.

I said, "We're talking damage control, D.F. You worked on Milo and he didn't tell you much. Maybe he just didn't know, or maybe he was tougher than you thought. In either event, you figure I'll be a softer touch. And maybe I will—but not if you're going to kill him anyway."

"You and he have something going, do you?"

"It's called friendship."

"Right." He smiled, lifted his right arm, and brought the knife up to my chin. And under.

"It's your kind of decadence that brings a society down," he said. "Softness. Putting it and taking it up the ass." Probing with the knife.

"All soft," he whispered. "Every inch of you." A tiny flick of his wrist and the blade came away red-tipped and wet. He turned again, holding it so that it caught the light—and stared at the candy-apple glint.

No pain for a moment, then a throbbing pang just above my Adam's apple. Wet heat. Like a wasp sting.

"This is you—this is all you are." Blood-entranced. I wondered how many animals he'd tortured as a kid. How many people . . .

I said, "What can I do, D.F.? Sure, you've got most of the cards. But I've still got to use what I have. Survival. Just like you said."

His blunt face was motionless. Then amused once more.

Then something else, dark and empty.

He raised the knife high, stabbed down hard.

I stumbled back, away from the slashing blade, anticipating agony. But less afraid than a moment before. Less afraid than I imagined I'd be—nerves deadened, anesthetized. The same kind of anesthesia they say overtakes gazelles just before the hyenas rip them apart.

I was on the floor, curled, head tucked, trying to be tiny.

But still alive. He'd stabbed air. From the look on his face I knew it had been intentional.

He began laughing.

Latch laughed too. The Gestaposcouts joined in.

A regular black-shirt gigglefest.

Through the gaiety, Ahlward's voice, soft and boyish: "Get up."

The laughter died.

He nudged my butt with his boot tip. Shiny black cowhide; no lizard for him. Gold chain dangling from instep to ankle.

Deprived of arm-balance, it took me a while to get to my feet. I didn't want to see his face. Concentrated on his clothes. The battle ribbons looked phony. Homemade . . .

"Yes," he was saying. "We'll keep the faggot here, for efficiency's sake. I'll want both of you together anyway. The grand climax." Smile. Frown. To the junior SS: "Dump it there."

He crooked a thumb at the couch. Latch gave an uneasy look.

The Gestaposcouts dragged Milo over and dropped him next to Latch. The big bruised body landed on its belly, head on the armrest of the couch, mouth gaping, cabbage-arms flaccid, grubby feet brushing against Latch's slacks. Latch wrinkled his nose and scooted to the far end. The scouts waited at attention until Ahlward nodded.

Then they were gone and the door closed behind them.

Milo groaned, rolled his head, stretched, and was touching Latch again. Latch looked as if he'd been ordered to drink a cup of spit. He shoved Milo's foot away, wiped his hands on the arm of the couch, and squeezed himself farther into the corner. "Don't you think we should tie him?"

Ahlward's heavy jaw tightened and the hand holding the knife blanched. "Why's that?"

"Just in ca—"

"Do you feel he's a threat to you?"

Latch pushed his glasses up his nose. "No, not at all. I just wanted to be—"

"If there's no threat, then there's no need to worry, is there?" said Ahlward. "Let's keep things logical. And as for this one"—he put the knife in its sheath and used his right hand to take hold of my nose—"he's not going to be any problem, is he?" Finger pressure, cutting off my air. "He's white-collar all the way."

He gave Latch an amused look. "The talking class, right, Gordon?"

Latch gave a weak smile. "Absolutely."

Led by the nose, I was pushed down in one of the folding chairs.

Ahlward said, "Wet and gray. All over your shirt. Maybe *infected* wet and gray stuff—all those little fag-viruses just waiting to squirm out and swan-dive into your blood system. If you're not already infected. You like to eat men, turd? You'll be eating *men*."

I said, "Better give your knife a thorough cleaning afterward, D.F. Keep yourself healthy for the revolution."

He went back behind the desk, sat, picked up the black gun, and used a fingernail to scrape something off its barrel.

"Start," he said.

34

I pushed through my fear of him. Concentrated on the tacky ribbons. The costumes, the banner, the paramilitary bullshit.

D.F.

Play to his ego.

I said, "Well, one thing I've figured out is your previous identity. Dayton Auhagen. Darryl Ahlward. Which one's real?"

"When you ask questions," he said, "my mind wanders."

"Okay, let's go back to fashion, then. Your taste in clothes a few years ago: buckskins. Long hair, a beard too. Perfect image for roaming the wilderness. For surviving in places like the forests of southern Idaho. Surrounding Bear Lodge. You trapped, hunted, lived off the land. Using all those survivalist skills you figured would come in handy when the brown stuff hit the Armageddon fan. Nifty stuff, self-reliance. Where'd you learn it from?"

Latch said, "It's in the blood," like a child reciting a lesson.

Ahlward flashed him another sharp look. But it lacked energy.

He liked the attention. All those years of charade. Executive assistant. Waiting to be center stage.

I said. "In the blood, huh? That mean you're a second-generation storm trooper? Got roots in the Fatherland, D.F.?"

I expected him to brush that off, but he gave a slow, measured headshake. "I'm all-American. More American than you or that soft, sorry piece of shit over there could ever conceive."

"All-American," I said. "Ah. Was your father in the Bund itself, or one of the splinter groups?"

The amber eyes opened a bit. "You know about the Bund?"

"Just what I've read."

"In the establishment press?"

I nodded.

"Then you don't know shit. The Bund was the most effective citizens' lobby this country's ever known. The only patriots with the foresight to warn against getting involved in the kike-war. So instead of heeding the warning and rewarding them for their foresight, *Rosen*velt hunted them down like criminal scum. So he'd be free to send our boys over to Europe to die for the kikes and the commie-maggots and the pope-fuckers and faggot-scum like you."

Latch said, "Major blunder. Sociologically as well as politically. World War Kike was the first step toward mass mongrelization. Opened the sluices for all the Asian and Semitic sewage Europe had no use for."

I ignored him, concentrated on Ahlward. "Like I said, D.F., all I know about the Bund is what I've read. Which no doubt *is* biased. But you can see the establishment's point—a war going on, the public being told day after day who the enemy is. Swastikas and *sieg heil*s in Madison Square Garden wouldn't go over great."

Ahlward gave a petulant, impatient look and slapped the desk hard. "That's because the establishment was too *stupid* to know who the real enemy was. Mass stupidity fed by the Zionist-occupier media. Mass weakness due to drugs and toxins developed in secret labs by the Zionist-infiltrated Rosenvelt army. The Zionist-occupier doles out drugs and toxins like candy—that's why they all become doctors, to poison the *goyim*. That's what kosher *food's* really about—the little *U* they put on cans. You know what *goyim* means in serpent-tongue? *Sheep*. We're fucking sheep to them. To be shorn and slaughtered. You know what the *U* stands for? Some Yid-word that means poison. They use toxins and tranquilizers that *their* bodies can tolerate because they're constructed of toxic cells. But we can't and it gradually weakens us. Physiological hypnosis—it's been scientifically proven. Been that way for centuries in every society the Zionist-occupier infiltrates. Gradual mass passivity, decadence, then inevitable destruction. Every liberation movement has to overcome it by wielding the cleansing spear."

It reminded me of stuff I'd heard during internship. On the back wards of state hospitals. He reeled it off in the flat tones of a high school thespian.

I said, "Cleansing spear," and looked at the banner behind him.

Latch said, "The spear of Woden. The ultimate cleansing machine."

Once again I ignored him and asked Ahlward: "What about Crisp and Blanchard and the rest of them? They second-generation Bundists too?"

His eyes narrowed. "Something like that."

"No skinheads for you, huh, D.F.?"

Latch laughed and said, "Punks. Rank-amateur clowns. We prize discipline."

I said, "So, am I right about the mountain-man bit, D.F.?"

Ahlward sat back in the swivel chair and put his hands behind his head.

"Okay," I said. "So you're living off the land and hiding from the government. Just like some of your former enemies on the left. Your movement's in trouble. So is the left. Cointelpro, Nixon, J. Edgar. Divide and conquer and it's working. It gets you thinking. By squaring off against the left, you're giving the establishment exactly what it wants. Some people on the left realize it too. And you all come to realize that when you stop to think about it, the radical right and the radical left have lots in common. You both believe society has to be torn down in order to totally restructure it. That democracy is weak and inefficient, controlled by the international bankers and running-dog press— by the talking class. A new populism is called for—empowering the working man. And the main issue that used to separate you—race—is no longer that big of a stumbling block. Because there are white leftists enraged at the uppity blacks who'd tried to kick them out of their own move- ment. White leftists getting in touch with their own racism."

"A beacon of wisdom," said Latch, "shining through the shit pile."

I said, "I don't know who thought of it first, D.F., but somehow you communicated and a new concept was conceived. Wannsee Two. Pressing inward from the outermost edges in order to squeeze the center and crush it to death. Which is how you got together with old Gordie here."

A quick look at Latch, then back to Ahlward. "Though to tell the truth, D.F., I really can't see the appeal. You're clearly a man of action. He's nothing more than a hot-air purveyor living off his wife's money."

Latch swore and waited for Ahlward to defend him. When the redheaded man didn't speak, I went on.

"He's the proverbial empty barrel making lots and lots of noise. A lap dog—the ultimate *example* of the talking class. Do you really think he'll be able to cut it when the time comes?"

Latch jumped to his feet. The impact jostled Milo; his body rolled to the edge of the sofa, then rolled back. His mouth gaped. As I searched the battered face for signs of consciousness, I felt another wasp-sting on my cheek. A new layer of pain veneering a three-year-old jaw injury. Memories of wires and putty . . . My head shot back. Another layer.

Latch was standing over me, spittle collecting in the corners of his mouth: a lap dog gone rabid. He raised his arm to hit me again.

And starring as the punching bag in tonight's school pageant is little Alex Delaware. . . .

He struck out, and the rattling in my head reverberated like acid rock pumped through a cheap amplifier.

After the knife, petty annoyance.

I looked up at him and said, "Temper, temper, Gordie."

He ground his teeth and drew back his fist. Just before impact, I feinted to one side. His hand grazed me. He was caught off balance and stumbled.

Ahlward looked disgusted. He said, "Sit down, Gordon."

Latch righted himself, stood there panting, his hands bunched. High color in the freckled cheeks. The welfare glasses askew.

My head hurt, but not that badly. My arms were numb. Gazelle-anesthesia, or loss of circulation?

I said, "Why don't you sit down and toot your harmonica, Gordie?"

He balled his hand, started to retract it. Ahlward's voice froze it mid-motion like a blast of liquid nitrogen.

"*Later,* Gordon."

Latch looked back and forth between the two of us. Spat in my face and returned to the couch. But no more casual leg-cross. He sat on the edge, hands on knees, huffing with rage.

A gob of his saliva had landed on my cheek. I lowered my head, wiped it as well as I could on my shoulder.

I said, "How impolitic, Councilman."

Latch said, "He's mine, Bud. When the time comes."

I said, "I'm touched, Councilman."

Ahlward turned to me and said, "That all you have to say, turd?"

"Oh, no. There's plenty more. Back to

Wannsee Two. The meeting no one believes ever took place. But it did. Somewhere rural and secluded—away from the *untermensch*-infested cities where the police and the Feds had control. Maybe somewhere like southern Idaho? The ranch that Miranda inherited from her father? How many people were involved?"

Ahlward's eyelids drooped. He touched his gun.

I said, "A redux of the Hitler-Stalin buddy bit. You even came up with a new insignia that said it all: red for the left, the spear for the right, a circle signifying the union."

I turned to Latch: "If the folks on Telegraph Avenue only knew."

He said, "You're an idiot. It *started* up in Berkeley. Back in the days when I was still brainwashed and toxified. I did hypnotic things without knowing why I was doing them. Taking African history, Native American studies, all sorts of contrived, useless bullshit the Jew-profs shoved down my throat. But even then I was starting to see through it. It wasn't working for me. I went searching for my own source material. Learned facts no one had the guts to come out and say in class. Like the *fact* that there wasn't a single written language in Africa before the white man came. No real *music* except for stupid chants a retardate could master. No fine cuisine, no litera-ture, no fine arts. We're talking an ape culture—

malaria, promiscuity, dung-eating, Mau Mau cannibals. They're nothing but a bunch of dung-eating baboons, brought to America by the Zionist-occupier in order to pick Zionist cotton. Trained by the Zionists to wear human clothes and mouth human words and masquerade as human peers. I'd dealt with them; I knew how impossible it was to get through to them using logic. All of a sudden it made sense. You can't use logic with an ape."

"Apes with rhythm? Like DeJon?"

He laughed. "That *was* fun. The *irony*. He and his fucking gorillas. Monkeys riding in lim-ousines. Thinking they're even a half-step above the dung heap. He actually *thanked* me for giving him the opportunity to serve."

"You have a taste for irony, don't you, Gordie?" I said. "Making speeches at the Holo-caust Center after the building was defaced. Serv-ing on their Board. Knowing all the time that it was D.F.'s storm troopers who did the defacing."

He laughed harder. "They're so gullible, all of them—the inferior classes. Poor self-esteem on a bio-ethnic level. It's coded genetically—on a *cellular* level they know they're inferior. Which is why, when the white man asserts himself properly, there's no competition. No resistance. They march straight into the ovens, shimmy right up to the lynching tree. All you have to do is pretend to like them."

Ahlward nodded in assent but I thought I spotted a hint of annoyance. Deprived, once again, of the limelight.

I shifted my attention back to him. "Wannsee Two went better than you'd imagined. You drew up a plan. But there were obstacles. People who stood in the way—who'd fight you to the death if they found out. People with charisma and drive and no compunctions about working outside of the system themselves. Norm and Melba Green, Skitch Dupree, the Rodriguezes, Grossman, Lockerby, and Bruckner. Time for some more damage control, and here Gordie came in handy again. Your inside track to the first cadre. Privy to *their* plan—New Walden. Black and white farming side by side, inviting the Indians back. Everything you despised. Gordie and Randy lured them up to Bear Lodge with tales of clean air and pure water and free rent. An old warehouse—another chunk of Randy's inheritance." I looked around the room. "Guess she likes warehouses. Didn't know they were such a good investment."

A flicker of impatience crossed Ahlward's eyes.

I said, "The Walden folks traveled up to Bear Lodge with stars in their eyes. And you were waiting for them. Dayton Auhagen, macho hippie. Communer with nature. The kind of stranger who could skulk around without arousing their suspicions. You watched them. Surveilled them. Get-

ting a fix on their habits, their routine. Same way
you'd track any prey. Getting into that warehouse
when they were gone and hiding explosive charges
among all that combustible produce."

Ahlward was smiling. Remembering.

I said, "Only some of the group was settled in
Bear Lodge. The others were farther north, negotiating for lumber. But that other group was
strictly second cadre. Without their leaders they
were likely to cut and run. And if they did prove
threatening sometime in the future, you could
always pick them off at your pleasure—small
game. So you fixed a date before the second cadre
was scheduled to arrive, got into the warehouse
again, poisoned their dinner meat. Returned to the
forest, waited until they were all inside, incapac-
itated, pressed a button, and boom. The FBI
dovetailed beautifully into your plans by jumping
on the bomb-factory explanation and feeding it to
the press. No doubt you helped them along with an
anonymous tip."

Smug smile on the blunt face. Nostalgia had
never looked so ugly.

I said, "That was a good touch. No one
mourned a bunch of urban terrorists blowing
themselves up with their own nitro. Only one
minor glitch: one of the second cadre people—
Terry Crevolin—arrived early. A *vegetarian*, to
boot. He didn't eat the meat, was spared, and
escaped the blast. But once again, no big threat.

He had personal problems—drugs, a weak will—likely to sap his political energies. And his hatred and distrust of the establishment led him to believe the explosion was government-sponsored. To this day he doesn't believe in Wannsee Two. So it was a nifty plan, D.F. As far as it went. But my question for you is, why *bother*? Why go to all that trouble for the first cadre when there were other radical leaders just as charismatic?"

Latch said, "They were scum. Fucking snobs."

Spoiled-brat rage.

Not-invited-to-the-party rage.

I knew then that the idea of the blast had originated with him. That for him it had been personal, not political.

All those lives lost—the horror—because they'd been smarter than he was. *Shut him out.*

His idea.

More of an idea man than I'd thought. Their relationship was complex. Made the one between Dobbs and Massengil look wholesome . . .

Ahlward was sitting up straighter. I decided to keep the insight to myself.

"After Bear Lodge," I said, "time to move forward. Pick a front man, sanitize him, and get him into public office—no matter how humble an office. You're a patient man, D.F., know your history. All those years it took the *first* Führer to progress from a jail cell to the Reichstag." I sat forward. "The only thing is the first Führer was his own front man. He didn't need a dummy on his lap."

Latch said, "Fuck you, you piece of shit."

I thought I saw Ahlward smile. "Times have changed," he said. "This is the media age. Image is everything."

I said, "Thought the Zionists controlled the media."

"They do," said Ahlward.

"More irony, huh?"

He yawned.

I said, "Okay, granted, got to consider images. But is *he* the best you can do, image-wise?"

Furious mutters from the sofa. A hint of movement that Ahlward stilled with a sharp look.

As if to compensate, he said, "He's doing just fine." Mechanically. His gaze floated around the room. Not much of an attention span. I wondered how many classes he'd flunked in school.

I said, "Gordie and Miranda retreat to the ranch for a few years, confess their Vietnam sins, reemerge as environmental activists. Meanwhile the ranch is also used for meetings. Other conferences. Recruiting the sons and daughters of your dad's old buddies. Just like the summer camps the Bund used to run. You also get a little publishing business going—all those boxes outside. *Printed*

Material. Probably hate stuff shipped at discount rate courtesy of Uncle Sam, right?"

Another smug smile.

"Aren't you worried someone's going to trace it back to one of Miranda's dummy corporations?"

He shook his head, still smug. "We write it here, print it somewhere else, then bring it back here, then truck it to other places. No way to trace. Layers of cover."

I said, "And the other boxes: *Machinery*. What is that? Hardware for the revolution?"

Latch said, "Guns and butter."

Ahlward coughed. Latch shut up.

The redheaded man played with his gun some more.

I said, "You picked L.A. for Gordie's renaissance because Miranda had connections here— show biz, the whole radical chic thing. Love-the-Earth rhetoric went over big with that crowd, so Gordie became Mr. Environment. Scrubbing pelicans while dreaming of cleansing the world. And got elected. So far, so good. The fact that Crevolin had also settled in L.A. was a bit of an annoyance, but all those years of silence meant he didn't suspect a damn thing. What *was* a shock was learning that someone *else* had escaped Bear Lodge and resurfaced in L.A. Norman and Melba Green's son. The FBI had declared him dead— *assumed* him dead, rather than proving it with a body. Because you assured them two little kids had been part of the group. Now here he was, seventeen years later. Returning to live with Norman's mother. His grandmother. A suspicious, unapologetic *Old* Leftist who had no trouble believing a new Holocaust was just around the corner. No trouble suspecting her son and daughter-in-law had been murdered. Though, like Crevolin, she thought the government had been behind it. She fired up her grandson with Nazi history and conspiracy theories. He started doing his own research. He was a smart kid and took to it."

Latch snorted and said, "Smart baboon."

I said, "Book research wasn't enough for him. He tried to meet his rescuer, couldn't get through to Crevolin, and went to the next-best source. Someone who'd also been a comrade of his parents. Another second cadre guy, but one who'd climbed. A public man."

I turned to Latch. "What a bummer, Gordie. The timing, I mean. Here you are, having bought all that respectability. Sure, you're only a sandwich sign for D.F.'s dreams. But sometimes you allow yourself to pretend it's real and you're the boss and that feels really good, doesn't it? And sure, City Council is relatively penny-ante, but it's a giant step forward for someone who committed sedition on national television. You're moving up. The rhythm is there. Things are *finally* fitting *together,* and along comes this mixed-race mongrel *black Jewish kid* knocking on your headquarters door, using his parents' names as passwords to get through the front office. Names you thought you'd never hear again. Coming face to face with you and asking questions about the bad old days. Wannsee Two. You try to put him off, play the old game you've learned so well and answer his questions without really answering them. But he's persistent. Pushy. Full of the kind of youthful fire that just might be able to incinerate you. That's how it always starts, isn't it? Small fry nipping at the big fish. A night watchman got Nixon. So it's time for a quick stall and an emergency meeting with D.F. D.F. instructs you to handle it in a time-honored manner: Lull the prey into complacency with phony friendship, feed him carefully measured bits of disinformation, then move in for the kill when the time's right.

"So you play compassionate liberal for Ike, spin him a tale about Wannsee Two in which the story remains intact but the characters are altered. Making someone else the chief bad guy. It wasn't exactly casting against type. Massengil had right-wing sensibilities; he'd been tooting his quasi-racist horn for some time. You probably made up some yarn about his having been a government agent. With your resources—your own printing press—it's no problem furnishing Ike with some impressive-looking bogus documents. And the beauty of it was that it served a double purpose.

Ocean Heights is part of your district. Getting Massengil out of a job he's had a lock on for almost three decades will allow you to run for his seat. Still penny-ante compared to your ultimate goal, but state assemblymen have been known to go to Washington. How many councilmen have ever gotten out of City Hall? You'd had your sights on him for some time, planted Bramble on his staff—your inside track. So when Ike showed up asking questions, everything clicked. You took him into your confidence, swore him to secrecy, fed him lies—fed his revenge fantasies and tried to work him up to the point of violent retribution. You figured that wouldn't be much of a challenge, because he was black—and blacks are inherently violent, aren't they?"

Latch said, "Sounds like the turd has some capacity to learn."

Ahlward didn't even bother to fake interest.

When you ask questions, my mind wanders.

I said, "First choice was for Ike to assassinate Massengil and get himself killed in the process. Second choice was for one of your junior SS boys to bump off Massengil, *frame* Ike for it, and kill him too. Same result, slightly less efficient. The only problem was, Ike resisted. Despite that kinky hair and all that melanin in his skin, he just wasn't the violent type."

"Fifty percent kike-blood," said Ahlward. "Programmed for cowardice."

"Or maybe Gordie just screwed up. Pushed too hard and got Ike suspicious. Made him wonder why a city councilman was so eager to get involved in murder. In any event, he refused to go along and turned himself into a serious liability. So you lured him to that alley with the promise of something—probably some new information about his parents. From another source. A black source—what better place to do it than Watts. Must have been fun making the call, putting on the patois."

"Yowza, massuh," said Latch. "We sho' good at talkin' that nigra talk. Ceptin' we po' culluhds have such a bay-ad tahm luynin to *di-al* that phone."

Turning to Ahlward for approval. The red-headed man's smile was obligatory. He fingered the black gun's barrel and yawned.

I said, "Ike walked into the ambush and one of your SS-kateers shotgunned him, injected him with a dope cocktail, and set it up as a drug burn. Because, after all, blacks are all dope fiends, right? Who's going to get suspicious about a junkie getting snuffed in South Central? And, by golly, you succeeded again. It went down that way in the books. Now there was only Grandma to deal with. Despite Ike's pledge not to talk, you figured he'd confided in her. You plucked her off the street and left her body where no one will ever find it. Just for the record, where was that?"

Blank stares from both of them.

I said, "Considering you've got all the cards, you guys are pretty stingy."

Ahlward said, "Sounds like you're running out of material."

I said, "Perish the thought. There's plenty more. After you dispose of Sophie, you break into her place and look for any evidence she might have left behind—notebooks, diaries. Doing the neighbor's place, too, to make it look like a burglary. But why the stuff on the walls? The Kennedy message?"

Latch couldn't resist answering that one. "Dessert. For the troopers who performed the mission. Reward for a job well done."

"Even revolutionaries have to party," I said. And caught movement from Milo. An eye-blink. Volitional?

Neither of them saw it. Milo's back was to Latch. And Ahlward was preoccupied with his gun.

Another blink. Or had I just imagined it?

I kept talking. "With both Ike and Sophie Gruenberg gone, your immediate problems finally seemed over. But there was still the matter of Massengil. You'd already started thinking of him as a dead man. So it was *annoying* to have to change that mind-set. And if the deed was going to be done, the timing was important. He was well into his current term, had already been nominated for the next one. So it was to your advantage for him to be eliminated before the next election. Too late for the governor to appoint someone else. The seat would lie fallow for a few months, giving you time to build up political steam and enter yet another image-stage: great conciliator, mature statesman. Sure, the widow would get first dibs, and if she didn't want the job, some hack or crony would move in. But you had plans to take care of that, per the lovely Ms. Bramble."

Latch said, "I do believe Ocean Heights and I will reach our own rapprochement."

I said, "Better do it soon, before Randy pulls the purse strings closed. Or were you intending to ask for alimony?"

Sudden panic in his eyes.

Ahlward's eyebrows were hot-pink crescents of surprise.

I said, "Oops. Sorry. I thought you knew, D.F."

Ahlward looked at Latch.

Latch said, "He's full of shi—"

I said. "Little Randy definitely wants out, D.F. She's filed papers. Check for yourself—it's public record."

Ahlward swiveled slowly in his chair and stared at Latch.

Latch said, "It just went down, Bud. I was going to bring it up, had it on the agenda."

"Oops again," I said. "Not quite true, Gordie

Pordie. She filed two weeks ago. Not the greatest thing to happen at a time like this, is it, D.F.? Vis-à-vis public relations. And money-wise." To Latch: "What happened, Gordie? Did her political enthusiasm wane? Or is it just you she's tired of? Guess all that discipline and bondage stuff wears thin after a—"

Latch said, "Shut your filthy mouth."

Ahlward cleared his throat.

Latch said, "It's not a problem, Bud. She can be taken care of. She's on so much fucking Seconal, nobody'll—"

Ahlward's turn to say, "Shut up! You know, Gordon, it's real pleasant hearing it this way."

"C'mon, Bud, you can see what he's—"

"And you're giving him exactly what he wants."

Latch sank back down and played with one of his cuffs.

Milo winked. This time I was sure.

I said, "We're talking thick coats of tarnish on your rising star, D.F. You might start thinking about a replacement."

Ahlward raised the gun and sighted down it again. To my surprise I felt no fear, only weariness at his Little Dictator routine.

He said, "I've heard enough."

Two winks from the couch. Milo's big body remained motionless.

I said, "You mean you don't want to hear the rest? The part you took charge of personally?"

He lowered the gun. "Go on."

"Shortly after Ike and Grandma were taken care of, another unpleasant surprise came your way. Someone else Ike had confided in. So much for pledges of secrecy—guess Gordie wasn't very convincing. A mentally dull shut-in who welcomed the cheer and conversation Ike brought with him when he delivered the groceries. Who appreciated the time he took to get to know her. And as he got to know her better, he lapsed into his favorite topic: politics. Not that she had more than a hazy idea of what he was talking about. Social justice, the evils of capitalism. But she was able to pick out the juicy parts. Conspiracies, murder. Wannsee Two. She sat there and listened. The perfect soundboard. Because Ike's visits filled the emptiness in her life, she didn't want them to stop.

"Then one day, they did stop. Forever. She found out he was dead. Murdered. People were saying he died buying dope, but she knew that was a lie because he didn't take dope. He hated dope. She knew something was wrong—probably one of those conspiracies Ike had talked about. She withdrew further, confused. Just like when her mother died. But this time she came out of it angry. Wanting to understand why bad things happen to good people. To talk to someone who could explain it to her. Not her father—they never talk; he treats her like a servant. And she barely knows her brother. But she does recall a name Ike mentioned consulting. A former comrade of his parents who's gotten famous—even been on TV. Someone Ike had suspicions about but didn't share with Holly because he didn't want to put *her* in jeopardy.

"Would someone like that talk to her? She was afraid. But she couldn't forget Ike—his death. So she built up her courage and called the famous guy's headquarters. One of the famous guy's staff answers and hears her babbling about stuff no one's supposed to know about, and knows this is a job for the High Command."

I looked at Latch. "What'd you tell her?"

He smirked. "That she'd done the right thing by getting in touch with me. That I was investigating Ike's death and she had to promise to keep everything secret until I got back to her." He laughed. "She ate that up like cornflakes."

I glanced at Ahlward. He'd put the gun down on the desk, had taken the knife out again, and was cleaning his nails.

"Proud of yourself, huh?" I said to Latch. "But D.F. here wasn't too proud. He figured you'd fucked up. Decided to handle this one personally." To the redheaded man: "You met with her—as Gordie's assistant. Debriefed her to find out exactly what she knew, found out it was just enough to make her a threat, and realized she was custom-made for another try at Massengil. A *better* dupe than Ike, because she lacked the intellect to think critically. She was *ripe* to obey. So you went to work on her. Building rapport, gaining her confidence. Putting on the old para-military thing. Secret meetings in out-of-the-way places when her father was out of town. Night walks. You'd pick her up and drive her away. She had no job, no schedule, no one to miss her, no one else to confide in. You fed her secret codes, high intrigue—giving her a sense of purpose for the first time in her life. Resurrecting the old Massengil-as-Satan fantasy. Massengil as the vicious murderer of her friend. Feeding her rage, nursing it, bringing it to bloom. Making her sense of self-esteem contingent upon carrying out her mission. And she did eat it up. Snow White gobbling a poisoned apple. She was so eager to act, she told you she even had her own weapons— a closetful of guns. You got into her house when her father was away and took a look. Most of them were antiques, unusable. Except the Remington. But in her hands it might as well have been a flintlock."

More winks from Milo. *Keep going, pal.*

"You spelled out her assignment, went over it with her, putting her through dry runs, until you were sure she had it down. Her sister-in-law saw her holding the gun, weeks before, muttering about Wannsee Two. Which she thought was gibberish. As would anyone else hearing it. The worst that could happen was she'd freak out before the big day and start rambling on about conspiracies. Who'd believe her? As it turned out, she didn't talk to anyone. Never saw anyone. And the big day drew near. You notified her with a coded call. Monday morning. Perfect time and place for a hit. Bramble had informed you of Massengil's plans to use the school for a press conference. You knew exactly what time he'd show up, precisely where he'd be standing. But getting Holly out of the house was a problem. Her father was an early riser, so sneaking out early on Monday was out of the question. You had her do it Sunday night, while he was still asleep. Told her to take the Remington out of the closet and wrap it in something, close the door to her bedroom so he'd think she was still asleep, then sneak out really quietly, sure to close her bedroom door. Disengaging the alarm, resetting it, and slipping out of the house with the wrapped rifle. Though Ocean Heights is so deserted at night, she could have carried it out in the open.

"You picked her up a couple of blocks away, brought her a change of clothes, a paper cup for elimination. The two of you drove toward the school, parked a few blocks away, and walked over. Hand signals. High adventure—she must have loved it."

Ahlward gave a disgusted look. "She was a pain to work with, took a long time to learn everything. Pure Mengele fodder, destined to live and die as shit. I gave her the gift of immortality, more than she could ever hope for."

"Real act of kindness," I said.

"Sometimes," he said, stroking his gun, "it's cruel to be kind."

I said, "You popped the lock on the storage shed and camped out for the night. She with her rifle, you with your pistol. Waiting. Stalking. Just like Bear Lodge. Telling her to go to sleep—you'd take first watch and wake her when her turn came. Letting her sleep until sunrise and then letting her know there'd been a change in plans: *You* were going to do all the shooting, just to make certain everything went smoothly. Not to worry, she'd still be a hero. Your assistant. Maybe she accepted that. Or maybe she put up a fuss—wanting *personal* revenge. You thought you had her convinced. But when the time actually came to shoot—when Massengil and Gordie and the kids poured out on the yard, she pulled a fast one on you. Grabbed the rifle. Second cadre wasn't good enough for *her*."

I gave Latch a smile, turned back to Ahlward before I could see his reaction.

"Her shot went wild. Of course. The recoil knocked her down and she dropped the rifle. You got hold of it, had to think fast, consider your options. The optimal choice would have been taking aim, squeezing off a good one at Massengil, and then doing her. But looking out the window you could see the moment of opportunity had been lost—panic, everyone screaming, running for cover, no clear shot. Not that you'd have minded a few dead kids, but that would have complicated matters. Vis-à-vis P.R. So you took your pistol and shot Holly in the face—kept shooting her. Eight times. Shot three rounds from the Remington—all of it together sounded like war to those out on the yard. Then you walked back to the yard carrying your smoking gun, ready to play savior. No one had seen you actually enter the storage shed, but the panic took care of that: No one remembered anything but their own fear. And the press hadn't arrived yet, with their cameras and their recorders. Besides, if anyone asked, Gordie and the troops could always be counted on to step forward as eyewitnesses to your heroic dash to the shed. Quick reflexes and calm under fire, D.F. Job well done."

Wink from the couch.

I said to Ahlward: "It must have been nice being the star for a change. Getting the credit you deserved instead of standing in his shadow—such a puny shadow at that. But after all your *planning*, you still hadn't managed to get rid of Massengil. The guy was turning out to be a goddammed Rasputin. Another assassination attempt soon after would look funny, raise all sorts of questions. Your instinct was to wait, let him live out another term, bide your time. But Gordie didn't like that. He pushed you. And now you know why: He knew he'd be losing his hope chest soon. Fortunately for him, the productive Ms. Bramble had gleaned another bit of inside info on Massengil: kinky sex with Cheri Nuveen on a regular basis, Dobbs looking on. Bramble even knew when the next appointment was. Given that, the rest was easy. A simple hit, Dobbs as dessert, no apparent connection to the schoolyard. First day, Gordie comforts the widow and plays Mr. Compassion. Next day, you leak the hooker stuff to the press and knock off the widow as a viable candidate. Along with any of Massengil's cronies: guilt by association. The voters would have to wonder if they'd attended any of Massengil's parties. Leaving guess who."

I leaned forward. "It's fine as far as it goes, D.F., but what do you really think it's going to accomplish? Let's say he gets elected. Even manages not to screw up for a term or two and goes on to Washington. There's no substance to him. Nothing to build an empire on. It would be like constructing a palace over a sump hole."

Latch swore.

Ahlward smiled. "You think he's the only one? I've got placements all over." He used the knife as a pointer. "Serious talent. Each of them young, photogenic. Courageously liberal. Until the time comes."

"Wannsee Three."

"And Four and Five and Six." Anger and impatience in the amber eyes; the knife stabbed air. "Whatever it takes to get the job done. Like you said, I'm a patient man. Long-term planner. Willing to wait until the time's right and the cleansing blood flows. Washing away all the anthro-pretenders and putting together a new age that's genetically honest and beautifully cruel."

"How poetic."

"Who else knows what you know?" he said.

"How about the police for starts? I sent them tapes."

He smiled and shook his head. "Bullshit. You believed our FBI scam. If you'd been in contact with the police they'd have called in the Feds, and the Feds would have interviewed you already. We've been watching you, know who you've met with. Try again, turd."

I said, "You're assuming greater efficiency on the part of the authorities than they deserve. Bureaucratic wheels turn slowly. The cops know. I was waiting for the FBI. That's why I opened the door for Blanchard and Crisp. And I *didn't* buy the scam. They had to sucker-punch me to get me here."

"I said Try again."

"That's it, D.F. Just the cops. There's no way you're going to pull this off."

"Negative thinking," he said. "Time for a little preliminary scrub."

He stood, holding the gun in one hand, the knife in the other. Running his eyes over Milo, he said, "Despicable. How can you live with yourselves, the things you do?"

He rotated the knife. "Here's the way it's going to go down. You and him doing filthy stuff—your filthy *friendship*. Things get out of hand. You beat him up badly. *Trash* him to death, then start feeling so guilty that you write a little note and blow your own faggot brains out."

I said, "Shame to dirty up your warehouse. Randy might not like that when it comes time to give it back to her. Not to mention the health hazard from faggot blood."

He smiled. "Not to worry, turd. We've got a nice little place all set up for you. Cock-sucky motel over in Pacoima."

"Another of her real-estate tidbits?"

He said, "C'mon, time for a butt-hole party. Up you go."

I remained seated.

The gun waved. The pink eyebrows climbed.

"I said Move it," he said.

Wink wink wink.

I ignored him.

All at once the blunt face was transformed into something livid and howling:

"I said Get the fuck up!"

I stood. Very slowly.

Latch rose, brushed off his trousers, and smiled at me. "Thought you might want to know we've also got something planned for Little Miss Principal. The snotty cunt—does she know you swing both ways? That you've been infecting her?"

I said, "She doesn't know anything."

I could tell from the way his face creased in a Kewpie-doll smile that I'd allowed my terror to show.

"Hey," he said, "you were balling her, which means pillow talk. She's a *liability* and it's *all your fault. She'll* be having a wild time tonight." He clicked his tongue. "Really wild. Shocking example of the burgeoning rise in crime on the West Side. Perfect timing for my campaign. I'll be showing up at the crime scene, pledging my troth to law and order. That's the way we work, you fucking piece of shit. Nothing ever goes to waste. Not even the squeal. And boy, will she squeal."

He giggled. I strained against my bonds.

"A *wild* time," he said. "We're sending someone to do her who really *enjoys* that kind of thing. Knows how to bring out the *best* in a woman. Try to get *that* image out of your mind. The look on her face when it actually happens and she realizes what's going on. The *sounds* she'll make.

Wink wink wink from the couch.

I said, "Bring out the best in a woman, huh? Then it sure wouldn't be a job for you. When's the last time Randy saw anything stiffer than her own upper lip?"

The Kewpie doll turned malignant. He began coming at me, arms up, boxer-style.

Ahlward said, "Not now," in a jaded tone.

Latch didn't seem to hear, kept coming.

Wink.

I backed away, danced on fear-laden legs. My turn to leer. "Sure, Gordie. Nothing like a fair fight. But who's going to protect *you* when D.F. finally realizes that without Randy's big bucks you're not very useful? Just a wimpy little piece of limp-dicked shit. Second cadre all the way?"

Latch said, "Give me the knife, D.F. I've had enough."

Ahlward raised the blade, holding it out of reach. "Don't be an idiot. It has to be done the right way."

Latch backed off.

I said, "Roll over, Gordon. Say bow-wow, Gordon."

Stuck out my tongue and dog-panted.

Latch charged me, swinging.

I moved to meet him, faked a shoulder butt, faded back suddenly just short of impact and caught him off guard. Again. He grunted in anger, regained his balance, and charged again.

Ahlward put the gun down, reached out, and restrained him with one hand. The other held on to the knife.

Gun on the desk. But no free hands.

I kept talking, bouncing on my feet. "Play *dead,* Gordon. Eat your *kibble,* Gordon. Don't wet the *rug,* Gordon."

Ahlward screamed at me: *"You shut the fuck up!"*

Latch shook off Ahlward's hand and lunged again.

At the same time a pale bulk rose from the couch, a polar bear coming out of hibernation. Taking hold of Latch's shoulders, shoving him forward.

Latch fell heavily. Toward Ahlward. On Ahlward. His weight causing the red-haired man to stumble backwards, onto the desk, a look of surprise on the blunt features.

Latch was on top of him, thrashing wildly. Ahlward tried to shove him off, cursing and twisting to get free. Trying to get to the gun.

Latch remained sprawled on top of him.

Screaming.

The two of them wrestling.

Then Ahlward's face was speckled with blood.

Showered with it.

Latch screamed. A terrible sound; more than just frustration.

Blood kept spurting, Ahlward thrashing away from it, spitting it.

Something shiny and sharp emerged from the soft freckled flesh on the back of Latch's neck. Worked its way through like a burrowing grub.

Silver, sharp-nosed grub. The knife point, ruby and silver.

Latch gurgled and tore at his throat.

The knife kept nosing its way out.

Ahlward gave a hard, two-handed shove. Latch came loose. Inertia threw Ahlward backwards, off the desk top, onto the swivel chair, stricken by astonishment.

Milo moved unsteadily toward the gun. Reached out for it, touched the butt, missed. The weapon skidded across the wooden surface and sailed away, landing somewhere on the floor.

Ahlward dove for it.

I felt a hand on my wrist, yanking. Freeing my hands. "C'mon!"

Milo limped toward the door. I followed him, dazed. Watching Latch sink to the floor, the knife still embedded in his neck. Hands grabbing the handle, gurgling, trying to yank it free.

Salivating blood.

His eyes rolled back. . . .

"C'mongoddammitalex!"

Yanking me.

The two of us out the black door, slamming it.

Into the hall. Four black-shirts, smiling, as if savoring the tail end of a joke. They saw us and the smiles hung in mid-air.

Milo howled at them and kept coming. The smiles vanished and they looked terrified. Naughty kids, unprepared for reality. One, a dark-haired fat boy with an old man's jowls, wore a holstered pistol and reached for it. I used my shoulder and hit him hard. Ran past the sound of pain-screams and cracking bone.

Running through a cardboard alley.

Warning shouts. The crackle of gunfire.

We took the first turn available, meeting up with two more Gestaposcouts—girls. They could have been sorority sisters discussing pledge night. One put a hand to her mouth. We hurtled past, bowled them over, heard girl-squeals.

Fuck chivalry.

More gunshots.

Louder.

I looked back as I ran, saw Ahlward, pumping his legs, screaming orders that no one was heeding. Calling for his troops, but the troops were frozen, unprepared for reality.

A cold rush of wind as something tore into a carton inches from my head.

Another turnoff, just a few yards away. We

ran for it. Above all the noise I could hear Milo gasping, saw him put a hand to his chest.

More gunshots.

Then a louder sound.

Earthquake loud, rumbling up from the cement floor. Rattling the floor as if it were paper.

Cartons tumbled in our path like giant, tantrum-stricken building blocks. Someone screamed.

More screams. Panic. The way the school-yard must have sounded.

Another rumble. Even stronger, bouncing us like toys, knocking us to the floor.

More boxes toppled. Cartons shot up in the air, tossed by an unseen juggler, and landed with dull, sickening thumps.

Milo tripped, was down. I helped him to his feet. He looked deathly, but resumed running.

No sign of Ahlward, a jumble of cardboard behind us, shielding us.

We made the turn. Black-shirts scattering. The auto-shop smell of seared metal . . .

Another roar.

The hiss of disintegrating plaster.

We climbed over boxes, ran around them. Milo stopped, hand on chest, legs bowed, head down.

I called his name.

He said, ". . . fine . . ." He swallowed

air, did it again, nodded dully, and began moving again.

Another explosion. The building shivered like a wet puppy. More cartons crashed down around us, a Vesuvius of PRINTED MATERIALS.

We swerved, dodged, managed to make our way through the rubble. Another turn. Past the forklift . . .

Metal clatter, more hiss. More thunder. Screams of agony.

The hiss grew louder. Joined by an unmistakable odor.

Burning paper. A sudden, burgeoning heat.

Demolition music. Tongues of orange licking the ground just a few feet away.

Filthy, inky smoke oozed from between the boxes, rising to the top of the warehouse, darkening it.

The heat intensified. Through it another cold rush.

Thunk. Shredded cardboard.

Ahlward emerging from the smoke, howling soundlessly, ignoring the smoke that churned behind him, mindless with hate.

He aimed again.

There was a clearing in the cardboard wall. I ran toward it, realized Milo wasn't with me. Looking over my shoulder, I saw him. Hand to chest.

A wall of smoke had risen between him and Ahlward. Shots came through it.

Milo looking from side to side, disoriented. I went back for him, grabbed his hand. Felt the resistance of his weight on my wrist, straining the sinews . . .

I pulled hard. He managed to get going again. I saw the sliding metal door of the loading dock just a few yards up. Shredded like foil and blackened around the edges.

Metal fragments scattered on the ground. Glinty treasure on a bed of masonry dust.

And something else.

A black-shirt. Prone. Blond crew cut. Pale, broad face. White eyes. Husky body stretched out, limp.

Two pieces of body. The trunk separated from the legs. Bifurcated by sliding-door shrapnel.

Closer to the door, another corpse, half buried in metal and offal. A charred head above hamburger. Four others, barely discernible, moist spots in the ash pile.

My gorge rose. I began to choke.

Chemical fumes.

The warehouse was a furnace, flames reaching to the ceiling, smoke thickening as it rolled toward us, a greasy tornado.

A black form emerged from the charcoal mass.

Ahlward, sooty and singed, jerking his head from side to side as if shaking off leeches.

Sighting us. Screaming. Lifting his big black gun.

I went for the largest hole in the shredded door, pulled Milo through it, slipping on the blood-slick floor, feeling the crunch of metal and bone beneath my shoes.

Outside. Fresh air. Gasoline-stink air.

The two of us lurched along the loading dock.

Fumes and flames poured out of the warehouse, out of shattered windows, the ravaged metal door. Shooting out of the gaping holes that had been blown in the wall.

Milo's breathing was raw and labored. I pulled him down the stairs, into the parking lot.

An incoherent scream rose at our backs.

Ahlward out on the dock, highlighted by the burning building. Looking very small. Aiming. A true believer.

Gunfire.

A frog-song ratatat.

Didn't know a pistol could make a sound like that.

Another burst. From our backs.

Trapped?

Frogs sang again.

I looked over my shoulder, saw Ahlward jerk and fall, saw the pistol go flying into the inferno.

The flames rolled out of the warehouse and ate him.

Dessert.

Then a voice, out of the darkness:

"You and your detective friend are safe, Dr. Delaware. I've saved you."

35

He stepped forward, orange-lit by the fire, wearing a dark windbreaker and holding an assault rifle that looked too big for him. A complicated-looking scope had been mounted on the weapon. His thin hair was blowing. Embers fell all around him. There was a look of deep contentment on his face.

I said, "Mr. Burden—"

"Mahlon," he said. "I'd say we've reached the appropriate degree of familiarity, wouldn't you? Alex."

Smile.

I saw Milo tense. I stood, rooted.

"Don't be afraid," said Burden. "I'm friend, not foe."

He looked past me at the burning warehouse, gave the satisfied look of a Boy Scout who'd just rubbed two sticks together successfully. Over the roar and crackle I could still hear people screaming. Ashes fell onto my sweaty face, lacy, foul-smelling snowflakes.

Burden said, "You don't look well, Detective Sturgis. Let's get you to a hospital."

Milo was working hard at taking in breath. In the shimmer of the firelight his bruises looked awful—congealed and livid as sloppy special effects.

Burden said, "Come on, Detective."

Milo said, "Forget that." Shaking his head and spreading his arms for balance. "Linda Overstreet. They've sent someone to her place. Gotta get to a phone, call it in."

He took several lurching steps.

Burden said, "I'll do you one better, Detective." Snap of fingers. Another face out of the darkness. Early thirties, handsome, big walrus mustache over a clipped beard.

"Doctor, *you've* met Gregory Graff. Photographically. Here he is in the flesh. Gregory, help me with Detective Sturgis."

Graff stepped forward, very big, very broad. A rifle similar to Burden's was slung over his shoulder. He wore camouflage fatigues that looked as if they'd been French-laundered. His demeanor was pure concentration—a surgeon tying off a capillary.

He put one arm around Milo's shoulder, the other on Milo's elbow. Dwarfing Milo. Six five at least.

I took Milo's other arm.

Milo tried to shake us off. "I'm okay, god-dammit. Get me a phone!"

"This way," said Burden. He turned his back on the inferno and began walking fast.

We followed him out of the parking lot, soot blowing in our eyes. Milo insisted on walking without assistance, but shakily, still breathing with effort. Graff and I stayed by his side. I kept looking at my friend. Finally his breathing regularized. For all the punishment Milo'd taken, he seemed in decent shape.

What shape was Linda in? I tried not to think of that, could think of nothing else.

Someone who knows how to bring out the best in a woman . . .

My own breathing grew clogged. I fought for composure. We made our way through the darkness. Then a hideous tidal wave of sound—monsters at feeding time—rose behind us, and the lot was engulfed in bloody light.

Still moving, I looked back. Flames had burst through the roof of the warehouse and were shooting into the sky, bloodying it.

A few people had made it out to the landing dock, engulfed in flames, arms flapping and throwing off sparks. One of them dropped to the ground and rolled.

More screams.

Burden turned nonchalantly, raised his rifle to his shoulder, and squeezed off a frog-burst.

Milo said, "Forget that, goddammit. Move!"

"Covering our tracks," said Burden. "Always sound strategy in this type of mission." But he lowered the rifle and sprinted ahead.

Milo cursed and tried to walk faster. His legs gave out. Graff lifted him, slung him over his shoulder as if he were a straw man, and kept going without breaking step.

Milo protested and cursed. Graff ignored him.

"And *here* we are," said Burden.

The sheet-metal gate was propped open by a crowbar. Just beyond it, parked at the curb, was a van. Dark-gray, one blackened window on each side, the roof coiffured with antennas. Tongues of reflected fire from afar created the illusion of a low-rider mural along the slab sides. Dancing mural . . . hell on wheels . . .

I heard the shriek of sirens from somewhere in the distance. It reminded me of something . . . a crack alley . . . Dogs began howling.

Burden took something out of his pocket and pressed a button. Metallic click. The van's rear doors swung open.

Milo looked up at the antennas. "You have a phone. Put me down and let me use the fucking thing!"

Burden said, "Gregory, see that the detective's comfortable in the back."

Graff lifted Milo, bride-over-the-threshold style, and slid him into the back of the van.

Milo disappeared from view, cursing. The doors slammed shut.

I grabbed Burden's shoulder. "Stop playing games and let's get to the phone!"

Burden smiled and peeled my fingers off. "Oh, this is no game, Doctor. I feel I've done a very fine job of saving your life. The least you could do would be to trust me." He went around to the driver's side and said, "Hop in."

I opened the right-hand door. Two Recaro racing bucket seats in front; between them, a console bearing a mini-computer and phone modem. I got in the passenger seat and lifted the phone. Dead.

Burden was behind the wheel.

I said, "Activate it, damn you!"

Burden was expressionless. He handed his rifle back to Graff and put a key in the ignition. I looked back; the rear of the vehicle was a carpeted shell. Milo lay on the floor, sharing space with several metal boxes and some electronic gear that I couldn't identify. Graff knelt beside him, his big head brushing against the ceiling. A gun rack covered one wall of the shell. Semi-automatic handguns, rifles, something Uzi-like.

Milo forced himself up and grabbed the back of Burden's seat. "You sadistic little asshole!"

Graff pulled him off and held his wrist.

Milo cursed.

Burden said, "Such gratitude," and turned the key. The engine started and the dashboard became a light show: meters, dials, graphic displays, LED readouts. A row of circular dials on the front edge of the ceiling, parallel with the windshield. Still more dials on the console, on both sides of the computer, and surrounding the phone. Enough hardware to fill the cockpit of a 747.

Burden said, "Welcome to the official mobile testing lab of New Frontiers, Limited. Components come and go. I get free samples all the time, keep only the best."

I thought of Linda. Now his narcissism was deadly. Fighting down the urge to strangle him, I said, "*Please*. It's life and death."

He touched dark space to the right of the steering wheel. A square yellow screen the size of a cocktail coaster appeared. Black numbers flashed: a two-digit combination followed by seven more numbers that kept changing. Below the screen a key pad. The light from the screen revealed two more phones, freehand, dash-mounted, their buttons banana-yellow.

"Police scanner," said Burden, playing the pad with four fingers. "Programmable for any region of the world. Which in and of itself is nothing out of the ordinary. But this one has been modified—it can be used to interface with police dispatch systems and *place* calls." Smile. Gorging himself on power. "Totally illegal. Please don't tell on me, Detective Sturgis."

I said, "For God's sake, call it in!" and shouted Linda's address.

"I know the address," he said. "Would you like me to place the call or would you prefer to do it yourse—"

"Just do it!"

He clucked his tongue, punched another button that froze the numbers on the scanner, and picked up one of the dash phones.

"All West L.A. units," he said in a voice not his own. "All West L.A. units and"—peering—"Eight A-twenty-nine. ADW in progress, possible attempt One-eighty-seven." He rattled off street and number, specified Linda's apartment. "Code Three. I repeat . . ."

The radio talked back via a speaker on the ceiling. A patrolman's voice confirmed taking the call. Within seconds two more units had called in Code Six—assisting.

"There," Burden said, pushing a button that darkened the dash, "that should take care of it."

"Drive there, asshole," said Milo.

"What about your injuries, Detective Sturgis?"

"Just get the fuck over there."

Burden's seat swiveled. He looked back. "Gregory?"

Graff lifted one of Milo's arms, flexed it gently.

Milo said, "Get the fuck off me, Paul Bunyan. Drive, Burden, or I *will* bust you for something."

Graff said, "Doesn't look like anything's broken, Mr. Burden." A basso befitting his size. Good elocution. New England inflections.

The sirens grew louder.

Burden said, "The last thing I want is to be accused of medical negligence. Particularly with regard to an officer of the law."

Milo said, "Get moving, you smug little fuck."

Burden's face turned stony in the dashlight. "I'll put that down to shock, Detective."

Milo cursed some more.

Burden's face got harder.

I said, "Look, it's been a long night for all of us. We appreciate what you've done—saving us. But let's make it perfect by trying to save Linda too."

He looked at me. "Perfect? No, I don't think so."

He sat with his hands on the steering wheel as the sirens grew deafening. Finally he fastened his seat belt, gave the van gas, and pulled away from the curb. Just as we turned out of the winding alley, the fire trucks came charging through.

I said, "Where are we?"

"Van Nuys," Burden said. "That red light is Victory Boulevard."

Milo said, "Shoot the light."

Burden said, "Such a bad influence, Detective," but he sped through the blackened intersection.

I said, "How about we turn the scanner on, hear what's happening."

He shook his head. "Not necessary. Have some faith, Doctor."

At first I thought it just another power play, but a block later he said, "No doubt you'll want to know how it was done. Your liberation."

From the back, Milo said, "The fucking punch line." He began to cough.

Graff said, "Here, drink some water."

"Sure water is all it is, Paul?"

"That's all it is," rumbled Graff, babysitter-patient.

Burden said, "Detective Sturgis, you're a hostile, ill-mannered man. Too many years of being on the outside?"

The therapist in me yearned to turn that back on him.

"Christ," Milo said.

I heard him gulping, looked back, and saw Graff holding a canteen to his lips.

Burden said, "It's water, all right. Pure spring water from Washington State. Artesian springs, water with a natural mineral composition miraculously matched to the body's own electro-chemical requirements. What page, Gregory?"

Slowing the van as he talked. The streets were desolate; clear sailing. I wanted to shove my foot down on the accelerator.

Graff said, "Seven, section two."

"Beauty and Balance," I said.

Burden said, "Very good, Alex."

Another red light. Riverside. This time he stopped. "Let's see, freeway or canyon—at this hour, I'd say freeway."

He headed west.

I said, "Of course I want to know. How'd you do it?"

"Any hypotheses?"

"A few."

"Let's hear them."

"For starts, you tapped my phone. The time you dropped in at my house."

My very nice *home*. Asking to use the *facilities* so he could have time alone in the rear of the house. Crying and spilling his coffee in order to have time alone in the living room. Me adding to his worktime by waiting in the kitchen so that he could compose himself . . .

"Very *good*," he said. "But actually it went far beyond the phones. I installed listening devices in several locations in and around your house—under furniture and beds. Near the front door. Today's technology permits incredible ease of installation. I've got units no bigger than a grain of rice—though the ones I used for you were larger. Lentil-sized. Self-adhesive. Long-distance, super-high resolution, tunable—"

I said, "Section five. Life and Limb." Stroking him while realizing all he'd heard. Phone conversations. Pillow talk. The violation . . .

He was my liberator but I didn't like him any better for it.

Being saved by him was like finding out God existed but that He had a bad personality.

He said, "Actually, these particular components haven't been featured in the catalogue yet. So you got a sneak preview. I'd be happy to leave them installed, show you how to use them for your own benefit."

"No thanks."

"No doubt you're feeling intruded upon. But monitoring your input and output was necessary. You were my informational conduit. To the school, the police—all of them. No one would help me. Everyone treated me as if I were a pariah. I needed good data—that was my *right*. I knew I had to be thorough. I pretuned the units to receivers in *my* house. Identical receivers were also installed in this van. No one else could possibly receive the transmission, so you needn't be concerned that anyone else was monitoring you. And the tapes will be destroyed very shortly."

"I appreciate that."

Unable to keep the sarcasm out of my voice. But he missed it or ignored it.

We were on the Sherman Oaks/North Hollywood border now, approaching Coldwater. A few cars on the street. Late diners heading home from the restaurants on Ventura. More lights, then the on-ramp to the 134 West.

He said, "The lentils are manufactured in *Poland,* of all places, though I suppose the actual research and development came out of the Soviet Union. Glasnost and perestroika have been a boon for those of us interested in the free exchange of advanced technology. The distributor in Hong Kong was more than happy to send me a boxful of the little devils at great discount in the hopes that I'd feature them in the next catalogue. It didn't work out that way, did it, Gregory?"

"No, Mr. B. Too expensive for our target audience."

"Very expensive—even at discount. But only the best for you, Dr. Delaware. Because I respect you. Your tenacity. I had high expectations of the quality of information you'd be able to shunt to me. And I was right, wasn't I? So I'd say the lentils paid for themselves. As did the homing tracers I placed in your Seville and in Detective Sturgis's Matador and Fiat. Unfortunately, I couldn't quite get to the Ford he traded for the Matador, but by that time I had enough data to be able to trace his abduction."

"What a guy," said Milo.

No longer hoarse now. Clear and quiet and enraged.

I knew what he was thinking: Burden had let him endure the interrogation. Waiting. Listening.

I said, "Howard was your conduit too. You dropped in on him and waited in his office so you could install your lentils."

And hear every hateful word his son had spewed.

"Absolutely," he said. A little too nonchalantly. "Holly's behavior had been puzzling— distant, preoccupied. Due to her communication problems, I couldn't draw it out of her. I knew she'd snuck over to Howard's, both of them thinking I didn't know about their little attempt at rapport-building. I thought Howard might be able to shed some light on the change in his sister, now that the two of them were *communicating*."

"But you couldn't simply ask Howard about it, because he also has communication problems."

"Exactly."

I remembered the loathing that had filled Howard's office. How was a father able to deal with that—to defend against it?

I looked over at him. Placid. Blocking it out. Narcissism in service to the soul.

He made a left turn onto the freeway. All six lanes were as empty as Indy the day after the race.

"Howard's a bright boy," he said, "but he's got many, many problems. Blind spots. You saw how obese and nervous he is. How he sweats. He gets eczema too. Gastric discomfort and insomnia. Clear signs of unhappiness. Constitutional weakness made worse by a poor attitude toward life. If he'd allowed me, I could have helped him with all of it. Perhaps one day he will. In the meantime, I couldn't let his weakness get in the way."

"That's why you were so eager for me to meet with him. Hoping he might open up to me and you'd get it all on tape."

He smiled. "More than hope. Data-based prediction. The conversation between the two of you ended up being a very useful transmission."

"Wannsee Two," I said. "Howard described how Holly had babbled about that the day her sister-in-law came over. I set out to learn what it meant. You listened and taped and followed along."

"No, no," he said, annoyed. "I didn't need you for that. I was one step ahead of you. I know enough history to understand exactly what *Wannsee* was. Vahn-say is the correct pronunciation, of course. Gregory knows about Wannsee too, even though he's from your generation. Because a good deal of Gregory's family was eliminated by the Nazis. So when I called and told him we were dealing with Wannsee Two, he was more than eager to get involved in this project. Weren't you, Gregory?"

"Absolutely, Mr. B."

"Good ventriloquism," said Milo. "Where'd you find a dummy this big?"

Graff gave a deep loose laugh.

"Hardly," said Burden. "Gregory's got training in electronics and biophysics under his belt, a year of medical school at an Ivy League university, a law degree from that same university, and graduate studies in business."

Pride. Paternal pride.

His real son.

I said, "Sounds like a real renaissance man." One part of my brain thinking about Linda and running at Methedrine pace. Another making small talk, trying to get information from the odd, scary man in the driver's seat.

"Bet he has military training, too," I said. "Former intelligence officer, same as you. That's how you found him, isn't it? Not some modeling agency. When it was time to recruit a partner, you knew precisely where to go."

"I'm not a partner," said Graff. "Just a figurehead." More laughter.

Burden laughed too. The exchange to the 405 appeared. He took it going south, and moved into the center lane, maintaining a steady seventy miles per.

I said, "How about going a little faster."

He didn't answer, but the speedometer climbed to seventy-five.

Wanting a hundred but knowing that was all I was going to get, I said, "Here's another hypothesis: Between the two of you, New Frontiers has access to military computers. Ahlward had a military background. You checked him out."

"Military background," said Graff. Bear-growl laughter.

Burden didn't join in. "He was the *first* one I researched. Before I approached *you*. The press was painting him as some kind of hero. I wanted to learn about the one who actually pulled the trigger. The hero who'd killed my daughter. What I found out smelled bad. He'd lied about being a military man."

His tone said that was the ultimate felony.

"All he had was seven months in the Marine Corps. April of 'sixty-seven to November of 'sixty-eight. A good part of it in the brig before he was dishonorably discharged for moral turpitude. A closed file that I managed to open. Two separate incidents. Sexual harassment of a sixteen-year-old girl—a black girl—and attempts to organize a white-supremacist gang among other new recruits. It was the latter that made me research him further. After his discharge he enjoyed brief stints in local jails for theft and burglary and disorderly conduct. I decided he was scum, looked into his family history. His father had been a Bundist war criminal. Ran one of their summer camps. Schweiben. Ahlward Senior was imprisoned for sedition in 1944, released in 1947, only to die a year later of cirrhosis. Alcoholic scum. Multigenerational scum. Which led to another question: why would a supposedly liberal-minded city councilman hire someone like that? So I researched the city councilman too. Found nothing there but a piece of lint masquerading as a man. Good family, all the privileges, not a trace of hardship in his background. Not a trace of character either. Addiction to the path of least resistance. Needless to say, he found his way into the latrine we know as politics."

Angry words but a conversational tone.

"I monitored Latch's headquarters. Easy as pie, right, Gregory? But that didn't teach me much. Latch's people displayed a modicum of discipline—tended to be circumspect over the phone. But you were doing a fine job as my conduit, putting it all together: Novato, the old woman, that pathetic washout Crevolin. For a brief period I thought the vandalization of Ms.—Excuse me—*Dr.* Overstreet's car was related to it. But Detective Sturgis proved me wrong. Congratulations, Detective."

"Fuck off and drive."

"Nevertheless, the rest of it proved what I'd known all along: that my daughter had been a victim herself. A dupe. I put it all together before either of you did. And in answer to the question you asked of Howard, Doctor, my political beliefs are antithetical to fascism. I believe in unrestrained free enterprise, minimal government control. Live and let live. On condition the other side behaves itself."

"Die and let die," said Graff. "Never again."

"Gregory and I had no trouble believing in Wannsee Two. Because of our military background, our access to classified data. We knew what had gone on in various army bases during the late seventies. Racist cells that the armed forces broke up swiftly. But at the cost of discharging the fascists into the weak, civilian world, where irregularities couldn't be dealt with as efficiently. That insight and experience gave me the edge. I knew from the careful way Latch's people handled themselves over the phone that there had to be some other place they did their dirty work—a secret headquarters where the swine spoke freely. But they never let on, not through all the monitoring. Then I thought of Latch's wife. Began tracing properties deeded to her. Burrowing through the layers of corporations she'd wrapped around herself. Piercing that kind of cocoon is absurdly easy if you know how, and I quickly came up with several possibilities—despite the fact that she's a very well-landed lady. I was in the process of narrowing down the list when you made my job easy. Calling Detective Sturgis last night and leaving him the message about your being followed. That license plate. I have trace capacities better than most police departments—millions of licenses in my data bank. I matched your number to one of my possibilities, a company listed as a printing facility. Gregory and I were there just after sundown. Saw Detective Sturgis being delivered there. Listening. Show him, Gregory."

Graff lifted something from the floor of the van. Glass cone with a microphone in the center.

"This is a Stevens Twenty-five-X long-range parabolic microphone," said Burden. "Good up to two miles."

I said, "Another sample of Eastern Bloc creativity?"

"Perish the thought," said Burden. "This one's all-American."

"Born in the U.S.A.," said Graff.

Burden said, "When you arrived, trussed and shackled, Detective Sturgis, we were waiting. You held up nicely. Your own military background, no doubt—quite impressive. Rest assured that had you been in any serious danger, we would have saved you, but we knew from our previous monitoring that they planned to keep you alive, finish both you and the doctor off in a sexually suggestive manner. You, however, had no way of knowing that and you did very well."

"Aw, shucks," said Milo.

"I'd suggest," said Burden, "that you conserve your anger for those who deserve it. For example, why do you think they came after you in the first place, masquerading as FBI?"

Silence from the back.

"Are you truly ignorant, Detective? Or just repressing?"

No answer.

Graff said, "Your own people sold you out. Extremely bad form."

I said, "Frisk."

Burden nodded. "Another piece of lint. When he came to interrogate me, the day of the shooting, he actually attempted to install a monitoring device in my living room. Primitive piece of junk. Needless to say, I left it in place. Talked to it, played the cello for it. Leading Frisk exactly where I wanted to lead him: in circles. Because he's a moron, I could see right away there'd be no use working with him. The next time I saw him at his office, I returned the favor. So I have a very clear picture of what he's been up to. And it's nothing I would tolerate if I were you, Detective."

"Polish lentils at Parker Center?" said Milo.

"Our vaunted Anti-Terrorist Division," said Burden. "If it wasn't so sad, it would be funny, the incompetence. You see, Latch and company have

been under investigation for quite some time. But
not for the right reasons. Frisk hasn't the slightest
inkling, no suspicions about Wannsee Two. *He*
suspects Latch of being a communist subversive,
an unrepentant left-winger—because Latch's political enemies have been feeding him that."

"Massengil?" I said.

"Among others. The late assemblyman was a
prime source of disinformation on Latch, because
he knew Latch had designs on his job. Dr. Dobbs
helped him compose little false reports of Latch's
supposed subversive activities. Dr. Dobbs actually
made direct phone calls to Frisk. Using a code
name. Santa. Talking on pay phones. All of it
very malicious and childish. Cinematic cloak-and-
dagger nonsense. But our Lieutenant Frisk took it
very seriously. Compiled a file on Latch—a classified file."

Chuckles. Echoed by Graff.

I said, "Why didn't he move against Latch?"

"He considered it," said Burden. "I have
recordings of him talking to his dictaphone, thinking out loud, considering his options. Playing
every angle against the other, ruminating end-
lessly. But he was afraid to confront Latch without
solid evidence, yet unable to get any evidence,
because A, he didn't know how, and B, the whole
thing was a sham. The man really is incredibly
stupid. That's why he was so eager to take over the
Massengil murder. He suspected Latch might be

behind it—this would be his big chance. And he was right."

"But for the wrong reasons."

"The idiot," said Burden. "He actually believed he had a chance to be promoted to deputy chief. You, Detective Sturgis, were considered a threat to that ambition. The possibility that you might solve the case yourself. You threaten him because down deep he knows you're what he isn't—a competent investigator. And also, of course, on another level. I believe 'despicable fag bastard' is the way he generally refers to you. If you'd like, I can play you the tapes."

Milo was silent.

Burden got off the freeway at the Pico exit and headed east, toward Westwood.

"During the course of my brief surveillance," he said, "I haven't been mightily impressed by the Police Department. Too much time spent on what officers do in bed, whom they do it with, religious beliefs, other irrelevant issues. That's not the way you win a war. It must be an awful strain on you, Detective Sturgis."

Milo said, "Thanks for the sympathy, Mother Teresa." But I could tell he was digesting what Burden had told him.

Burden drove smoothly and rapidly. "Like a true politician, Frisk used you. Called Latch. As a supposed confidant. Informed him that *you* were the one who was suspicious about him. *Apolo-*

getic. You were an embarrassment to the Department. A rogue cop. Rogue fag cop, with a drinking problem. The Department only kept you on the payroll to avoid lawsuits and political hassles. It was only a matter of time before you'd be drummed out in disgrace. Frisk told Latch you'd been asking questions about him, were unstable, prone to violence. Warning the good councilman. So Latch began having you—and Dr. Delaware—tailed. Meanwhile, Frisk tailed Latch. You were his decoy, Detective. Had you died tonight, he might have blundered into a solution, maybe even had glory and his promotion. Deputy Chief Frisk. Wouldn't that be lovely?"

Milo thought out loud: "He didn't tail me tonight."

"No, not tonight. Tell him why, Gregory."

"He and his staff are having a retreat," said Graff. "Lake Arrowhead."

Burden said, "To share feelings. Outline management strategy. Frisk is a modern policeman. Reads his textbooks and knows his operations manuals."

I said, "Sounds like something out of Dobbs's book of tricks."

"They're all the same," said Burden. "Pencil-pushers. In any event, don't you think I'm a hundred percent correct, Detective? About focusing your anger properly?"

Two blocks of silence.

We approached Sepulveda.

Burden said, "Do you want to know what we used to demolish the building?"

On the edge of my seat. Linda, Linda . . . "Sure."

"Selectively applied dabs of plastique. Not Semtex. Something better. Brand-new."

"A little dab'll do you," said Graff.

"A *very* little dab," said Burden. "Complete with a tiny little detonating cell stuck smack in the middle. They didn't see us because the entire front wall of the warehouse was windowless. Their idea of security, but they ended up hoist on their own petard. Gregory dabbed, then retreated to the van, where we relaxed, ate sandwiches, and listened. You were very good, Doctor. Trying to play them off against each other. Holding onto your nerves. Then, when the time came, we pushed buttons."

"Boom," said Graff.

"I'd say it was poetic justice," said Burden. "Wouldn't you? Too bad Mr. Latch wasn't around to see it. What exactly happened to him? We heard some sort of commotion."

I waited for Milo to reply. When he didn't, I said, "He fell on Ahlward's knife. It went through his neck."

"Splendid." Big smile. "*Literally* hoist on his own petard. What a pretty picture. My only regret was that I wasn't there to see it. All in all, a very productive adventure, wouldn't you say, Gregory?"

"A-one, Mr. B."

"Lots of people died," I said. "There'll be questions."

Burden took one hand off the steering wheel and made a whoop-de-doo spinning gesture. "The more questions the merrier. City and state commissions, senate subcommittees, our beloved press. Bring them all on. I love Washington, D.C., in the winter. A certain bleakness sets in on the Capitol Mall that matches the spirit of the petty bunch who work there. I especially love it when I go there with something to trade."

"The unmasking of Ahlward's other covert Nazis?"

"It should prove to be quite a revelation," he said. "After I supply the names, I guarantee you I'll be a hero. *People* magazine. *Entertainment Tonight. A Current Affair.* Popular enough to run for office and win, if I had the poor taste to harbor such ambitions. I, however, will choose to avoid the limelight and most of my fame will fade fairly quickly—that's the age we live in. The public has no attention span, craves constant novelty. Meanwhile, Gregory and I will be mapping out a strategy for harnessing whatever good will we've garnered in Washington. For business purposes. I've been thinking about increasing my Weaponry division for a while, anyway."

"Makes sense," I said. "Life and Limb. Buy your AK-forty-seven from the man who knows."

"Very good, Alex. Have you ever thought of applying your psychological skills to marketing?"

"Not this year."

Westwood Boulevard came into view, backed by the night-gloomed mass of the Pavilion. We turned right.

I said, "Sounds like you've got it all figured out."

"That's my business. Anticipating. Under-standing trends, mapping behavioral patterns." Pause. "Not that I can ever be compensated for my loss."

I looked over at him.

"They took what was mine," he said. "Fatal error."

36

Ambulances. Crime-scene van. Another domino spill of squad cars, roof-flashers pulsing in counterpoint to my heartbeat.

All the old mechanical vultures, familiar as pets . . . A street without them would look naked.

Burden pulled the van behind one of the black-and-whites. A very young-looking cop came over to the driver's window and said, "If you people don't live around here, you'll have to move."

Milo said, "It's okay, Sitz." Propping himself up on his elbows, his face just visible over the driver's bucket seat.

The officer tensed and peered in.

"It's me, Sitz."

"Detective Sturgis? You okay, sir?"

"Big trouble out in Van Nuys. Fire, multiple deaths. I was lucky—all I lost was my shirt and ID. These good citizens helped get me over here.

Possibly related to one of my cases. What's the situation?"

"Attempt One-eighty-seven. Detective Hardy's up there. We haven't heard much—"

As Milo reached over and opened the door, Sitz backed away from it. I was out of the van like a bandit, running, hearing Milo's voice behind me: "It's okay, let him go."

Racing up the walkway to the apartment, past a pair of technicians carrying crime-scene kits, a handful of gawkers in nightclothes lounging behind a tape line.

Ducking under the tape. Someone said, "Whoa, *he's* stressed out."

Another cop came forward, one hand on his gun. Tall, thin, beach tan over pimples. Heavy underbite. God, they were hiring them young.

I said, "I need to get up there."

He held me back with one arm. "Are you a resident of the building, sir?"

"Yes."

He raised the clipboard. "Name and apartment number?"

My heart threatened to burst out of my chest. I contemplated violence.

Underbite sensed it and touched his gun.

A voice at my back. "It's okay, Stoppard."

Milo was trying to look dignified with his wounds and his tattered undershirt.

Underbite stared at him and said, "Sir?"

"I said it's *okay*, Stoppard."

Underbite stepped aside.

I raced forward, legs churning. Into the green-foil lobby. Another uniform holding the closet/elevator open. When he saw me, he touched his pistol too. A second later, when he saw Milo, he gave a B-movie double take.

Milo said, "Out of the elevator, Buell. Stay in the lobby."

A silent, maddening ride up three flights. So slow. Endless. Me punching the walls of the elevator. Milo just standing there, close to me. I knew he could smell my fear, but he made no effort to distance himself.

When the elevator finally bumped to a stop, I squeezed myself through the door before it was completely open. More green foil. Racing to the far end.

Cop at the door. Always cops. Suspicious eyes. Milo giving the okay.

"Yes, sir."

Through her door, now tagged with an LAPD crime-scene label. Into her living room. Bright lights. Perfume smell. Oyster walls. Fresh vacuum tracks in gold carpeting—what an organized young lady. Stretched out on the carpet, something human-sized in a black zipped bag.

I broke down, sank to my knees.

A gray-haired, bearded man in a bottle-green blazer and gray flannels sat at the butcher-block table holding a mini-recorder. Black Gladstone bag at his feet. Stethoscope around his neck. Different kind of house call.

He looked up at me. Diagnostic appraisal. But no sympathy—just curiosity.

Sounds from the bedroom.

I got up, staggered in.

More perfume. Cloying.

A slender balding black man in a navy-blue suit stood by the brass bed, holding a note pad and gold pen. The covers were in disarray.

Linda sat on the bottom sheet, shoulders hunched, knees drawn to her chest, wearing a pink quilted robe. Staring off into space.

I ran to her. Held marble.

The man in the navy suit turned. Such a nice suit. He'd always had a thing for clothes. Dapper half of the "odd couple" when he'd partnered with Milo. Tonight no exception . . . sky-blue broadcloth shirt with white pin collar, red-and-blue paisley tie . . .

Rust-red. Just a shade lighter than the muddy spots on the mirror above the dresser.

Rust on the plaster too. Three holes, radiating spider-leg cracks, left of the mirror, tight formation. The top surface of the dresser a wasteland of tipped perfume bottles, free-form blood blotches, shattered mirror-tray. Blood looped down the front of a drawer. The carpet was a collage of glass shards, more mud, something metallic. A snub-

nosed revolver with a walnut grip. To my unprac-
ticed eye, identical to the one Milo carried when
he carried.

Delano Hardy looked at me with surprise and
said, "Doc. She talked about you. Was worried
about you."

"I'm fine."

"She's gonna be fine too." The power of
wishful thinking.

I held her tighter, stroked her back. Still
frozen.

". . . and she did a good job," Del was
saying. "Protected herself, which is what it's all
about, right?"

He pointed to the revolver.

I'm a crack shot. . . .

Very softly, he said, "Tough lady. She's got
my vote for sheriff. Gave her statement really
coherently. Then, when we were through, she got
real quiet, sank into the way she is now—the
shock's settling in, according to the coroner. Not
physical shock, psychological—*your* neck of the
woods. Physically she's okay, the vital signs and
everything. Coroner checked her out, said she was
tough, gave her something to take the edge off,
make her sleepy. Said she looks fine physically,
but should go in for a couple days observation.
Ambulance from UCLA is on its way."

Talking faster than I'd ever heard Del Hardy
talk. Despite all the years, all the bodies, still able

to be affected. I remembered why I liked him. Apart from the fact that he'd saved my life. Once upon a time . . .

I said, "It's down there already, Del."

"What's that?"

"The ambulance. It's here."

"Oh." Del looked at me diagnostically too.

I held Linda closer, tried to engulf her, be everything for her. Finally she molded to me, but remained cold and inert as modeling clay.

Milo came into the room.

Del's eyes widened. "Must have been some kind of party, guy."

Milo said, "Hot time in the old town, Del. Shoulda been there." Battered, but oddly authoritative. His gaze rested on Linda. He and Del traded cop-to-cop eye signals. As in the past, I felt like an outsider. Didn't mind.

Hardy repeated the few facts he'd just told me, seemed to be talking even faster. Pushing comfort.

Linda began to tremble violently. I held on to her but it wasn't enough to make her stop.

Milo's big face drooped with pain and empathy. He said, "Let's talk outside, Del."

Del nodded, put away his pen and pad and said, "Keep her warm, Doc. Pull the covers over her. She's supposed to be resting."

They left.

I lowered her down on the bed and gathered

the comforter around her. Stroked her face, her hair. She was still shaking. Gradually it slowed, then ceased. She began breathing rhythmically. I touched her cheek. Kissed it. Kissed her eyes. Waited until I was certain she was deeply asleep before returning to the living room.

Del and Milo were walking the green-jacketed coroner to the door. His trousers had a sharp crease. Everyone had dressed for tonight.

Milo had on a couple of bandages.

After the coroner was gone, Del pointed to the body bag.

"Intruder got in by picking the lock," he said. "B-and-E tools, professional set. But he made too much noise doing it and woke up the victim—Dr. Overstreet. Not that it was a particularly sloppy job—pretty good, actually."

Pointing to the doorjamb. I couldn't see any scratch marks.

Milo examined it and said, "Spick-and-span, no print dust. No dust in the bedroom either. I saw the print boys down there. What's the delay?"

"My orders," said Del. "Haven't authorized them yet. The uniforms who got here don't think they touched the jamb but they did touch the knob and they trampled the bedroom pretty darned good charging it—it was a Code Three. They were after prevention, not preservation."

Milo said, "Yeah."

Del said, "Let me ask you. Any reason to go through the whole shebang, trash her place? Most of it's light surfaces—that means the black dust. You know what a godawful mess that makes. Seems like a clear-cut self-defense situation. Coroner says height of the spatters backs up everything she said."

Milo thought and rubbed his face and said, "No reason."

"I mean, if we're going to get into a giant hassle, let's do it, Milo. But I just don't see the point."

"No point," said Milo. "I'll handle any procedural hassles." Glance at the body bag. "Tell me a bedtime story, Del."

Del said, "Okay, so she hears the door opening, wakes up. She's normally a good sleeper but tonight she was jumpy because of the doc's call." He looked at me. "Something about your being followed, some weird Nazi stuff that I couldn't really make out. What I did get was that 'cause *you* sounded worried, that worried her."

"Goddam good reason to be worried," said Milo.

Del stared at Milo's wounds and said, "Your hot party's related to this?"

Milo let out a long sigh; suddenly he looked weak and wasted. "It's a long story, Del. You wouldn't believe it if I tried to give it to you for free."

"I'm open-minded," said Del.

Milo smiled. "It's a *four*-drink story, Delano. You buy; I tell."

"After the paperwork?"

"Fuck the paperwork."

Hardy shrugged. "You're the D-Three. Someone gets on my case, I blame it all on you. You sure you don't want a blanket?"

"I'm fine," said Milo. "Tell the story."

"Where was I," said Del. "Yeah, she was jumpy—so jumpy she took her gun out of storage. S and W Police Special. Apparently it used to belong to someone named Mondo back in Texas where she's originally from—she didn't want to talk about that. I couldn't get that part real clear. If the reg isn't kosher, I imagine we can work that out, too, right? No Bernie Goetz illegal weapons bullshit. Anyway, she had a box of bullets for it, loaded it up, put it on her night stand, and had it ready to grab when she heard the intruder out in the living room. Intruder came tippy-toeing in. There was light from the window above the bed. She could see the intruder swinging something— we found it over in the corner. Louisville Slugger with nails sticking out of it, real pretty. She yelled at the intruder to stop. Intruder kept coming. She yelled again, kept yelling. Intruder didn't pay any mind. So she emptied the gun. Three slugs in the intruder, three near-misses in the wall. She's a damn good shot, considering the situation. Hope she doesn't waste too much time on guilt."

He knelt beside the bag. "Now for the interesting part." Tugging down and parting a foot of zipper. It sounded like something ripping.

A face stared up at us.

Female. Capuchin-monkey face under dirty-blond hair. Mussed hair. Eyes closed, the left one puffy and plum-colored. Skin tinted gray—the greenish-gray reserved for Death's palette. A quarter-sized, black-edged ruby hole in the left cheek. Dry lips, parted. Between them a sliver of corn-niblet tooth.

"A woman," said Hardy. "Can you top that? No ID, nothing on her. One thing we *should* have them dust is the bat. Hopefully we'll pull something off of that."

"She calls herself Crisp," I said. "Audrey Crisp. That may or may not be her real name."

"Yeah?" said Del. "Well, Crisp got herself crisped." Shaking his head. Tugging the zipper another inch lower. "Want to see more?"

"Anything to see?" said Milo.

"Just two more holes down below."

Milo shook his head.

Del zipped up the bag. "Lady with a baseball bat—all those spikes, like one of those medieval things. Mace, or something. Gotta be one for the books, right? Ever see that before, Milo?"

I walked back into the bedroom. Sat on the

bed. Linda opened her eyes, muttered something that could have been my name.

With no evidence to the contrary, I decided it had been my name.

The power of wishful thinking . . .

I brushed hair away from her brow and kissed it.

She whimpered and turned on her side, facing me, looking up at me.

I lay down beside her and closed my eyes. When the ambulance attendants came for her, they had to wake me. Had to pry my arm from around her waist, and hers from mine.

37

Her father flew in the next morning from Texas. I'd expected Gary Cooper and got Lyndon Johnson out of a trash compactor: short, stout, big ears with banjo lobes, whiskey nose, crinkle chin. The only genetic link to Linda I could discern, a pair of small, delicate hands that he kept plastered to his sides. Nothing Texas Rangerish about his clothes either. Powder-blue sport coat, yellow golf shirt, white seersucker slacks, brown patent-leather loafers.

He called me *sir* a lot, not sure who I was. Not sure who his daughter was. When he walked into the hospital room, she gave a weary smile and I left the two of them alone.

She left with him the following day, promising to call when she got to San Antonio. Following through that evening, but sounding tentative herself, as if someone was listening in and she was unable to talk freely.

I told her to take her time healing. That I'd check to make sure the kids at Hale were okay. That I was there for her whenever she needed me. Working at making it sound convincing—putting a little therapist in my voice.

She said, "That means a lot to me, Alex. I know the kids are going to be okay. The person they're using for substitute principal is really good. I went to school with him—he'll do a good job."

"I'm glad."

"Can he call you? For advice?"

"Of course."

"Thanks. You're so terrific."

"My head is swelling swelling swelling."

"I mean it—you are. By the way, Carla has your gift—we got a gift for you. Last week. It's a set of Mark Twain. The complete works. I know you like books. I hope you like Twain."

"I love Twain."

"It's an old leather set, really pretty. I found it for you myself, in an antiques store. Wish I could be there to give it to you. But Carla will send it to you. Unless you're at the school. Then you can pick it up. In my office. On the desk."

"I'll go by. Thanks."

Pause.

"Alex, I know this is nervy, but do you think

you could possibly come on out here, spend some time with me? Not just yet, but maybe a little later?"

"Sounds good to me."

"Great! I'll take you around. Show you a good time. I promise. You can have grits for the second time. As soon as things settle down."

"Look forward to it. Remember the Alamo."

"Remember me."

Later that day Robin came by, with deli sandwiches and jug wine, a beautiful smile and a soft quick kiss on the lips.

We sat facing each other at the ash burl trestle table she'd hand-carved years ago.

First time in a long time we'd been in the same room. If we'd scheduled it, I'd have spent hours dreading it. But it ended up nice. Nothing physical, nothing covert or calculated or stiff. No excavation of old wounds, debridement of damaged flesh. It wasn't denial. There just didn't seem to be any scars either of us could see or feel. Or maybe it was the wine.

We sat talking and eating and drinking, discussing the piss-poor state of the world, occupational hazards, occupational joys. Trading bad jokes. The space between us smooth, soft. Baby-smooth. As if we'd birthed something healthy.

I started to believe friendship was possible.

When she left, my loneliness was tempered by the pleasant confusion of hope. And when Milo came by to pick me up, I was in an amazingly good mood.

38

Surveillance. Numb butts.

But nice to be on the other side.

The first couple of days yielded no results. I learned about cop boredom, about self-doubt. About how even the best of friendships get strained by too much of nothing. But I refused Milo's repeated offers to drop out.

"What? Your year for masochism?"

"My year for closure."

"If your guess is right," he said.

"If."

"Lots of ifs."

I said, "If you don't want to bother, I'll do it myself."

He smiled. "Joe Detective?"

"Joe Curious. You think I'm reaching? It was just a look."

He turned to me. The swelling down, his wounds greening, but one eye was still puffy and wet and his gait was stiff.

"No, Alex," he said softly. "I think you're worth listening to. I've always thought so. Besides, what do we have to lose except sanity, and not much of that left, right? It's only been forty-eight hours. Let's give it at least another couple of days."

So we sat in the rented car until our butts turned downright frozen. Ate stale fast food, did crossword puzzles, engaged in inane chatter that neither of us would have tolerated under different circumstances.

The second day it happened. The maroon Volvo rolled away from suburbia, the way it always did. But this time it abandoned home territory and headed for the 405 Freeway.

Milo hung back until it had climbed a northbound on-ramp, then followed, hanging back several car lengths.

"You see," he said, turning the steering wheel with one finger. "This is the way it's done. Subtly. No way short of psychic powers he's going to see us."

Bravado in his voice but he kept checking the rearview mirror.

I said, "How're *your* psychic powers?"

"Finely honed." A moment later. "I knew the Department would buy my story, didn't I?"

His story. Post-traumatic stress reaction. A need for seclusion.

Escape from L.A.

He'd been thorough. Buying an airplane ticket for Indianapolis. Showing up at LAX only to duck out of line just before boarding. Picking up a rental Cadillac and driving into the Valley. Checking into a motel out in Agoura under the name S. L. Euth.

Then surveillance. The other side.

Picking me up at a preassigned place that changed each day.

Watching. Making sure *we* weren't being watched.

Today he had on a brown polo shirt, tan cords, white sneakers, and an old felt Dodgers cap on his head.

"Umm, nice leather," he said, fondling the mocha-colored armrest that bisected the sedan De Ville's bench seat. "Nice, even if it does drive mushy. I can see why you hold on to yours."

"Not too obtrusive for a tail?"

"L.A. Chevy, pal. Your pricier neighborhoods, this is what the *help* drives." He smiled. "Besides, it's brown. Like my fashion statement. Blends in with all the bullshit."

We followed the Volvo onto the 101 toward Ventura, stayed with it all the way through the west Valley. When it switched to the 23 North just past Westlake Village, Milo sat up straighter and smiled.

I said, "Let's hear it for educated guesses."

We sped past an industrial park with high-tech leanings. Vaguely ominous limestone and mirror-glass buildings with nondescript logos, security-gated parking lots, and streets with names like Science Drive and Progress Circle. The Volvo kept going.

When traffic thinned out at Moorpark, Milo pulled over to the shoulder and stopped.

I said, "What is it?"

"Now we *are* too conspicuous. Gonna give him a mile, then get back on."

"Not worried about losing him?"

He shook his head. "We know where he's going, don't we?"

"If our information's up to date."

He said, "The *Colonel*'s information." Frowned and checked his watch and got back on the highway. The highway became Grimes Canyon and evolved into a narrow, serpentine mountain pass. No other cars going our way; a few huge tankers coming from the opposite direction. The curves challenged the Cadillac and Milo put two hands on the wheel. Shifting his weight, he said, "Now the mushiness isn't fun."

I said, "You could have borrowed the Colonel's Honda."

"Right. God knows what kind of crap and gizmos he's packed it with. Would you feel comfortable talking in something he owned?"

"Nope."

"Him and his *data* banks. Guy's got more

info than the IRS. You see how fast he came up with what we wanted? But try to get something on *him*, and other data banks dry up real fast. I had a very reliable source on it, Alex. Same guy in Washington who helped me trace Kaltenblud. All his computer had to say about the *Colonel* was name, rank, date of discharge. Ditto with Major Bunyan."

I said, "New Age warrior becomes New Age entrepreneur. I wouldn't have pegged him for a colonel."

"What then? Some clerk? He's *exactly* what a colonel is. A general, even. Forget the George C. Scott stuff. Go high enough in any organization, and what you get is assholes exactly *like* him."

Suddenly angry again.

I said, "He thinks he saved our lives."

Milo grunted.

I said, "Maybe he did. But I think we had a pretty good chance without him. That sleeping-beauty act you pulled took *me* by surprise."

He grunted again. The road straightened and we were in agricultural country: mountain-rimmed, ruler-edged plots of flat dry lowlands, ready for harvest. Cows grazing side by side with bobbing-grasshopper oil wells. Pig and egg farms; horse breeders, where gorgeous Arabians pranced arrogantly around roadside corrals; acres of citrus being cultivated for Sunkist.

The end point of the view from Howard Burden's office window.

The maroon Volvo was nowhere in sight.

"Nice," I said, looking up through the windshield at clean blue sky. "If you have to run, do it in style."

We crossed a green-hooded bridge over a dry bed of the Santa Clara River and kept going to the 126 junction at Fillmore. Past a business district consisting of well-preserved two-story brick buildings on spotless, empty shopping streets striped with meterless diagonal parking spaces, full-service gas stations staffed by attendants in hats and uniforms, and a Frosty Mug root beer stand that could have been part of the set for *American Graffiti*. Then a continuation of the highway and more citrus groves, working ranches, and produce stands advertising nuts, olives, tomatoes, corn, and "all natural" beef jerky.

Just a few more miles to the base of the mountains and Piru. The outskirts of town was abandoned railyards and citrus warehouses, derelict auto bodies and lots of dust. A hundred yards in were clumps of small, poor houses. One- and two-room structures set in chockablock randomness on fenced dirt lots. Untrimmed trees lined the road—date palms, plums, beeches, and stocky-limbed carobs that emitted a spermy perfume which insinuated itself into the car's air-conditioning system and lingered. Chickens in the front yard. Toddlers in hand-me-downs making toys out of found materials. Inflatable wading pools. The few adult faces we saw were sunbeaten and solemn, tending toward elderly and Hispanic.

Main Street was a couple of blocks that crawled past a one-story bank so petite it resembled a county-fair model. Yellow brick, tile roof, gilt script on the windows over drawn Venetian blinds. CLOSED. Then a general store, a couple of saloons, one with a handwritten MENUDO TODAY poster taped to the front window, and a silvered-wood barnlike structure advertising auto repair, tack and ferrier supplies, bait and tackle.

Milo drove another half block until we reached more empty freightyard. Stopping and consulting his *Thomas Guide*, he jabbed a finger at a map page and said, "Okay, no problem. No problem finding anything here. We're not talking Megalopolis."

"No problem," I said, "if you know there's something to look for."

Circling the tack shop, he drove down a back street, crossed Main, and coasted for another couple of blocks before turning off onto Orchard. The road took on a mild grade, turned to dirt, and ended at a bungalow court. Flat-roofed buildings of yellow stucco. Half a dozen of them, less than a foot of separation between the units. In the center, a plaster fountain that hadn't spouted for a long time. The Volvo was parked at the curb, windows open, unoccupied, with a cardboard sunscreen stretched across the windshield.

We got out. The air was broiling and smelled like marmalade. Milo pointed again, this time for direction. We walked past the bungalows, taking a dusty path that ran along the right side of the court. Behind the units, in what would have been the backyard, was another building, fenced by waist-high pickets that needed priming and painting. White frame cottage, green sash and shutters, tar roof, warped porch, plank swing hanging lopsided from one piece of rope. To the left, a weeping willow grew out of the dirt—dreaming the impossible dream. Huge and rich with foliage it imprisoned the tiny house in a wide black ellipse of shade.

The drapes were drawn. Milo pointed to the left of the big tree and I followed him. Two-step cement porch. Rear panel door. He knocked.

A voice said, "Who is it?"

Milo said, *"Naranjas."*

"Sorry, we've got."

Milo raised his voice and gave it a plaintive twist. *"Naranjas! Muy barato! Muy bonito!"*

The door opened. Milo shoved his foot in it and smiled.

Ted Dinwiddie stared out at us, startled, his ruddy face mottled by patches of pallor.

He said, "I—" and remained frozen. He was

dressed the same way he'd been at the market, minus the apron: blue broadcloth shirt rolled to the elbows, rep tie loosened at the neck, khaki slacks, rubber-soled cordovans. Same good burgher's uniform he wore every day . . .

He kept staring, finally managed to move his lips.

"What is it?"

Milo said, "Even though my mother spent years trying to convince me otherwise, I never developed a taste for asparagus. So I guess we're here to see your other special."

Dinwiddie said, "I don't know what you—"

"Look," said Milo, his voice gentle and scary at the same time, "I was never any fashion model—I need all the help I can get to be able to walk down the street without freaking out little kids. This"—he pointed to his eye—"ain't exactly help."

Dinwiddie said, "I'm sor—"

"Can the apologies," said Milo. "Your being a little more forthcoming in the first place might have prevented substantial pain and suffering to my person."

I said, "He's understating. The two of us nearly lost our lives trying to figure it out."

Dinwiddie said, "I know that. I read the papers, for God's sake." He bit his lip. "I'm sorry. I never meant for it to—"

"Then how about you let us in out of the heat?" Milo said.

"I— What purpose would that really serve?"

Milo turned to me: "What's that word you used, Dr. Delaware?"

"Closure."

"Closure, Ted. Dr. Delaware and I would like some closure."

Dinwiddie bit his lip again and tugged his straw mustache. "Closure," he said.

"You took psychology," said Milo. "Or was it sociology? Either case, that should mean something to you. Man's search for meaning and finality in a cruel, ambiguous world? Man trying to figure out *what the fuck is going on?*"

He grinned and put his hand on the doorknob.

Dinwiddie said, "And after that, what?"

"That's it, Ted. Scout's honor."

"I don't believe much in honor anymore, Detective."

Milo lifted the bill of his baseball cap and wiped the sweat from his forehead. Brushed away black hair and exposed white, sweaty skin, knobbed and scraped and scabbed.

Dinwiddie winced.

Milo tapped his foot. "Lost your innocence, huh? Well, bully for you, Mr. Clean, but there's still plenty of explaining to do."

A voice sounded behind Dinwiddie, the words incomprehensible but the tone pure question mark. The grocer looked over his shoulder and Milo took the opportunity to grasp his shoulders, move him aside like a toy, and walk into the house.

Before Dinwiddie realized what was happening, I was inside too. Small kitchen hot as a steambath, with white cabinets and counter tops of yellow tile laid diagonally and bordered with wine-colored bullnose. Open doorway to a paneled room. Yellow enamel walls, white porcelain sink, four-burner gas stove, a Pyrex carafe half-filled with water on one of the burners. Five big paper double-bags printed with the name of Dinwiddie's market sitting on the counter. A sixth bag, unpacked: boxes of cereal, bags of whole wheat flour and sugar, sausages, smoked meats and fish, spaghetti, tea, a jumbo mocha-colored can of deluxe-grade Colombian coffee.

Holding the can was a boy wearing a baggy T-shirt and cutoff jeans. I knew his age, but he looked younger. Could have been a high school senior. Varsity letter in basketball.

Mocha-colored himself. Very tall, very thin, light-brown hair worn in a two-inch Afro—longer than in his photo. Full lips, Roman nose. His father's nose.

Almond eyes full of terror.

He lifted the can as if it were a weapon.

Milo said, "It's all right, son. We're not here to hurt you."

The boy darted his head at Dinwiddie. The grocer said, "These are the two I told you about, Ike. The cop and the psychologist. According to the papers, they're on the right side."

"The papers," said the boy. Aiming for defiance, but his voice was reedy, uneven, adolescent in its lack of confidence. Big hands tightened around the can. His legs were skinny and hairless—cinnamon sticks perched on bare feet.

"I don't want to talk to you," he said.

"Maybe so," said Milo, walking up to him and standing on the balls of his feet to go eye to eye. "But you owe us, son. You owe someone else, too, but it's too late for that. At least this is a debt you can pay."

The boy retracted his head and blinked. The hand holding the can faltered. Milo reached up and took it from him. "French roast," he said, examining the label. "Only the best for a super-hip fugitive, huh? And look at all this other good stuff." Motioning toward the counter. "Granola. Pasta—what is that, tagliarini? Looks like you've got yourself hunkered down for the long haul, son. Comfy. Lot more comfy than where Holly ended up."

The boy clenched his eyes shut and opened them, blinked again. Several times. Harder. A tear rolled down his cheek and his Adam's apple rose and fell.

"Ike," said Dinwiddie, alarmed, "we've

been through that. Don't let him guilt-trip you." A cold look at Milo. "Hasn't he been through enough?"

Milo said, "Tell it like it is, Ted. Wasn't that an axiom you once lived by?"

The flush had returned to Dinwiddie's complexion and his thick forearms were lumpy with tightened muscle. He was sweating heavily. I realized I was sodden. All four of us were.

Dinwiddie tugged at his mustache and lowered his head like a bull about to charge. I smelled confrontation. Said to the boy: "We're not your enemies. Once in a while the papers do get it right. We know what you've been through, son. The running. Looking over your shoulder. Never knowing who to trust—that's got to be hell. So no one's saying anyone in your shoes could have handled it any better. You did exactly what you had to. But what you know can be useful—to get rid of the evil that remains. Draining the whole swamp. Terry Crevolin's agreed to talk, and he's not exactly Mr. Idealistic. So how about you?"

The boy said nothing.

I said, "We're not going to force you—no one can. But how long can you go on like this?"

"Lies," said a brittle voice from the doorway.

A very small old woman, wearing a gray-and-pink print shift and over that, despite the heat, a coarsely woven porridge-colored cardigan. Beneath the shift, bowed legs encased in supp-hose ended in flat sandals. Her face was wizened and sun-spotted under a halo of white frizz. Big dark eyes, clear and steady.

I wasn't surprised by her appearance. Remembering Latch and Ahlward's reaction when I talked about their plucking her off the street and disposing of her body.

Blank stares from both of them. No smirking, no jumping to take the credit . . .

Just a look.

My educated guess . . .

But something did surprise me.

Steady hands in one so tiny and old. Gripping a very big shotgun.

She said, "Cossacks. Lying bastards."

Clear eyes. *Too* clear. Something other than mental clarity.

Beyond lucidity. A flame that had burned too hot for too long.

Ike said, "Grandma, what are you doing! Put that down!"

"Cossacks! Every Christmas a pogrom, raping and killing and giving the babies to the Nazis to eat."

She aimed the weapon at me, held it there for a while, shifted it to Milo, then to Dinwiddie. To Ike, then back to Dinwiddie.

"Come on, Sophie," said the grocer.

"Back or I'll blast you, you cossack bastard," said the old woman, eyes jumping from one imaginary foe to the other. Hands shaking. The shotgun vibrating.

Ike said, "Grandma, enough! Put that down!"

Loud, a little whiny. A teenager protesting unfair punishment.

She looked at him long enough for confusion to finally settle in.

"It's okay," said Dinwiddie, pushing down with one hand in a calming gesture and taking a step forward.

Her eyes shot back to him. "Back! I'll blast you, you goddammed cossack!"

Ike called out, "Grandma!"

Dinwiddie said, "It's okay," and walked toward the old woman.

She pulled the trigger. Click.

She stared down at the weapon with more confusion. Dinwiddie put one hand on the walnut stock, the other on the barrel, and tried to wrest it away from her. She held on to it, cursing, first in English, then louder and faster in a language I guessed was Russian.

"Easy does it, Sophie," said Dinwiddie as he carefully pried her fingers from the gun. Deprived of it, she began shrieking and hitting him. Ike ran to her, tried to restrain her, but she struck out at him, continued to curse. The boy struggled with her, absorbing blows, taking pains to be gentle, tears streaming down his face.

"Unloaded," said Dinwiddie, handing the shotgun to Milo as if it were something unclean. To Ike: "I took out the shells last time I was here."

Ike gaped at him. "Where? Where'd you put them?"

"They're not here, Ike. I took them with me."

Ike said, "Why, Ted?" Talking loud to be heard over the old woman's invectives, his tall body canopied over her tiny sweatered frame. Trying to contain her with his spidery arms while fixing his attention on Dinwiddie.

Dinwiddie held out his hands and said, "I had to, Ike. The way she is—how she's gotten. You just saw that."

"She didn't even know how to use it, Ted! *You* just saw *that*!"

"I couldn't take a chance, Ike. She was so much worse the last time, so . . . you know that's true. We talked about it—your worries. I didn't want anything to happen. It's obvious I was right."

The boy's face was a battlefield. Comforting calm for the old woman warring with the pain and rage of betrayal. "What about our *protection,* Ted! Our *arrangement?* Where did that *leave* us? Tell me *that,* Ted!"

"It was a judgment call," said Dinwiddie. "What could I do? I couldn't take a chance she'd—"

Ike stamped his foot and began shouting. "We need *protection*! *Shotgun* protection! I know what a shotgun can do—I saw what a shotgun can do. That's why I asked you for a *shotgun,* Ted, not some stupid metal tube that clicks and blows *air*! You got me a shotgun because that's what I *needed,* Ted! Now you pull it out from under me without— How could you *do* that, Ted!"

The words rushing out, followed by short, harsh breaths. Fugitive panting. Fugitive eyes.

His passion had silenced the old woman; she'd stopped struggling, was looking up at him with the innocence and bafflement of an infant on a first outing.

Dinwiddie shook his head, turned away, and rested his elbows on the counter. One of his hands brushed against a package of pasta. He picked it up, looked at it absently.

Milo inspected the shotgun. "This thing's right out of the box, never been fired."

Silence filled the kitchen, choking it, draining the air of oxygen.

"Such a good boy," said the old woman, reaching up and touching Ike's cheek. "The cossacks come, you protect your *bubbe*."

"Yes, Grandma."

"Yes, *Bubbe*."

"Yes, Bubbe. How are you feeling?"

The old woman shrugged. "A little tired, maybe."

"How about a nap, Bubbe?"

Another shrug. She took one of his hands in both of hers and kissed it.

He escorted her through the doorway.

Milo began to follow.

Ike turned around sharply. "Don't worry, Mr. Detective. I'm not going anywhere. Can't *handle* going anywhere. Just let me take care of her. Then I'll come back and you can do whatever it is you want with me."

We waited for him in the living room. Knotty-pine panels, working fireplace under a fieldstone mantel, brick-a-brac that had once been meaningful to someone, hooked rug, overstuffed chairs, tree-stump end tables, a couple of trophy fish on plaques over the mantel. Next to them, a snapshot of a beaming white-haired boy holding an enormous trout. It brought to mind the shot of the two children I'd seen in Dinwiddie's office. But this one was black-and-white, the boy's clothes two or three decades out of fashion.

Below that, a shot of a heavyset man in wading boots, his arm around the same boy. A string of fish hanging from the other arm.

Dinwiddie saw me looking. "We used to come up here a lot. Dad owned lots of the land around here. Bought it up after the war, thinking he'd combine growing with selling, avoid the middleman, become serious-rich. A couple of cold years killed off the profit margin in citrus but the mortgage stayed the same. The big outfits could wait it out but it dampened Dad's enthusiasm, so he sold a lot of his acreage to the Sunkist co-op. We continued to come up for a couple of weeks each year and fish, just the two of us. Lake Piru used to be jumping with rainbows and bass. Last few years the rains have been weak and everything's dried up—they're not releasing anything out of the Fillmore hatchery until they can be sure the survival rate'll be high. I'm sure you saw that, coming over the Santa Clara. The dry beds."

Milo and I nodded.

"Can I get you coffee or something?" said Dinwiddie.

We shook our heads.

He said, "In the early sixties Dad got into another cash-flow problem and sold off most of the land he still owned in town—like the bungalows in front of us, the plot where the school is now. All of it gone, fast and cheap. He kept only this house—guess he was more sentimental than he'd ever have admitted. When he died I inherited it, started bringing my own boys up here. Until the drought. I figured it would be a good place—who bothers to come out here except truckers? Lots of Mexicans and old people—the two of them wouldn't stand out."

I said, "Makes sense."

"I did it because I had to. There was no choice. Not after Ike raised my consciousness."

He stopped, waited for a challenge, and when none came, said, "He'd talk about the Holocaust, how so few people had hidden Jews. How only the Danes had stood up as a country. How the whole thing could have been prevented if more people had stood up, done the right thing. You hear that, you start to wonder. What you would have done. The depth of your own principles. It's like this psych experiment they did years ago—I'm sure you know it. Telling people to shock other people. For no good reason. And most people did it. Just to obey. Shocked total strangers, even though they knew it was wrong, didn't want to. I'd always told myself I'd be different, one of the noble few. But I was never really sure. How can you be when it's all theoretical? The way my life had gone, *everything* was theoretical. So when Ike called me, middle of the night, so scared, told me what they'd tried to do to him, I knew what I had to do. And I know I did the right thing. I'm sorry if it caused you—"

Milo said, "You pick up the old lady too?"

Dinwiddie nodded. "Both of us did that. She wouldn't have gone with me alone. Ike was taking a chance, coming back to town, knowing they were after him. But he loved her, was worried about what might happen to her—especially worried because of the way she'd become."

"What is it, Alzheimer's?"

Dinwiddie said, "Who knows? She won't go to a doctor." To me: "Her age, it could be anything, right? Hardening of the arteries, whatever."

I said, "How long has it been going on?"

"Ike said just a few months. Said she was such a bright woman—before the change—that most people didn't notice anything different. Because when she talked she still made sense. And she'd always gone on about conspiracies—cossacks, whatever. So if she did it a little more, who'd notice? The way she is now, of course, you'd notice, but that's just been the last few weeks. Maybe it's the stress. Of hiding. I don't know."

He lowered his head, rested his forehead in his hands.

"So the two of you came back to town and got her," Milo said.

"Yeah," said Dinwiddie, talking to the hooked rug. "When she wasn't home, Ike figured she'd either be at the synagogue or walking around. She'd always loved to walk, had started doing it even more—since the change. In the dark, when it wasn't safe. We drove to the synagogue, saw there was some kind of party inside, and waited until she left. Then we picked her up and brought her here. She didn't want to come, was yelling at us a lot, but Ike managed to calm her down. He's the only one who seems to be able to calm her down."

He looked down again, knitted his hands and swung them between his knees. "There's something special between them. More than just family. The bond of survivors. He's not even twenty, has been through way too much for someone that age. For anyone. So bear that in mind. Okay?"

Ike came back into the room and said, "Bear what in mind?"

Dinwiddie sat up. "I was just telling them to keep things in perspective. How's she's doing?"

"Sleeping. What kind of perspective?"

"Just everything that's been going on."

"In other words, coddle me out of pity?"

"No," said Dinwiddie. The boy looked away from him. "Ike, about the shotgun—"

"Forget it, Ted. You ended up saving your own life. What could be better?"

Generous smile, startling in its suddenness. But largesse tainted by bitterness. Dinwiddie picked up on it, knew what it meant—an immutable change in the bond between them—and his expression turned to misery.

Milo said, "You ready to tell us what happened, son?"

Ike said, "How much do you know?"

"Everything up to Bear Lodge."

"Bear Lodge," he said. "Rural nirvana, some

pipe dream, huh? All *I* know about that is what I've been told. By Grandma."

"Where'd you live afterward?"

"Where'd I live?" The boy smiled again and ticked off fingers. "Boston. Evanston, Illinois. Louisville, Kentucky. I was a regular ramblin' man."

Another smile. So forced it was painful to look at.

I said, "Not Philadelphia?"

"Philadelphia? Nope. I'm with W. C. Fields on that one."

"Terry Crevolin said your father's family was from Philadelphia."

"Family." The smile opened and twisted and turned into an angry laugh. "My father's *family* was wiped out fifty years ago. Except for one distant cousin. In Philadelphia. Fat-cat lawyer, I've never even talked to him—couldn't imagine he'd welcome me with open arms." Another laugh. "No, Grandma wouldn't have sentenced me to Philadelphia."

I said, "Those other places—was that your mother's family?"

He cocked a finger at me. "You guessed it, smart person. *You* get the rubber duckie. A progressive series of nice middle-class *Negro* neighborhoods, where I wouldn't stand out like chocolate syrup in milk. Nice hospitable relatives who tolerated me until they got sick of me, or got scared of what it meant putting me up, or things just got too crowded—the middle class likes its comforts."

Dinwiddie said, "Why don't you sit down, Ike?"

The boy wheeled on him. "What, and *relax*?" But he did lower himself into an armchair, stilt-legs stretching out onto the hooked rug.

A long silence. When Milo didn't break it, I said, "Any reason you chose a Spanish surname?"

"Spanish? Oh yeah, that. I'd been using Montvert—some of my mom's family were Creoles, so it seemed appropriate to go French." Another joyless smile. "Then when I moved here I needed a new one. Covering tracks. I thought of Russian, for Grandma. But who would buy that on me? I didn't want to attract attention. Then one day I scoped out Ocean Heights—it had been in the news, Massengil's Jim Crow bullshit. I wanted to take a look at the place, see what KKK territory looked like in the eighties, took a drive through. Beaver Cleaverland. But I noticed they had all these Spanish names for the streets. Stone hypocrisy. So I thought, why not? Do 'em one better, go for Español. Which would be *Verde*. But that sounded wrong—like it wouldn't be someone's name. So I checked out a Spanish-English dictionary. *Green*. Slang for 'novice.' Which I was. An L.A. novice—go west, young man. *Novato*. Had a cool ring to it. The rest, as they say, is Will and Ariel Durant territory."

Milo had started to squirm halfway through the speech. He said, "How'd it happen? The alley."

"Boy," said Ike, "you're a real master of subtlety."

"Fuck subtlety," said Milo. "Let's aim for truth."

The boy's turn to be startled. Then a genuine smile.

He said, "By the time they told me to meet them in the alley, I'd started to suspect something weird. Latch was *too* nice. I mean, the guy was an elected official and we were talking about murder, blowing things up. Him being really casual. As if it were no big deal. As if he were still a revolutionary. Not that I ever really trusted him in the first place. Grandma didn't trust him—said the fact that he'd gone into establishment politics said plenty about him. So when he told me about the meeting, new information, I said sure, faked being all gung-ho. But I was suspicious from the outset."

"Why down there? In Watts."

Ike nodded. "Exactly. That bothered me too. Latch's story was, the source I was going to meet was someone who lived there. From Mom and Dad's past, the Black Liberation Army. Someone still wanted by the authorities, needed the cover of Watts, couldn't afford to leave home territory."

"Latch give you a name?"

"Abdul Malik. But he said that was just a code. He liked codes. Like some kid playing *I Spy*. I never really bought it."

"The real reason for Watts," said Dinwiddie, "was that a black body there wouldn't cause the police to blink an eye. And that's exactly what happened, isn't it?"

Milo ignored that, said to Ike: "So in spite of it smelling bad, you went down there."

"I had to know what was going on. I figured if they were going to pull something, they'd do it another time, another place. Might as well be prepared, see what was going on. So I showed up early, hid my bike in the next alley, and found a hiding place next to this garage, behind some garbage cans. The bulb was out and that part of the alley was really dark. And *rank*. Something out of a nightmare." He grimaced, remembering. "Junkies sneaking in and out, all these low whispers, deals going down, people shooting up, snorting, taking leaks, taking dumps. I started to get scared, wondering what I'd gotten myself into. But as it got later, closer to the time I was supposed to meet this Malik, the action started to slow."

"When was that?" said Milo.

"About three A.M. I heard somewhere that's

the killing time of day, time the life forces are weak. Hiding in that place, you could really feel it. Everything going dead. Anyway, the junkies and dealers started to go home, only a few stragglers. Real losers nodding off, not caring if they were sitting in dog shit or whatever."

He gave a sick look. Stopped.

Milo said, "Go on."

"One of them—one of the stragglers—was about my size. Maybe a little shorter but almost the same size. And really skinny, like me. I noticed him because of that, kind of identified with him, thinking about what led him to get that way, there but for the grace of God, and all that kind of stuff. I mean this guy was really pathetic— totally wasted. Walking back and forth, muttering, stoked on God knows how many different kinds of poison.

"I'm watching him, watching all of this, the smells seem to be getting worse, and the darkness starts to get really heavy—crushing down on me. I know now it was my anxiety. I start thinking anxiety-thoughts, like is someone going to steal my bike and am I going to get stranded here? Who knows who's out there. Watching. Then the guy they sent to do the job shows up. He's early too. Half hour early. I can tell 'cause he's dressed in black, wearing this long black coat even though it's summer—that's one thing that tipped me off, though by itself it didn't mean much. Junkies get cold. But he stepped under a garage light and I saw that he was a white guy. Real cracker face, turned-up pig nose, but with stuff on his face. Greasepaint. To make him look black—like a minstrel act. In the darkness it almost worked. The few junkies who were left never noticed—they just wanted their dope. But I was looking out for it, so I caught it right away.

"This guy just kind of saunters in, walking cool, head-bopping, trying to look as if he belongs there. But overdoing it. *Playing* black. Then, when he saw no one was paying attention to him, looking at his watch, showing how jumpy he was. I stay behind the garbage cans. Then this tall thin junkie spots him, says, 'Yo, bro,' and starts ambling up to him. Talking really slurred—stoned out of his mind. Maybe he was trying to buy or sell or just hitting the white guy up for a handout. The guy in the coat says my name—'Yo, Malcolm?' Like that. And the junkie mutters something back, doesn't say he's not me, and keeps coming at him. Maybe he even wanted to mug him or something, I don't know. He was pretty big, must have looked pretty scary to old Whitey. So old Whitey pulls something out of the coat. Sawed-off shotgun. And blasts the tall guy, from right up close— maybe he was two feet away, if that. I could see him fly back, as if he'd been hit by a hurricane. Just fly back and fall. The other stragglers started running—it was weird, no screams, no one talk-

ing. Just silent running, like rats. Like they were
used to it—this was no big deal. Then the white
guy in the coat runs away and I hear a car start at
the end of the alley and drive off. I wait awhile,
scared out of my mind but knowing I should go
over to the junkie, see if there's anything I can do
for him. Even though I know there isn't—the way
he was thrown back, the way he exploded. But
finally, I do. When I see what the shotgun did to
him I get really sick. For him and also, I guess,
because I know this is what they meant for *me*. I'm
dizzy, I feel like throwing up, but I know I've got
to get out of there before the police show up, so I
hold it in. My stomach's really killing me, churning, I need to go to the bathroom. Then I think of
something—some way to take something good out
of this. Make the junkie's life meaningful. I put
my hands in his pockets. It's disgusting—they're
all wet. With blood. And empty except for some
pills. No ID. I slip *my* ID in and split. Hoping the
way he looks—what the shotgun did to him—us
being around the same size, no one will figure it
out. Later, riding away, I get real paranoid about
it, start to shake. Tell myself it was the most
idiotic thing I *could* have done. What if they *do*
figure it out? There's my ID right on the body—
I'm cooked. I could be busted for *murder*. So I call
Ted from a pay phone. He gets out of bed and
drives me here. And I wait, scared out of my
mind. Out here in Nowheresville. For the cops to

come looking for me. For Latch's Nazis to come looking for me. The next day the cops do come around talking to Grandma, asking about my involvement with dope. Accepting the dead body as me. So I'm officially dead." Smile. "Never thought it would feel so good."

The smile faded. "But I can't stop thinking about the junkie. His dying for me. Like the Azazel goat in the Bible—almost as if he were my Jesus. If I *believed* in Jesus. I think about the fact that he was someone's little kid once. Maybe someone loved him; now no one will ever know what happened to him. Then I rationalize it, saying it wouldn't make him any more alive to tell the story. The way he was—so far gone— probably everyone who'd once loved him had given up on him."

Looking to us for confirmation. I gave a supportive smile and nodded. Milo nodded too.

The boy clenched and opened his hands. Blinked. Wiped his eyes. When he spoke again, his voice was small and tight.

"I know what you're thinking," he said. "Holly. Another sacrifice. But I had no idea she'd do what she did—it wasn't as if the two of us were confidants or anything. I felt sorry for her, so lonely, so closed in, that father who treated her like a slave. If I had known, I would have called her, warned her not to do anything stupid."

Milo said, "What did the two of you talk about, son?" Using the voice I'd heard him use with victims.

"Things," said the boy. Wretched. "All kinds of things. She didn't talk much herself—she wasn't very bright, just a step above retarded, really. So I did all the talking. I *had* to do all the talking."

He held his hands out, supplicating. Zeroing in on Milo. Wanting a cop's forgiveness.

Milo said, "Absolutely. If you didn't talk, it would have been like treating her the way everyone else did. Shutting her out."

"Exactly! Shining her on—everyone shined her on, treated her like some kind of subhuman creature. Even that father of hers, going around doing his own thing with his computers, pretending she didn't exist. She told me that, told me how he expected her to do his housework. His scutwork. For no money. After we got to know each other she said her dad had been in the army, a general or something. Demanded everything perfect. That she could never be perfect, so she knew he'd never like her."

"Ever meet the father?" said Milo.

"Just in passing. He walked by me once or twice. Pretending I didn't exist. Whether it was racism or just the way he was, I didn't know. Until Ted told me."

He looked at Dinwiddie and our eyes followed.

The grocer looked uncomfortable. "What I told him is that Burden was strange, to be careful. The whole family was strange."

"And the other stuff," Ike said softly.

"Rumors," said Dinwiddie. "About Burden having been some kind of government spy—rumors that were going around back when I was in high school. We used to ask Howard about it. He always said he didn't know, but no one believed him—why wouldn't he know about his own father? We figured he was hedging. This was the sixties—it was uncool to be military. Not that I really believed it. But I just wanted Ike to know that he was dealing with a possible risk factor. So as not to get into trouble."

"You wanted to make sure I didn't sleep with her," said Ike, smiling. Without malice. "Which is cool—that would have been stupid. But there was never any *chance* of that. It wasn't . . . She wasn't like that—wasn't feminine. More like a kid. Gullible. It would have been like sleeping with a kid. Perverted."

Milo nodded again and said, "How much detail did you give her? About Wannsee?"

"More than I realized, I guess. When I'd come over there, she'd be so happy to see me—set out food, start to make a big deal about it. I was the only one who gave her any attention. So I guess I just kind of went on. Talking my head off."

"You mention Latch's name?"

He looked down. Muttered something that passed for "Uh-huh."

"And Massengil's?"

"All of it." Still downcast and muttering. He looked up suddenly, wet-eyed again. "I had no idea she was really listening! Half the time she was so spaced-out I felt like I was talking to a wall! Talking to myself! Almost a stream of consciousness thing, just letting it all out. I don't even remember what I told her, how much I told her. If I'da known . . ." He broke off, shook his head. Wept. Dinwiddie went over to him and patted his shoulder.

Milo waited a long time before saying, "It wasn't your fault."

The thin brown face shot up like a jack-in-the-box. "No. Nothing like that. Whose fault was it?"

"You want to torture yourself with guilt, son, wait until you're a bit older. After you've given yourself some good reason."

Ike stared at him. Dried his eyes. "You're weird, man. For a cop. What is it you want from me?"

"That's up to you," said Milo. "Latch and Ahlward and a bunch of the others are dead. Mrs. Latch is being looked into. But quite a few of them—too many of them—survived. We've got very little to hold them on—nothing that'll do serious damage in terms of jail time. And maybe that's no big deal. They're all a bunch of sheep—with the leaders gone they'll forget politics, go into real estate or growing dope or writing screenplays, whatever. But maybe not."

"Meaning?"

"Meaning you were an eyewitness to a homicide. Maybe you saw enough of the asshole in the coat to be able to match him up to a face. Match that pig nose. If you don't want to bother, I understand. You can't buy beer legally and you've been through ten lifetimes' worth of shit. You still don't trust anyone, know who's right, who's wrong. But if you can ID him, there's a chance we can put the Nazi fuck away, get some of the others for conspiracy. Get them really scared. And talking."

"That's it?" said the boy. "Match a face?"

" 'Course not," said Milo. "If you do get a match, there'll be depositions, subpoenas, the whole legal ball of twine. If it gets that far the Police Department will offer you protection, but the truth is, that can be kind of half-assed. So I'll protect you myself. Make sure it's done right. I'll also make sure your grandma gets protection. And good medical help. I've got close medical connections."

"Why?"

"Why what?"

"Why go to all the bother?"

Milo shrugged. "Part of it's personal. I'm still plenty pissed at them—what they did to me." He ran his hand over his face. Removed his baseball cap and scratched his head. Sweat and pressure had turned his hair into something black and oily and sodden. "Also, maybe I'm curious. The way Ted was. How I'd react. Being asked to shock someone."

He yawned, stretched, put his hat back on. "Anyway, I'm not going to pressure you, son. Tell me to forget it and I drive back to L.A., you go on to your next hidey-hole, sayonara."

The boy thought for a while. Bit his nails, gnawed his knuckles.

"Match a face? It was a long time ago, pretty dark. What if I can't?"

"Then it's bye-bye and good luck."

"Do I have to see them . . . him . . . in person? Or can I just look at some photos?"

"Photos for a start. If you come up with an ID, we'll do a lineup. With full security. Behind a one-way mirror."

The boy got up, paced, punched his palm with his other hand. I couldn't help thinking how much he reminded me of Milo. Wrestling. Always wrestling.

"Okay," he finally said. "I'll look at your photos. When?"

"Right now," said Milo. "If you're ready. I've got stuff in the car."

39

It ended the way it started.

"Turn on your TV, Alex."

I'd been sitting at the dining room window, watching the sun set over the Glen. Reading Twain. Then poetry—Whitman, Robert Penn Warren, Dylan Thomas. Stuff I'd neglected for too long. Stuff with body to it. Music and lust and despair and religion.

"Is it important, Milo?"

"Quick, or you'll miss it."

I got up and switched on the tube.

Six o'clock news.

Tape of Lieutenant Frisk at a podium; below him, a microphone audience. Fawn-colored suit. Cream shirt, green tie.

Grinning and blathering about long-term investigations, interdepartmental task forces, multiple indictments the result of careful coordination with federal and state agencies.

Using the word *hero*. Looking as if he had to force his lips around it. Holding out a hand.

Milo stepped up to the podium.

Frisk shook his hand, handed Milo a piece of paper.

Milo took it, looked at it, gave the camera a *Hi, mom!* smile. Pocketed the commendation.

Frisk stood away from him. Stood back, waiting for him to leave the stage.

Milo stayed there, still smiling. Frisk looked puzzled.

Milo mugged for the camera again, turned and faced Frisk. Drew back his arm and hit Frisk, hard, in the face.